Shaman

Shaman

KELLY Z. CONRAD

Sharon —
Hope you
enjoy the book!
Best Wishes!
Kelly Z Conrad

iUniverse, Inc.
Bloomington

Shaman

iUniverse books may be ordered through booksellers or by contacting:

iUniverse
1663 Liberty Drive
Bloomington, IN 47403
www.iuniverse.com
1-800-Authors (1-800-288-4677)

ISBN: 978-1-4620-7327-6 (sc)
ISBN: 978-1-4620-7328-3 (ebk)

Printed in the United States of America

iUniverse rev. date: 01/04/2012

For Marcus, my sweet moleque.
Agora eu sei o que é o amor.

ACKNOWLEDGMENTS

My deepest gratitude is extended to the following people . . .

Mrs. Jane Souders, my creative writing teacher in high school, who told me years ago, "Hold on to this story. You may want to do something more with it someday."

Fellow writers Deb Rempert, Eileen Sugg, and Toby Eberly for being so generous with their feedback, suggestions, and support. Barbara Bamberger Scott for her insightful editing that made my story so much better. Ray and Bettz Whitehead, and Adam Roberson for being interested when few others were.

Most of all, Marcus, for always being my first read, biggest fan, gentlest critic. And for finally making me see that I am, in fact, a writer.

PART 1

January 1867
Northwestern Pennsylvania

CHAPTER

1

She lay shivering on the frozen ground, the night's damp chill piercing her bruised body. A fire crackled and men's voices laughed nearby. The cries of her sister had long since quieted. Had she finally died? Tears stung her eyes. She prayed that her own death would soon rescue her.

She could not remember the last time water passed her lips. When she tried to moisten them with her tongue, she tasted blood. Tight around her neck was the coarse rope her captors used to lead her, sometimes drag her, as they traveled through the day. Tonight, bound at the wrists and ankles, flat on her back, she knew what she would soon endure again. The raw burning between her legs was excruciating when she moved, so she lay perfectly still.

Rustling footsteps approached and stopped beside her. In the dim light, she saw him bend toward her feet, then felt the blade of his knife slice through the rope around her ankles. She was careful not to move. Without warning, a strong kick to her ribs sent a searing pain shooting through her body. The rope around her neck was wrenched, and with one quick motion, she was sitting up. She pushed against him, struggling to breathe. Fresh blood trickled from the open wounds around her neck, down between her breasts. The stench of sweat and gin filled her nostrils as she stared into the bearded face of the older captor, his malicious grin exposing brown and broken teeth.

"Please, no more," she begged in a hoarse whisper.

"Shut up!" His hand exploded into the side of her face with a loud crack, causing her to momentarily lose awareness. "You're the only dirty squaw left alive."

He fumbled with the buttons on his trousers, and shoved her tattered skirt above her hips. A panicked cry rose in her throat when she felt his hands on her buttocks, the cold night air brushing the most intimate part of her body. She pulled frantically at the ropes that bound her wrists, mindless terror flooding her. He lowered to force her legs apart, and she screamed in pain when he shoved himself into her. She smelled sweat and dirt on his neck as he thrust back and forth into her, her bound hands crushed between them. Trying to push against him was futile, her arms too weak, his body too heavy. His rancid breath in her face, he suddenly slowed his movements. He closed his eyes and collapsed on top of her. Fearing her chest would cave in under his weight, she tried to shift from beneath him. Though still breathing, he was not moving. With great effort, she pushed his body to the side and he rolled to the ground. When he settled onto his back, his coat fell open and she saw the knife hanging from his belt. She sat up and reached quickly to pull it from its sheath, glancing toward the fire to be sure the other man was not approaching. Her heart pounding, she turned the knife against the ropes at her wrists. After several awkward attempts with shaking hands, the blade finally cut through the rope. Keeping a wary eye on her captor passed out at her side, she pushed her skirt back down, then cut the rope from around her neck.

On her hands and knees, she crawled a few feet away, still clutching the knife. She tried to think what to do next. The other man at the fire was still quiet, but if he came to her and discovered what had happened, the weapon would be of little use. Her only chance was to wait here in the shadows and hope he remained at the fire.

The man near her began to stir. She watched him closely. He lifted his head and looked around. When he saw her a short distance away, he frowned.

"How'd you get over there?" His speech slurred, he seemed disoriented. Struggling to sit up, he finally managed to stand unsteadily, holding his unfastened pants at the waist. He stumbled over to her. "Get up," he ordered. When she did not move, he reached down to grab a handful of her hair. She cried out as he pulled her to standing.

In one quick motion, she brought the knife from behind her skirt and plunged the long blade as far as it would go into his abdomen. He grunted with the force of the blade. His mouth dropped open, shock registering on his face as he soundlessly put his hands to his stomach, dropped to his knees, then crumpled at her feet.

Frozen, she stared down at him for several long minutes. She did not know if she had killed him, and didn't care, as long as he stayed quiet and could no longer hurt her. His eyes in a petrified stare, the handle of the knife protruding from his stomach, his blood ran into the dry grass. He was not breathing. She bent down and wrenched the knife from his body, wiping the bloody blade on his pants. Still watching him, she moved beyond his reach, and sat for a moment on the hard ground. Only now realizing how cold she was, she considered removing her dead captor's coat, but decided against it. She was afraid to go near him, and did not want to endure his stench just to be warm.

The men's horses stood a few yards from the encampment, tethered to surrounding trees. Quietly, she circled the outer perimeter of the camp, toward the animals. She untied both horses and gathered the leather straps in her hands, praying they would not make enough noise to waken the other man. Approaching the smaller horse, she put her hand against his neck to calm his agitation at her unfamiliar touch. When his stomping subsided, she jumped and hoisted herself onto his bare back, grimacing with intense pain that radiated throughout her body. A firm grip on both tethers, she turned the horse, kicked his sides, and hung on as they bolted through the trees.

Behind her, she heard a man shouting but did not dare look back. She kicked the horse harder and he picked up speed.

"Hey! That squaw bitch is stealin' our horses!" She heard a shot and felt a searing shard hit her left leg just above the knee. Either the shot or her loud shriek spooked the horse. He jumped and began to gallop faster, the other horse following close behind.

For a time, she continued to kick the horse's sides, urging him on through thick trees and along open fields, until he would gallop no longer. Toward daybreak, she forced herself to look back. Seeing no one, she let go of the other horse, and allowed her mount to slow to a walk, knowing he needed rest. Small creeks they had passed were frozen solid, and with no sign of a larger body of water from which to drink, she wasn't sure how far she could go. The pain in her leg was agonizing, the bullet wound bleeding profusely through her skirt and onto the horse. His left flank was sticky with her blood. She knew she should try to bandage the wound but she was afraid to stop and dismount, for fear she would not have the strength to continue if she did. Instead, she gathered as much material of the bloody tatters of her skirt as she could and held it over the wound. A foggy vision of her grandmothers came to her, offering the petals of the tiny white flowers in the field to stop the bleeding, just as they had done many years ago. She knew it was only a matter of time until she joined her grandmothers in the spirit world.

She was feeling weaker by the hour. The feeble January sun did little to warm her, but slouching against the horse, at least she could benefit from his body heat. She remained wary, always scanning her surroundings to see that no one was approaching. If the other captor somehow caught up to her, as he had done the last time she escaped, he would surely kill her.

By late afternoon, she was slipping in and out of awareness. At times, she leaned to rest her face against the horse's neck, feeling his warmth beneath her cheek. She was strangely comforted by images of her father teaching her to ride when she was a girl.

"Your horse must always know that you are his master, Degan," her father had said. "Then he will do what you want, go where you want."

A brave Seneca, respected among his people, her father had always been gentle and loving with her, as well as with her brothers and sisters. She wondered what he would say if he could see her now, crumpled over this horse's neck, unable to sit up, allowing the animal to ramble wherever he chose.

At sunset, the intense thirst had invaded her mind and her body. Neither she nor the horse could go much further without water. The trees were beginning to thin and soon she could distinguish two dark structures in the distance. She made out a log cabin and a barn in the gloom, with no signs of activity on the property. Perhaps there would be water there. The horse seemed to read her mind, as he quickened his pace toward the barn.

At the barn door, she slid from the horse's back to fall against the crossbar. Putting all her weight on her right leg, she could barely stand, but managed to push the heavy crossbar aside. The barn door swung open. In a shaft of moonlight, she could see a bucket and a feed bin in a stall along the back wall. She collapsed on the dirt floor just inside the door.

The horse entered past her, making his way to the unfamiliar stall to drink loudly from the bucket.

She crawled toward the back wall, as far away from the cold night air as possible. In the moonlight from a small window overhead, she saw the yellow straw under her turning red with her blood. Lifting her torn and dirty skirt, she could see the bullet wound in her leg was still bleeding. She wondered how long it would be before death would take her. She expected it would be very soon.

Removing the knife from the waistband of her skirt, she placed it beside her in the straw. The useful weapon had saved her life last night, but if threatened now, she would be too weak to use it. She was too weak to crawl to the bucket to drink whatever water the horse had left her. Leaning her head against the splintered wood of the barn wall, she closed her eyes to sleep, but fear and despair had rooted themselves too deeply, and sleep wouldn't come.

She knew she would never see home again, and yearned deeply for her husband. Never again would she hear her father's laughter when he teased her. Thoughts of her mother came to her. Braiding her long dark hair when she was a girl, her mother had always said, "Degan, you will be a strong woman some day." Now her mother lay dead back home and she was here in this strange barn, shaking in the cold, bleeding, and waiting for death.

Matt Tyler urged his horse to quicken its steps, and soon came upon his log cabin and small barn, surrounded by towering pines. Crisp evening air slipped icy fingers beneath the collar of his coat. His breath preceded him in frosty puffs. Relieved to be home, he looked forward to a relaxing smoke in front of a warm fire.

Darkness had fallen hours ago. A multitude of stars illuminated the sky on this cloudless night, moonlight brightening the frozen ground. Though the Civil War had ended nearly two years before, these nights still evoked memories of the camps where his Union regiment had endured in the endless winter months. Tonight, with the cold penetrating to his bones, he was thankful to live less than a mile from the town of Sylvan, where he worked as a physician's apprentice.

As he approached his barn, Matt was surprised to see a horse standing just inside the open barn door. Dismounting, he withdrew the rifle holstered to his saddle and walked cautiously toward the stray. Despite the blood on its left flank and both sides of its neck, Matt quickly determined that the animal was not injured. He raised his rifle and cocked it.

"Who's there?" he yelled into the darkness. With the barrel of the rifle, he pushed the barn door open wide to allow the full moon to bathe the interior with pale light. It was then that he saw a small form crouched against the far wall.

"Who's there?" He stepped forward, and was stunned by what he saw.

A young woman, obviously injured, sat on the barn floor. She was shaking noticeably and kept wide eyes fixed on the rifle in Matt's grip. He lowered the gun and set it to lean against the barn door, then struck a match to light a lantern hanging just inside. When he turned the flame higher and advanced a few paces, she frantically glanced around as if looking for a means of escape. Finding none, she pressed herself tightly to the wall behind her as Matt came closer.

Looking at her in stronger light, he could see she was an Indian, he guessed in her mid-twenties. Her dark hair hung in tangled disarray about her face and shoulders, her dark skin smooth over high cheekbones. Her face, hands, and bare feet were covered with dried blood and dirt. A raw and bleeding stripe encircled her neck. She clutched the remains of her dress in the front, deep red cuts around both wrists. Her face was badly bruised and swollen on one side, and blood had soaked through her skirt, he presumed from a wound he could not see.

"My God, where the hell did you come from?" As if the sound of his voice shook him from a daze, he quickly unfastened his medical bag from his saddle. But when he approached her, he realized his foolishness in thinking she would be a cooperative patient. She quickly reached into the straw and produced a sizeable knife. He stopped abruptly and held up his hands.

"You won't need that," he said, keeping his tone even. "I won't hurt you."

She stared at him, her breath coming in rapid gulps, her fear palpable between them.

He knelt down and searched his medical bag, producing rolls of clean linen bandages which he held out to her. "Can you understand me? I'm a doctor. Let me help you."

After what seemed an eternity, she slowly lowered the knife, and placed it beside her in the straw. He carefully inched toward her, intending to inspect her injured leg. He thought it best to give her fair warning.

"I'm going to lift your skirt just enough to look at your leg. I think you're bleeding from there."

He touched the hem and pushed back the filthy garment. When she gasped and reached for the knife, he dropped the hem and lifted his hands.

"All right, you do it yourself then. I won't touch you. Just let me see the wound in your leg."

Brandishing the knife, she shook her head. "No, no more!"

"I can't let you sit here and bleed to death," he told her firmly. Deciding not to waste more time trying to elicit her cooperation, he reached forward to pick her up.

"No!" she shrieked, raising the knife. In a flash, he clasped her wrist and clamped down hard. She cried out, holding on in wild desperation to her only defense. But her struggle soon weakened and the knife dropped into the straw. Matt picked it up and saw dried blood on the blade and the handle. He tossed it to bounce off the opposite wall.

Terror engulfed her, but she found a small voice to beg, "Please," as he reached for her again.

"I can't let you die." He gathered her slight frame into his arms, easily lifting her off the barn floor. She struggled against him, but the fight proved too much. With a final cry, she passed out in his arms.

She hovered at the bottom of a very deep lake, trying to swim toward the surface. Her ears filled with the muffled sounds of rushing water. When she emerged from the black depths to realize the dim light of day, she heard her voice calling her dead husband's name in a mournful incantation. There were gunshots and screams from her family as they fell around her. Friends and other families in neighboring lodges had met the same fate. Viewing the carnage, she wished for her own death.

Then she heard the white man's voice again, quiet and pleading, from a different place. His gentle words soothed her. She caught the scents of whiskey and sweet tobacco. She felt something cool, distantly soothing on her face. But she had broken the surface for only an instant before sinking again to the bottom.

Early daylight filtered through the pines behind the cabin. Matt sipped fresh coffee, watching a blanket of twinkling frost come into view over the clearing outside. Sleep had been intermittent at best the night before. He had tried to doze at his desk, not allowing himself the comfort of his bedroom. He knew the injured woman would require his skills throughout the night. And though the last few hours had passed fitfully for him, they had been agonizing for her.

She had raved in delirium for long periods, fallen into restless sleep, only to stir and cry madly again. At one point, she had put a hand out to him, staring with wild, unseeing eyes. She'd repeated a word he did not understand, as if calling a name. But when she touched his face, she jerked back as if his whiskers burned her fingers.

He had tried to console her by talking. When he did, she would quiet. The fever that had raged for hours finally broke, and now she slept peacefully.

She lay on a small bed in one corner of the great room of his cabin where Matt kept an infirmary. Complete with an apothecary cabinet filled with medicines and bandages, this corner held every accoutrement required to care for the sick or injured.

A fire blazed in the hearth, its warmth filling the room to the opposite wall where his desk and full bookshelves occupied another corner. Two armchairs and a soft leather sofa sat before the hearth, along with a low table of polished mahogany. The furnishings of the cabin were distinctly masculine, dark and heavy, down to the thick rugs on the floor. Unlike other log and wood-frame houses in the area that were Spartan and drafty, Matt's home was a testimony to the luxuries of his upbringing.

He sat down in the bedside chair. With the possibility of her death behind them now, he watched the woman as she slept. The ordeal she'd barely survived had taken a considerable toll.

During the night, she had remained unconscious for more than an hour, which had allowed him time to examine her thoroughly. Aside from the injuries he had observed in the barn, she had two broken ribs, and her back bore the raw welts of a recent beating. He knew she had been brutally violated, but his greatest concern remained the bullet wound in her left leg.

He had bathed her and wrapped her ribs with strips of linen, then tossed her torn, bloody skirt and blouse aside. Having no suitable replacements, he retrieved one of his own shirts from his armoire and dressed her in that. His shirt seemed to swallow her slight frame, but it sufficed.

The white linen bandages that encircled her wrists contrasted sharply with the dark skin of her hands. A mass of long hair tumbled over the edge of the small bed. Her face, though bruised and swollen on one side, looked soft and delicate in sleep. He reached to remove the damp cloth from her forehead and rinsed it again in the basin of cool water. Gingerly, he touched it to her battered cheek and she stirred.

She awoke with a frightened gasp and stiffened beneath his touch. Instinctively, she tried to move away and sit up, her dark eyes wide with terror.

"Easy, don't be afraid," he said. He put a firm hand on her shoulder and pressed her back down to the bed. "You have a couple of broken ribs. You'll feel less pain if you don't move too much."

She quickly glanced around.

"You're in my home. You're safe here."

She touched the bandage around her neck and it seemed to distress her. Clawing at the fabric, she tried to tear it off, until Matt took hold of her hands to stop her.

"It's just a bandage," he said, pointing to the cloth around her wrists, "like these. It helps the medicine work."

His words seemed to calm her. She pushed back the sheet that covered her and, seeing what she was wearing, stared at him curiously.

"Your clothes were ruined." He pointed to the shirt. "Sorry, but this was all I had."

She pushed the sheet back further, and touched the bandage that encircled her left thigh. Putting a hand to her side, she felt the fabric wrapped snuggly around her rib cage.

As she slowly reclined again, Matt took the sheet and covered her. "I know you can understand me. What's your name?"

She put both arms under the sheet and began to shiver. He reached for a woolen blanket at the foot of the bed and spread it over her. Taking a cup from the bedside table, he slipped a hand under her head and tilted the rim to her mouth.

"Take some water."

When the cool liquid touched her lips, she drank ravenously until the cup was empty.

"You're starving." He gently squeezed her forearm before rising to fill the cup with warm broth from a pot on the stove. At the bedside, he raised her head again. When she tasted the broth, she grabbed the cup with trembling hands and gulped hungrily, choking and coughing, dribbling some of the liquid down her chin.

"Not so fast," he said, pulling the cup away with difficulty. "You can have as much as you want, but not all at once." He waited a moment to give her stomach a chance to accept nourishment before allowing her to drink again.

The broth finished in short order, he set the cup aside. A scowl of pain crossed her face as she reached to touch her bandaged leg.

"Lucky for you, somebody's a bad shot. I assume they were trying to either kill you or shoot the horse. The wound wasn't infected yet, but it needed some attention. The bullet's out. You'll be all right now. What happened? Who did this to you?"

Her eyes welled with tears. She put a hand over her mouth, shaking her head.

"All right, try not to think about it." He reached to touch her shoulder. "No one's going to hurt you here."

She shrank from his touch, trying again to move away. Glaring at him, she swallowed hard to find a small, raspy voice.

"Why do you help me?" she asked suspiciously.

Pleased to hear her speak, Matt replied, "Because you need it. What's your name?"

"Degan."

"Well, Degan, I'm glad you finally decided to talk to me."

"You are . . . the shaman?"

"I'm a doctor. In your language, I think 'shaman' is the word." Now that communication had been established between them, his mind flooded with questions. "Are you from one of the Iroquois nations up in New York?"

"I am Onodowohgah of the Haudenosaunee. Iroquois is the white man's word."

"Ono-do-?"

"The white word is Seneca."

"I see. From the Allegany Reservation?"

She nodded.

"How did you end up in my barn?"

"I rode from the North one day," she said carefully, searching for words. "I saw the barn. They shot me and the blood did not stop. I needed water and rest from the cold. I would rest only a short time, but I could not go on. I am waiting for death."

"You're not going to die."

She turned her head away. "Many in my family died. Killed by the white men."

"How did you survive?"

"They took us . . . my sister . . . we could not get away. They tied our necks and our hands. No food or water. They came and . . . forced us—" Her voice broke into a cry, and she covered her face with both hands.

"Shhhhh. Where's your sister now?"

"She is dead."

"I'm sorry." He put a hand on her forearm, but she quickly pulled away.

"What will you do to me?"

"I'm going to take care of you until you're well."

Her distrustful glare quickly dissolved under a fresh wave of pain. She reached to touch the bandage around her wounded leg.

"I'll give you something to ease the pain." He rose to pour her another cup of broth, to which he added a dose of laudanum. When he returned to her side, she drank the broth, more slowly this time.

He eased her head back to the pillow. As the sedative began to take effect, she visibly relaxed, frowning at him with drowsy eyes.

"Why do you help me?" she murmured.

"It's my work. I tend to people when they're sick or injured. You're safe now. No one will hurt you here."

"If I do not die, Shaman, it is because the Creator brought me here to be healed by you."

"Well, I don't know what the Creator is doing these days," he said softly, "but you can call me Matt."

She whispered his name just before closing her eyes, allowing sleep to take her.

CHAPTER

2

"Three complete surgical theaters, Matthew," Dr. Henry Bowman said. "Over two thousand beds in all when the hospital is complete!"

Matt couldn't remember the last time such boyish glee had sprung from his sixty-five-year-old mentor. The younger doctor poured each of them a cup of coffee. Their office was slowly warming from a fresh fire in the wood stove.

"And the new procedures now available, well, you must see for yourself."

Despite Dr. Bowman's robust physique, his white hair and full beard added years to his appearance. He had just returned from a two-week visit in Washington to tour the new Hamilton General Hospital currently under construction. Dr. Adam Tyler and his wife, Kathleen, had hosted the doctor during his stay. Matt settled into the chair at his desk to hear the latest news of his parents.

"They're doing well," Dr. Bowman said, "though I think your father is working much too hard."

Matt grinned and took a sip of steaming coffee. "You must have been talking to my mother."

"Ah, Kathleen . . . such a lovely woman, your mother." Dr. Bowman smiled wistfully, stroking his whiskers. His blue-gray eyes, pale with age, looked somewhere far away, as they always did when Kathleen's name was mentioned. Sometimes Matt wondered had it not been for his father, if Dr. Bowman might have pursued his mother romantically. Margaret Bowman, the doctor's wife of three decades, had died some years earlier, and Dr. Bowman had never remarried. "Kathleen was busy managing your parents' social calendar."

"As always," Matt said with resignation. "And how is Daisy?"

Dr. Bowman frowned briefly in confusion. "The housekeeper? She seemed fine to me," he said with a shrug. "Why do you ask?"

"I received a letter from my mother a few weeks back, saying Daisy had been ill, so I've been concerned about her," Matt replied, though he would have asked about her in any case. The daughter of former slaves, Daisy had raised Matt and his sister from the time they were infants.

"Caroline arrived home from Europe while I was visiting. She looks wonderful. She's the picture of your mother, except for that beautiful blond hair of hers."

"Caroline's home?" His younger sister had planned to spend the winter in Europe. He was surprised that she had returned so soon after the holidays. "Did she say why?"

"She didn't. Perhaps she was homesick. She seemed a little sad to me. Your family is doing well, Matthew. They send their love and best regards to you. They're looking forward to your visit." He chose his next words carefully. "And after speaking with your father and Dr. Duncan, I believe a position at the hospital could be yours for the asking when the construction is finished in the spring."

Matt leaned back and propped his feet atop his desk. The prospect of his joining the staff of Hamilton General had been mentioned before.

"I've thought of what it would be like to work at the hospital. But I've been satisfied here. I love this town and I love my work here. It's been like a refuge. It's quiet and no one ever talks about the war. I don't know that I could go back to the city where people will start asking questions. Questions about what happened . . ." He almost shuddered at the thought, then his eyes rested on a horse-drawn wagon passing outside in the frozen dirt street. The farmer driving the wagon had come to town for supplies. The back was loaded down with sacks of flour and sugar, alongside bolts of colorful fabric that would soon be dresses on his wife and daughters.

"I understand your reluctance to leave Sylvan," Dr. Bowman was saying, "but the doctors at Hamilton General will be on the leading edge of new techniques and procedures. The opportunities would be tremendous. You're a gifted physician, Matthew, and still young. When I offered you this position, I never expected you'd stay here for the rest of your career. I knew you needed a quiet place to recover from the war. I know what war is like."

Matt took another sip of coffee and met Dr. Bowman's stare. "Did Dr. Duncan mention the charges against me?"

"Not directly, but I think he's aware of what happened. Being your father's son will go a long way toward overcoming any past indiscretions."

"My accusers would hardly call it an indiscretion. I believe the term they used was murder."

"Nevertheless, the government has its hands full with the Indian wars out west, and Reconstruction in the South. They won't be chasing down an inconsequential case from several years ago."

"I wish I could be sure of that."

"Dr. Duncan seemed enthusiastic about meeting you when you travel to Washington later this spring. You must have more faith in your father's attorneys."

"Some would say my absolution has been purchased. In a way, they're right. Maybe I don't deserve forgiveness for what happened."

Dr. Bowman shrugged. "You served honorably in the war, and you've done good work here."

Matt took a deep breath. "This town has been a refuge to me. But you're right, the opportunities would be vast at Hamilton General. I've been here in Sylvan more than a year. Perhaps it's time to move on. Take on some new work at the hospital."

"There will always be a need for our services, Matthew, no matter where we are. You could do excellent work at the hospital. And it would make your father very proud to have you on his staff."

Matt nodded in agreement. "You make a strong argument. I'll think about speaking with Dr. Duncan when I visit Hamilton General." Rising from his desk, he donned his coat and hat. "I have patients to see this morning." He did not mention that it was the patient he'd left sleeping in his cabin who was occupying his thoughts as much as any other.

Matt spent the morning checking on a young boy who had broken his arm two days earlier when he fell from a tree, and a farmer who had required stitches to close a wound he'd sustained while chopping wood.

His final stop was the Miller Hotel on the edge of town. Often the site of late-night drunken brawls, the Miller Hotel was considered the seediest establishment in town. Its proprietor, forty-year-old Charlotte Miller, was openly shunned on the street. Most people were aware of her "business on the side" as the genteel preferred to call it in gossipy whispers.

"Stay off your feet for the next few days," Matt told Charlotte as she lay in her upstairs bedroom. He placed his stethoscope back into his medical bag and looked at her pointedly. "No keeping company with the gentlemen for at least a few weeks. Your recovery from this will take a long time."

Charlotte's face flushed as red as her hair. "Thank you, Matt, for all you did for me yesterday. I got scared when the bleeding wouldn't stop."

"And the next time you want to end a pregnancy, for God's sake, don't try to do it yourself. Come to the office to see me, or send for me."

"Matt, I got no money to pay you—"

"You know I don't care about that," he said firmly. "I don't want you bleeding to death from a botched attempt to end your own pregnancy. You've been lucky up to now. Next time, send for me."

She nodded her compliance under his stern demeanor. Then his face softened. "I'm glad you're feeling better."

He looked around the starkly furnished bedroom. The place had taken on a chill from a dying fire and lowered blinds, so he bent to pick up several logs from the side of the hearth. He carefully stacked them atop glowing embers in the grate, and watched as the wood caught and the fire crackled anew. At one window, then the other, he raised the blinds to allow the feeble, mid-winter sunlight to brighten the room.

"Emma stayed right by my side all night," Charlotte told him with pride in her voice. "She's a good girl, Matt."

The doctor did not comment as he put on his coat and picked up his hat.

"I never got a chance to talk to you about what happened between you and Emma. I know she hurt you, but she didn't mean nothin' by it."

"There's not much to talk about. And if you know anything about what happened, you must know I was justified in ending our courtship."

"She didn't care nothin' about that boy she was with, Matt. She was just tryin' to bring in some extra money to the household, that's all."

When Matt made no reply, Charlotte lowered her pale blue eyes. She fingered the tattered edge of the quilt that covered her, looking despondent. He knew she blamed herself for the person Emma had become. She had raised her daughter alone, and though she had done her best, she had often known disappointment.

Charlotte blinked back tears. "Emma doesn't always think straight, especially when it comes to the gentlemen. It's because she never had a daddy."

Matt resisted the urge to defend his decision to Emma's mother. Though he still felt the sting of Emma's betrayal and humiliation, he had grown fond of Charlotte and remained determined not to burden her with his side of the story. She would either empathize with him and feel greater disappointment in her daughter, or she would feel compelled to rationalize her daughter's actions. He was interested in neither. He could foresee no positive outcome of bringing Charlotte into the mix.

Matt leaned over and put a warm hand over both of hers. "Don't worry, Emma will find someone to care for her."

She looked up at him and smiled sadly.

As he left the bedroom, he latched the door quietly behind him. Making his way down the narrow hallway to the back stairs, he heard footsteps racing up from the first floor.

"Matt!" Emma called breathlessly. "Rebecca just told me you were here."

"I was checking on your mother," he said flatly, stopping in the hallway to face her.

"Why don't you stay and eat?" Emma's cheerfulness sounded forced, and her blue eyes held the hard glint of determination. "Rebecca has a roast of beef in the oven—"

"Thank you, no. But I'm sure your mother would appreciate it if you brought her some lunch, and maybe a cup of tea."

Ignoring the look of irritation on Emma's face, Matt turned toward the stairs.

"When will you be back?"

"In a few days," he called back as his steps faded to the first floor.

Emma reluctantly turned toward her mother's bedroom. Then, remembering that the windows in that room face the street, she burst through the door, carelessly allowing it to bang against the adjoining wall. At the window, she scanned the street below and quickly caught sight of the departing doctor. He was fastening his medical bag to his saddle before reaching to untie his horse from the hitching post. One of the local merchants approached him and the two men began to converse.

Emma watched Matt intently. She watched the mist of his breath in the cold air as he chatted amiably with the other man. Her heart quickened at the sight of him, just as it always had.

He was unlike most other men Emma had known. At six-feet-two-inches tall, he stood well above his companion in the street. His broad shoulders narrowed to a lean waist. Always well groomed, he emanated a polished, yet relaxed and unassuming quality. Despite his family's rumored wealth and prominence in Washington, from the first day he arrived in Sylvan, Matt had been friendly and approachable. The townspeople soon grew to consider him one of their own.

She knew intimately the lines of his face when he was laughing, his soft green eyes that were always so expressive and kind, the strong line of his jaw, and his easy smile that revealed even, white teeth. She remembered tasting that mouth and feeling his hands on her body. She still quivered when she recalled his unselfish expertise. Considerate and imaginative, his love-making was often gently demanding, yet always responsive to her wishes and her needs.

She remembered running her fingers through his dark brown hair that was thick and just long enough to touch his collar in gentle waves. It had been a long time since she had kept company with the young doctor. As she watched him now, she realized her desire for him had not diminished since he abruptly ended their courtship some months ago. Despite his silly jealousies, she was determined to get back into his good graces.

She smiled to herself, her fingers toying with a blond curl that had escaped her chignon. Still stinging from his cold, authoritative demeanor in the hallway just now, she knew it would take patience on her part.

He's going to make me work for it, but when I win him back, I know it will all have been worth it.

"What are you doing?" her mother's voice from the bed startled Emma from her thoughts. She whirled quickly from the window.

"Watching Matt," she said, turning back around.

"He was just here. Did you talk to him?"

"We spoke a little in the hallway." Emma's breath made a frosty circle on the glass.

"You hurt him, honey. You should apologize."

Emma spun around, angry impatience on her face, her icy-blue eyes piercing. "Why should I apologize when it's his fault? I don't see why he should care if I keep company with other gentlemen. We're not married yet."

Turning again to the window, Emma scanned the street.

"Damn it!" she cried, stomping her foot. "Now he's gone."

As she headed for the door, Charlotte pleaded, "Honey, would you put another log on the fire? It's going to get cold in here again."

Emma barely slowed her pace. "Mama, I don't have time to be your nurse. I have better things to do, like run this hotel. I'll send one of the boys up to take care of it."

She marched out, slamming the door behind her.

CHAPTER

3

Riding back to his cabin at mid-day, Matt thought about his earlier conversation with Dr. Bowman. Working at the new hospital would benefit his career tremendously, though it would be difficult to give up his quiet life here in Sylvan. Three years as a surgeon in the Union Army had instilled a deep need for a peaceful existence. Sylvan had indeed been a refuge. No one in town knew anything about the events of that hellish day when Colonel Garrison had died under his care in the field hospital. Afterwards, the Garrison family had called it murder, and Matt's spotty memory of that day could not confirm that they were wrong. *If anyone deserved to die, it was that bastard.* But was it possible he could have purposely withheld medical care from this officer who had been widely despised by his men for sending them to their deaths in battle without planning or preparation?

Dr. Bowman seemed confident that the matter would never be pursued. Yet Matt couldn't shake the fear that one day, he would have to defend his conduct of that time with very little accurate recall. *Why can't I remember?*

With effort, he pushed that worry aside. As soon as the worst of winter was past, he would travel to Washington for the grand opening of Hamilton General. It was a dream for which his father had been working tirelessly. And he would speak to the hospital administrator while he was there. The war had ended nearly two years ago. Perhaps enough time had passed now and no questions would be asked. His work in Sylvan had been most fulfilling. He had come to love the people of the town and felt a sense of fulfillment in helping them, even though most could never pay. He would look forward to the opportunities at the new hospital, but not to the inevitable inclusion into Washington's social circles. He had always found his parents' contemporaries to be pretentious and artificial. Daisy had taught him to be polite and respectful toward them, but he had no desire to befriend them. Especially now, since returning from war, he needed to feel a sense of belonging among people who led simple lives and found joy in simple things. And yet, the idea of exploring opportunities at Hamilton General was intriguing.

Even before he dismounted, Matt could hear Degan's desperate cries from inside the cabin. He secured the gelding to the porch post, flew up the steps, and burst through the door. Still asleep, she was crying and thrashing about in the bed, clearly in the grip of a nightmare. He quickly tossed his coat and hat aside and sat down beside her.

"Degan," he said. He pulled her upright and said louder, "Degan, wake up."

Her eyes flew open, and she shrank back.

"It's all right. You were having a nightmare."

Shaking and gasping for air as if she had been running hard, she looked down to see her wrists encircled with clean linen. She reached to clutch the bandage around her neck.

"It's just the bandages. You're safe now."

Panic-stricken, she shook her head. "No, they come for me. They are coming for me!"

"No one is coming for you—"

"They will find me here. They will follow me and take me again. They will kill me!"

"No, they—"

"Don't let them take me, please!"

"I won't let them take you. I won't let anyone hurt you."

She bent to press her face against clenched fists, and sobbed uncontrollably. Instinctively, Matt reached to gather her in his arms to comfort her, but this upset her more. She stiffened and recoiled, pushing him away.

"I won't hurt you." He let go, suddenly feeling awkward and useless. He had treated frightened patients before. During the war, Confederate soldiers had always held distrust and suspicion in their eyes when he approached, unsure of the true intentions of an enemy surgeon. But

Degan's extreme reaction made him uneasy. Though he had cared for her physical injuries, he realized the horrors she had endured would continue to bring frightening dreams. Occasionally, such nightmares still haunted his sleep too. Other soldiers had confided to him of similar terrors since the war. From experience, he knew it would be many months, perhaps longer, before her dreams would return to normal.

When she finally quieted and sat up, she dragged a bandaged wrist across her wet eyes. With a grimace, she put a hand to her ribs. Keeping her head down, she seemed to brace herself before murmuring, "Please, water?"

"Of course." He offered her the cup from the bedside table, but she was clearly afraid to take it. The idea that she could ask for something from a white man and be given it without punishment remained foreign to her. He waited patiently until she finally reached for the cup and backed away. She kept watchful eyes on him as she drank.

When the cup was drained, she reclined again, pulling the blanket to her waist.

"Let's see how this leg is healing," Matt said, reaching to lift the blanket.

She stiffened again, her eyes wide. "No!" she said firmly, seizing the blanket and clamping it tightly over her lower body.

"Degan, I'm only going to look at the wound and change the bandage, that's all."

"No, no more!" Her eyes burned with angry defiance and she looked ready for a battle.

Irritation rising, he leaned forward and met her stare. "I understand your need to protect yourself. I know what they did to you. But I have no intention of hurting you in that way. I have no interest in what's under that blanket except for the wound in your leg. If I meant to harm you, why would I be taking care of you? Why would I be tending to your wounds?"

For a moment, she seemed to consider the logic of his questions, but she did not release her grip.

"Degan," he said evenly, "I'm going to look at your wound and change that bandage whether you allow it or not. Don't fight me, I don't have much patience today. If I have to, I'll tie your hands to this bed so I can do my work."

When she still refused to yield, Matt tore two strips from a roll of linen. He slipped one end around her left wrist and quickly secured it to the wooden bed frame beneath her. When she reached to free herself, he looped the cloth around her other wrist and pulled it to the other side of the frame.

Anger quickly dissolved from her face, and panic descended. "No, don't." He stopped to look at her skeptically. "Please . . . don't tie my hands," she pleaded, surrendering her grip and lifting her fingers from the blanket.

"You'll let me change the bandage?" He watched as she struggled with the choice. "Answer me. You'll let me change the bandage?"

She hesitated, then whispered, "Yes."

Freeing her hands, the assurance that he would not harm her rose again to his lips, but he said nothing. He knew his words held no meaning for her. Only time would teach her that she truly had nothing to fear from him.

He pushed the blanket aside, and unwrapped the soiled linen from her leg. The deep hole from which he had extracted the bullet had stopped bleeding.

"You're lucky. I don't see any infection," he told her, pouring warm water from the stove into a basin. As he prepared to bathe the wound, she turned her head away and squeezed her eyes shut. With trembling hands, she gripped the hem of the shirt in tight fists. Matt sensed she was on the verge of hysteria, but she made no further move to interfere. He wet a towel in the warm water, and pressed it carefully over the wound. She flinched in silence.

"I'm not trying to hurt you. I have to keep the wound clean so infection doesn't set in. This won't take long."

She turned her head to scowl at him. He wondered how long it would take for trust to replace fear. *Surely, she's had positive contact with white people in her lifetime.* But he realized her recent ordeal at the hands of the criminals who brutalized her had wiped out any good impressions she might have had of white men.

He finished by wrapping her leg with clean linen.

"There, that wasn't so bad." When he reached to remove the bandage from her neck, she shrank back. "Shhhhh, be still." He untied the linen strips and saw that the salve he had applied the night before had begun its healing. Wrapping fresh cloth around her neck, he was careful to lift her long hair away from the binding. "Is that too tight?" he asked as he secured the ends of the bandage. She only stared at him. He put a hand under her jaw and turned her face toward the light. "Your face looks better. The swelling is going down. In fact, all your injuries are beginning to heal nicely."

Matt leaned back to consider her for a moment. The fact that she would eventually be up and around presented a dilemma he hadn't thought of until now: she would soon need clothes to wear. Before long, he would have to stop at one of the dress shops in town to make the purchases. His next thought was how he would explain his mission to a confused shop girl, as no male he'd ever known had ventured into a ladies' dress emporium, even in the city.

A grimace of pain distorted Degan's face, shaking Matt from his thoughts. He rose to stoke the fire in the belly of the stove. The pot of broth quickly warmed again. He uncapped a small brown bottle from the apothecary cabinet, and mixed a dose of laudanum with the warm broth.

"This will help ease the pain," he told her, positioning an extra pillow under her back, which allowed her to sit more upright. She took the broth without protest. "I'll find you something to eat."

In the kitchen area, he removed a cotton towel from a basket of cornbread and biscuits that had been given to him the day before. Knowing he lived alone, the town matrons often indulged him with homemade baked goods. He prepared a tray, arranging biscuits and squares of cornbread on a plate, adding butter and a small bowl of honey.

"Something here should appeal to you," he said, placing the tray on the bedside table. To his surprise, she seemed fearful and reluctant to partake. She backed away, her wide eyes darting from his face to the food. He sat down again.

"Go ahead, eat all of it if you want."

With shaking hands, she seized a piece of cornbread and shoved it into her mouth with reckless urgency. Barely taking time to chew, she swallowed, and a second piece was in her hand, then her mouth. She closed her eyes and savored the sweetness of the coarse, yellow bread. For the first time, she seemed not to care that Matt was sitting so close, watching her.

Astonished at her fervor, he asked, "When's the last time you had anything to eat?" She opened her eyes and, without answering, stuffed a third piece into her mouth. "Maybe you should slow down. I'd hate to see all that come back up."

He picked up a biscuit and pulled it apart, exposing the fluffy-white softness of its center. When he reached for the butter knife, she shook her head.

"No? This?" he asked, taking the spoon from the honey dish.

She nodded.

"Ah, she likes honey," he said, drizzling the amber syrup onto the biscuit. When he offered her the honey-soaked half, he thought he saw the beginnings of a timid smile peeking from the corners of her mouth. Keeping her eyes down, she reached for the biscuit, careful not to touch his fingers. He witnessed her actually chewing this piece instead of swallowing it whole.

By the time the plate was empty, the laudanum had taken effect, drowsiness descending over her like a warm cloak. Matt removed the extra pillow from behind her.

"Get some rest," he told her as she lay back.

She was asleep before he pulled the blanket to her shoulders.

"Degan."

A man had called her name, but it was not her husband's voice, nor her father's. Was she dreaming? She heard the winter wind howling outside, but the warmth of the lodge fire embraced her. She felt a gentle hand across her forehead, coaxing her from the depths of slumber.

"Degan, wake up."

She stirred and opened drowsy eyes to see the white shaman standing over her. Startled, she tensed, then remembered that she could relax. For the past two weeks, he had roused her in the early morning to offer her food and medicine before he left.

"I always hate to wake you when you're sleeping like that," he said, placing her breakfast tray on the table beside her.

The aroma of fresh bread and fried potatoes wafted toward her as she oriented herself once again to the shaman's lodge. The white shaman had told her from the beginning that she was safe here with him. So far, he had not given her reason to believe otherwise. He had provided her with food and water in abundance, and had not hurt her in any way when she ate and drank. He allowed her to sleep as much as she wanted, and always awakened her gently, as he had done this morning. When he sensed that she was in pain, he gave her medicine to take it away. Tending to her injuries, he had touched her body many times, but had never struck her, or forced himself on her. His hands, always warm and clean, had touched her only to treat her wounds, never to torment her, or for his own pleasure.

Reaching for a piece of bread from the tray, she watched him gather papers from his desk. He assembled his medicine bag, and lifted his coat from the rack by the door. Ready to leave, he came to sit beside her, the familiar look of concern in his eyes.

"Do you have any pain?" he asked. "I can give you medicine before I go."

"No," she replied. "Today is better. No medicine."

"All right. Try to get some more rest. I'll check on you later."

At day's end, while she took her supper, Matt sat at his desk across the great room, reading his medical journals and updating patient notes from the day. One evening, she questioned this routine.

"You do not eat?"

He stopped in mid-fluff of her pillows. "I ate in town before I came home." A look of disappointment briefly crossed her face. "I think you'll like this," he said, positioning the tray before her. "It's Mrs. Bradley's chicken stew. She's the best cook in Sylvan."

"Why do you eat in the town?" Degan asked, dunking a spoon into the steaming bowl of thick stew.

Matt shrugged. "It's just my habit. I don't like eating alone. I prefer the company of other people."

He settled comfortably at his desk across the room, reaching for a leather pouch of tobacco to fill his pipe. With the flick of a match, gray smoke puffed gently from his mouth. The sweet aroma of burning tobacco soon filled the room. Spreading his work before him, he glanced up to see Degan watching him with rapt attention.

"Do you need something?" he asked.

She pointed to his pipe. "This is your medicine?"

He frowned, his mind racing to make sense of her question. Then from the recesses of his memory, he recalled that many Indian tribes considered smoking to be a spiritual activity, reserved for the elders of the tribe during religious ceremonies. Natives believed their prayers were transported upward by the smoke.

"No," he said, amused at the notion that his smoking might somehow assist him in his work. "The body heals itself. Whatever I do just . . . helps it along."

"You are the shaman." Her tone reverent, she seemed unconvinced by his modest claim.

Matt made no reply, meeting her earnest stare with a smile as she resumed eating. He was pleased with the progression of her recovery. She had gradually grown more comfortable with him, and each day her personality emerged more. It had been two weeks since he found her in his barn that cold night. It was remarkable what plenty of rest and good food had done to restore her physical health. He still pulled her from the depths of an occasional nightmare, and he expected they would remain with her for a while. Physically, she was healing well. Soon she would not be spending her days sleeping in recovery, and would be eager for companionship by the end of the day. Perhaps that was why she looked disappointed when he told her he had taken his supper in town. With that in mind, he decided to join her for dessert.

When she finished the last spoonful of the stew, he set his pipe aside. In the kitchen area he retrieved two china plates and two forks from the cupboard. He then carefully removed the cotton cloth Mrs. Bradley had used to wrap a fresh cherry pie she had proudly presented to him earlier that afternoon. The matrons of the town often treated him to delectable desserts. It had not taken long for Matt to discover that Degan had a penchant for sweets. He cut two slices of the pie, served them onto the plates, and took them to the bedside.

"Try this," he said, offering her one of the plates and a fork. She smiled shyly at him as he sat down. Tasting the confection, pleasure blossomed on her face.

"Mrs. Bradley is an excellent cook. There's a group of ladies in town who make such things for me. They think that until I take a wife, I need to be looked after. That seems to include supplying me with home-cooked meals and desserts. I never turn them down," he said with a grin.

"You live alone here? No wife? No people?"

"My family lives in Washington. That's where I grew up. It's a long way from here."

"Why do you live away from your people?"

"I was a surgeon in the war. When the war ended, I was offered an apprenticeship here."

Degan frowned. "Appren . . ."

"Apprenticeship. It's a time of training. There's an older doctor in town. I work with him."

"The old shaman teaches you?"

"That's right," he said, silently wondering how Dr. Bowman would feel about being called an "old shaman." "I've been curious, how did you learn English? Who taught you?"

"The friends. Many years ago."

"Friends?" Matt thought for a moment, then realized what she meant. "You mean the Quakers?"

"Yes. They came to us and said they will teach the white words and the white ways. They make a school for us. So we will be like the whites."

"I see," Matt said. Her dark eyes were fixed on his face, as though she had more questions.

"You have no wife?"

"No."

Empathy saddened her expression. "My husband died also."

"No, I . . . I've never had a wife. Was your husband killed when you were taken from your village?"

"He died before. He was hunting and fell from the mountain. He lived two days. The shaman could not heal him."

"I don't suppose he could with no medical training and no knowledge of the human body," Matt said with an edge of scorn in his tone. He had heard stories of native healing ceremonies that included burning herbs, shaking rattles, and chanting over the sick and injured. "It's a miracle anyone survives illness or injury under those conditions."

Degan kept her eyes down. "The shaman heals many. But it is not the white way." When she finally looked up, she asked, "You healed many in the war?"

"We did our best. It was a long damn war," he said quietly, gazing into the distance as if watching a scene unfold. "We patched up the bodies as best we could. Sent them back to the fighting, only to come back maimed and bloody again. Others, we cut off arms and legs and sent them home." He closed his eyes and grimaced. He could still hear the cries of soldiers, some grown men, some just boys, begging him not to saw off their limbs. Many became enraged, screaming "butcher!" at him just before they fell asleep under the chloroform. He wondered if he would ever be able to silence the voices that still tortured him. "War is such a goddamn waste.

So many young boys massacred, and for what? Families never recover from the loss and misery. It makes no sense."

Silence hung heavily between them before Matt broke from his daze, took a deep, uneasy breath, and met Degan's eyes.

"No more," she murmured, placing the remains of the pie on the tray.

He rose to take the tray to the kitchen. Returning to the infirmary, he withdrew a wood-framed screen from the corner and positioned it around the bed, creating a more private enclosure. She watched as he filled a porcelain bowl with hot water from the stove and placed it on the bedside table, along with a bar of soap and thick towels.

"I'm going to remove your bandages so you can bathe," he told her.

He sat down on the edge of the bed, and began to unwrap the strips of linen from her wrists. She sat quietly, holding her wrists out to him. He suddenly realized that she had not cringed in fear as he approached. In fact, it had been several days since he had seen utter terror on her face when she looked at him.

"You don't seem so frightened of me anymore," he said. "I'm glad."

Her dark eyes met his. "I was afraid you were like the other white men who hurt me."

"I understand."

"Maybe you want a slave. Maybe you heal me so I will be strong to work for you."

Matt chuckled at the idea of keeping a slave, though he knew that to be a reality for many captured natives and whites alike.

"I don't want a slave," he said, reaching under her hair to loosen the bandage around her neck. "And I don't want you to work for me. That's not why I'm taking care of you."

"When I am healed, what will happen to me?"

"I suppose that's up to you."

"I want to go home," she said firmly, "back to my people."

"Then I expect that's what will happen to you."

"You will let me go?"

"Of course, why wouldn't I? You're my patient, not my prisoner. You can leave as soon as you're recovered." When he looked up from his work, he saw bewilderment on her face.

He touched the warm skin of her neck. The rope burn, so bloody-raw that first night, would soon be healed. Moving to sit behind her, he said,

"I'm going to lift this shirt, and remove the binding from your ribs. You'll be able to breathe easier."

He gathered her long hair in both hands and swept it forward over one shoulder. He then lifted the shirt to expose the snug fabric that bound her ribs. She sat very still. Unwinding the material, he noticed the fading welts across her back. She stiffened when he reached to unwrap the loosening fabric from the front of her body. He took great care not to touch her breasts.

"I'm going to press against your ribs. I'm not trying to hurt you. It's the only way I can tell if your ribs are healing." He pressed both hands firmly down her bare back and around her sides, careful to avoid the healing abrasions. "Do you feel any pain?" he asked.

"Yes, a little."

"Take a deep breath." When she complied, he asked, "Any pain?"

"A little. But please, no more binding. I want to breathe like this."

"All right, as long as you're just resting, I can leave the binding off." He was quiet for a moment, then, "How did you get all these wounds on your back?"

She pulled the sheet protectively to her chest. "I ran away before. They found me and brought me back. They tied my hands and beat me."

Horrified, Matt could barely speak. "My God, the bastards." He now understood why her nightmares often resulted in her insistence that her captors would find her and take her back to be punished. With a measure of guilt, he also remembered the panicked look on her face when he tied her hands to the bed so she couldn't interfere with his work.

He decided not to pose any more questions, not wanting to traumatize her further. He shuddered in helpless rage. During the war, he had witnessed so many acts of unthinkable brutality, soldier against soldier, and had often repaired the damage brought about by those acts. But this seemed far worse. From the first night, his heart was full of sympathy for Degan, and outrage at the savage treatment she had suffered. He knew a feeling of protectiveness that was stronger than he had ever experienced with any other patient.

He took a moment to stroke her back, as if by his touch he could undo the harm and cruelty she had endured. Then he pulled the shirt down and collected the discarded bandages.

"I'll let you have some privacy. I'll get you a clean shirt to wear," he said, turning to leave her to her bath.

"Matt," she said. He stopped and looked down at her. She was still clutching the sheet to her body. Her dark eyes were soft with unguarded sincerity as she searched for words. "Thank you . . . for giving me food and water, and caring for me."

He stood frozen in place and swallowed hard. "You're welcome," was all he could think to say, suddenly feeling self-conscious and uncomfortable with her gratitude. He dropped his eyes and made a quick exit from the enclosure.

Seated at his desk, Matt lit his pipe again, and puffed leisurely while the sounds of splashing water came from behind the screen. He found it difficult to keep his mind on his work. He had decided to stop at a dress shop in town the next day to purchase clothing for Degan.

Though her time here is temporary, she's now recovered enough to be up and around. She should have proper clothes to wear.

He tried to think of all the items she would need. He realized he would have to rely on the shop girl to help him. Never before had he purchased a dress of any kind, much less ladies' undergarments. But Degan would need everything. No matter how awkward and embarrassing his shopping trip proved to be, he would have to be the one to provide for her.

CHAPTER

4

The clanking bells on the door of Connor's Ladies Emporium the next afternoon announced the arrival of a customer. Young Jessica Connor scurried from the back room of her mother's dress shop and stopped abruptly in her tracks when she saw Matt. She smoothed her dark auburn curls back into a semblance of tidiness, and self-consciously straightened the bodice of her green-print dress.

"Dr. Tyler!" she said, unveiled surprise in her wide brown eyes. "Good afternoon. Were you looking for someone?"

"Hello, Miss Connor. Ah, no, I'm here to . . . purchase some clothing." He tried his best to sound nonchalant, but his face suddenly felt hot and he had a sense of disorientation, as though he had just stepped onto the surface of another planet.

"Oh . . ." her voice trailed off, and she looked confused. "Are you buying a gift for someone? We have the measurements for many of the ladies in town. If you tell me who it's for, I can help you choose material, and we'll have it made . . ."

"I don't think you'd have the measurements of the lady I'm shopping for, but I might be able to guess her size. In fact," he looked more closely at the young clerk's figure, "I'd say she's pretty close to your size, Miss Connor. You do have dresses for purchase that are already made, don't you?"

"Yes, of course," she said, flustered by his obvious scrutiny of her form. "Mrs. Tanner sent over some outwork just yesterday."

"Outwork?"

"Dresses she made to sell in our shop. She's an excellent seamstress, one of our best."

"Excellent! In that case, I'd like to see Mrs. Tanner's work, please."

Still perplexed, Miss Connor hesitated.

Matt cleared his throat and with a nervous eye toward the door, said sheepishly, "I don't suppose many of your customers are men."

Her cheeks turned pink and she smiled uneasily. "You're the first. Come this way."

They began at the front of the shop where wooden racks held dresses on display, some made of cotton, some of linen, a few dressier styles made of silk and taffeta. Not sure how many outfits to buy, he recalled from his boyhood that no fewer than twelve steamer trunks had always accompanied his family when they traveled. His mother's extensive wardrobe had occupied all but two of those trunks, even for a brief excursion. As his sister Caroline grew, the number of steamer trunks increased. He had once questioned his father about this as they watched a weary porter unload the trunks and stack them on the back of a wagon for transport to the family's accommodation. With resignation in his voice, his father had told him simply, "Ladies like to have an abundance of selection among their frocks."

Degan will be returning home in a few weeks, there's no need to purchase more than a few items. He chose two cotton dresses, one in a rich shade of blue, the other pale yellow. He then picked out two skirts and two blouses to be worn interchangeably.

As Miss Connor held up each garment, Matt tried to envision Degan wearing it. He was reasonably sure his choices would fit her small frame. He rejected a number of more elaborate styles. In Washington, as well as in Sylvan, he often saw ladies wearing dresses and bonnets adorned with bunches of flowers, feathers, or other garish ornamentation. Bustles attached at the waist created a great shelf atop their backsides upon which yards of fabric gathered to form a cascade to the ground. Though these latest styles were popular, he thought they looked ridiculous. For Degan, he chose simpler dresses that suited her.

Miss Connor took her time wrapping each piece in brown paper. She then began to total the purchases, easily the largest single sale she had ever made.

"Wait," Matt held out a hand, "before you do that . . . what about . . ." he leaned forward and muttered the word "undergarments?"

Miss Connor's eyes grew large again. A crimson flush that began at the base of her neck surged quickly to her hairline. "You want undergarments too?" she finally choked in disbelief.

"I'm afraid so. Would you help me please?"

Miss Connor shook her head, shrinking under the weight of embarrassment. "Dr. Tyler, I don't think I can help you." Though they were alone in the store, she leaned forward to whisper, "How is it that you're buying all these personal things for a lady? It just isn't proper."

Matt lowered his voice as well. "She has no means, and no one to look after her. I'm just helping her out, that's all. She does need . . . everything."

"Oh."

Nervously, he looked again toward the door, surprised and very grateful that no other customers had entered while he was there. He wondered how long his luck would hold. "Please, would you reconsider? I'd certainly be lost without your assistance."

She took a deep breath, her face full of compassion, as though she were reaching to help a wounded animal out of a trap. "Well, all right. Follow me."

The young clerk whisked her customer into a private room at the back of the store where shelves were stacked with neatly folded ladies' underclothing. The more expensive items were made of silk, the less expensive made of cotton and linen. Clearly enduring a measure of shame, Miss Connor held up a beautifully crafted silk chemise, and another made of cotton. Running his hands along both, Matt pronounced the silk decidedly softer and purchased seven, the store's entire stock. Miss Connor recommended petticoats, six pairs of pantalets, and five pairs of stockings.

The uncomfortable task of choosing undergarments completed, Matt felt a bit more at ease. Perhaps there was nothing inherently odd about a man purchasing ladies' dresses and undergarments. In his new, relaxed mind-set, and with a sense that the worst was over, he took the liberty of wandering around the back room unescorted. He perused all the available merchandise, including shoes and boots, hats and bonnets, and hair accessories.

"What about a corset?"

He turned to see Miss Connor holding up a frightfully stiff, form-fitting bodice with long strings attached in the back for lacing tight.

Matt scowled and shook his head. "That looks far too uncomfortable."

"It is very uncom—!" she blurted, then immediately clamped a hand over her mouth, and blushed deeper for revealing such an intimate detail to a gentleman she barely knew.

Matt chuckled. "Rest assured, Miss Connor, I won't be sharing your secret with any men I know."

His arms stacked high with bundles of brown-paper packages, Matt made his way to his wagon. He looked up to see his friend, Jonathan Monroe, crossing the street, a perplexed look on his face.

"Matt! Need some help?" Jon leaned over the side of the wagon.

"That's the last of the packages, Jon," he replied, purposely ignoring his friend's quizzical expression.

"Looks like you bought out the store. What is all this?"

"I'm helping one of my patients get back on her feet after a terrible accident."

"Oh," Jon said, looking confused. He turned to see Miss Connor standing in the doorway of the shop, a soft smile on her face. "You bought her all of this?"

"She needs everything."

"Where's her family?" Jon asked, watching as Matt hastily mounted the driver's seat of his wagon and picked up the reins.

"Sorry, Jon, I don't have time to talk. I'll see you tomorrow." Matt snapped the reins, and his horse pulled the wagon into the street. He turned to wave to his friend who stood bewildered on the wooden sidewalk.

A crisp gust of wind swept into the cabin when Matt pushed the door open. Weighed down with parcels, he threw a quick "hello" in Degan's direction, passing into the bedroom. He dumped everything unceremoniously onto his bed.

Degan sat up and slowly swung her feet to the floor. Covering her lower body with the blanket, she watched as Matt made another trip from his wagon into the bedroom with an armload of packages.

"How are you feeling?" he asked, bending to stoke the wood in the stove.

"I feel better today," she said, smoothing her hair as if it looked unkempt when she sat up.

He sat down to face her. "Those packages I took to my bedroom are for you. Now that you're feeling better, you'll be up and around more. You'll be needing clothes to wear. Would you like to see what I bought?"

With a shy smile, she nodded and started to get up. Matt quickly rose and put one hand under her elbow and the other around her waist, helping her to her feet.

"Can you walk?" he asked, as she gingerly shifted some weight to her left leg.

"I am not strong on this side. But I want to walk . . . to be strong again."

"Lean on me," he said. "We'll take it slow."

A sizeable four-poster bed dominated the bedroom, with a leather armchair before the fireplace, a polished armoire, and thick rugs. A wood-framed screen partitioned one corner of the room. Atop the bedside table lay a book, and smoking accoutrements, including a pipe stand and an ashtray. The rugs and curtains of deep red gave the room a cozy, masculine ambiance. The quilt covering his bed was barely visible beneath the multitude of packages. Degan turned to Matt in wide-eyed astonishment.

"It's mostly dresses, skirts and blouses," he said. "Go ahead, open them. I'll help you."

They began tearing at the brown paper. As each new garment was revealed, Degan examined the material, running her fingers over the sleeves, the collar, the buttons, the fine stitching. Matt had also bought her a pair of leather ankle boots and a hooded cloak of dark blue wool. She had never seen so many articles of clothing at one time. Though everything looked quite different from the ornately beaded and layered clothing her people wore, she had to admit that all were skillfully made.

Several smaller packages lay to the side, unopened. Matt reached for them.

"These are the . . . undergarments," he said. Avoiding her eyes, he added stiffly, "I trust you won't need any assistance."

Degan silently took the packages. The clothes displayed across the bed, she stepped back to look at everything. "You are very kind. I can never repay you."

He reached for yet another small package buried under the dresses. "I don't expect you to repay me." He unwrapped the package to reveal a hairbrush, its ivory handle adorned with delicately painted flowers. He offered it to her.

She whispered, "Thank you," as she took it.

"You're welcome. Now, I'm going to leave so you can try these things on. There's a mirror on the washstand behind that screen. I'll be in the other room if you need anything, all right?"

At the washstand behind the partition, Degan peered into the mirror. She could see only faint traces of her injuries. Pale red lines were all that remained of the ropes that had bound her at the neck and wrists. She looked closely at her face. The swelling had gone completely. Only a few fading bruises remained. She could discern no permanent physical damage from her ordeal. Still holding the hairbrush, she began to brush her long hair and was surprised at how good it felt.

She unbuttoned Matt's shirt, one of many that had served as her only articles of clothing for the last two weeks. Gazing at her naked body from the waist up, she could only imagine what she must have looked like that first night, ragged and bloody, when Matt found her. She remembered waking up in the small bed, seeing the clean bandages on her wrists and leg, and realizing he must have washed the blood and filth from her body before clothing her in his own shirt. If the shaman had not tended to her injuries, she certainly would have died.

Suddenly, the nightmare came rushing back. She covered her face with her hands, and fought back a panicked cry. It seemed like only yesterday—and yet a lifetime ago—that the savage white men invaded her home on the reservation in the middle of the night. She knew they had shot her mother dead, but the men had taken her and her sister away before she could tell if other family members had survived the attack, or if they had all perished. With some difficulty, she pushed those thoughts from her mind to focus again on her recovery.

She looked up and caught a glimpse of the bed laden with all the new clothes, and marveled again at Matt's generosity. She could not imagine the cost of everything. She would never be able to repay him for everything he had done for her. But she resolved to think of something she could do that would express her gratitude for saving her life, and caring for her all this time. For as long as she had been living with him, Matt's kindness had never wavered. He had treated her with care and respect. Even when she had been helpless to defend herself, he had not harmed her. In fact, he had worked hard to heal her, frequently offering her medicine to take away her pain as she recovered. He was not at all like the other white men. Only the Quaker missionaries who lived among her people when she was a girl had shown such kindness. She remembered the school they had built, and how they had taught her and the other children in the village the white man's language. They had taught the white customs so that she and the rest would be "civilized," they had said. They had been respectful and she knew they meant well, but her grandmother had been determined to teach her the Haudenosaunee ways as well.

Abruptly, tears of loss and agony welled, threatening to drown her. She closed her eyes tightly and pushed the memories and the sadness back down inside. Everything was too much to think about now and she was not yet strong enough to grieve. She stroked her hair again with the brush. Though intense anguish lingered just beneath the surface, she forced herself to think of the present moment, and that she was now in a safe place. The shaman had assured her that no harm would come to her here. She thought of his strong, gentle hands that were always warm and clean. She found comfort in his easy smile and his striking green eyes that were so kind.

A short time later, Degan emerged from the bedroom wearing the dress of light blue print. Feet propped atop his desk, Matt was enjoying a cigar. When he saw her, an approving smile spread across his face.

"Very nice," he said softly. "That color suits you."

Unexpectedly, his expression pleased her. She was glad she had taken the time to brush her hair to shining. It felt good to be dressed and standing, even if she was still very weak.

"Does everything fit?" He came around the front of the desk to sit on a corner. It was then that he looked down to see her bare feet beneath the hem of the dress.

"Yes, everything is right."

"Everything except the shoes?" He pointed to the floor where she stood.

She looked down. "Yes, the shoes fit, but I . . . they . . ." She struggled to find the words to explain that she had never grown accustomed to the shoes of stiff leather that were common among the white people.

Matt waved his hand. "It's all right, I think I understand. They're not what you're used to wearing."

"But I will learn to wear them," she assured him, not wanting to seem ungrateful, or insulting of his generosity. "And I will work for you . . . for the clothes. And for healing me."

Matt frowned as he exhaled gray smoke. "No, you won't. I told you, I don't want repayment for anything. I don't want you to think about anything but resting and getting completely well. Do you understand?"

She nodded.

"Good."

"Where do I put everything? Your bed is covered."

"Ah, good question . . ." He rose from the desk, muttering something about making space in his armoire as he returned to the bedroom. Following him, Degan began to gather the skirts and blouses as Matt opened the massive wooden doors of the armoire, and pushed some of his own clothing to one side. "We can put everything in here for now."

She stroked the material of a blouse before handing it to Matt. Then, with a sudden cry, she took a step back, her eyes wide with panic.

"What's wrong?" Matt asked, following her stare which seemed fixed on his clothes hanging in the armoire. He looked in the armoire, then back at her, confused. "What is it?"

Paralyzed with fear, she seemed unable to breathe or look away.

"Degan, tell me what's wrong," Matt said urgently, reaching to touch her arm.

As if stung by his touch, she jumped back and shot him a look of terror that he had not seen since the first night he found her. She pointed wordlessly to the dark blue frock coat of his Union Army uniform that hung among his other garments, its golden shoulder straps faded but prominent.

Her voice quivering and barely audible, she said, "The men who . . . hurt me . . . wore this."

"My uniform?" Alarm and confusion dissolved into a relieved chuckle. "You had me worried there for a moment."

Still shaking, she staggered back onto the edge of the bed and put her head in her hands. Matt came to sit next to her, but she quickly moved away from him.

"Degan, there's nothing to be afraid of, it's just the coat of my uniform that I wore in the army. I don't even know why I still keep it, except that it's the warmest damn coat I've ever had." He waited to see if his words would calm her, but they didn't. "Look, if it's that upsetting to you, I'll store it someplace else while you're here. I need the extra space in the armoire now for your clothes anyway."

As if afraid to look up at him, she kept her eyes fastened to the floor. "You are not one of them?"

"Of course not. I was an officer in the Union Army. If they wore coats like that, they were in the army also, but that's the only way we're the same. There were thousands of men in the Union Army. We all had coats like that."

When she said nothing, he rose from the bed, removed the coat and took it to the great room, out of her sight. When he returned, she was still sitting motionless on the edge of the bed.

He came to stand beside her. "Better?"

She did not look up.

"Degan, you're safe with me. No harm will come to you here." When he saw no reaction from her, he said, "Have I hurt you in any way since you've been here?"

"No," she whispered.

"And I won't. I told you, you can stay here as long as you need to. When you're fully recovered, you'll go home."

His assurances finally seemed to penetrate her fear. "When the men took me, I was afraid of death. Then I prayed for death to take me. Now that I will live, I want to go back to my family. I don't know what I will find. I know my mother is dead. But maybe others live."

"I'm sorry about your mother," Matt said softly. "When you're well, I'll make arrangements for you to travel back to your home."

"But I could go back on the horse I took from the men. I would need only food and a blanket to sleep on—"

"Degan, the Allegheny Reservation is hundreds of miles from here. You're much too weak to make a journey like that. And it's too dangerous for a woman to travel alone, especially in the wintertime. I have to go to Washington in a few weeks. By the time I come back, winter will be over and you'll be well enough to travel. I'll arrange for you to return to your reservation."

Just then a frantic pounding at the front door startled them. Matt rushed out to open the door and Degan heard him say, "Jeremy, what happened?"

"Dr. Tyler," said a young boy urgently, "it's my ma. Pa hit her and now she won't wake up. Can you come?"

"Yes, I'll get my bag." Matt rushed back to the bedroom and told Degan in a low tone, "I have to go. It's an emergency. I'll be back as soon as I can."

CHAPTER

5

A dog barked wildly at the sight of an unfamiliar visitor as Jeremy reined the wagon to a stop in front of the farmhouse. The Boyds lived on a few acres just west of Sylvan. Matt had spoken briefly with Jeremy's father, Charles, on several occasions, usually when he came into town for supplies.

"Pa's drunk," Jeremy said. Matt wondered if this was an explanation or a warning.

"Where's your mother?" he asked as they mounted the porch steps.

"Inside." Jeremy opened the front door, cautiously peeking around the edge.

Matt entered swiftly. "Mrs. Boyd?" When no answer came, he said, "Show me where she is."

Jeremy took hold of the doctor's sleeve and led him through the kitchen to a chilly back room. Mrs. Boyd lay on a tattered and stained divan that sat against the far wall. Her eyes were open now, and without saying a word, she wrapped her arm around the waist of her young son when he came within reach.

"Hello, Mrs. Boyd." Matt smiled as he sat down on the edge of the divan. He quickly pressed two fingers firmly to her neck to measure her pulse. Her face and hands looked weathered, aged well beyond her years.

"I think under the circumstances, Dr. Tyler, you can call me Laura," she said, returning his smile weakly.

"What did he hit you with?" Matt asked.

"My hand," a gruff voice answered from the doorway.

Matt looked up, and Jeremy spun around to stare at his father with large, terrified eyes.

"Jeremy, why did you bother the good doctor this evening?" Mr. Boyd's speech was slurred. The small room quickly filled with the strong smell of whiskey. Though his voice was quiet, Matt sensed an excruciating tension just beneath the surface that, given the smallest opening, would explode like a bursting dam.

"Your wife is hurt, Mr. Boyd." Matt kept his tone even. "Jeremy did the right thing by coming for me. Now I'm going to examine her and—"

Before he realized what was happening, Matt found himself nose to nose with Mr. Boyd, whose red face and bloodshot eyes flamed with rage. "Who the hell do you think you are, comin' into my house? If you think I'm lettin' you look at my wife you're—"

Without thinking, Matt grabbed the drunken Mr. Boyd by the collar and shoved him hard against the wall, his own rage barely contained. He looked sternly into the red eyes of the older man, and through clenched teeth, issued a warning. "Thanks to you, your wife needs a doctor tonight. Now, while I'm in this house, she's my patient, and I'm going to do whatever I can to help her. And I will not tolerate any interference from you. Is that clear?"

As Mr. Boyd lowered his eyes and made no move to fight back, Matt suddenly realized the risk he had taken in allowing his blind fury to control his reaction. This man was many pounds heavier, with broad shoulders and thick arms that come only from years of hard, physical labor. He knew instinctively that on another day, when not impaired by too much alcohol, Mr. Boyd could have easily overpowered him.

Matt slowly let go of his shirt, and stepping back, asked Jeremy to fetch him a basin of cold water and a cloth. Awe mixed with grim satisfaction on his small face, the child sprinted to the kitchen to fulfill the doctor's request.

Mr. Boyd skulked silently from the room. Matt listened for an angry voice from the kitchen as Jeremy pumped water into a basin, but no disturbance ensued. The boy returned momentarily, placing the basin on the floor next to the divan, then hovered nervously over his mother. Matt listened to Laura's heart through his stethoscope. Looking up to meet Jeremy's worried eyes, he smiled reassuringly.

"Your mother's going to be fine, Jeremy."

The youngster let go a sigh of relief at this prognosis, as if the weight of the world had been lifted from his small shoulders.

"You see, Jeremy?" Laura said sweetly to her son. "I'm good as new."

"Does this sort of thing happen often?" Matt asked, dunking the cloth in the cold water, and placing it carefully across Laura's forehead.

"He never knocked me out before."

"Where are the other children?"

"I sent them upstairs to bed."

More than a hint of pride leapt from Jeremy's voice as he explained, "I stay up later 'cause I'm the oldest."

"I see," Matt said. His eyes met Laura's and they both stifled a grin.

"You're probably going to have a headache for a few hours," Matt said. "I don't think it's any more serious than that. Get a good night's sleep. If you feel worse in the morning, send for me."

She nodded, then reached for her son again. "I'm sorry if Jeremy bothered you, Dr. Tyler. He was just scared." She looked lovingly up at her son. "He's my special boy. He takes good care of all his brothers and sisters, bless their hearts."

"It's no bother," Matt said, putting his hand on the child's shoulder. "You come for me anytime you feel it's necessary, all right?"

"Yes, sir," Jeremy answered. Matt sensed that Jeremy now viewed him as an ally, and realized it must have felt good to see someone stand up to his father in a way he could not.

Later, Matt came out of the back room to find Mr. Boyd sitting motionless at the end of the long table in the kitchen. The tablecloth was threadbare and stained. A bowl of half-peeled apples sat unattended, the exposed flesh of the fruit now brown and dry. Several cooking utensils and dishes lay scattered and broken across the floor, the scene of violence sometime earlier. Walking past the older man, he stopped when he heard a hoarse voice.

"How is she?"

"She's going to be fine," Matt said. "She's got a headache right now, but that will pass. She'll feel better after a good night's rest."

"I didn't want to hit her."

"Then why did you?"

"She was asking for it. She just has a way of . . . pushing me."

Matt knew he should walk away and say nothing, but he was suddenly envious of Charles Boyd. This man did not seem to appreciate all that he had.

"Charles, she's given you five children, all the while working hard alongside you on this farm. You have a loyal wife, a beautiful family. You have what most men really want."

Mr. Boyd's tenuous composure finally crumbled. He folded his arms on the table and buried his face in his sleeves. As Matt left the house, he heard him sobbing.

With relative calm restored for now in the household, Jeremy drove Matt back to his cabin under a crisp winter night's sky full of stars. As they bounced along the rough road, Matt reflected on the fact that the Boyd family was not unique in their troubles. Many times, when he treated a woman for an illness or injury, he would notice abrasions and bruises on her arms, shoulders, or face. When he commented on the injuries, the woman would awkwardly insist that she had sustained them in a fall, or by some simple act of clumsiness. But Matt surmised the real culprit was her husband. The notion that a man would strike a woman was unacceptable to him.

"Dr. Tyler, can I ask you somethin'?" Jeremy turned to Matt with a frown.

"Of course."

"Do you think it's all right for married folks to hit each other?"

"No, Jeremy, I don't."

"My ma and pa yell at each other all the time. I think they hate each other."

"It might seem that way. But I'll bet down deep inside, they really care for each other. Maybe they just can't get along sometimes."

Jeremy still looked confused. "Maybe if they didn't have us children to get in the way, they'd treat each other better."

Matt sensed a great vulnerability in his young companion, and he chose his next words carefully.

"I think you're wrong about that. Didn't you see your ma's face tonight when she saw you? Her face lit up like an angel when she put her arm around you. You and your brothers and sisters bring her a lot of joy, there's no mistaking that."

"What about my pa?" Jeremy looked intently now at Matt, hanging on his every word.

"I think your pa sometimes worries he's not providing for his family like he'd like to. Maybe he can't show he loves you all the time . . . doesn't mean he doesn't feel it."

Jeremy sat in silence, allowing the conversation to sink in.

"When I grow up and have a family, I'm gonna treat them real good," he finally said. "I won't hit them or make them cry, ever."

"I think that's a good plan."

"You know, for somebody who doesn't have a family, seems like you know a lot about them."

Matt chuckled. "Well, don't forget, I grew up in a family. And I know a lot of families around here."

"Oh yeah," Jeremy said, this wider perspective freshening his viewpoint. "You think someday you might have a family of your own?"

"I hope so."

As the horse pulled the wagon to the front steps of the cabin, Jeremy reined the animal to a stop.

"You know what, Dr. Tyler?"

"What's that?"

"I wish you was my pa."

Matt could not remember ever feeling so profoundly complimented and undeserving at the same time. He met the boy's innocent stare and was grateful for the limited view of a child, in which the most fallible of men can wear a suit of honor, even if it doesn't fit. "Well, maybe I can't be your pa, but I'm happy to be your friend. Friends help each other out when it's needed and I'm glad I could help you out tonight. If you need me again, you just let me know."

Jeremy squared his shoulders. "And if you ever need me, Dr. Tyler, you just let me know."

"I will do that," Matt said solemnly as he retrieved his medical bag and climbed down from the wagon.

As he ascended the three steps and crossed the porch, he saw the dim glow of a dying fire in the fireplace, and realized that Degan must be asleep. She had dozed off on the sofa before the hearth, and she roused when he entered.

"Everything is all right?" She sat up and rubbed sleep from her face. Matt hung his coat and hat on the rack by the door. He came to settle in the chair across from her and sighed heavily. "What happened?"

"I treated a woman tonight who was knocked unconscious by her own husband's hand." He shook his head in bewilderment, and sank deeper into the chair. "How can a man allow himself to do that?" He looked up to meet her dark eyes. She did not seem upset by his account of events in the Boyd household. "Does that happen with your people?"

"No," she said. "In my people, women and men are the same."

"What do you mean?"

She shrugged. "It has always been this way. Seneca women and men are the same with each other. In the whites, the man owns the woman, like a horse or a dog. In my people, the women are the leaders of the clans. The men do not own them. The clan mothers choose the men who will sit at the council fires. The council says what will happen in the people, but if the council makes a mistake, the women say no."

"So the council governs the people, but the women choose the council. Women have equal power to the men?"

"They are the same."

"Are there ever disagreements between the council and the clan mothers?"

"They talk about what will happen in the people. The clan mothers say yes or no. In my people, the man treats the woman with honor. White men treat their women with hatred. The old ones say many years ago when the whites gave our people the strong drink, the men began to beat their wives. Our prophet warned the people and told them never to drink this again, so they stopped. But the white men still beat their women. This is not allowed in my people."

"Not all white men beat their women," Matt said firmly. "There are many white men who are as outraged by that as I am."

"You have not beat a woman with anger?" she asked pointedly.

Matt cringed. "No. And I wouldn't."

"You do not feel the anger to hit?"

"Yes, I feel anger at times, but hitting is . . . just not acceptable. It's wrong, especially hitting a woman." He leaned forward, meeting her gaze with intensity. "I think the bastards who captured you and hurt you should be shot for what they did. In fact, I think shooting's too good for them. And I think the man who hit his wife tonight should be punished for it in some way." He waited for his words to sink in before he spoke again. "You told me this afternoon that I haven't harmed you in any way since you've been here."

"I feel safe here."

"You are safe here."

She studied his face. "I believe you. You are very kind to me. Maybe not all white men treat their women this way."

"No, not all white men," Matt said, sitting back again. "There are many white men who love their wives and would never hurt them. But after what you've been through, I can understand your strong feelings against white men."

"You hurt me only one time. In the barn that first night." She massaged her wrist to illustrate her words. "When you made me drop the knife."

"Oh," he replied sheepishly, remembering how she had cried out when he clamped down on her wrist. "I'm sorry about that. But I thought you were going to plunge that knife right into my chest."

"I was."

Caught off-guard by her abrupt candor, he had to laugh, the tension between them broken. "Well then, I'm glad I stopped you!"

"I am glad also," she said, smiling back at him.

In the warm glow of the dying fire, she was watching him. As if seeing her for the first time, he suddenly realized how lovely she was. She still wore the light blue dress he had bought her earlier in the day, the bodice of which outlined her breasts and hugged her small waist in a most flattering way. She sat with her legs stretched out on the sofa so that only her bare feet peeked out from under her hem. One slender brown hand was propped at the side of her face, and disappeared into silky dark hair that flowed freely about her shoulders and down her back. Long black lashes rimmed her dark eyes that turned up slightly at the outer corners, especially when she smiled. High cheekbones gave a classic elegance to her face.

"The woman you helped tonight will be happy if she has children. This boy who came here today is one of many children?"

Matt could only nod, momentarily enthralled by a new awareness of Degan.

"Maybe this woman finds joy in her children," she said, a notion that had a familiar ring to him, as it was the same reasoning he had presented to Jeremy earlier. Somehow, it sounded more plausible now that she had said it.

"You seem to know the situation, though you've never met the family," he said, amazed at her insight.

"Families are the same. Children always make mothers happy."

He returned her smile. "I think you're right." He still considered Charles Boyd's behavior inexcusable, but realizing his wife found great joy in her five children made her circumstances seem a little less bleak. "Did you and your husband have children?"

"No," Degan said, her eyes downcast. "No babies."

Matt went to the humidor on his desk and withdrew a cigar. He snipped the ends, and with the flick of a match, gray smoke soon wafted around him.

"You're still young," he said, sitting down again. "You could still have children. Do your people remarry if a husband or wife dies?"

"Yes. The time to cry is one year. When I return to my home, I will marry again. The clan mother will say who it will be."

"The marriages are arranged then?" When she frowned in uncertainty, he clarified. "Someone else says who you will marry?"

"Yes, the clan mothers say who will marry."

"You don't get any choice in the matter?"

"The clan mothers are old and wise. They know what is best in all things. It is not the white way."

"No, it isn't. We prefer to choose our own mates. I can't imagine anyone I know agreeing to marry a woman who was chosen by someone else." Then he smiled. "But maybe for some of us, it would be better if a wiser person chose our mate for us."

"This is why you do not have a wife? You are not wise to choose?"

"No, I mean . . ." His voice trailed off, but when he glanced up, he saw that she was waiting for him to continue. "I finished my medical training in Washington shortly after the war broke out. When the war was over, I came here. There was someone here for a while . . . Emma . . ." He drew on the cigar as he searched for words to describe his courtship and its ending with Emma Miller. The few people who were closest to him knew the story, so he had never explained to anyone what happened. Degan waited patiently for him to gather his thoughts. "She turned out to be . . . someone I hoped I could trust, but . . . she did something I couldn't stand for."

"No trust?"

"That's right." Relieved that she might understand, Matt found it easier to tell her more. "My friends told me not to trust her. But I thought maybe she'd be different with me. Why, I don't know." He smiled ruefully. "She wasn't different with me."

"What happened?"

"I found out she was . . . keeping company with other men at the same time I was courting her," he explained with difficulty, feeling again the sting of betrayal. "One day, I found her with another man. They were . . . together . . . intimately."

"What is 'intimately'?"

He drew a deep breath. "They were together . . . like a husband and wife."

Degan's eyes widened with sympathetic outrage. "You saw this?"

Without looking up, he nodded. "I was a complete fool."

"No, Matt, you are not a fool," she said gently. "A man should trust his woman. But she was not your woman. She is still part of you?"

"No. I ended my courtship with Emma when I saw what kind of person she is. The whole thing still bothers me, though. I often see her in town, and I know I shouldn't still be angry with her, but it feels like I am." Confused by these lingering emotions that still pricked him, he shrugged. "It doesn't make any sense."

"Maybe when you forgive yourself, you will feel better."

He frowned. "What do you mean?"

"Maybe you are angry inside . . . with yourself."

Taken aback by her observation, Matt reflected in silence. Perhaps that was the reason he still carried the burden of Emma. Deep down he wished her no ill will, and yet he often found it difficult to be civil to her. He now realized that perhaps he needed to forgive himself for choosing to ignore the warning signs that had been abundant. Having learned from his mistakes, he would not be so foolish again.

He held Degan's stare for a long moment. The last bits of charred wood popped and hissed in the fireplace. The room was growing darker as the lamp on the table now burned brighter than the fire. She reached for the blanket draped across the back of the sofa, and spread it over her legs. Matt shook himself from his thoughts, and quickly got up to feed more wood into the fire.

From behind him, Degan said, "You will take a wife someday."

He watched a bluish-gold flame lick its way between the logs. At her prediction, he smiled to himself. "You think so?"

"Yes. And she will not hurt you like this Emma."

The fire crackling anew, he rose from the hearth and sat down at her feet. "And I think you'll remarry and have . . . a dozen children."

"How many is this?"

"Twelve."

Realizing he was teasing, her eyes flew wide with shocked amusement. "No, this is too many! If I have this many children, I will be old and fat like the clan mothers."

Matt laughed. "I can't picture you old and fat."

He unfolded the blanket and tucked it snugly at her waist, under her legs, and around her bare feet. Resting a hand on her covered ankles, he said, "I'm tired. I'm going to turn in. I'll be out later to put more wood on the fire."

"Thank you," she said, "for everything. You are very kind to me."

Silently, he patted the blanket over her feet. He rose, retrieved his smoldering cigar from the ashtray and retired to his bedroom.

Just before noon, snow had begun to fall lightly, silently coating the frozen dirt streets, and the roofs of Sylvan. The soft white blanket had a quieting effect on the mid-afternoon activity of the town.

"They're saying it's going to be a bad one," Dr. Bowman reported to Matt when the younger doctor returned to the office from his early rounds. Removing his coat, he brushed the wet snow from the sleeves and collar, then draped it on the back of a chair in front of the woodstove that roared its warmth to the other side of the room.

"That's what I heard," Matt said. "It's starting out tame enough, but for late February, it's still too early to hope we won't get another few feet before spring."

The winter months, typically harsh and long for northwestern Pennsylvania, always brought a succession of fierce snowstorms. Howling winds battered the area, with frigid temperatures and many feet of snow accumulating throughout January and February, even into March. Every year, as the gray days of winter passed, bleak and bitter, the townspeople of Sylvan predicted the farmers would soon enough find themselves enduring the punishment of another hot, dry summer.

On this winter's day, Matt knew he would need to leave town earlier than usual to get home before the storm became too severe, rendering travel impossible. During previous winters, if the weather made his ride to the cabin too unpleasant, he would often spend the night in the treatment room at the back of the medical office, or upstairs in the infirmary if it was unoccupied. But this winter was different. Since Degan had come to live with him, he found himself more compelled to return home at the end of each day, regardless of his schedule or inclement weather.

As anticipated, the afternoon and early evening hours brought a heavier snowfall and stronger winds. By six o'clock, the streets and wooden sidewalks of the town were buried under eight inches of powder, with drifts blowing higher against the buildings and doorframes.

"You'll be staying here tonight?" Dr. Bowman asked just before they heard a frantic pounding on the glass of the front door. The doctors looked at each other, silently wondering what emergency would bring someone out on such a night. Passing quickly through the front office, Matt could see Jacob Howard standing on the porch with his coat collar pulled up against the frigid wind and stinging snow. When Matt opened the door, Jacob quickly ducked into the warmth.

"Dr. Tyler," he said breathlessly, "I hate to trouble you on a night like this, but Elizabeth is in a bad way. She started her labor pains last night, and she's been bad all day. Ma's with her, and she's saying she can't have the baby without your help. Can you come?"

"Yes, of course. I'll get my bag," Matt said, grabbing his coat from the chair at the woodstove.

Back in the treatment room, Matt explained, "Elizabeth Howard went into labor last night," and opened a drawer at the base of the apothecary cabinet to pull out a pair of forceps.

Dr. Bowman was shaking his head. "This is her first. I knew she'd have trouble. She's too small," he murmured under his breath as he watched Matt place the forceps into his bag.

Without another word, Matt threw on his coat and hat and followed Jacob Howard out the door and into the storm.

CHAPTER

6

"Dr. Tyler, we surely do thank you for comin' out in this terrible weather," Joseph Howard said when he opened the front door, allowing his son and Matt swift entry. "Margaret is with Elizabeth upstairs."

Margaret Howard greeted Jacob and Matt at the bedroom door with a weary look of concern on her face. Wisps of iron-gray hair had escaped from the tight bun atop her head. Her usually tidy appearance had deteriorated over the long hours.

"Elizabeth's in a bad way, Dr. Tyler," she said in a low, anxious voice. "I've done everything I know of. She's worn out, poor thing, and this baby just won't come."

Matt touched her shoulder reassuringly. "I'll see what I can do."

In the bedroom, he placed his medical bag on a chair and rolled up his sleeves. Nestled between the damp sheets, Elizabeth looked pale and exhausted. Dark circles had settled under her closed eyes. Her chestnut-brown hair was wet with perspiration from hours of fruitless exertion.

"Elizabeth?" Matt said softly. She looked up at him. "I'm here to help you have this baby."

She shook her head, tears spilling down her face. "I can't," she whispered, "I'm going to die."

"You're not going to die. You're going to have this baby. I'm going to help you, and so is Jacob. The two of you are going to be parents before this night is over, do you understand?"

She nodded feebly, but Matt saw no hope in her eyes.

"Jacob!" Matt shouted, opening his medical bag and pulling out the forceps.

"You need some hot water or somethin' from the kitchen?" Jacob asked, peering around the edge of the bedroom door.

"No, I need you to come in here and help Elizabeth birth this baby," he said sternly. A mixture of shock and dread descended on the young man's face as he looked nervously at his wife, then back at the doctor.

"I-I never heard of a man helping to birth a baby, un-unless he's the doctor." Frozen in place, he risked no further advance into the bedroom.

"Well, you're not just any man, you're the father. Now take off your coat and get in here. We're running out of time," Matt commanded, repositioning the pillows under Elizabeth's back.

"Yes, sir," Jacob mumbled halfheartedly, glancing back at his mother who stood speechless in the hallway.

"Mrs. Howard?" Matt called. "We'll need you as well."

Margaret Howard marched dutifully back into the room in which she had spent the last twenty-four hours coaching her daughter-in-law. She appeared ready for instructions.

"Jacob, I want you to kneel on the bed behind Elizabeth, put your hands under the pillows, and lift her to a sitting position when I tell her to push. Understand?"

"Yes, sir," Jacob said, looking more ashen than his young wife.

"And, Jacob," Matt said in a voice so low only he could hear, "encourage her. She needs you to be strong, not scared."

He nodded before taking his post.

Matt bent over the bed again. "Elizabeth, I'm going to use forceps to deliver this baby. When I tell you to push, I want you to bear down as hard as you can, understand?"

"I'm not strong enough anymore," she cried.

"Jacob will help you."

"I'm right here, honey," Jacob said sweetly, then looked to Matt, who nodded his approval.

"Mrs. Howard, when I start to pull on the baby, I want you to apply pressure just above Elizabeth's ribs. I'll tell you when. All right, Elizabeth," the doctor said, "let's bring this baby." He wasted no time throwing off the sheet that covered her, shamelessly pushing her soiled nightgown above her sizeable belly. With a gentle hand, he opened her legs wider and quickly inserted the forceps. Elizabeth cried out in pain.

"Take a deep breath, you're doing fine," Matt told her, giving Jacob a dour look.

"You're doing fine, honey, just take a deep breath," Jacob repeated. "You're gonna make me a daddy tonight, Elizabeth. I love you so much."

Matt glanced up and was disappointed to see no reaction from Elizabeth.

"All right," he said, firmly grasping the wooden handles. "Now on three, I want you to push. Ready? One, two, three, push!"

Jacob lifted Elizabeth's upper body, and she bore down with a hard grimace on her white face. As Matt pulled on the forceps, Elizabeth's body began to slide toward him. He raised a hand to signal Jacob to stop.

"It's not working!" she cried miserably.

"That's only the first try," Jacob said. "We'll get it, don't you worry."

"Mrs. Howard, I need you to apply pressure just above her ribs," Matt said. "That'll help to keep her from sliding toward me, and will move the baby at the same time."

With everyone in place, he gave the directive again. This time when Elizabeth pushed, the baby moved.

"The baby moved, Elizabeth, did you feel it?"

Jacob let out a whoop and nearly jumped off the bed before Matt drew attention back to the task.

"Let's give it another try. Ready? One, two, three, push!"

The baby moved again, and Elizabeth seemed to find renewed strength in her progress.

"I think it's working!" She turned to give her husband a weak smile of triumph before her expression changed to concern. "Is it hurting the baby?"

"It's not hurting the baby," Matt said. "One more push will bring the head."

"Just one more push, honey!" Jacob chimed in.

"Do you need a moment to rest before we try again?" Matt asked.

"No," she said, jaw clenched, "I'm ready."

"All right then, let's go, one, two, three, push!"

With the team effort and a long, throaty growl from Elizabeth, Mrs. Howard finally cried, "The head is out!"

Matt tossed the forceps aside, and gently grasped the baby's head. "One more push for the shoulders, Elizabeth, ready? Push!"

Grunting through gritted teeth, Elizabeth bore down hard a final time.

"You did it!" Matt said, guiding the baby from Elizabeth's body onto the soft towel under her hips. Cradling the tiny newborn in his hands, he held the child up for mother and father to see. "You've got a son."

The expressions of astonishment and joy on the faces of the new parents brought tears to everyone's eyes. Matt carefully placed the baby on Elizabeth's stomach, then reached to wipe the tiny face clean.

"He's perfect," Elizabeth whispered in awe, hesitantly touching a miniature hand.

"Is he all right, Dr. Tyler?" Jacob asked.

Before Matt could respond, the newborn let out a wail and began to squirm atop his mother's belly.

"He's fine."

Descending the stairs later, Matt heard the mantel clock in the parlor chime half-past eight. Joseph Howard was nowhere in sight. Matt reached the bottom step and placed his medical bag, coat, and hat by the door. Reaching to part the sheer curtain at the glass, he peered out. The snow had stopped but the wind howled angrily, blowing drifts of white powder higher around the porch railing.

"How is she?" Mr. Howard asked anxiously, rushing from the parlor into the foyer.

"You have a grandson," Matt said with a tired smile. "Elizabeth and the baby are just fine."

Mr. Howard clapped his hands together triumphantly. "Thank you, Dr. Tyler! I don't know what would've happened if not for you."

"I was glad to help, but Elizabeth did all the work."

Mr. Howard slapped Matt on the back and announced, "I feel like celebrating!"

Matt chuckled at the enthusiasm of the usually staid Joseph Howard, who had already made his way to the kitchen. He heard the creak of a cabinet door and the clink of glasses.

"Come on in the kitchen, Dr. Tyler," Mr. Howard called. "Seems like the birth of my first grandchild is a fitting time to break out the spirits, don't you agree?"

Taking the proffered glass half-full of amber liquid, Matt smiled. Mr. Howard hastily threw back his first shot, then poured a second.

"You and Mrs. Howard are fortunate to have your children, and now your grandchild, all living in the same house with you," Matt said, taking a sip of the whiskey that burned all the way to his stomach.

"We wouldn't have it any other way," Mr. Howard said proudly. "Elizabeth is a good girl. Where is Jacob, anyway?"

"He's still upstairs. He did a good job helping Elizabeth birth the baby."

Mr. Howard froze. "He did what?"

"He helped his wife bring their son into the world."

"I . . . I heard you ask fathers to help birth babies, but I thought it was just gossip. I couldn't believe it."

"Neither could Jacob. But I think he was glad to be a help for Elizabeth. She needed him." Mr. Howard remained silent so Matt continued. "About a year ago, I was delivering a baby and the husband asked me if he could help. He was worried about his wife, and wanted to help her. At first I was surprised and refused him. Then I thought about it and I realized, who better to help a woman birth a child than her husband? He was so thankful afterwards, to be present to see his child born. Now when I deliver a baby, I do ask the husband to help. Some turn me down, but as far as I know, no man has ever regretted being there to witness the birth of his child."

Wide-eyed and speechless, Joseph Howard quickly downed his second shot.

"Joseph!" Mrs. Howard cried out from the doorway, "at least have the decency to ask Dr. Tyler to sit in the parlor!"

Mr. Howard quickly retrieved another glass, poured a third whiskey, and handed it to her. "We're celebrating. Here, have one."

Chuckling self-consciously, Mrs. Howard gave Matt a quick glance before taking the glass. "I suppose a new grandfather can be excused for forgetting his manners just this once." She threw back the whiskey with unmistakable expertise.

Matt placed his empty glass atop the cabinet. "Thank you kindly for the drink. I'd better be on my way."

"Oh, Dr. Tyler, the weather is so bad, won't you stay the night with us?" Mrs. Howard asked. "It's not safe to be out."

"Thank you, but I'll be fine. It stopped snowing and it's not that far to my cabin."

"Are you sure? Let me make you something to eat before you go."

"Thank you, but I couldn't trouble you," Matt replied graciously. "You'll want to spend time with your family, and I really need to get home."

The new grandparents accompanied the doctor to the foyer and watched as he donned his coat and hat, and picked up his medical bag.

"Dr. Tyler!" Jacob called out from the landing before descending the stairs, his hand outstretched. "Thank you for helping Elizabeth, and for letting me help. I'll always remember this night, seeing my son being born."

Matt offered his hand, which Jacob pumped vigorously. "I'm glad you were there. I believe it makes all the difference."

Jacob's chest swelled with pride.

"Thank you again, Dr. Tyler," Mrs. Howard said, taking his hand. "Please be careful on your way home."

"I will. Good night." Turning the collar of his coat against the wind, Matt stepped onto the snow-covered porch.

In pleasant weather, the two miles between the Howards' home and his cabin would have been an easy ride. But tonight, enduring a strong wind that mercilessly whipped its icy sting against his body, Matt soon realized that perhaps spending the night at the Howards' would have been the more prudent decision. However, his horse seemed to know the way home, and stepped as quickly as possible through the swirling drifts. Just minutes into the journey, Matt could no longer feel his face or hands, bare to the punishing lash of icy needles that pierced his skin. *Why am I taking such a damn fool risk?*

Somewhere deep inside, he knew the answer.

CHAPTER

7

Degan fed more wood into the belly of the stove, wondering how much longer she should keep supper warm. Countless times, she had paced to the window, but it was impossible to discern any form in the darkness outside. Though the wind continued to wail, the snow had stopped and the unbroken clouds of the storm had begun to drift apart. Now in the moonlight, the naked trees swayed like black ghosts against the deep white blanket.

Kneeling at the hearth, she carefully placed fresh wood on the charred and shrunken logs that had been burning in the grate. With each passing hour, she had grown more concerned that the storm would render Matt unable to come home. She hoped his absence meant that he had stayed in the town tonight. But she could not quell a nagging fear that perhaps he had attempted to reach the cabin, and had become stranded in the storm.

Suddenly, a loud thumping noise on the porch startled her. She turned abruptly to see Matt stumble into the cabin along with a burst of swirling snow. Slamming the door behind him, he fell against it, allowing his medical bag to drop to the floor. He brought his hands stiffly to his mouth. Encrusted with snow from head to foot, he was barely recognizable and seemed unable to move from the spot.

Rushing to him, she reached to remove his hat, and hung it on the rack by the door. Brushing off the wet snow caked on the front of his coat, she quickly unfastened the buttons, then pushed the heavy garment from his shoulders. She took a frozen hand, led him to the chair before the fire, and nudged him to sit down. His arms crossed in front of him, he was shivering noticeably. Pulling the woolen blanket from the back of the sofa, she wrapped it around his upper body.

She knelt before him, placing her hands on his knees, her eyes filled with concern. "I will bring food for you."

"No," he said in a shaky whisper, "need to get warm first."

"I thought tonight you will stay in the town."

Slowly flexing his aching fingers toward the fire, he grimaced. "Prob'ly should have. Somehow . . . my horse found his way here. I couldn't see a thing."

"You have a smart horse."

"Smarter than the rider?"

"Maybe."

He looked down and saw a playful light in her eyes, but his face was too stiff to smile. "I tried to warm up in the barn . . . but the wind . . . cut right through me."

She pulled the ends of the blanket around his legs and tucked it more snuggly about his shoulders. Her attentiveness was as unexpected as it was comforting.

"I'm not accustomed to . . . coming home to . . . someone who's been waiting for me."

"Your home is not empty now," she said, holding his gaze.

"Don't look so troubled. I'll be all right. Just need to get warm."

"You have nothing to cover your hands?"

"I left the office in a hurry this evening," he said, speech coming more easily now that his face was beginning to thaw. "I left my gloves behind." He sat up straighter and looked around. "Something smells good."

"I have supper for you. You must eat something warm."

"I'll get out of these wet clothes first. Then I'll eat." He patted her hand on his knee, then rose to make his way to the bedroom, still holding the blanket around his shoulders.

Degan went to the kitchen area to fetch the pot of soup she had prepared. Earlier in the day, she had found vegetables and salted beef in Matt's well-stocked larder. Food and other supplies were offered to him regularly in exchange for his services. Other items he purchased from the town's general store. Fruits and vegetables, canned throughout the previous summer and fall by neighboring homemakers, sold well alongside baked goods, fresh eggs, milk, and butter.

Matt soon emerged from the bedroom, wrapped in his quilted dressing gown that looked soft and warm. The appetizing aroma of fresh-baked bread filled the room.

"You were cooking today?" He sat down and leaned over the steaming pot to look inside.

"I found the food," she said, pointing toward the larder. "I make soup like you bring to me." She ladled a bowl full and placed it in front of him. "I ate before, but I keep it warm for you."

"Do you feel strong enough to be doing all this?"

"I feel stronger now," she said, sitting next to him. "I no longer want to rest all day."

"I suppose it does get tedious, just resting all the time. But don't do too much. You're not fully recovered." She waited for his reaction as he took his first bite. When he nodded and said, "Very good," his appreciation pleased her.

"You healed someone tonight?"

"I delivered a baby. The woman was in labor since last night. She couldn't have the baby, so I helped her."

"How do you help her?"

"Forceps."

She frowned. "What is this?"

"It's a device that grips the baby's head at one end, then I pull on handles at the other end. I use the forceps to pull the baby out of the mother," he said matter-of-factly, demonstrating the motion with an imaginary instrument. Degan cringed, which brought a smile to Matt's face. "It doesn't hurt the baby or the mother, and sometimes babies can't be born otherwise." He reached for a piece of bread that was still warm from the oven. "Anyway, the new mother and the baby are doing fine."

"In my people, only the women help bring babies."

"That's generally true among the whites also. But sometimes when women have trouble, they call the doctor. This woman tonight is very young, and this is her first baby. The first birth is often troublesome."

"She was very scared," Degan said, her voice tinged with sympathy.

Matt nodded. "She was afraid she was going to die."

"You helped her."

"I told her she wasn't going to die, and that she would be a mother before the night was over. She just needed encouragement, to hear some hopeful words."

"And now she is happy with her child."

"Sometimes I think no matter how many babies I deliver, the miracle of birth will always amaze me. And when the parents see their newborn for the first time . . . the looks on their faces . . . I can't describe it. This couple tonight, they're so young, been married only a year. Now they have a child to raise."

At the last spoonful, Matt leaned back in his chair and put a hand across his stomach. "That was good, thank you."

"I will cook for you until I go home. In my people, the women gather wood for the fires, and cook the food, and clean the clothes—"

Matt put up a hand. "You don't have to do any of that. You're still recovering. I don't want you doing anything strenuous."

His rejection of her offer disappointed her. "You have made me well when death was very near. I feel stronger now. I can do this work for you."

"I never expected you to repay me for anything," he said, rising to pour a cup of coffee from the pot on the stove. "Besides, in the beginning, you were afraid I would force you to work for me. Now you're offering to do just that?"

She smiled at her own inconsistency. "Before, I was afraid of you. But not now. You helped me. Now I help you."

He sat down again, taking a sip. "I'm glad you're not afraid of me anymore, and I do appreciate the offer, but—"

"In my people, everyone has work to do. I see work here to do, and you have no wife. I cannot rest all day until I go home."

"All right, I can see you're determined, so I'll make a bargain with you. You can do whatever work you want, as long as it's not too hard, and you don't get tired. If you feel any pain in your leg, or if you feel tired, I want you to stop and rest." He extended his hand to her. "Do we have a deal?"

She looked down at his hand, confused as to what he expected.

He explained, "When two people agree to something, they shake hands. Do you agree with what I've said?"

"Yes. I will work, but not too hard."

"That's right. So give me your hand."

She placed her palm against his, her small hand disappearing in his grip.

"This means we agree?" she asked.

"Yes. Except the part about cleaning my clothes," he said, releasing her. "My clothes are often a bloody mess because of my work. I don't want you to labor with that. You'll have enough to do just keeping your own clothes clean. There's a woman in Sylvan who takes in laundry for payment. I take my clothes to her. She's a widow and needs the money."

"This woman cleans your clothes for money?"

"That's right. She cleans Dr. Bowman's clothes as well."

"The old shaman? He has no wife also?"

"No, his wife died years ago."

"Other women in the village care for white men who have no wife?"

"That's right. Women have a caring nature about them, especially when it comes to men who are alone. They have a tendency to want to look after us."

"This is the way of my people also, but we do not take money. The white woman takes money for this caring?"

"Sometimes," he shrugged. "Depends on the woman."

Curiosity suddenly swept over her. "Some white women give their bodies for money. This is so here?"

Matt shifted uneasily in his chair. "There are a few."

"You have been with them?"

"No." He looked away, clearing his throat, and took another sip of coffee.

"Why?"

He paused to think about his answer, as no one had ever asked him why he did not purchase the services of prostitutes. "It's not something I would do . . . now. A few years ago, during the war, I was . . . with such a woman." He lowered his eyes. "I realized then that if I'm going to be with a woman . . . in that way, I want it to mean something to both of us. I don't want her to be . . . intimate with me because I'm paying her, but . . . because she cares for me."

Degan studied his face, captivated by his honesty. He was a strong man, and yet, vulnerable at times. He looked up at her, as if waiting for her reaction. His green eyes held a trusting sincerity, and the silence between them felt safe and comfortable.

Unexpectedly, a chill from the floor caressed her bare feet and she shivered. Lifting her knees to her chest, she wrapped her feet in the hem of her skirt. At this, Matt rose and returned to the bedroom, emerging moments later with a pair of his thick socks. He sat down again. Pulling one bare foot, then the other from under her skirt, he slipped his socks on her feet.

"If you ever decide to wear the shoes I bought you, you won't need these to keep your feet warm," he said with a teasing smile, pushing the tops of the socks toward her knees.

"You are very kind," she said, smoothing the soft yarn with her hands. She reflected his playful expression. "Do I give you money for these?"

"No, everything I do for you is free."

After supper, Matt bent at the hearth to feed fresh wood into the fire. Its bright warmth roared to challenge the howling winds outside. Snow lashed against the windows, accumulating in frosty triangles at the corners of the panes. Matt filled the bowl of his pipe with tobacco before striking a match to light it.

"You will go to the people tomorrow?" Degan asked, settling onto the sofa.

"I'll try to get into town. The wind should quiet down by morning, then I'll be able to tell how deep the drifts are. The town will be pretty quiet for a day or so until everybody starts digging out from the snow."

"After the snows in winter, my people are also quiet."

"How do you spend the winter? How do you pass the time?"

"We play games in winter. The people say who will win. If they win, they are given things like blankets or beads." She frowned. "I forget the white word for this."

"It's called gambling."

"Gambling, yes, this is the white word."

"Gambling or wagering. What kinds of games?"

Her face brightened. "My favorite is snow snake."

"Snow snake? How do you play with snakes in the wintertime? Aren't they frozen?"

Degan burst out laughing. "Not a real snake!" she said, putting a hand over her mouth, laughing harder. Catching her breath, she extended her arms to illustrate. "It is long and thin. It is made of wood. You run with it, then slide it in the snow. If it goes very far, more than the others, you win. If the snow is ice on top, the snow snake goes very far."

"I would imagine so. Do you play, or is it only the men?"

"Only the men play. But the women . . . gamble . . . to say who will win."

Matt grinned, tamping the tobacco in his pipe. "So you're a gambler, are you? Do you often win?"

"Yes, many times. I am good at games," she said, delighted that this declaration seemed to amuse him.

"Well, I'll have to teach you to play poker."

"Poker? This is a game in snow?"

"No, it's a card game. It involves gambling based on the cards you're given. The aim is to have a better hand than everyone else. Or make them think you do."

Comprehension dawned. "Ah yes, I have heard of this. But I have not played. Do you win at poker?"

"Once in a while. I've probably lost more money than I've won. The whites usually play for money, not blankets and such."

"Maybe you will teach me to play poker. Maybe I will win."

"Or maybe *I* will win," he said, a glint of mischief in his eyes. "What will you give me if I win?"

Her smile faded. "In my home, I have many things. But here, I have only what you have given me."

"I don't think any of your dresses would fit me," Matt said dryly.

She thought for a moment, then caught his humor and giggled. "If I lose, I will work for you longer to pay you."

His face softened. "I wouldn't do that to you. I'd forgive the debt."

"You are very kind to me."

"You'd do the same for me, wouldn't you?"

"No," she replied earnestly. "If I win, I always want to be paid."

Caught off-guard by her frankness, Matt chuckled. "You're a hard woman, Degan."

He was watching her, amused appreciation on his face. She sensed that he was pleased, so she returned his smile.

By morning, the wind had settled. The twinkling crust over deep snowdrifts glistened in the pale winter sunlight. After breakfast, Matt had gone to the barn to tend to the horses, while Degan swept powdery snow from the porch.

Finished clearing the front porch, she was sweeping the back porch when she heard Matt calling her name. Something in his voice alarmed her. She leaned over the back porch railing to peer around the side of the cabin. Without his coat, he was tramping through the snow toward the cabin, holding a bright red cloth around his right forearm that she realized, to her horror, was soaked with blood. With each step, the snow at his feet reddened with blood that dripped profusely from his arm.

She rushed back into the cabin and opened the front door just as he was mounting the steps.

"What happened?"

Breathless, he grimaced with pain. "I was reaching for a shovel hanging on the wall. There was a saw blade hanging next to it. Somehow I . . . dislodged the blade and it fell on my arm." When he removed the blood-soaked cloth, Degan gasped.

"It is very deep!"

"Get a basin of water. We'll get a better look once it's cleaned."

She hurried to the pump in the kitchen to fill a basin. He collapsed onto a chair at the table and pulled the lamp closer. Turning the flame higher, he said, "There are more towels in the drawer of the apothecary. Get them, please."

Placing the basin on the table, she handed Matt a towel, which he dunked into the cool water. He dabbed at the sizeable gash, which continued to bleed freely. In no time, half a dozen towels were soaked with blood.

"Damn it," he muttered, reaching for yet another towel, "it's going to need stitching." He looked up. "You'll have to sew it up for me."

Aghast, she staggered back. "I . . . I cannot!"

"Degan, you have to help me. I'd try to stitch it myself, but it's my right arm. I'm right-handed, I can't do it with my left."

"But . . . in the town, the old shaman—"

"There's no time for that, I'm bleeding too much. Look, I'll tell you what to do. You know how to sew, right?"

"Yes, but . . . not a man!"

"It's no different. It's the same as sewing cloth, or . . . have you ever sewn deerskin?"

"Yes, but—"

"It's the same. Skin is skin. I'll tell you what to do, but I can't do it myself. You have to help me."

Stricken and shaking, she finally nodded, looking as though she might faint.

"All right. You'll find needles and sutures in the other drawer of the cabinet, beside where the towels were."

"Sutures?"

"Thread. There are rolls of bandages there, you'll need those as well."

She hastily gathered all the supplies from the infirmary and laid them out on the table. Too stunned now to remember how to sew, she looked helplessly to Matt for direction.

"Just thread the needle like you normally would," he said.

With trembling hands, she took a length of suture and made a number of failed attempts at threading the needle. At last, the string went through the tiny eye. Everything ready, she stood poised with the needle. Matt removed the wet towel from his arm.

"Start at the upper end of the gash. Hold the edges together, and make your first stitch. You're going to sew the wound shut, just like you would a tear in fabric. I'll try to keep the wound clean for you as you work."

Her jaw set, she took several shallow breaths and touched the needle to his arm unsteadily. She looked up at him with panic in her eyes.

"Try to calm down," he said with a stiff little smile. "It's hard to sew if your hands are shaking."

She took a deeper breath and held the needle just above his arm, unable to move.

"Stick the needle in, right here," he instructed, pointing his finger to the spot to begin. When she pushed the needle into his skin, he braced himself against the table, trying not to react. She stopped and looked up. "I am hurting you," she said miserably.

"It's all right. It's better than bleeding to death."

She made the first stitch, then the next. To her surprise, it was indeed very similar to sewing deerskin.

"Go a little deeper. That's it, pull the thread tight." Though his tone was even, his voice sounded taut and strained. She knew he was in great pain. His breathing was loud, and when she looked up, his face was tense and very pale.

"Maybe I'll hire you as my assistant," he quipped through a clenched jaw. "You're doing fine, just keep going."

As she sewed the wound shut, the bleeding subsided. Matt cleaned drying blood from the edges of the gash while she slowly progressed toward his wrist. At the sixteenth and final stitch, he said, "Good. Now, cut the thread and knot it."

She complied with hands that were no longer shaking as noticeably.

"Unwind a good length of the bandage," he told her. "You're going to wrap the wound securely, but not too tight. Start here," he pointed to his forearm a few inches above the wound, "and work your way down."

She pressed the end of the strip to his forearm and began wrapping. "This is right?"

"Ease up a little. We don't want it too tight. That's it. When you get down to my wrist, leave enough of the bandage to fold the end under the wrapping." She followed his instructions, and soon, the bandage was secure.

He let out a forceful sigh. "That's it. You did it."

She sank into the chair next to his and exhaled loudly.

"Are you all right?" he asked. When she nodded, he said, "You did a good job."

"Now we watch for infection," she said, "as you did with my leg."

"That's right."

Renewed concern washed over her. "What will we do if infection comes?"

Matt leaned forward to take her hands in his. "Let's not worry about that right now. I know what you just did wasn't easy. I'm very grateful for your help, Degan." She sat motionless, staring at him. "Are you sure you're all right? Do you want a brandy or something?"

She shook her head. "Please be more careful next time."

He smiled at her, his natural, more relaxed smile. At that moment, she thought he looked like a little boy. "I'll be more careful next time."

CHAPTER

8

Matt had fallen into the routine of ending most days at sunset in the late winter afternoons. But during a brief respite of balmy weather in March, he surprised Degan by returning home shortly after noon one day. He burst through the door carrying his coat and a good measure of cheerful enthusiasm.

"It's such a warm day," he said, "let's go for a walk."

His cabin sat at the edge of a thickly wooded grove, secluded on three sides by the trees. The winter's dry leaves swished and crackled loudly under their feet as they walked, a thick layer of brown pine needles providing a soft cushion for each step. Spotty sunlight filtered through the bare trees, brightening the ground. Small, oddly shaped mounds of snow still clung desperately to life.

After a time, Degan requested a few minutes of rest. Matt led her to a fallen tree that had surrendered weeks ago to strong winter winds. Settled on the craggy bark, they sat in silence, listening to the awakening woods. The breeze was chilly, as if winter would not yet accept dismissal. But the air smelled of early spring, fresh and sweet, as it rustled through skeleton trees. Though feeble, the sunlight felt warm.

Turning her face toward the sun, Degan closed her eyes, a peaceful smile softening her features. Matt watched as the breeze picked up a few strands of her hair, and deposited them across her folded arms.

"It must feel good to be outside in the fresh air after so many weeks."

She kept her eyes closed. "Where my people live is a forest like this. When I am young, my grandmother taught me to come to the woods for food, for everything. Everything is here for life."

Matt silently studied her face.

"I will return home soon," she said, turning toward him. "I'm glad I have worked for you for this time. It's good I work for you because you healed me."

"You didn't have to do anything for me," he said, feeling the familiar discomfort of being the recipient of another's generosity. His thoughts turned to the winter's approaching end. He would soon travel to Washington for the grand opening of the new hospital. In fact, he had received a letter from his father just yesterday, asking about his travel plans. He had promised to take Degan back to her people upon his return. By that time, winter storms would be behind them, and she would be strong enough to make the trip. Explaining that women never travel unescorted, he had said he would accompany her. But as the days passed, he had to admit he would be reluctant to see her go, reluctant to go back to living in his cabin without her. Now, bringing up the subject was more difficult than he had expected.

"Degan, there's something I need to talk to you about," he began. "I have to go away for a while, back to Washington." Her expression barely changed, but the space between them felt heavier. "My father has been in charge of building a new hospital in Washington. I promised him I'd come to see it when it opens and, well, it's scheduled to open soon."

"When do you go?"

"In a few days."

She nodded. "How long?"

"I'll be gone three weeks, maybe four. We planned for you to return to the reservation when the weather broke, and you were fully recovered. By the time I return from Washington, we'll be able to make the trip."

"You said I will not go back to my people alone. It is too dangerous, and I cannot travel alone. So I will work for you until you come back."

"You don't have to do anything for me, Degan—"

"You saved my life," she insisted. "It's good I work for you." There was a softness in her eyes that he hadn't seen before. "I will wait for you."

The plan confirmed, he now felt a strong aversion to his trip. Despite feeling out of place in his family's world, he usually looked forward to his visits to Washington. He enjoyed his father's company, and spending time with Daisy and Caroline was always pleasant. His visits were infrequent and, for the most part, a welcome break from his routine. However, this time was different. He realized that being apart from Degan for several weeks was not something he wanted.

"I have a good friend in town. His name is Jon. I'll ask him to check in on you while I'm away."

Suddenly, her expression changed, her dark eyes wide and pleading. "No, Matt, please tell no one in the town about me."

He smiled, understanding that he needed to put her fears to rest, as she had not yet met his friend. "You don't have to be afraid of Jon, he's a good man. He would never hurt you."

"No, please say nothing about me."

"Degan, Jon would never do anything to harm you. I've known him for years. He's a good man. You don't have to be afraid." His attempts to reassure her seemed to be falling on deaf ears. He had not known her to be obstinate. Her reaction to Jon was taking him by surprise.

She searched frantically for words. "Maybe your friend is a good man, but if he knows I am here, he will tell others in the town. They will come for me."

"No," Matt took both of her hands and leaned closer. "I don't think anyone would come here to hurt you—"

"There are many who would hurt me. They have already done this. I see the men coming for me in my dreams. If you are not here, no one will protect me."

"But that's why I want Jon to look in on you while I'm gone—"

"Please, Matt! Say nothing to Jon about me."

The idea of going away for several weeks, leaving Degan to fend for herself was unthinkable. If something were to happen to her while he was gone, she would have no one to turn to. Additionally, she would have no way of restocking her supply of food and other necessities during his absence. Of course, he had planned to insist on Jon's discretion. There was no question in his mind that Jon would respect his wish for privacy. What she was asking felt like abandonment, and he knew he could never abandon her.

She closed her eyes tightly. "Please tell no one in the town about me. I am afraid of what the white men will do."

"I understand that, but there's nothing to be afraid of with Jon. If I ask him not to say anything, he won't."

She shook her head stubbornly.

Becoming more exasperated, Matt tried to explain his reasoning. "Degan, even if I thought it too dangerous for Jon to know about you, you have no way of getting supplies while I'm gone. You would run out of food here by yourself."

Her face brightened. "I will find food to eat in the forest. For many years, my people—"

Giving in to his rising frustration, Matt's tone was loud and harsh. "I won't have you foraging in the woods for food like an animal, that's ridiculous!"

She flinched as though he had struck her, and he instantly regretted his outburst. He could not have named which was more pronounced on her face, hurt or insult. His growing irritation of just a moment ago had suddenly dissolved. She pulled her hands from his and moved away.

"I'm sorry, Degan. I didn't mean that."

Without looking at him, she jumped to her feet and tramped away through the trees.

"Degan, I'm sorry," he called after her, but she did not look back. He sighed heavily and muttered, "Damn," under his breath, then rose to go after her.

Picking up her skirts, she quickened her steps to stay ahead of him, stomping deeper into the woods, where the undergrowth grew thicker, slowing her pace.

When Matt caught up behind her, he reached to touch her shoulder. "Degan—"

She spun around, rage burning in her eyes. She backed away, her breathing labored from exertion and anger.

"For many years, the Haudenosaunee were a strong and prosperous people . . . without supplies from the white man. You come to us with promises and . . . papers to sign and . . . lies, always lies! You take away our land and how we live. You trick us and never do what you say you will do!"

Clearly favoring her injured leg, she leaned against a tree to steady herself and catch her breath. Grimacing, she reached to massage her thigh. Matt took a step toward her, but when her eyes darted to his face in warning, he moved back. A strained silence hung like poison in the air between them.

"Degan, I admit I haven't paid much attention to what the whites have done to your people over the years. But I do know I'm not responsible for it. I can't do anything about the lies or the broken treaties or whatever crimes the whites have committed against your people. All I can do is take care of you now as best I can."

"Why does the white man always think we need him to save us? My people need to be saved only from the whites!"

"I'm not talking about my people or your people," he said firmly. "I don't care about my people or your people—" He knew instantly by her expression that he had said the wrong thing.

"The white man never cares about the people, only himself!"

"That's not what I meant, goddamn it! How can you say I only care about myself? I'm trying to—"

"How can you care for me all this time, then tell other whites about me? They will come for me—"

"For God's sake, Degan, no one is coming for you!" He took her shoulders and turned her to face him, his frustration mounting again. "After all this time, why do you still insist they're coming for you?"

"I see them in my dreams."

"That means nothing, it's just a nightmare. Everyone has nightmares."

"I killed him!" she cried, pushing against him. All the terror of her captivity suddenly came rushing back. "With the knife. He came to me and forced me . . . and I killed him. I took the horses . . . so the other man could not follow me."

Startled by her admission, Matt quickly put his arms around her and pulled her closer. Shaking and crying, she fought against him at first, but he held onto her until her arms were around his waist, and she was clinging to him. He felt her body convulsing with sobs.

"I was . . . the only one alive," she muttered into his shirt. "They tied me down and forced me—"

"Shhhhh," he murmured, hoping she wouldn't say more. "I'm glad you killed him. They deserved to die for what they did to you." He held her tightly, stroking her hair, until her trembling subsided. Her face pressed against his chest, she finally quieted.

"I have been safe here with you," she said, tightening her hold around his waist. "You said . . . you said . . . you will not hurt me. If you tell, this will hurt me."

She took several deep breaths, relaxing in his embrace. After a time, she raised her head and looked up at him. Her face wet with tears, she dragged a sleeve across her cheeks. He looked into her dark eyes, wondering how his anger and annoyance at her could have been so intense.

"Degan," he said quietly, "the last thing I want to do is abandon you. When I leave you here by yourself, I have to know that you'll be all right."

"I will be all right if no one knows I am here. I can make a fire. I can find food. But I cannot survive if the white men take me again."

He sighed heavily and tried to imagine feeling at ease with granting her determined wishes.

"All right," he conceded. "I won't say anything to Jon."

Her face softened with relief. The wind picked up and the sun disappeared behind a bank of clouds. Chilled by the cool breeze, Degan crossed her arms and brushed her wind-blown hair from her face.

"Let's go back," Matt said, touching her forearm. She stepped beyond his reach and remained several paces from him as they made their way back to the cabin. Well aware that he had insulted the age-old ways of her people, he looked around and realized that these woods undoubtedly provided a variety of food sources if one knew where to look and what to look for. He suddenly felt foolish for implying that if not for his efforts, she would be doomed to starvation. But at the same time, the thought of her hungrily scrambling in the woods for food filled him with dread.

When they had almost reached the edge of the clearing, Matt looked over at her.

"Degan," he said, putting a hand out in front of her. She stopped but kept her eyes fixed straight ahead. "I am truly sorry for what I said earlier. I know I insulted you and, for that matter, all of . . . your people. I hope you can forgive me."

Without turning, she looked up at him and her demeanor seemed to relax. The corners of her mouth turned up in not quite a smile.

By the time they reached the cabin, the sun had slipped from behind the clouds, and it felt once more like spring. Matt settled next to Degan on the top step of the porch. His mind raced to think of everything he would need to accomplish before his trip.

"I'll make sure you have plenty of food and supplies before I leave." His firm tone conveyed no tolerance for discussion. He had agreed not to enlist Jon's help in providing for her in his absence, but he resolved to leave her well stocked prior to his departure. "Don't light a fire during the day while I'm gone. If anybody in town sees the smoke from the chimney, they might ride out here to see what's going on. And I'll teach you to shoot my rifle before I leave." In answer to her questioning look, he explained, "I'll feel a little better about leaving you here by yourself if you know how to shoot."

The following days proved busy. Each morning, Matt traveled to town in his wagon and each evening he returned, the back loaded down with supplies from the general store. He packed his larder with dry goods, meats, cheeses, canned fruits and vegetables. He knew Degan would be unable to obtain fresh ice for the icebox, so he purchased a variety of salted meats that would remain unspoiled for a few weeks. Many times, he thought that providing for her would be much easier if he could simply ask for Jon's help. But he had promised her he would say nothing to Jon, and he intended to keep that promise.

On the day before his departure, Matt took advantage of the continuing pleasant weather to set up a makeshift shooting range at the edge of the grove of trees behind his cabin. He retrieved several empty bottles and jars from the barn that he had planned to use for target practice, and set them carefully atop a fallen tree a few dozen paces from the back porch.

Degan emerged from the back door, confusion on her face.

"Ready for your shooting lesson?"

"I will shoot bottles?" she asked, noting the glass targets in the distance.

"That's the idea." He mounted the back porch steps, and disappeared into the cabin. He returned with his rifle and a small wooden box packed with neat rows of bullets.

"Here, take this," he said, handing her the gun. He showed her how to load the weapon, placing fifteen bullets in its magazine just beneath the barrel. Standing beside her, he instructed her on the proper way to hold the rifle, to sight it, and demonstrated the lever mechanism that would quickly place the next bullet in the chamber after firing.

"Now, when you fire it, it's going to kick," he warned, moving behind her.

She turned toward him, looking down at the gun in puzzlement. "How can it kick?"

"You'll see. Don't worry, it won't hurt you, but you'll have to get used to the feel of firing it. When you're ready, sight the bottle on the end like I showed you, and squeeze the trigger. And try not to hit the outhouse."

She planted her bare feet firmly on the wooden planks of the porch floor, took careful aim at the first bottle, and squeezed the trigger. The rifle cracked loudly with an explosion that knocked her back forcefully against Matt's chest. He caught her shoulders to steady her. Peering through the cloud of white smoke that had burst from the rifle upon firing, he could see no sign of the first bottle.

"You got it!" he said. Degan spun around, meeting his astonished expression with a gleeful smile.

"Try to hit the next one."

She lifted the rifle again, snapped the lever down and back, took aim, and fired a second shot. Shards of glass flew in every direction as the next bottle blew apart.

"Excellent!"

She finished off the remaining bottles in quick succession, missing only one. His ears ringing now, the acrid smoke from the shots filling his nostrils, Matt took the rifle. "I can see I don't have to worry about you being able to defend yourself. You're a damn good shot. Have you done this before?"

Looking up at him, she grinned impishly. "My father taught me to shoot. He said I am very good."

"I'll be damned," Matt said, chuckling at her ruse. "I guess I assumed . . . well, your father was right. You're a dead-eye."

With a bit of challenge in her voice, she said, "You try."

He barely hesitated. "All right, I think I'm up to a little competition. As long as we don't run out of bottles."

He set the rifle aside before stepping down from the porch to arrange six more targets.

The bottles replaced, Matt returned to the porch and took the rifle. Pressing the brass buttplate against the front of his shoulder, he took aim. On the first shot, he hit the first bottle, but hit nothing with his second, third, and fourth shots. The fifth shot hit nothing, and his final shot shattered a board on the roof of the outhouse.

"We will not run out of bottles," Degan muttered dryly beside him.

He looked up from the sight to see a teasing gleam in her eyes. Lowering the rifle, he turned to face her. With mock indignation, he asked, "Are you making fun of my shooting?"

She put a hand to her mouth to stifle a giggle.

Trying to hide his own amusement, he asked again, "Are you now laughing at my shooting?"

With little success, she attempted a serious expression. "You teach better than you shoot," she said, then covered her mouth again to hide her laughter.

Her amusement was infectious, and Matt couldn't help but laugh at her reaction to his lack of prowess with the weapon.

"Now you know why I was on the Army's medical staff and not in the infantry," he quipped, enjoying more of her musical laughter. "Your lesson is over."

That night, Degan was relaxing in her bed in the great room, listening to a rain shower that had begun just after sunset. Following the evening meal, Matt had packed his bags for his trip, and would leave early in the morning. He had explained that he would take a stagecoach from Sylvan to the train depot in the neighboring town. His journey to Washington would take three days. He said he would be returning in a few weeks, and thinking now of spending all those days without him, she realized that a few weeks felt like a very long time.

She had closed her eyes and begun to drift into sleep when she heard the sound of Matt's voice coming from the bedroom. His words were muffled and indistinguishable, as if answering an imaginary interrogator. She lay very still, breathing silently, listening closely. But except for the softly hissing fire in the hearth, and the rain tapping gently against the window, all was quiet. In a few moments, she closed her eyes, and dozed again.

Suddenly, a loud crash from the bedroom shattered the silence, and Matt's voice now rang out forcefully. She sprang upright to look at the closed door of his bedroom, and heard him shouting "No, no!" many times over. Momentarily paralyzed, she sat very still and listened, then heard him yell again. Without thinking, she threw back the blanket, jumped from the small bed, and rushed to open the bedroom door.

When she entered, she saw him lying in the bed, the sheet pulled just to his hips. His bare torso glistened with sweat, and his breathing was labored. She cautiously approached the bed.

"Matt?" she said. When he did not respond, she reached to touch his arm. Suddenly, he jumped up and took her shoulders in a firm grip, shaking her. His eyes were open but he was not awake. She shrank back, but he held her tight.

"There's no morphine, no chloroform! I can't amputate without—"

Then he broke from his trance and looked at her curiously. Releasing his hold of her, he swallowed hard, confused and embarrassed.

"I . . . I'm sorry." he whispered hoarsely. He dragged a hand across his eyes and through his hair and looked around the room as if trying to reorient himself to the present. "I don't know . . . what just happened."

The book he usually kept on his nightstand now lay on the floor beside the bed, along with two of his pipes and a small, empty glass. She knelt to gather the items and placed them back on the nightstand. In picking up the glass, she remembered that he always offered her water when she awoke from a nightmare.

"Do you want water?"

"No, something stronger. There's a brandy snifter on the washstand. Would you get it, please?" Then he added contritely, "I would get it myself, but . . . if I get out from under this sheet, we'll both be embarrassed."

She nodded, now realizing he wore nothing when he slept. She took the glass to the washstand and poured it half-full of brandy, then carried glass and snifter to the bedside. She handed him the glass, then sat down gingerly, tucking the tail of his shirt in which she always slept around her bare legs.

He took a sip and sighed, "Ah, that's more like it." He reached to pull the sheet to his waist before sitting up. Repositioning the pillow under his upper body, he seemed more alert now. "I'm sorry I startled you."

"I heard you shouting before."

He sighed heavily. "It's been a while since I've had those dreams. I had nightmares almost every night just after the war."

Degan nodded. "Sometimes I am afraid to sleep. The men still come to me in my dreams."

She watched as his leisurely sips of brandy calmed him further. He closed his eyes and leaned against the massive headboard, resting the glass on his stomach. She took in his broad shoulders, muscular arms, and the generous amount of dark hair across his upper chest. His face was relaxed and peaceful in repose, and she stared at him, wanting to memorize his handsome features. She noticed for the first time how dark his eyelashes were. His lips, open just slightly as he breathed, were full and well formed. She watched his bare chest move up and down rhythmically. His clean, sturdy hands that had cared for her so tenderly were now very still.

Sitting at his side, she silently watched this man who had saved her life, her heart full of gratitude and caring of a measure she had not felt before. Not only had he saved her life, but he had allowed her to live here in his home over the last few months, feeding and clothing her abundantly. He had treated her with sensitivity and respect that she had not thought white men capable of.

She noticed a small scar high on his chest near his right shoulder. Leaning forward, she stroked light fingers across the raised mark. He awoke abruptly and she pulled back.

"How did you get this wound?"

"Gettysburg," he said, taking the final sip of brandy. "I got too close to the fighting and took a stray bullet."

"Another shaman saved you?"

"Yes. I was lucky."

"The whites have many holy men to heal them."

Matt smiled. "The whites don't consider surgeons holy men."

"In my people, you are very special, apart from the rest."

A strange eagerness came into his eyes. "Is that what you think?"

"I think you are very special. The Creator has chosen you to heal."

She reached to take the empty glass and placed it on the nightstand. Standing, she pulled the blanket over the sheet that covered his lower body. As she tucked it loosely around his waist, he reached out to take her hands. Their eyes locked and for a moment, they seemed frozen in time. She saw something in those striking green eyes.

"Don't go, Degan," he whispered, "stay with me."

His words washed over her, flooding her senses. Losing herself in the depths of his eyes, she could only stare at him, unable to speak, with perceptively weaker knees and a quickening heartbeat.

"I won't force myself on you, I hope you know that," he said. "I only want to hold you."

She drew an audible breath. In a moment of hesitation, her eyes swept over his body. She knew he was naked under that sheet.

He patted the blanket at his side. "Just lay on top of the blanket," he said, as if reading her mind. "Put on my dressing gown there on the chair. It'll keep you warm."

Nodding her consent, she looked around, and saw the dressing gown draped over the armchair before the fireplace. She reached for it, and when she put it on, it was soft and warm and smelled wonderfully of him. Drawing the silky folds of fabric around her body, she climbed on top of the bed, and carefully settled at his side. He wrapped an arm protectively around her, and she rested her head on his shoulder.

They lay together for a while, Degan listening to the comforting sound of sputtering logs in the fireplace, to the rain dripping from the roof over the back porch, and to his steady breathing. Closing her eyes, she savored the embrace of this white shaman, and the trust she had come to know with him. After so many weeks, she knew she could relax against him. She placed a tentative hand on his chest, her fingers lightly stroking the crisp hair.

He sighed deeply. "That feels good."

When she reached to touch his scar again, she thought of his earlier bad dream, and of her own nightmares from which he still rescued her.

"We both have wounds from cruelty we did not choose," she said softly.

He pulled her closer.

"I will miss you," she said.

"I'll be back as soon as I can."

The pale light of early morning awakened her. For an instant, she had forgotten where she was, then remembered the night before. Now she lay alone in the large bed, and Matt was nowhere to be seen.

She heard a splash of water, followed by barely audible scraping sounds coming from behind the partition around the washstand, and knew that Matt was shaving. She sat up and rubbed sleep from her eyes.

Matt stepped from behind the partition. His face partially covered with soapy white foam, he held a razor in his hand, and a towel draped over one bare shoulder. Dressed from the waist down, he wore dark trousers and boots. He looked well rested, as though he had been up for hours.

"Good morning," he said with a smile.

She returned his greeting with a shy smile, smoothing her hair with her hands. "Good morning."

He quickly stepped back to the mirror to finish shaving, then she heard him splashing water on his face, and drying himself with the towel.

Reemerging from behind the partition, he said, "I made coffee," and went to the great room. He returned a few minutes later with a steaming cup, which he handed to her. When she reached for the cup, a quick flash of pain twisted her face.

"Your shoulder hurts from shooting yesterday?" he asked.

She nodded, massaging her upper arm. "This I remember from when my father taught me. When you say the gun kicks, now I understand."

He smiled. "It'll feel better in a day or two."

"You woke early?" she asked, taking a sip of coffee. In the light of day, she found herself once again admiring his physique. She took in his broad chest and narrow waist. His back was smooth and muscular when he turned to select a shirt from his armoire.

"I've been awake since five," he said. "I have to leave soon for the train depot."

Degan climbed out of bed, and leaned against the foot post. She still wore his dressing gown from the night before, but it now hung loosely open from her shoulders, revealing his shirt in which she always slept.

"That day I bought you those clothes," he said, "I should have bought you a proper night dress to sleep in." Removing a necktie from a drawer, and threading it under his collar, he leisurely looked her up and down with a mischievous grin. "But I think I prefer you in my shirts."

She couldn't help but smile at his boyish honesty. His approving perusal of her body filled her with a rush of warmth.

Now fully dressed, he reached for his coat, and putting it on, came to stand before her. His attire rich and striking, the dark material of the coat and the dark-patterned tie contrasted sharply with the crisp white shirt he wore. But there was a longing in his eyes, and she thought his smile seemed a little sad.

Placing his hands on either side of her neck, he tilted her face upward and looked into her eyes. He hesitated for a moment, then leaned to press his mouth gently to hers. She drank in the fresh scent of him. His kiss was tender and too brief. When he released her, she felt a raging fire coursing through her body.

"You be here when I get back," he whispered against her cheek. After a time, he stood back from her. She was too breathless to speak. Finally he said, "I have to go."

Picking up his bags, he turned and left.

CHAPTER

9

A shiny black carriage rolled to a stop a few feet from the massive front door of Tyler Mansion. Matt emerged from the plush interior and waited while the driver retrieved his bags, placing them on the gravel driveway.

"Enjoy your stay, sir," the driver said with a bow, touching the brim of his hat as he accepted a generous tip.

Matt picked up his bags and mounted the steps of the porch that wrapped around his boyhood home. Shafts of late afternoon sunlight slanted across the columns that stood imposingly at the base of the porch and extended to the second floor. A cool breeze rustled budding maple branches at either side of the landscaped lawn. Matt tapped the brass knocker twice before hearing footsteps approach from the other side. A white-haired gentleman in pristine livery pulled the heavy door open.

"Master Matthew!"

"William, it's good to see you!" Matt said, extending his hand to the butler who had been the distinguished, lone male of the household staff for years. "How are you?"

"I'm well, sir, thank you. Let me take your bags—"

"No, thank you, William, I can manage." He quickly grasped the handles of his luggage before the butler could reach down. Stepping further into the foyer, he looked up to see his mother descending the expansive staircase.

"Matthew, darling, you're finally here!" Kathleen Tyler floated gracefully into the foyer, demurely embraced her son, and accepted his kiss on her cheek. He took a step back. Her dark hair was piled high in curls atop her head, with just a few tendrils framing her face, the latest style of the day. Clear sapphires sparkled at her ears, nearly matching the blue of her eyes. Her complexion looked as smoothly porcelain as always. Matt could never discern signs of age in his mother, save for a few gray hairs mixed among the dark that had become more numerous with each visit.

"You're looking well, Mother."

"Thank you, dear," she replied, "how kind of you to say so."

They walked arm-in-arm into the parlor. Once settled on a richly upholstered sofa, Matt glanced around the room. Everything looked the same as it had on his last visit the previous year, from the beautifully plush furniture, to the thick, Persian carpets under his feet.

"How was your trip, darling? You look so tired," his mother said as she adjusted the lacey folds of her bodice and the voluminous dark blue taffeta of her skirt.

"It was uneventful, though long. I'm sure I'll sleep well tonight."

"I do hope so. Now tell me, what's the latest news from your little town? How is dear Dr. Bowman? He so enjoyed his visit when he was here over the holidays. It was just delightful having him. Such a lovely gentleman. And he was so impressed when he toured Hamilton General. He said he couldn't wait to get back to tell you all about it. He says you're both kept very busy."

When she paused to take a breath, Matt took advantage of the opening. "Yes, we've had several new families move to Sylvan, and of course, the families that are there continue to grow. The town itself just completed construction of a new school, and there's talk of another church to be built soon."

"Oh, I do want to mention, dear, tomorrow evening, your father and I are hosting a little soiree for some of the more generous donors to the hospital fund, as well as the doctors on staff and their wives. Of course, with your father taking the position as chief of staff, I expect we'll do our share of entertaining. I'm so looking forward to it, and I know you'll enjoy seeing everyone again. Everyone knows you're visiting, and they're all quite eager to—"

"Matty!" came a squeal of delight from the parlor door. Matt turned to see his younger sister, Caroline, rushing toward him with her arms outstretched. He stood and they embraced warmly, his hug lifting her off the floor. When he set her back down, he held her at arm's length for a better look. She wore her blond hair pulled back in a simple chignon at the nape of her neck, her hazel eyes flashing.

"Look at you, Cara, you're as beautiful as ever."

"Thank you, Matty. It's good to have you home," she said, settling into an overstuffed armchair across from the sofa.

"You returned from Paris early this past winter. I thought your plans were to stay until summer."

Before Caroline could answer, their mother offered her own version of events. "She's nursing a broken heart, Matthew," Kathleen whispered, as if she thought her daughter too fragile to hear the words spoken aloud. At twenty-two, Caroline's prospects for marriage were dwindling, nowhere faster than in her mother's mind. Engaged at seventeen, her fiancé had been killed at the Battle of Antietam, and it had taken the heart-broken Caroline a long time to recover. Since the end of the war, she had taken several trips abroad as a means of diversion. On one such trip, she had met a Parisian man with whom she had become romantically involved.

Matt turned to Caroline with an expression of genuine concern. "I didn't mean to bring up a difficult subject—"

"But not to worry," Kathleen interjected, putting a hand on Matt's arm, this time with a look of triumph on her face. "Tomorrow night there will be several eligible bachelors attending our soiree, and our Miss Caroline will have her pick of *la crème de la crème!* As will you, Matthew. Dr. Duncan's lovely daughter, Lilly, is very anxious to see you again. You remember Lilly . . ."

Matt opened his mouth to inquire about his mother's plotting, but Caroline was too eager to change the subject.

"How have you been, Matty? Does your practice in Pennsylvania keep you busy?"

"Yes, I was just telling Mother how the town is growing, with new families moving in. The farmers are planting their crops and preparing for a busy harvest at the end of the summer. We had a hard winter, but this time of year is always hectic."

"What do those poor country people do for amusement in the wintertime?" Kathleen asked. "It seems they'd be so isolated."

"In winter, activities mostly center around the two churches in the town," Matt explained. "They host music festivals, socials, and dramatic plays on the weekends. Church services are held mid-week and social events always follow. After a big snow, farmers will invite their friends and neighbors for sleighing parties. The farmers hitch their horses to sleighs and take their guests riding through the woods. Afterward, everyone goes back to the house for dessert."

"How fun!" Caroline said. "To be part of a large farm family that works together and has fun together . . . it sounds lovely."

"Well, dear, that life is suited to some," Kathleen said, "but it's a very hard life. And those poor people never travel more than five miles from their homes their entire lives. They certainly don't have the opportunities you've had, poor things."

Matt shrugged. "They seem happy enough," he replied. During his time in Sylvan, with the exception of Emma, he had never met anyone whose desire was to leave the area.

"I'm sure they're very happy," Caroline said.

Kathleen let go an uneasy, disdainful laugh. "Now Caroline, please, don't get any ideas about traveling to the wilderness of Pennsylvania, and finding yourself a farmer to marry and have twelve children with!"

Matt watched his sister's smile fade, and he felt the familiar distaste for his mother's perspective. *I'm barely in this house ten minutes and already I'm irritated.* Why did Kathleen never miss an opportunity to deflate a notion that did not conform to her ridiculously snobbish standards? As always, she seemed interested only in the upkeep of appearances, not in the true happiness of those around her.

He turned to his mother, and as respectfully as he could muster, replied, "I'm sure whomever Caroline chooses to marry, they'll be very happy together, no matter what he does for a living."

Caroline smiled gratefully at her brother as he rose to his feet.

"I must go say hello to Daisy." Passing Caroline's chair, he put a hand on her shoulder and squeezed affectionately.

Only one year older than Kathleen, Daisy, the daughter of former slaves, had been employed by the Tyler family since before Matt's birth. As a boy, Matt had found comfort in Daisy's kindness and occasional gentle discipline. He had spent many hours sitting at her worktable in the kitchen, watching as she chopped vegetables, stirred ingredients for a sauce or a soup, or kneaded dough to make bread. She always welcomed his offers of help, taking the time to teach him her expert culinary techniques. While Kathleen Tyler was immersed in managing the active social life expected of prominent couples in the community, it was Daisy who provided an always-present maternal figure for the Tyler children.

Daisy frequently held the Tyler children spellbound with stories of her parents, who had been born into slavery near Richmond, Virginia, but managed to escape. With the help of devout abolitionists in Philadelphia, the couple had traveled north to Pennsylvania, where Daisy was born in 1809.

Through mutual acquaintances, the young Dr. and Mrs. Adam Tyler had learned of a daughter of former slaves, who had been raised in Philadelphia, and had displayed an early talent in the kitchen. Upon meeting with Daisy, they decided to offer her employment, and she had been a loyal member of the household ever since.

This afternoon, Matt's mood was lifting and he was already feeling more at home as he made his way down the narrow hallway that led from the downstairs foyer to the kitchen. Taking a shortcut through the darkened, formal dining room, he picked up the familiar scent of the buffing wax the servants used on the furniture, blended with the delectable aromas wafting from the kitchen. Twelve high-backed chairs stood at rigid attention, as if awaiting marching orders, around the long dining room table of polished walnut. Heavy brocade draperies stood guard at the windows, protecting the room from the harsh intrusion of daylight. With quickening steps, he passed into the bright and spacious kitchen.

"My mouth was watering even before I reached the kitchen," he said, crossing the work area with open arms.

"Well, young man, you'll just have to wait until dinner," Daisy admonished, returning his warm embrace. She stretched on tiptoe to plant a kiss on his cheek.

"How are you, Daisy?" he asked, making himself comfortable at the worktable. A skinny, dark-haired girl of about thirteen was stationed on the opposite side.

"I'm fine, Matthew," Daisy replied before nodding toward the girl. "This is Sara. She's been with us for about two months now. Her parents work at the Clark residence, and they asked if I'd train her. She's picking up on things real fast. Sara, this is Dr. Tyler's son, Matthew. He's a doctor also. He lives in Pennsylvania. He's the one I told you was coming for a visit."

"Hello, Sara," Matt greeted her with a smile. "You're a lucky girl to be training under Daisy. She's a good teacher, as well as an excellent cook."

Sara's cheeks turned rosy and she giggled softly, keeping her wide blue eyes fixed on the young Dr. Tyler. She was preparing fresh asparagus for the evening meal, picking up each stalk, breaking off its pinkish-white end, then placing it into a separate bowl filled with ice water. To her surprise, Matt grabbed a handful of stalks, dumped them on the table in front of him, and began snapping away, tossing the shortened stalks into her bowl.

"What smells so good?" he asked, looking around the kitchen.

"I have pastries in the oven that you'll have for dessert this evening," Daisy said, reaching for a copper saucepan from the rack that hung over the massive cook stove. As always, she wore a spotless white cobbler's apron over her charcoal gray uniform, attire she had insisted upon from her first day of employment. She was not a large woman, but had always been of sturdy build that had served her well, allowing her to work energetically for long hours when necessary. Over the last few years, her hair had turned to match the color of her dress. Even so, she had retained a youthful grace and her dark, laughing eyes still reflected a buoyant personality.

"What's the main course?"

"Your favorite," she said, turning to see the look of delight on his face, "honey-glazed salmon."

"Ah, you know how to spoil me, Daisy!" He turned to Sara. "I can see I'll be putting on weight while I'm here."

"Matty." He turned to see that Caroline had entered the kitchen. "Father has come home, and he's asking for you."

He rose immediately from the table and, wiping his hands on a linen kitchen towel, nodded in Sara's direction.

"It was a pleasure to meet you, Sara," he said with a gentlemanly bow.

"Yes, sir," she managed, seeming pleasantly flustered.

Matt crossed the room to the stove where Daisy was stirring what would eventually be custard filling for the pastries. He put an arm across her shoulders and bent to kiss her lightly on the temple. "Thank you, Daisy, for all your hard work. I know dinner will be delicious."

In the foyer, William was carefully brushing the pile of Adam Tyler's frock coat before hanging it in the closet. The patriarch of the family was asking of any additional household news of the day, besides the fact that his son had arrived home for a visit. Before William could answer, Adam Tyler looked up to see his son emerging from the hallway leading to the kitchen.

"Hello, Father." Matt extended his hand to the tall, white-haired, elder Dr. Tyler. His father gripped his hand vigorously, then wrapped his arm around Matt's shoulders and pulled him close.

"Matthew! How are you, son?"

"Very good, sir, and you?" His father did look tired, just as Dr. Bowman had reported.

"Well, your mother says I'm working too hard, but I think she's secretly glad I've been staying out of her hair," Adam Tyler said with an impish chuckle. He kept a hand affectionately on his son's back.

Matt turned toward the parlor, but his father redirected him to the opposite side of the foyer. "Let's go into the library. If Mother catches us smoking in the parlor, she'll refuse us dinner, and I hear Daisy is preparing your favorite salmon dish. It's not to be missed."

Matt laughed at his father's assessment of unacceptable behavior in the household, as he pulled open the sliding wooden door, and stood back, allowing entrance into the dark, cool library. The room was patently masculine, with heavy, mahogany furniture upholstered in deep brown leather. Persian rugs of intricate patterns in rich hues of dark blue, hunter green, and gold covered the floor. Thick wine-colored drapes hung from windows on either side of the fireplace, obscuring the last faint shafts of early evening light.

William followed them into the room, making his way to a selection of decanters on the sideboard. "May I serve you both a brandy, sir?"

"Yes, please, William, and pour one for yourself while you're at it," Dr. Tyler said, retrieving a handsomely carved wooden box from his desk at the far end of the library.

William laughed in his reserved way. "I'm afraid I couldn't do that, sir, not while I'm on duty."

"Later, then," Dr. Tyler said, holding the humidor open while Matt chose a plump cigar from its depths.

"Thank you," he said, and watched his father turn and hold the box open for William.

"Here, take a cigar to enjoy with that brandy later," Dr. Tyler told his servant.

Without hesitation, William quickly chose a cigar and slipped it into the pocket of his livery coat in one easy motion, a gesture familiar to Matt. His father had never given a second thought to sharing the pleasure of his vices with William, for years a point of contention between his father and mother, who disapproved of such familiarity between servants and their employers.

"You'll enjoy these," Dr. Tyler told his son as he chose a cigar for himself and sank comfortably into a leather armchair opposite Matt. William was immediately at his side with a burning taper, touching the tip of the cigar while Dr. Tyler rotated it gently between his fingers as it lit. The butler then did the same for Matt.

"Tell me about the hospital." Matt eased back, stretching an arm across the back of the sofa. Clouds of gray smoke began drifting aimlessly between them.

Dr. Tyler waved a hand. "If you don't mind, Matthew, I'd much rather talk about your practice in Sylvan. We'll have plenty of time to talk about Hamilton General. For now, frankly, I'd love to talk about something else for a change."

As his father relaxed, Matt detected the unmistakable weariness in his demeanor. He was, most likely, working too many long hours to coordinate all the decisions and last-minute projects that needed to be handled before the hospital's official opening day. Matt proceeded to share with his father all the news of his practice in Sylvan.

"It was good to see Henry when he was here a few months ago. He was quite excited to tour the hospital," Dr. Tyler said, a measure of pride surfacing through fatigue.

"I know he was enthusiastic when he returned to Sylvan. He talked about his trip for days."

"He and Dr. Duncan, our administrator, got on quite well. I believe they even discussed you and your career."

"Yes, he mentioned that."

Dr. Tyler took a sip of brandy before carefully posing his next question. "Is that something you would consider? Coming to work at Hamilton General? Your skills would be most welcome."

"I'm not sure coming back to Washington would be wise right now. Dr. Bowman said he thought Dr. Duncan was aware of the charges against me."

"I spoke with Mr. Cunningham just a few weeks ago at his office. I was having some legal documents drawn up for the hospital. He spoke with assurance that the matter had been postponed indefinitely. An attorney for the Army Medical Corps had told Mr. Cunningham that the government has not been pursuing any such cases."

"That doesn't mean it's been dismissed, just that they aren't currently acting on the charges."

"Mr. Cunningham doesn't think you have anything to be concerned about," Dr. Tyler said calmly. "Besides being stale charges at this point, it was always an entirely political exercise. The Garrison family is quite influential in the Buffalo area, but beyond that, they would have a difficult time convincing anyone to take up such an insubstantial case."

"I know, you've said that before, but—"

"Colonel Garrison and I were colleagues at one time, so I am well aware of the gentleman's character, or lack thereof. I cannot imagine that his offspring have strayed far from their father's path. I believe, and Mr. Cunningham agrees, that the Garrison heirs presented their original complaint as a means of avenging the colonel's death. They simply want someone to blame."

"I'm afraid I don't have quite as much confidence in your attorney as you do."

"Matthew, as you well know, in time of war and in the aftermath of battle, men often do and say things that run contrary to their character. Those who would pursue these charges against you are aware that the evidence is slim at best, especially now, after so much time has passed. They would be relying on the memories of witnesses who were so traumatized by battle that their testimony would be deemed unreliable."

His father's words did little to assuage Matt's fear that one day he would have to face the consequences of his actions—actions he couldn't even remember clearly. He stared down at the glass in his hand without really seeing it. With an absurd detachment, he briefly pictured himself standing to face his accusers and a judge during a court martial, and wondered how he would retain adequate counsel in Sylvan. When he looked up, his father was watching him.

"Didn't you tell me that the colonel who died under your care was already suffering from typhus when he was brought to the field hospital?" Dr. Tyler asked. "Didn't you tell me that there were hundreds of wounded and dying men brought in that day, and only three surgeons to tend to them?"

"Yes," Matt whispered, quickly taking a sip of brandy. The memories of battle rushed back, so vivid he could almost feel the ground shaking beneath his feet from cannon explosions more than a mile away. He wanted to recount more of the story, but could not put that day into words.

"Matthew, I've been in war. The idea that anyone could hold you accountable for the untimely death of a man under those conditions, officer or not, is senseless."

"But you don't know the whole story, Father. At the time, I wanted to tend to the soldiers who had borne the worst of the fighting at the front lines. I made them my priority. I wanted to patch them back together as best I could . . . to send them home to their families with some semblance of who they were before they went into the fighting. Perhaps I could have done more for the colonel. I just can't remember."

"No one can be certain of what happened in a situation like that." Dr. Tyler reached to tap the end of his cigar against the rim of a heavy ashtray on the side table.

"His family feels certain enough to pursue medical negligence and dereliction of duty against me. They aren't content to blame the colonel's death on the natural consequences of warfare and disease."

"I know they feel that Colonel Garrison, being an officer, should have received priority care that day. But Mr. Cunningham believes that the Army Medical Corps has no intention of pursuing such charges. It's ridiculous, two years after the end of the war. Even if they do pursue the charges, the worst that's likely to happen is a change of the status of your discharge to dishonorable and you would not receive a pension."

"Unless their attorneys plan to pursue murder charges, and they're able to convince the court that my neglect was intentional."

"Was it?"

"I'm not sure," he muttered. "I just can't remember."

"They can prove nothing." Dr. Tyler sounded resolute. "I believe, at worst, you need only fear a dishonorable discharge."

"That would bring disgrace to this family."

Dr. Tyler's eyes were downcast and a look of dismay came over his face. "Your mother would have a difficult time with it, I fear." He raised his eyes, looking more hopeful. "But Mr. Cunningham believes that eventually, the Garrison family will drop their accusations and the case will be formally dismissed and forgotten."

"I hope you're right," Matt said, unconvinced. "In any event, I'd feel more at ease remaining in Sylvan for the foreseeable future. It's been the safe haven for me that I'd hoped it would be. Except for Dr. Bowman, no one there knows anything about these charges. Here in Washington, I'd be more likely to encounter someone from the Army Medical Corps who might start asking questions."

"I understand. And the Garrison family being from Buffalo, it's not likely their influence will reach as far as Sylvan." Dr. Tyler leaned forward to make his point. "I want you to know, Matthew, that I'm very proud of you and your service in the war. You did good work and saved many lives. I'll always be proud of you and the work you do."

Matt looked up to meet his father's eyes. He was filled with gratitude and love for the man he had admired above all others his entire life. "Thank you, sir."

Dr. Tyler sat back in his chair, now seeming more relaxed, and amenable to sharing details about the new hospital.

"Hamilton General has been a very long, arduous road, but I feel a sense of accomplishment," he said, a pleased expression on his face and satisfaction in his tone. "I know the hospital will make a difference in this community. We've got three surgical theaters completely equipped. Once our roster of physicians is complete, we'll be at full staff, including our Matron of Nurses, Mrs. Bloom. You'll meet her at the party tomorrow evening. Mother did mention we're hosting a little get-together tomorrow evening here at the house, didn't she?"

"Yes, she told me about it."

"Our guests are looking forward to seeing you again. They will likely inquire of your joining the staff of Hamilton General, now that it's almost complete. You should be prepared for the subject to come up."

Matt smiled. "I appreciate the warning."

The library doors slid open and William announced that dinner was being served. The men rose, extinguished what was left of their cigars, and followed the butler to the dining room.

It had always been the tradition of the Tyler family to enjoy the evening meal in a leisurely fashion, sometimes extending dinner over two or three hours, depending upon the conversation. Daisy embraced the philosophy that a late-day meal of fewer than five courses was simply not worth coming to the table for. Kathleen Tyler took great pride in choosing the most appropriate wine to accompany each course from the cool, dusty confines of the family's wine cellar.

However, this evening, Matt was unable to do justice to the delicious salmon that Daisy had prepared especially for him. His conversation lagged during dinner, and more than once he had to be pulled from his own thoughts to participate in the discussion. When Daisy emerged from the kitchen to ask if the family required anything further, she noticed that Matt had barely touched his dinner.

"Is the salmon not cooked to your liking, Matthew?" she asked.

"Oh, it's delicious, Daisy," he said, unconvincingly. "I'm afraid I'm just so tired from my trip, I don't have much of an appetite."

Following dessert, he apologized to his family and quietly retreated to his bedroom.

Alone in the place he once considered his private sanctuary, Matt opened his bags to unpack, but found them empty. When he opened the armoire, he saw that his shirts and suits were hanging neatly, and realized that William must have performed this task earlier. The bed had been turned down for the night, and a tray bearing a small, steaming pot of tea, a cup and saucer had been placed on the nightstand. Matt smiled at the butler's considerate forethought, and made a mental note to thank him in the morning. Looking around the bedroom, while grateful for the beautifully luxurious appointments, as usual, he found himself feeling out of place.

He settled on the bed, intending to read the book he had retrieved earlier from the library, but his mind immediately focused on Degan. It was not just his cabin and life in Sylvan that he missed. He missed Degan much more than he had expected to. If he closed his eyes, he could envision her lovely face, sweet smile, expressive dark eyes. He could almost feel her lying in his arms, as she had done the night before he left for Washington. How he longed for that again.

Many times in his life he had been alone and had not found it to be distressing or unpleasant. In fact, he had welcomed solitude on countless occasions. But tonight he was not merely alone, he was lonely. He felt an emptiness with an odd pain attached to it that he could not shake. He had scarcely realized how much he looked forward to coming home at the end of each day, knowing that Degan was waiting for him. He now missed the time they spent sitting before a warm fire, talking, laughing, and sharing an ever-deepening intimacy. When they talked, he felt she not only listened to him but truly heard him, accepting what he said without judgment or pretense. Unlike other women he had known, he sensed that instead of attempting to devise responses that he would find most palatable, she offered him honesty, and a reflection of her true self.

While he knew that her return to her people was inevitable, the thought made him acutely uncomfortable. He had grown to appreciate her unassuming, wise, and generous character. He would often discuss his day with her, sharing stories of his patients, their struggles, their successes, and how much satisfaction he derived from his work. When he was called out on an emergency, no matter how late the hour, she always stayed up until he came home.

Little by little, she had revealed to him aspects of her life on the reservation, how close and loving her extended family was, and how they worked together to make a life for themselves on what little land the U.S. government had allotted to them. He knew she felt a strong loyalty and affection for her family, that she missed them, and that she looked forward to returning to her home as soon as possible.

He had shared with her some of his life growing up, focusing not on his family's wealth, but instead, on Daisy's role as a surrogate parent, and her wisdom and influence on him. Daisy had taught him the importance of respect and deference for all people, not just those of means and rank. Those lessons had been reinforced by his father's tireless example of devotion to the sick and injured of all statures, a practice that rarely sat well with Kathleen.

Tonight, he thought of Degan alone in his cabin, and he worried about her. *She's a survivor, smart and resourceful.* But he couldn't keep his nagging fears at bay. He hoped that she had chosen to keep the rifle loaded and at the ready while he was gone. To shoot what, exactly, he couldn't think, but the fact that he knew her to be an excellent shot provided a small measure of comfort. As the clock on the mantel over the fireplace chimed eleven o'clock, he yearned for her. He turned on his side, and closed his eyes.

Sometime later, Matt awoke abruptly and sat up in bed, breathing heavily. Another of the nightmares that had relentlessly invaded his sleep since the night before his departure had struck once again. He sat for a moment, trying to calm himself. A shaft of moonlight shone on the face of the clock. It was just after one in the morning. The house was quiet and the utter darkness of the hour seemed to suffocate him.

Fleeting, cloudy images of his dream replayed in his mind. He was back on the battlefield, under a dirty canvas tent that served as a makeshift surgical ward. Black flies crawled on his hands, his bloody instruments, and his filthy uniform as he prepared to examine the next casualty. Faceless orderlies placed the stretcher precariously across the tops of two waist-high barrels, and Matt reached to remove the sheet that covered the patient's face. He gasped when he saw Degan on the stretcher, her body savagely beaten, bruised, and bloody. Her eyes were open, filled with horror and the certainty that he would violate her in the most gruesome and sadistic way. He froze, paralyzed with agony, unable to reassure her, unable to help her. Suddenly, Jon was beside him, saying, "You can't help her, Matt. I can't help her either. You cut off my arm, now I can't help her either . . ."

Then he woke up, drenched in a cold sweat and gulping for air. He knew well how nightmares played on his deepest fears, and he thought of Degan and her extensive injuries that first night he found her in his barn. He remembered how terrified she was, and how he had been unable to convince her that he would not harm her. He thought of his best friend, Jon, whose arm he had amputated on the battlefield some years ago. Trying to calm himself, he forced the garish, horrific images of his dream aside, and saw again in his mind's eye a healed and healthy Degan. He tried to comfort himself with the knowledge that Jon certainly would have died if not for the amputation.

Not relishing the idea of trying to go back to sleep, Matt got up, retrieved his smoking jacket from the armoire, and his pipe from the nightstand. He decided to go downstairs to the library for a brandy and a smoke.

The musicians were the first to arrive at Tyler Mansion, an hour before the party. Kathleen greeted them in the foyer before directing them where to set up for optimum sound quality throughout the downstairs. The household staff scurried from the kitchen to the parlor, the library, and the dining room, with silver trays of every dimension laden with hot and cold hors d'oeuvres. By seven o'clock, the flushed and slightly harried hostess pronounced everything "ready" and not long after that, guests began to arrive.

On the second floor, Caroline knocked gently on her brother's bedroom door.

"Come," she heard Matt call from inside. When she opened the door, her breath caught in her throat. Her brother was standing by the fireplace fastening the top button of his collar. He wore a black dress suit with swallowtail coat, a black vest cut low in the front, and a white cravat. The front of his white shirt was elegantly plain, with simple pearl studs and pearl cuff links at his wrists.

"Matty, you look so handsome!" She entered the darkened room, her stylish, royal blue ball gown sweeping behind her. The neckline of the gown rested just off her shoulders, lending radiance to her porcelain skin. "You'll have all the ladies swooning this evening."

"Well, at least there will be plenty of doctors in the house to tend to them," he replied sardonically.

"Here, let me do that," Caroline offered, reaching to finish adjusting his cravat. As she worked to tighten the knot, he made choking sounds. She looked up to see the familiar glint of mischief in his eyes.

"Cara, I'd like to be able to breathe this evening, if you don't mind."

"Oh, is that too tight?" she asked, feigning innocence.

"Is my face turning blue?"

"I hope not, you'd clash with my dress. There, it's finished."

"Thank God," he mumbled, running a finger between his snug collar and his neck.

Caroline chuckled. "I believe some of the guests have already arrived. Are you feeling better tonight?"

"I'm still a little tired, but I'll be all right," he said with no trace of enthusiasm in his voice.

"Let's go down the back stairs and see if Daisy needs any help in the kitchen."

In their youth, brother and sister had often tiptoed down the stairs at the back of the mansion to sneak into Daisy's kitchen for forbidden snacks late at night, or to hide from imaginary monsters. This evening, navigating the narrow stairway was no small feat for Caroline, draped as she was in yards upon yards of swishy crinolines, and the satiny material of her gown. Matt descended the stairs ahead of her, her hand firmly in his grip.

When he unlatched the door at the bottom of the stairwell, they felt the warmth of the kitchen wash over them.

"Tyler children reporting for duty," Caroline chirped brightly as a busy Daisy sent the final server from the kitchen carrying a tray laden with food.

With a wide smile that radiated pride and affection, Daisy clasped her hands to her breast. "Don't you both look stunning!"

"Thank you, Daisy," Matt said. "Now, what can we do to help?"

"Oh I wouldn't dream of asking you to help with anything! You both go out and enjoy the party. Some of the guests are already here, so I'm sure Miss Kathleen is looking for you."

Matt nodded, then turned to his sister. "Shall we?"

"I'll be along shortly," Caroline said. "I want to smooth my hair one last time."

As Matt ventured out, Caroline turned to Daisy with a look of concern and confusion on her face.

"Daisy, do you think Matty seems—oh, I don't know—not himself?" she asked with a frown.

Daisy shrugged. "He seems troubled. Maybe a little sad."

"I suppose he's preoccupied with his decision whether or not to transfer here to Hamilton General."

Daisy shook her head decisively. "Never seen a man get that far-away, gloomy look in his eyes over an offer of employment."

Now Caroline was even more confused. "What do you think is troubling him?"

Daisy turned to meet her questioning gaze. "A woman."

CHAPTER

10

Kathleen Tyler was well educated and well traveled. Aside from her two children, she counted foremost among her accomplishments a thirty-three-year marriage that had weathered few storms. Another forte was her organizational abilities that allowed her to manage two hectic social schedules, while running a household staff of a half-dozen servants. Successfully planning and hosting a social gathering of Washington's elite was certainly a feat she would have counted among her talents. Many agreed such events provided her with yet another opportunity to shine.

She approached these occasions like a general embarking on a military campaign. Daisy assumed the role of drill sergeant, giving instructions directly to the foot soldiers who comprised the staff. Kathleen took over as commander-in-chief, relying on her competent subordinates to carry out her orders. The two women worked well together. After many years, Daisy had learned to anticipate the preferences, as well as the whims, of the mistress.

When her guests began arriving at Tyler Mansion, Kathleen personally met each of them in the foyer, bubbled with welcome, then skillfully parlayed their greetings into seedlings of conversation with her other guests. The parlor was buzzing with scattered voices when Matt appeared in the doorway and was promptly spotted by his mother's keen eye.

"There you are!" she called out above the din, detaching easily from a small group of guests to sweep toward her son and take his arm. "Come, Dr. and Mrs. Clark were asking about you, as was their sweet daughter, Miss Abigail."

Matt dutifully allowed himself to be led to the center of the room where an older gentleman with a kind face, large belly, and short legs stood with two lavishly dressed women. With exaggerated ceremony, Kathleen presented her son to Dr. Daniel Clark, then to his wife, and their daughter, Abigail Clark, who giggled nervously and loudly as Matt took her gloved hand.

"It's so nice to see you again, Matthew," Dr. Clark said. "I believe we were traveling about the continent the last time you visited Washington."

"The pleasure is mine, sir. Congratulations on your success in the completion of the new hospital. You must be very proud."

Dr. Clark beamed, but spoke with a humble demeanor. "It's been hard work, and we're almost there. We'd like to bring another doctor on staff before our official opening—"

Mrs. Clark took a small step forward. "Your mother says you're considering joining the staff, Matthew. We're certainly hoping that you do." She looked too deliberately at Abigail, who nodded enthusiastically at her mother's statement.

Matt's gaze swept the floor briefly before he answered. "That's very flattering, but I'm afraid I haven't made any final decisions yet."

"It's a wonderful opportunity," Dr. Clark said, wagging his finger. "You should consider it very seriously."

"Daniel, have you begun your recruiting campaign even before you've finished your first drink?" Dr. Adam Tyler seemed to appear out of thin air at his son's side.

"I was just telling Matthew how much we need his skills on our staff."

"And he'd be a splendid asset to the Washington social circuit, Dr. Tyler," Mrs. Clark added, looking again to her daughter whose cheeks flushed a deeper shade of crimson. The tight ringlets that framed her plump face bobbed as she nodded.

Dr. Tyler turned to Matt. "If these compliments keep up, by the end of the night, we won't be able to afford you!"

Polite laughter infused the small group, and before he knew what was happening, Matt saw his mother swooping down on him once again. She excused them both before whisking him off to present him to other guests.

Charles Thomas had given several thousand dollars in memory of his wife who had died just two years before. Robert Carter and his wife, Ruth, had a son attending Georgetown University's medical school, undoubtedly expecting that their donation would secure their son a position on staff upon completion of his studies.

"And I don't believe you've met this handsome gentleman, Mr. David Lawson," Kathleen pronounced. An impeccably dressed, dark-haired young man with piercing dark eyes turned. "Mr. Lawson, please meet my son, Dr. Matthew Tyler."

Matt extended his hand, and Mr. Lawson took it firmly. "Dr. Tyler."

"It's a pleasure to meet you," Matt said.

"Mr. Lawson has just moved here from Annapolis, so he's brand new to the city, and to our social group," Kathleen explained.

"Yes, and I'm finding Washington to be quite an interesting little city," Mr. Lawson said, taking a sip of champagne. He bowed solicitously toward Kathleen as she excused herself to flutter among her other guests. "Do you live here?"

"No," Matt replied. "I have a medical practice in a town in northern Pennsylvania."

"A town in northern Pennsylvania?" Smug astonishment seeped into Lawson's tone.

"Yes, Sylvan. About four hundred people live in the town and outlying areas."

"How charming," he said acerbically, "but you must miss the city terribly. Isn't it—well, what's the word?—rather *rustic* up there?"

"Yes," Matt answered, feeling instinctual defenses rising. "The town is growing, but it's very rural. A large number of families in the area are farmers. The families tend to be quite large as there's always so much work to do on a farm, especially in the summer months, and during the fall harvest."

"Farmers you say? How very quaint." His voice oozed condescension, and he barely bothered to stifle a derisive smirk. "Have you also been able to apply your skills to the farm animals as well?"

Matt refused to be baited, and with earnest enthusiasm, cheerfully told the truth. "Actually, yes, I have. Last summer I assisted a farmer in birthing a large calf. The calf was in a breech position, which, as you may know, means it would have come out back feet first, and possibly suffocated inside the mother. So I opened her up from the side, and lifted the calf right out. It was quite a successful surgery."

Mr. Lawson turned pale and quickly excused himself, muttering that he needed some air.

Too far away to have heard the exchange, Kathleen swept immediately to Matt's side. "Is he all right?"

"He will be," Matt said, chuckling to himself. "I don't think the champagne agreed with him."

The hostess looked genuinely surprised, and a little offended. "Well, it's the best champagne money can buy. He should be used to it," she said, then lowered her voice. "His family in Annapolis is very well-to-do. They're the largest ship-building concern in three states. For being so new to the area, he gave very generously to the hospital."

Matt did not reply, but wondered if David Lawson had an ulterior motive for his generosity. He always found the political maneuverings of such occasions at once fascinating and distasteful. He could only imagine the wrangling his father and other members of the administrative team of Hamilton General had endured—not to mention the egos they had stroked—to get the hospital built, equipped, and operational.

"Oh, Dr. Duncan and Miss Lilly are here!" Kathleen announced. Matt's attention was drawn to the parlor entrance where Gerard Duncan now stood with his grown daughter, looking around the room. Dr. Duncan's wife, Lydia, had died some years earlier. He had never remarried, but had come to rely on his unmarried daughter as a social companion, presumably until she took a husband.

"Dear Mrs. Tyler, how nice to see you! Thank you so much for inviting us." Dr. Duncan bent to deliver a light peck on the back of Kathleen's hand. He was a tall, balding man with broad shoulders, white hair, and a bushy moustache that nearly obscured the lower half of his face. "And Matthew, good to see you again."

"Good evening, sir," Matt said as the older gentleman firmly pumped his hand.

"Your father and Dr. Bowman have kept me informed of your career, Matthew. Oh, forgive me, you remember my daughter, Miss Lilly Duncan."

A blushing Miss Duncan stepped forward, and allowed Matt to take her hand as they exchanged greetings. She was a small woman with auburn hair, hazel eyes, and a generous sprinkling of freckles across her cheeks and the bridge of her nose. She had been away at boarding school for several years, and had returned to Washington since Matt's last visit. From a prominent family, and attractive, Miss Duncan had known no shortage of suitors as she came of courting age, but had yet to settle on one to marry.

"Dr. Duncan, let's leave these two to get reacquainted," Kathleen was saying, and Matt recognized the familiar look of calculated planning in his mother's eyes as she led the older doctor toward an array of hors d'oeuvres across the room.

"When Daddy told me you were visiting from Pennsylvania, I was so excited to attend Mrs. Tyler's party this evening," Miss Duncan began, her lips curving into a pleasant smile. "I wasn't sure you'd remember me. It's been a few years since we've seen each other."

"Of course I remember you," Matt said, putting a hand up to catch the eye of young Sara who was passing with a tray of champagne flutes. "Thank you, Sara." He selected two glasses from the tray, and offered one to Miss Duncan.

"I'm sure your family is glad to have you here," she replied, raising a gloved hand to take the glass, "particularly your father. I know he couldn't be more proud of you."

"That's very gracious of you to say. It's my pleasure to be here."

"You must miss Washington terribly. You've been away since the end of the war."

"Yes, a colleague of my father's, Dr. Henry Bowman, offered me a position working with him in his practice in Pennsylvania. I must say I've never regretted my decision. Sylvan is a very peaceful town, and quiet."

"Still," she said, taking a step closer, "how does a refined and cultured gentleman such as yourself find contentment in such a *pastoral* setting?"

Images of his cabin flashed quickly through his mind, and it was Degan his thoughts settled on. Suddenly, he felt very lonely, though he was standing in a room full of people. With difficulty, he pulled himself back to the present. "I've always known I could return to Washington if I chose to. But after the war, I needed some peace, a slower pace."

Miss Duncan smiled politely and nodded, but Matt could see in her eyes that she did not really comprehend his meaning, and cared little about his reasons for living in Sylvan. It was always difficult to talk about how the war had changed him. He actually preferred not to discuss it at all. Only those who had experienced it themselves could understand. Those who had not lived through the battles, the hardships, and the unimaginable suffering, could never understand the need for distance and serenity afterwards.

"But Daddy said you might be joining the staff of Hamilton General," she said, sounding almost petulant.

"That does seem to be the rumor that's circulating."

"I certainly hope you do!" She looked up at him with a suggestive pout. "What can a lonely city girl do to convince you to leave the wilderness, and come partake of all that Washington has to offer?"

Taken aback by her boldness, Matt replied as courteously as possible. "Miss Duncan, you flatter me with your attention. However, I'm afraid I find myself at a loss to offer any solution to your dilemma."

Undeterred, she pressed on, "Well I'm sure we can think of something that might lure you from the countryside—"

"Lilly Duncan!" came a squeal from the other side of the room. "I didn't know you'd be here this evening!" When Matt looked up, he saw another young woman making her way toward them through the swarm of chattering guests.

Obviously irritated at the interruption, Miss Duncan icily greeted the interloper, and with reluctance, introduced her to Matt.

"This is Dorothea Wilson. Her father, Dr. Nicholas Wilson, just joined the staff of Hamilton General. This is Dr. Matthew Tyler."

"Well, hello," Miss Wilson gushed, extending her hand to Matt. She was a few inches taller than Miss Duncan, with light brown hair pulled back tightly from her face, and wound around her head like a turban. Large, gold earrings swayed with each move of her head, and Matt noticed her plump cheeks were overly rouged.

"It's a pleasure to meet you, Miss Wilson," Matt said with a slight bow.

"I saw the two of you over here with your heads together, and I just had to come over and introduce myself. Any chance I could get one of those?" Miss Wilson asked, nodding at the half-empty glasses that Matt and Miss Duncan were holding.

"Of course," Matt said, waving a hand in Sara's direction. She came over immediately, and held the tray steady while he chose a third glass.

"Thank you, Dr. Tyler," Miss Wilson said, sampling the fizzing liquid. "This is a lovely home your family has. Did you grow up here?"

"Have you not visited Tyler Mansion before, Dorothea?" Miss Duncan asked with a lift of her chin. "Daddy and I have visited many times. Daddy and the elder Dr. Tyler are quite good friends."

"Now Lilly, how could you have visited many times when you've been away at school for so long?" Miss Wilson challenged with a flip of her hand. "Silly!"

Before an annoyed Miss Duncan could retort, Matt said, "My parents moved into this house right after they married. My sister Caroline and I grew up here." He now had to raise his voice, as the room had grown more crowded in the last half-hour.

"I understand you live out of town," Miss Wilson said. "Do you come back to visit often?"

"No, not often. The trip from Pennsylvania takes several days by train."

"We'd love to see more of you, Dr. Tyler," Miss Wilson proposed, then turned to Miss Duncan, whose own seductive tone of moments earlier seemed to have evaporated. "We'll just have to convince the good doctor to move back here to the city, won't we Lilly?"

Miss Duncan did not answer, nor did she bother to hide her displeasure at Miss Wilson including herself in any plans to ensnare the young doctor.

"Have you toured the new hospital yet?" Miss Wilson asked, turning to Matt. "Dr. Tyler, are you all right?"

The room had grown smaller as more guests arrived and the noise of a thousand conversations in the tiny parlor seemed to close in around him. Fighting to keep his breathing even, Matt forced himself to focus on answering Miss Wilson's question.

"No, I haven't yet, but . . . I'm looking forward to it," he replied, startled that his own voice sounded so far away. "I'll be visiting later this week."

"Daddy says it's quite impressive," Miss Duncan interjected. "He's been telling me all about it. In fact, Dr. Tyler, I'd be happy to accompany you on your visit, and personally show you the various innovations of the facility—"

"Oh, that sounds wonderful, Lilly, I'd love to join you! I haven't yet seen the hospital myself," Miss Wilson announced, seemingly unaware of the sharp daggers that were flying her way from Miss Duncan's frosty eyes.

Matt could take no more. "If I may beg your pardon, ladies," he murmured. "I'm afraid I must excuse myself to get some air . . ."

Without a backward glance, he quickly made his way past the other guests, and into the foyer where the air was already cooler and pleasantly free of the heavy perfumes that clouded the parlor. He crossed the foyer into the library, and when he found the room empty, he closed the door quietly behind him and went straight to the brandy snifter atop the sideboard. His hands shook as he poured the amber liquor into a glass and quickly took a sip. Wishing fervently that he could just stay here, alone in the darkened library until the party was over, he knew it would be only a matter of time before an overflow of guests made their way across the foyer as he had. So he wasted no time escaping through the hallway to the kitchen, out the back door, and onto the moonlit terrace that extended from the rear of the mansion.

Relieved and grateful to find himself alone, he stood motionless for a moment, listening to the welcome quiet of the night. The crowded parlor, the loud buzzing of the guests, and the suffocating loneliness of being surrounded by strangers had filled him with an intolerable agitation that he had to flee. He filled his lungs with evening air that was crisp and fresh, then walked a few paces away from the house, onto the lawn. The grass had already taken on its nighttime moisture, and in the manicured shrubbery nearby, crickets chirped.

Reaching for a cigar in his coat pocket, he struck a match, and was soon enjoying the relaxing habit that always calmed him. He sat down on the low brick wall that edged the terrace, and gazed up at the stars. It was getting late and he wondered if Degan had turned in yet, and how she was spending her days and evenings at the cabin. She was never far from his thoughts. As each day passed, he grew more eager to make the trip home to resume his normal life that had come to include her. With a weight of sadness that was heavier than he expected, he remembered his promise that he would escort her back to her village upon his return. His frequent thoughts of Degan always resulted in the depressing reality that she would understandably want to go home as soon as possible when his visit to Washington was over.

He heard the back door open. When he turned, he was thankful to see Caroline peeking out to scan the back yard. When she spotted him, she quietly closed the door behind her and, crossing the terrace, came into the yard to sit next to him.

"I thought I might find you here," she said. "But I didn't expect to find you alone."

"I had to get some air," he confessed, sounding worn out.

"And a respite from all the female attention, I suspect," she added, grinning. "There are several women in there who are wondering where you've disappeared to."

Matt rolled his eyes and exhaled cigar smoke into the cool night air.

"So tell me, dear brother, which young lady strikes your fancy?"

He took another leisurely draw on his cigar and exhaled before answering casually, "She's not here."

Caroline looked surprised, and let go a laugh. "Well, aren't you being mysterious!"

He smiled and quickly changed the subject. "And what have you been doing all evening while I've been keeping the ladies entertained?"

"I've been circulating among the guests, making sure everyone is pleasantly engaged in conversation and having a superb time."

"I thought that was Mother's job."

"I guess I'm second-in-command. Actually, I was conversing earlier with Mr. David Lawson. I do find him quite charming."

"Ah yes, Mr. Lawson," Matt growled. "I had a conversation with him earlier as well. I found him to be quite insufferably condescending."

"Really?" Caroline seemed taken aback. "When I spoke with him, he was a perfect gentleman."

"I'm sure he can be when he wants to be." Matt sometimes worried about his sister, as he had often known her to be far too trusting and vulnerable, especially where men were concerned. He was glad she had not endured much of life's pain and misfortune that often toughens the tender-hearted. Still, he would have preferred she be a bit more protective of herself.

"You know what Daisy always says: 'Don't listen to what people say, watch what they do,'" Caroline reminded him.

"Good words to live by."

"Father seems to be enjoying himself more than anyone," Caroline said. "He loves parties, having people over to the house, with plenty to eat and drink, and lively conversation among his friends."

"Yes, he's really at his best when he's entertaining," Matt said, enjoying the mental picture of their father happily circulating through the crowd of guests. "We've had a lot of good parties here over the years."

"Yes, we surely have."

They sat in silence for a moment before Matt began to chuckle at his own thoughts. "Remember at Christmastime when we were young? How Auntie Beatrice always drank too much wine before dinner?"

Caroline smiled. "Yes, I remember! She would have several glasses before she ate anything, and she became tipsier with each sip. She always spoke French when she had too much to drink."

"The more she drank, the more French she spoke," Matt said. "By the end of dinner, her pronunciation was so poor, I think Mother was the only one who could understand what she was saying!"

Caroline put a hand to her mouth to muffle her laughter. "I remember how you and I got into so much trouble for laughing at her, but she sounded so funny. Proper French pronunciation is just impossible when you've had too much to drink."

"Oh?" Matt turned to look at her askance. "Are you speaking from experience?"

Caroline was suddenly shamefaced. "Ah . . . oui?" she confessed, then laughed again.

"Cara, Cara," Matt scolded with a teasing gleam in his eye, "have you completely forgotten your upbringing?"

Still giggling, Caroline looked up to see David Lawson striding across the terrace toward them.

"I see you're having a grand time all by yourselves!" he said as he drew near. "I thought our soiree took a definite downturn a while ago, and now I see the reason. The most radiant person at the party is here on the terrace!"

"Why thank you, Mr. Lawson, that's so kind of you," Matt joked, and Caroline burst out laughing again.

"I was referring to your sister," Lawson said, not amused in the least. He turned purposefully toward Caroline. "I'm wondering, Miss Tyler, if you might kindly consider taking a stroll with me, and showing me the rest of the grounds of the mansion. It's such a lovely evening."

Obviously pleased, Caroline rose to her feet. "I'd be happy to. Matty, will you excuse us?"

"Of course," Matt said with a wave of his hand, and a stern glare in Lawson's direction. He thought he saw triumph in the young man's eyes as the pair turned, and Caroline took his arm.

Matt could hear the music and the voices getting louder as he reluctantly made his way back into the house. Entering the foyer, he caught sight of

Miss Duncan standing outside the parlor looking angry and disgusted. Sara stood facing her, begging forgiveness while fretfully dabbing at the bodice of Miss Duncan's dress with a clean, white cloth.

"Give me that!" she spat, snatching the cloth from Sara's hand.

"May I be of assistance?" Matt asked as he approached the two women.

Sara's fearful expression intensified and she stepped back, silently fastening her eyes to the floor.

"This clumsy little fool spilled champagne all over the front of my dress," Miss Duncan said, her cheeks flushed, her hands shaking with rage. "Now I'm trying to repair the damage so I can return to the party without being completely humiliated! I intend to speak with Mrs. Tyler about this!"

"I'm sure it was simply an accident," he said. "Perhaps you'd allow me to escort you to the kitchen where Daisy can help you—"

His suggestion ignited fresh rancor. "I'm not going to be trotted off to the kitchen to be dealt with like a common servant! Why, I'd be no better than . . . than this simpleton!" she screeched, waving a hand in Sara's direction.

Intense, familiar anger rose quickly in Matt's chest. On too many occasions as a child, he had witnessed self-important house guests belittling Daisy for minor mistakes or accidents. When he impulsively jumped to her defense, he had been scolded by his mother for his impertinence. While the Tylers did not look kindly upon a member of their household staff being treated disrespectfully, it was never considered acceptable behavior for Matt to give voice to his feelings of protectiveness toward Daisy or any other servant. Now as an adult, he savored the freedom to throw aside that old rule and speak his mind.

"Miss Duncan," he said evenly, "if champagne spilled on your dress is the worst thing that ever happens to you, you will be quite fortunate indeed. Sara has apologized to you for what happened. Now I think you owe her an apology for being discourteous."

With that, Miss Duncan wordlessly swelled with offense, spun around and marched toward the downstairs powder room, leaving Matt and a trembling Sara in her wake. He took a step toward the young servant, but she did not look up.

"You'll be dismissin' me now, sir?" she managed in a shaky whisper, in envious awe that he could speak so freely to one of Mrs. Tyler's guests, when a servant doing so would quickly result in termination, no questions asked.

"Of course I'm not going to dismiss you, Sara. Would you look at me, please?"

She lifted her head ever so slowly, her face white, her pale lips quivering.

"Everyone has accidents from time to time, don't they?" he asked, smiling gently.

"Yes, sir."

"Don't give it another thought."

"Do you think she'll tell Mrs. Tyler that I ruined her dress?"

Matt shook his head. "After what I said to her, Miss Duncan won't even remember how the accident happened. In her mind, my offense was far greater than yours." He took a step closer and lowered his voice. "And honestly, I thought her dress was much improved by the spilled champagne."

Sara's eyes grew large with disbelief as she clamped a hand over her mouth to smother a giggle. Matt patted her shoulder before returning to the parlor.

Not until well after midnight did the last guests depart, leaving the mansion quiet once again. Adam and Kathleen Tyler slowly climbed the stairs to the second-floor master bedroom after bidding their son goodnight in the library. Matt had decided to stay up a while longer to unwind from the evening. He settled comfortably into the leather armchair at the fireplace, loosened his cravat and top collar button, and touched a flame to the tobacco in the bowl of his pipe. He sat for a while, listening to the silence of the house that was pierced occasionally by the delicate clinking of crystal as the servants gathered the remains of the event to be taken to the kitchen for washing.

"Would you mind some company?" came Caroline's voice from the doorway.

"Please," Matt replied, waving a hand toward the sofa a few feet across from him.

"I would've thought you'd be exhausted and on your way to bed." Still in her gown that rustled softly as she crossed the room, she relaxed onto the sofa.

"I haven't been sleeping well lately," he said, taking a leisurely draw on his pipe.

"Yes, I've noticed you have seemed . . . troubled," she said. "I thought perhaps you were trying to make a decision about whether to leave your practice and come to work at the new hospital. But Daisy disagrees."

Matt looked up, an inquisitive grin on his face. "Oh? What does Daisy say?"

Caroline hesitated before replying. "She says you're troubled over a woman."

He let go a full laugh and shook his head in amazement. "That Daisy . . . she's one of the wisest people I know."

When he looked up again to see anticipation in her eyes, he answered her unspoken query. "I have been thinking of someone."

Caroline waited for him to continue. Before he could say more, Daisy stepped into the doorway of the library.

"Would either of you like some tea before I turn in?" she offered.

"No, thank you, Daisy," Matt answered quickly. "You've worked hard today, go on to bed. If we need anything, I'll get it myself."

"Now don't you go making a mess of my kitchen, young man," she admonished, stifling a smile.

"No, ma'am!" Matt replied solemnly.

As the library door closed with a soft bump, Caroline turned her attention back to Matt. "You were saying?"

After a moment of reflection, he said, "I don't know where to begin."

"At the beginning?"

He suddenly felt relieved to be able to talk about how his life had changed in the last few months. There had always been an honesty and a safe acceptance inherent in his relationship with his sister that he appreciated, never more so than now. He had not allowed himself the luxury of talking openly to anyone about his growing feelings for Degan, and he felt the secret getting heavier by the day. He met her captivated stare and took a deep breath.

"In early January, I came home from town one evening, and found this young Indian woman in my barn. She was badly hurt. She had been captured by white men who raided her home on the Allegany Reservation in New York where she lives with her family and her people."

"A reservation in New York? That's a long way from where you are, isn't it?"

"A few hundred miles. They raided her home in the middle of the night, killed many of her family, captured her and her sister, and were traveling south. Her sister died, and after a few days, she managed to get away. She took one of their horses and just started riding. They had brutalized her pretty badly. One shot her as she was escaping, hit her in the leg. She was riding and needed a place to rest when she saw my property."

A stunned Caroline was taking in the story, her hand over her mouth and her eyes wide as if barely able to imagine the ordeal.

"When I found her, Cara, she was in bad shape. I didn't know if she'd live," Matt said, his voice thick with emotion. "They had beaten her badly. Her leg was bleeding from the gunshot wound. She was cold and hungry. Her clothes were in shreds. I know they . . . violated her."

Caroline cringed, closing her eyes, and held up a hand. "Please, Matty."

"Sorry. Anyway, I took her into my cabin and cleaned her up. I treated her wounds and took care of her. In a few weeks, her wounds healed and she started regaining her strength. She was terrified at first. I tried to be as gentle with her as I could, but she would look at me with big eyes, full of fear. Every time I got near her, she would draw back, as if she expected me to strike her . . . or worse. It took some time for that to go away."

"Does she speak English? How did you talk to her?"

"She speaks English. She told me Quaker missionaries lived among her people when she was a child. They actually built a school and provided some education for the children."

"And she's been . . . living with you since January?"

He nodded. "By the time she started feeling better, she had learned to trust me. Obviously, we've spent a lot of time together. We've talked a great deal, gotten to know each other, and . . ." his voice trailed off.

"And?"

Matt sighed, not sure how to verbalize his feelings. He leaned his head back against the soft leather of the chair, searching for words that could accurately convey the complexities of what had taken place over the last few months.

"I'm at a loss, Cara, it's so powerful. Without her, I feel like I'm walking around with a big hole in my chest."

Mesmerized, Caroline said, "I've never spoken with anyone who actually knows a hostile. I've read stories in the newspapers. Is she wild?

Aren't you afraid to go to sleep at night? What's she like? Does she scream a lot?"

Matt suppressed the urge to take exception to the term 'hostile,' then had to chuckle at the disparity between Caroline's impressions and the woman he'd come to know.

"Her name is Degan. She's sweet and quite intelligent. More than intelligent, she's wise. She's usually reserved, but she has a playful side that often surprises me. I just want to be with her, protect her. It's as though she's . . . part of me now."

"I've never heard you speak so of anyone."

"I've never felt this way about anyone. It's powerful, Cara. I didn't realize how powerful until I left her to come here. I miss seeing her every day. I miss her waiting for me when I come home." Matt pictured Degan plainly in his mind, and a smile came readily to his lips. He found her beauty intoxicating and realized he would have given anything to see her walk into the room and smile at him. "She's lovely. She has black hair, and dark eyes. My God, I could get lost in those eyes."

"Matty, I can't imagine how or why, but . . . you seem to have deep feelings for this woman. The way you're talking, it almost sounds as though you're . . . in love with her."

He met her steady gaze as she waited for a response. Having now heard the words spoken, he knew with certainty that he was, in fact, in love with Degan. He had a strong sense that confessing it aloud would bring a profound fulfillment unlike any he had known before.

"I am," he whispered, experiencing a release deep in his soul that he could not have described. "I do love her."

They sat silently for a time, each taking in the magnitude of their conversation. Hearing his feelings spoken from his own mouth, Matt now wondered how he had not consciously realized before that he was in love with Degan. It suddenly seemed so obvious, so natural, and so enormous that it was difficult to imagine a time when he had not loved her. Then the familiar sadness washed over him.

"Unfortunately, my feelings for her are immaterial. I promised her that when she was recovered, I'd see that she returns to her people. When I get back to Sylvan next week, I will have to fulfill that promise, and take her back to her reservation. After that, I'll probably never see her again."

Caroline's tone was sympathetic, but resolute. "Well, forgive me for saying so, but I think that's for the best. After all, it's one thing to take in an injured woman and nurse her back to health. I do admire you for that. But it's quite another to—well, you must realize it would be a hopeless situation. Your station doesn't permit such associations."

"My station?"

"Yes. I mean," Caroline searched for words, "I'm sure your feelings for her seem very real right now, but she can't possibly be your equal on any level."

"She's my equal on every level. On every level that's important to me."

"But how can she be? You wouldn't seriously entertain the thought of her socializing among white people! A hostile? Wearing animal skins and feathers in her hair?"

"She doesn't look like that," he said defensively. "She wears regular clothing. In fact, once she was well enough to be up and around, I bought her several frocks at a dress shop in Sylvan."

"Even so, no matter what she wears, she would never belong in our circles. Polite society wouldn't be at ease with her, and she certainly wouldn't be at ease with us."

"I'm not sure I'm at ease in 'polite society,'" Matt confessed. "I thought I would die this evening, trying to make conversation when I have absolutely nothing in common with these people, and they care nothing about who I am."

"And this Indian woman does?" she asked skeptically.

"Yes, as a matter of fact, she does. We talk about things that really matter, not whose latest tour of Europe was more luxurious, or whose donation to charity was larger—"

"But can you picture her attending an opera, or a ballet, or a soiree of any kind?"

"We don't have many operas, ballets, or soirees in Sylvan," he said dryly.

"Even in Sylvan, you talked about the church activities, the dances, and socials. I think it's admirable of you to consider trying to make a civilized human being out of her, but would the townspeople accept such a . . . woman . . . as your companion? Think about what you're saying!"

Matt had no answers, and could think of nothing to say to counter his sister's claims that he reluctantly realized were valid. He had to admit that he couldn't predict how white society would receive Degan. Though Caroline's arguments were based in reality, they did nothing to diminish his feelings for Degan. If anything, those feelings were now intensified.

"I'm sorry, Matty," Caroline said, "but once she's back with her people where she belongs, and you're able to look at it from a less emotional viewpoint, you'll see that it's for the best." Both were quiet for a long moment before Caroline spoke again. "Sometimes resigning yourself to doing what's best is painful, but it's the only thing to do."

He recognized that his sister's train of thought was taking another direction and he was relieved to change the subject. "Mother said you were nursing a broken heart. Is that true?"

Caroline shrugged. "I suppose you could say that. When I was in Paris, there was a gentleman, Michael, who was courting me for a few months, but . . . it didn't work out."

Matt silently debated how far to probe. "What happened? Did your courtship end badly?"

She drew a long breath before answering. "I was hoping for a proposal of marriage. I had very deep feelings for him, and I thought he felt the same about me. I kept waiting for him to propose, or at least express how he felt about me. But he never did."

"I'm sorry."

She leaned forward, her tone suddenly impatient and frustrated. "Why do men find it so difficult to express their feelings for the woman they're courting? Don't they understand that a woman needs to hear certain things? Are they afraid? Or just heartless?"

Her questions swirled through his mind, and he found himself at a loss to defend his gender. "Maybe he was afraid you didn't feel the same. Or maybe he assumed that you already knew how he felt."

She seemed dissatisfied with his explanations. "Or maybe he simply didn't have the same feelings for me that I had for him," she said dismally. "At any rate, he was quite upset with me when I said I was returning home, but my mind was made up."

"It must have been difficult for you."

"It was hard to leave him. Mother's friend from church, Mrs. O'Neil, was my chaperone in Paris. She said he'd come back to me once he realized

I was serious about returning home. But he didn't. If he had expressed any measure of affection for me, I would have stayed."

"I'm sorry, Cara," Matt said softly. He could think of nothing to say that would ease his sister's pain.

"Mr. Lawson asked me if he could call on me again soon. I'm sure he and Father spoke this evening."

Matt would have expected happy excitement in her voice and on her face, but it never came. "Are you agreeable to this?"

Caroline shrugged. "I know I should be, but . . ."

"But?"

Her face suddenly blossomed with enthusiasm. "I've been thinking about something for a while—a project that I want to get involved with."

"What kind of project?"

"I want to work at the dispensary that's run by the church down on Alexander Street. I was discussing it with Mrs. O'Neil during our travels abroad. She told me the church wants to expand its operation. They own the property adjacent to the dispensary. A vacant building that would serve the purpose quite nicely."

"Alexander Street used to be a very poor and run-down section of the city."

"It still is. That's exactly the point. The poor come to the dispensary to receive medical care that they couldn't afford otherwise."

"Have you discussed this with Father?"

"No, he's been much too busy with getting the new hospital ready to open. I haven't wanted to bother him. And Mother will find out soon enough, as she and Mrs. O'Neil are good friends. Though Mother has stated many times that Mrs. O'Neil does have the occasional radical thought."

"You'll face stiff resistance from Mother," Matt said, knowing this observation to be completely unnecessary. Caroline knew as well as he that Kathleen's objections would be vocal and unrelenting.

Passion draining from her features, she gazed at her hands in her lap. "I know Mother would prefer to see me get married and start producing children as soon as possible. I know that's what I should want as well."

"Cara," Matt said, "you should do what you feel strongly about. If working at this dispensary is something you believe in, then do it."

She looked up and her excitement had returned. "Mrs. O'Neil said I could work at the dispensary and, if I want, be extensively involved in the expansion also. I see you and Father making a difference in people's lives with your skills as physicians. I want to do something similar."

"Then you will."

Caroline sat up straighter, squared her shoulders, and smiled at her brother. "I appreciate your encouragement, Matty."

"Just . . . be careful," Matt said.

She frowned. "What do you mean?"

A familiar protectiveness toward his younger sister rose in him and Matt found it difficult to choose only one potential danger to warn her about. He could picture her working long hours at the dispensary, too tired to bother with asking someone to escort her home.

"The area in which you'll be working is a dangerous one. Alexander Street is not a section of town for the uninitiated. Make sure you always have an escort."

"Matty, you're sweet to worry about me," she replied with a smile.

"Just promise me you'll be careful."

"Of course I'll be careful," she said, then put a hand to her mouth to stifle a yawn. "I think I'm going to turn in. It's been a busy night."

"Cara, I would prefer that we keep our earlier conversation here tonight just between us. I'm sure you understand . . ."

"Yes, I understand. And I'd appreciate the same." She got up and bent to give her brother a light kiss on the cheek. "Are you staying up?"

"I'm not sure I could sleep. But you sleep well. I'll see you in the morning."

"It is morning," she said with a drowsy grin.

"Then I'll see you at breakfast," he said as she left the room.

Alone now, Matt listened to the absolute silence of the house, and reflected on their conversation. He was proud of Caroline and her desire to help the poor in the church's dispensary. And he couldn't help wondering if there was a point to be taken from her experience in Paris with Michael. Her statement, "if he had expressed any measure of affection for me, I would have stayed," echoed in his mind. He thought of his own situation with Degan. He could never go back on his promise to help her return to her people when she chose. But he also knew that unless he confessed his feelings to her, he would never know if her choice might have been different.

He was filled with apprehension at the thought of telling Degan how he felt about her. Though he had never met his sister's Parisian suitor, he empathized with Michael's struggle in his courtship of Caroline. *A brotherhood of fear,* he thought wryly. Nevertheless, he was determined to learn from his sister's observations about the sentiments women need to hear from the men who love them. He resolved to be forthcoming with Degan upon his return, no matter how uneasy the prospect made him.

CHAPTER

11

The days leading up to the grand opening of Hamilton General Hospital were hectic ones for Adam Tyler. As the new chief of staff, Dr. Tyler was expected to attend a number of dinner parties, luncheons, and last-minute meetings, while continuing to conduct regular staff conferences to resolve unending conflicts large and small.

"I must tell you, son," Dr. Tyler said late one evening as he and Matt were sipping brandy in the library. "I will be very glad when the Grand Opening is over, and we can settle into the daily routine of running the hospital."

"You do seem tired, Father," Matt said. "Perhaps Mother is right, you've been working too hard." He had grown more concerned about his father's health in recent days, noticing not just his fatigue, but that he appeared, at times, to be experiencing pain. When asked, his father had dismissed the notion that he was ailing, and changed the subject.

The day of the Grand Opening finally arrived, and the event was a great success. The public had been invited to tour sections of the new facility, including one of three surgical theaters, the sizeable kitchen, and the back terrace complete with manicured gardens, and a pond with a waterfall. Many of the city's dignitaries attended, expressing to the crowd their pride in the innovations that would now serve the local citizens in ways that could not have been imagined just a few years before.

All staff physicians were on hand, along with the hospital's chief cook, laundress, and the women who would comprise the nursing staff. The building fund's major donors attended, shaking hands, slapping backs, and congratulating one another on their accomplishment. Aside from their own contributions, what impressed them most was finding their names immortalized on a bronze plaque displayed in the hospital foyer, which promised to provide them adulation and respect for generations to come.

The festivities now behind them, Matt wasted no time in finalizing his plans to return to Sylvan. The day prior to his departure, his mood almost giddy, Daisy observed that he reminded her of an excited child on Christmas Eve. He had decided to relax from the busy week by visiting some of the shops in the city to purchase a few items before his return home. In particular, he wanted to stop at the local confectionery to pick up chocolates for Degan. He was well aware of her sweet tooth, and he suspected she had never tasted chocolate. He invited Caroline to join him on his shopping excursion.

Following a breakfast of Daisy's waffles, brother and sister made their way to the merchant district. They stopped at several stores along the way, Matt heeding Caroline's suggestion that they purchase the chocolates last so the candies could be taken directly back to the house and kept in the icebox.

It was late morning when the two returned to Tyler Mansion juggling armloads of multi-colored boxes of all shapes and sizes. When William opened the front door, Matt peered around his stack of boxes.

"William, would you please help Caroline with her packages?"

"Yes, of course. Miss Caroline, let me take those for you," William offered, reaching toward her.

"Thank you, William," she said, stepping into the foyer.

"I'll take these straight to my room. I have to finish packing," Matt said, then saw his mother coming from the parlor.

"Matthew," Kathleen said, "when you go upstairs, please tell your father it's time to get up. I convinced him to sleep late this morning because I knew he was exhausted. But we have a luncheon to attend this afternoon, and you know I cannot tolerate being late."

Matt quickly deposited the packages in his room, then made his way down the hallway to his parents' bedroom and knocked on the door. When there was no answer, he knocked again.

"Father?" he called.

He slowly opened the bedroom door and saw his father, still in his nightshirt, sprawled motionless on the rug between the bed and the armoire.

"Father?" He rushed to kneel at his side, and pressed two fingers under his jaw to feel for a pulse. Adam Tyler's skin had a grayish cast and was cool to the touch. Matt knew that he had been dead for at least an hour.

At that moment, an enormous weight descended onto Matt's shoulders, and he sat unmoving beside his father. His blurred mind had already begun to shut down, refusing to take in what was obviously before him. Impulsively, he put an ear to his father's chest, but heard nothing.

"Matthew?" Kathleen's voice rang from the staircase. "Matthew, did you awaken your father?"

Matt wanted to get up to intercept her at the door, but he could not move. Then she was standing in the doorway of the bedroom, her mouth open, as reality began its cruel possession of her.

"He's gone," Matt heard himself saying in a voice that sounded small and distant.

"No, no, no," Kathleen murmured, rushing toward him, falling to her knees, and collapsing over her husband's body.

The next moments, the next hours, the next days, were an indistinguishable haze in Matt's mind, and would remain so for a long time. He had somehow broken the news of his father's death to everyone, beginning with Caroline, Daisy, and the rest of the household staff. He found himself, by default, in charge of making all the final arrangements, as his mother and sister had withdrawn to their bedrooms to grieve.

He postponed his return to Sylvan following a conversation with his mother that had escalated into an argument. She begged him to stay in Washington indefinitely, now that Adam was gone. Her reasoning was that the family needed him now and surely Dr. Bowman could handle the practice in Sylvan by himself. The one clear memory he did have was his mother asking, with rising indignation, "What else could you possibly have to go back to?" He had fallen to silence at that and had left the room, knowing from years of experience that an explanation would be pointless. His mother would never understand his strong desire to return to Sylvan, to the one who awaited him there. She could never put her own needs aside for his, particularly if it involved something she would vehemently disapprove of, such as her son having developed feelings for an Indian woman he had taken in. Only imagining his mother's reaction to this news made him cringe.

He knew he had to get word to Degan that because of his father's death, he had been forced to extend his trip. His first thought was of Jon, and though he had promised her that he would not tell his friend about her, there was no one else he could trust. The struggle over whether to keep his word only added to his anguish.

Finally, on the morning of his father's funeral, he hastily penned a letter to Jon, and delivered it personally to the local post office a few blocks from his parents' home.

CHAPTER

12

The first days of Matt's absence did not require a significant adjustment for Degan. She had grown accustomed to spending her days by herself while he worked in the town. But when night came, she missed him deeply. A warm fire in the hearth banished the chill of the early spring evenings, and as she sat alone watching the flames, her thoughts unfailingly turned to Matt. She missed the sound of his voice, and the way he looked at her when she said something that amused him. If she closed her eyes, she could imagine him there with her, his long legs stretched out toward the fire, sweet-smelling pipe smoke floating around his chair, his presence satisfying her hunger for safety and protection.

She had come to anticipate his sharing of his day, entertaining her with animated stories of his patients, his friends, and news of the town. She had come to realize through these stories, that the whites were much like her people in their relations with one another, their struggles, their hopes for their children, and their resilience. He illustrated for her an aspect to the whites that she had not known existed, and she began to see that the whites were mostly honorable people, with whom her own people had much in common. But these exchanges also were bittersweet, as they deepened her sense of isolation. Among her people, she had been part of a larger society, an active participant in the workings of daily life.

Chores around the cabin kept her busy. Beyond the back porch, and quick trips to the barn to tend to her horse, she grew more comfortable being outside. Though Matt's property was less than a mile from the town, it was secluded, surrounded by mature trees. She felt safe outside, but still kept a watchful eye on the open fields that lay between the cabin and Sylvan, as an approaching rider on a horse would not make much noise. The rifle was always loaded and within her reach. Knowing she could defend herself if necessary gave her a small measure of confidence, but she remained alert and vigilant.

Spring brought warm days, cool nights, and an abundance of rain. One afternoon, Degan sat on the front porch of the cabin, listening to the sounds of the awakening woods around her. This was the time when the women of her village would be planting the crops. For as long as she could remember, Degan had helped her grandmother, her mother, and her sisters, along with the other women in the village, plant the corn. A few weeks later, they would plant beans in the same location so that as the corn stalks grew, the beans would climb the stalks. To keep the soil moist, they would then plant squash or pumpkins, the broad leaves shading the ground.

She smiled, remembering all the women of the village working together to plant, nurture, and harvest the Three Sisters, as the crops were called. Several times a year, the entire village would celebrate to mark the growing seasons and, finally, the harvest. Though the whites had relegated her people to the small reservation, they had preserved as much of the old ways as possible.

Degan tried to let her memories cheer her, but it was still too soon. For now, they brought only sorrow, and intense homesickness. Hot tears stung her eyes, and a heaviness swelled in her chest. She had not yet permitted herself to mourn the loss of family members, fearful that if she gave in to her need to cry, she would never be able to stop. Though it frightened her, she knew that today, she could no longer push the grieving aside for another time.

A powerful wave overtook her. Sitting there on the porch, she doubled over, covered her face with her hands, and cried with a force she could not control. For a long time, she was unaware of her surroundings, and watching for approaching intruders was forgotten. She only knew a profound loneliness, a sense that she had been thrust into a strange new life in which she had to find her way.

To her surprise, she realized that what she wanted more than anything was to feel Matt's strong arms around her, comforting her, holding her until the grief passed. He had promised to take her back to her people upon his return. While the prospect of going back to her former life should have filled her with happy anticipation, she could not deny a sadness at the thought of leaving the white man who had been so kind to her, and who was now such an integral part of her life.

She sat up and wiped her wet face with her sleeve. Exhausted from crying, she took several deep breaths and looked around. Everything remained as before. The birds still sang from nearby branches, the sun still slanted across the porch, warming the floorboards at her feet. The breeze rustled through new leaves on the trees.

She rose from the porch and decided, without a conscious purpose in mind, to walk around the sides of the cabin. The land around her was relatively flat, one side thick with grass, the other side less so. She thought the grassy side would be an excellent area to allow her horse to graze, so she went to the barn, and led him from his stall. As the animal munched contentedly on these new tufts of greenery, she walked to the other side of the cabin to look again at the sparsely covered ground there. The afternoon sun shone brightly on this side and, looking more closely at the ground, she realized this area must have once been a garden, possibly tended by a previous occupant of the cabin. Matt had told her that the cabin was vacant when he came to town. Perhaps a family had lived here before, and had made a vegetable garden.

Her mind filling with possibilities, she walked the perimeter of the now-obvious plot of ground. She figured the area to be about twenty paces on each side, a good space in which many rows of corn could be planted. The soil would need much work before it would be ready to receive and nurture seeds. She would have to remove the sparse clumps of grass, and the many weeds that were aggressively reaching for the sky. Her spirits brightening, she decided to go to the barn to see if she could find tools that could be used to work the soil.

She discovered a collection of tools, possibly left by a previous owner, or, more likely, given to Matt as payment for his medical services. Many people could not afford to give him money for his help, but instead gave him produce from their farms, or extra items that they might have. She found a hoe, a rake, and a few hand tools that would be useful in preparing the ground. By the time that task was completed, Matt would be back, and she would ask him to bring her seeds from the town that she would plant before she returned to her people.

Back at the cabin, hoe in hand, she stood at the edge of the parcel of earth, and surveyed what she now hoped would, in a few weeks, be a thriving vegetable garden. For the first time in a while, she knew a feeling of hope and expectation.

This garden, she thought, would serve as a bridge of sorts between her people and the white world. By preparing the soil, planting, and nurturing the crops, she would be honoring her family and her ancestors, and their ancient way of living that had sustained her people for centuries. It would also be an important contribution to Matt's life, a way of showing her gratitude. By harvest time at the end of summer, she would be back with her people, so she resolved to leave the harvest to Matt's care.

She closed her eyes and silently asked the Creator to watch over this plot of ground, and bless it with an abundant yield. Once the crops were planted, she would burn tobacco as an offering of thanksgiving and hope for a good harvest.

Her prayer complete, she opened her eyes, and began her work.

Typical rainy spring weather was the only cause for a break in the hard work of tilling the soil in Degan's garden. Reluctantly designating one skirt and one blouse to serve as her work clothes, she soon noticed they were showing signs of her labor. She hated to see any of the beautiful clothes get so dirty and worn, but it was a necessary sacrifice.

Each morning, she rose early to work for several hours before the sun grew too warm, then resumed her gardening in the late afternoon until the last rays of sunlight slipped behind the foothills. The greatest benefit of working the ground was that it rendered her bone-tired by the end of the day, and she could fall asleep early, not feeling Matt's absence quite so keenly during the evening hours. Since his departure, she had been sleeping in his bed, which she found immensely comforting.

After supper one evening, she warmed a kettle of water on the stove, then carried it into the bedroom, and filled the porcelain bowl on the washstand. Placing a thick towel under her feet, she removed her blouse, her skirt, and her undergarments. She turned the flame of the lamp higher, and studied her reflection in the mirror. Few traces of her injuries remained, and she marveled again at the shaman's skill and attentiveness in caring for her. She was thankful that the Creator had led her here that night so many weeks ago.

She took a leisurely bath, then slipped her arms through the fresh cotton of Matt's shirt and climbed into his bed. A deep sigh relaxed her as she closed her eyes, and imagined that Matt was just in the next room, and would soon join her, a gentle smile on his handsome face. Her thoughts drifted back to the night before he left, when he asked her to share his bed. He had kept the sheet discreetly over his naked body, and she remembered stroking his bare chest. Now, her heartbeat quickened at the thought of lying next to him. The cool sheets and pillowcase still held his scent, and his essence warmly embraced her. Her last thought was how vastly her life had changed because of him. Then she drifted into heavy sleep.

"Bring her over here!" a gruff voice bellowed. The rope around her neck grew tighter as they dragged her toward two wagons. She clawed at the rope to pull it from her neck so she could breathe, but had little strength left in her arms. Slipping in and out of awareness, she felt her upper body being lifted and she was on her knees. She heard the sound of ripping cloth and realized her blouse had been torn off, her arms tied at the wrists, she was stretched between the two wagons.

"This is what happens to runaways," another voice screamed in her ear, and she felt her hair pulled to the front of her body to fall over her naked breasts.

Then she heard a loud crack and felt the burning white pain of the first lash as it fell across her back. She crumpled under the force. Her lungs collapsed, and a violent power sucked all the air from her body. Before she could take another breath, the whip cracked again, and the searing pain blinded her. Unable to breathe, she felt a rough hand grab a fistful of hair and pull her head up.

"This is what happens to runaways," he spat, grinning maliciously.

She sprang upright in bed with a loud gasp. The darkness of the bedroom magnified the horror of her nightmare and she gulped for air, shivering in a cold sweat. Pulling the sheet up to her shoulders, she realized where she was. Her surroundings were quiet and she was alone in Matt's bed. She buried her face in her trembling hands and forced herself into the present, fervently wishing for the morning light.

"Matt," she whispered, "please come back. Please . . . come back."

As her breathing slowed to normal, she could once again hear crickets outside the open window. Matt's dressing gown lay at the foot of the bed. Reaching for it, she quickly brought it to her face to feel its softness against her cheek. The image of Matt calmed her. The rifle stood at the ready against the nightstand by the bed. She sat for a while, listening to the night sounds before reclining again, still clutching his dressing gown.

The next morning, she rose early to a cloudy day that threatened rain from the time of sunrise. She went to the garden as usual, but worked for only two hours before rain chased her back under the roof.

At mid-day, she was relaxing in one of the rocking chairs on the back porch, looking out on the grove of trees, wondering how Matt was spending his days with his family. She remembered her shooting lesson before he left, and how she had teased him about being a poor shot. A smile came unconsciously to her lips as she pictured him laughing at himself.

With a start, she stopped rocking and turned her head to listen. Thinking she had heard a knock on the front door, she instinctively reached for the loaded rifle. Sitting up stiff and tense, she waited, the rifle poised in her lap.

"Hello?" a male voice came from the side of the cabin, and she heard footsteps approaching through the wet grass. She jumped to standing, pressed the rifle's buttplate to her shoulder, and nearly fainted when she saw a white man round the corner of the porch.

She immediately took aim. The man stopped in his tracks and took a step back, holding up a hand. "Whoa there, ma'am, be careful with that thing!"

She held him in the sight of the weapon, noticing he had only one arm and a look of genuine panic on his face. He stood frozen, as if afraid to move. Eventually, he found his voice.

"Are you Degan?" When her stance did not change, he went on. "I'm Jon. Matt sent me out here to talk to you. I got a message for you . . . from him."

Without twitching a muscle, she held the rifle steady, but her mind raced. He had promised not to tell anyone in the town about her, yet here stood his friend, professing to have come at Matt's request.

Jon quickly pulled from his shirt pocket a folded piece of paper, rushing to explain. "Matt sent me this letter here." He unfolded the paper and held it out to her, as if she could read it from where she stood. "He'll be stayin' in Washington a while longer . . . because . . . his father just died. He asked me to come out here and tell you."

Degan tried to grasp all the implications of this sad news. Matt would not be coming home anytime soon because his father had died, and she knew the death had been unexpected. She suddenly felt unsteady on her feet, but kept the gun pointed at Jon's chest.

Long moments passed before Jon finally spoke again. "Ma'am, I got no weapon of any kind. I got no intention of hurtin' you or causin' any trouble."

She studied him. Matt's words from weeks ago came back to her. Jon was his friend and could be trusted, he had said. He's a good man and would never harm her.

Jon was watching her anxiously. Slowly, she lowered the rifle to rest against her waist. Visibly relieved, he finally exhaled.

"Mind if I sit?" he asked tentatively, pointing to the porch steps.

She watched him cautiously round the corner of the porch, turning to keep her eyes locked with his in unwavering vigilance, as two wary animals circling each other, distrustful and guarded.

"When?" her voice thick, she swallowed hard.

Jon hesitated. "Ma'am?"

"When did his father die?"

"Last week. He didn't say much more in the letter, just that he would be stayin' in Washington longer than he planned. He wanted me to let you know what was goin' on." Jon scrutinized her. "You live here with Matt?"

She nodded, carefully settling into the rocker. Placing the rifle across her lap, she kept her hand on the barrel and her finger on the trigger, knowing she could aim and shoot within seconds if she needed to.

"Since when?"

"Many months."

"*Months?*" He shook his head in disbelief and started to laugh. "Well I'll be damned! That damn Matt, he sure can keep a secret! How'd you come to live here?"

"I was badly hurt by white men. I found my way here. Matt saved my life."

"Well now, there's somethin' you and I have in common." He pointed to his armless left side. "See this? Matt took my arm. During the war. Fredericksburg. Gangrene ate my hand, and woulda killed me if Matt hadn't cut the rest of my arm off." Noticing her frown, he said, "You know what gangrene is?"

She shook her head.

"It's where . . ." his voice trailed off. "Well, I don't know how to explain it. But it eats your body unless you cut off the part where it left off. That's why Matt cut off as much'a my arm as he did."

She grimaced at the thought of having an arm cut off.

"You from one of the reservations up north?"

"Yes."

"What tribe?"

"Seneca."

He shook his head and chuckled again. "So you been here all this time with Matt? I'll be damned! I mighta guessed Matt would have himself a servant before it's all said and done." Before she could respond to his assessment, he asked, "Does anybody else know about you?"

"No. Please, tell no one about me."

Jon shrugged. "It's plain Matt doesn't want anybody to know you're here. I won't say anything." There was a resolute quality to his tone and Degan hoped fervently that she could trust him to keep his word. "I figure I wouldn't know about you myself if Matt's father hadn't-a died, and he has to stay away longer."

She would not have thought it possible, but suddenly she missed Matt even more. The knowledge that he would not be returning for a while was difficult to take in, but knowing that he was now struggling with grief over the death of his father broke her heart. And in the midst of his pain, he had sent word to her of his change in plans. It had been important to him that she understand why he wasn't coming home when he said he would.

She looked down and saw that Jon was watching her, and she felt the tears that had pooled in her eyes spilling down her cheeks. She quickly wiped her face with the sleeve of her blouse.

"He is feeling great pain," she said, remembering all too vividly the sorrow and profound sense of loss she felt when members of her own family died.

"Yeah." Jon looked out over the thick stand of trees before them. "The whole family is, I figure."

They sat silently for a time, as distant thunder gradually grew louder, and clouds swollen with rain darkened the mid-day sky. The showers started again, and water was soon dripping off the porch roof just beyond the bottom step.

"I'll be gettin' back to town," Jon said, rising to his feet.

Degan looked up. "Do you want to eat something?"

He hesitated, surprised and wary of her offer of hospitality, given that moments ago, she'd been pointing a rifle at his chest. "No. Thank you kindly. I don't want to trouble you none."

"You are Matt's friend. A good man, he told me. He would want me to offer food to you."

"He told you about me?"

Degan nodded. After a moment's consideration, he said, "Well, all right then. But don't go to any trouble."

Still clutching the gun, Degan rose and turned toward the back door.

"Ma'am?" Jon began tentatively. She turned to face him. "If you don't mind puttin' that gun down? I'd sure be able to relax a bit more. I ain't plannin' on causin' you any trouble."

"I will put it down inside."

"Yes, ma'am."

Jon followed a respectable distance behind her as they made their way to the great room. A pot of soup sat atop the warm cook stove, along with a loaf of bread. Retrieving two bowls from the cupboard, she ladled soup into both, then carefully set one before Jon who had seated himself at the table. Then she sat down a safe distance from him and watched closely as he took his first spoonful. She found herself a little surprised that he functioned so well with just one arm. His build was not as muscular as Matt's, and he was not quite as tall. His sandy hair was short, and his blue eyes held an innocent kindness. They ate in silence at first, each considering the other with caution, each inwardly acknowledging that their common thread was Matt, a man both had come to respect and care for.

Jon asked Degan in more detail about how she had come to live with Matt. She recounted her experiences many months earlier at the hands of the men who had captured her.

"How'd you get away?"

"One of the men came to me at night. He . . ." she stopped, searching for words.

Jon held up his hand, sorry that he asked. "You don't have to tell me."

"The man slept from the strong drink. I saw a knife on his . . ." she made a motion across her waist.

"His belt?"

"Yes, his belt. I took it and cut the ropes that held me and took a horse. The Creator led me here to be healed by Matt. I was very afraid at first, but Matt never hurt me. He said he would not hurt me, and he didn't. I trust him. He is a good white man."

"Yeah, he's a good man all right." Jon took another thick slice of bread and reached for the honey. "I've known him since the war and he's been a good friend to me. 'Course I was plenty mad at him for takin' my arm after the fightin' in Fredericksburg, but I knew he had to. They ran out of chloroform and ether, so he made me drink a whole fifth of whiskey before he got started. It still took four men to hold me down. You sober up pretty quick when somebody starts sawing your arm off."

Degan cringed at his description. Her own ordeal had been horrific, and she could scarcely imagine what Jon must have endured as a soldier in the war.

"Matt's a good doctor," Jon said. "He knows what to do for people when they need help."

"He tells me about his people in the town. He loves the work, helping the people."

"Which is pretty damn amazing considerin' he wouldn't even have to work if he didn't want to," Jon said, taking a bite of the honey-soaked bread. "Matt's family's got money. I mean, look around you," his eyes swept quickly over the furnishings. "Nobody else in Sylvan has a fine-lookin' home like this. Matt brought all these things when he came here. His granddaddy made the family fortune in the railroads back some years ago. That's how he can work and not worry 'bout the fact nobody can pay him much. I asked him once how he could afford all them fine cigars he smokes, and that good brandy he drinks. He told me about how his family came into their money. The Baltimore and Ohio Railroad, that's how."

Degan did not detect any jealousy or resentment in his tone. She watched as he popped the final bite of bread into his mouth and savored its sweetness. He pushed himself away from the table and, dragging the back of his hand across his mouth, thanked her for the meal.

"You need anything from town?" he asked.

She thought for a moment. "Matt brought ice for the box, but now it's gone."

"I can bring you a piece of ice," Jon said affably. "Anything else?"

Baffled by his generosity, she frowned. "Why do you help me?"

He seemed surprised by her question and shrugged casually. "Well, I figure you ain't goin' into town anytime soon. You got anybody else lined up to bring you supplies?"

"No. No one knows about me, only Matt. And you."

"How else you gonna get supplies with Matt away in Washington till who-knows-when?"

Suddenly, that day in the woods came rushing back to her, when Matt was insistent about enlisting Jon's help in taking care of her while he was away, and she had begged him not to say anything. Now she was sitting at the table with Jon, having just shared a meal, making her requests for supplies from the town, as Matt had intended all along. And there was something about Jon's demeanor, something in his face that told her he could be trusted not to give her away.

"Does the town have corn and beans to plant?"

Jon looked at her askance. "Corn and beans? Green beans?"

"Yes. I will make a garden. I will plant soon."

"All right. I'll bring the ice out tomorrow, and corn and beans."

As he got up to leave, he glanced out the front window to assess the fickle spring weather. "Looks like the rain stopped and the sun's tryin' to come out again." Then something caught his eye. He drew closer to the window for a better look.

"Degan," he said, and when she looked up, he motioned for her to come to the window.

She peered out and saw a wagon approaching in the distance. As it got closer, she could see a lone woman driving. It was obvious she was headed toward the cabin.

"Did Matt ever tell you about Emma Miller?" Jon asked with an edge in his voice.

"Yes." She watched as the wagon drew nearer. Tendrils of Emma's blond hair peeked out from under the emerald-green bonnet she wore, which perfectly matched her stylish dress and leather riding gloves. "This is Emma?"

"Yep, that's Emma."

"She is very beautiful."

"Only on the outside, trust me," he murmured, a look of disgust on his face. "There's no reason for her to be out here. The whole town knows Matt's away."

"What does she want?"

"Prob'ly to snoop around and stir up trouble," he snarled. "I'll get rid of her."

With that, he opened the front door just as the wagon pulled to a stop at the front steps. Degan stepped to the side of the window and pressed herself against the wall so that she could not be seen from the outside. The two voices exchanged tense pleasantries.

"Hello, Jon. What are you doing here?" Emma asked.

"Matt asked me to check on his place while he's away. Somethin' I can do for you?"

Emma seemed to stammer a bit with her answer. "I just . . . thought I'd drive out to see if anything needed tending to while Matt's gone." After a brief silence, Degan heard her speak again. "I wanted to leave this for him. I purchased it from a man who came through town selling books. I thought he would enjoy it."

Degan heard Jon cross the porch to accept the gift. "I'll see he gets it."

"And make sure he knows it's from me."

"I will." A loud burst of thunder cracked overhead. "You better be gettin' on back to town before the rain starts up again."

She hesitated, then said, "Yes, well, thank you, Jon."

Jon was silent, and Degan could hear the wagon wheels creaking an about-face as the horse turned the vehicle slowly back toward town. Degan took a small step to the window, just enough to peek out and see Emma driving away. Jon waited on the porch until their visitor was out of sight before coming back into the cabin carrying the small book. His eyes met Degan's as he waved the book in the air.

"She wanted to give this to Matt," he said, flipping absently through the pages. When Degan approached, she saw writing on the inside cover.

"Something is here," she said, pulling the front cover back. The message was penned in a delicate hand.

"To my dear Matt," Jon read aloud, *"I saw this book and thought fondly of you. Please come to call on me when you return. I miss you. All my affection, Emma."*

Jon snapped the book shut and, rolling his eyes, tossed it unceremoniously onto Matt's desk.

"She cares for him," Degan said quietly.

Jon shook his head. "The only person Emma Miller cares about is herself," he said with venom in his tone. "Matt knows that. He's not one to make the same mistake twice."

Degan was silent but Jon continued, delivering a stern warning. "Listen, if you see her comin' this way again, you hide or run into the woods or somethin'. I won't tell anybody about you bein' here, but she will. She's a troublesome little bitch—beggin' your pardon—and she's not to be trusted. The less she knows, the better. Understand?"

Degan nodded.

"I can't believe nobody's been around here to find out about you up to now," he said. "Anyway, I'll be back out tomorrow with your supplies." He thanked her again for the meal, and left.

As she stood at the window watching Jon ride away, she was thankful that Matt had sent him. She realized that if not for Jon, she would very likely have faced Emma Miller alone. She might not have seen her coming until it was too late, and then her presence would be known. Jon would also provide vital supplies for her garden. With Matt's stay in Washington now extended, the planting time might be over before he came home. The memory of her argument with Matt over not telling Jon about her now stung her conscience. She resolved to make amends with him when he returned.

The next day, Jon brought Degan a sizeable chunk of ice for the icebox, as well as butter, milk, fresh eggs, and corn and beans for her garden. Degan thanked him for his kindness. He asked her about her garden, and she offered to show him the plot of ground on which she had been working for many days.

"I will plant the corn first, then the beans. The beans will climb the corn stalks."

Jon was impressed with this ingenious method of planting which he had never heard of before. "Most folks plant the corn, then plant the beans someplace else, and put poles in the ground for the beans to climb. Your way makes more sense."

"My people always plant the two together. Then the squash is planted to cover the ground. When harvest time comes, Matt will have plenty of crops. Enough to give you," she said, watching an uneasy smile spread slowly across Jon's features.

"I'd appreciate that," he said, embarrassed by her kindness.

"You have a wife and children?"

"No, ma'am. I live with my folks. They got a farm on the other side of town. I help them out. Plus I work at the saw mill in town. Some men're afraid of losin' a hand or an arm workin' at the saw mill. I figure I'm already ahead of 'em on that account!" Jon said dryly, but his attempt at humor was lost on Degan.

"Like Matt, no wife."

Jon shuffled his feet uncomfortably and studied the ground. "Well, I don't suppose any lady would want to be courted by a man with only one arm. I ain't exactly what you'd call a whole man."

Degan's heart went out to him. "This does not matter. You are a good man."

A flush of color crept over Jon's face, and he took a step back, seeming reluctant to look up. "I should be gettin' back to town. I . . . I'll come out to check on you in a few days." With that, he began to make his way back to his wagon that he had left at the front of the cabin. Degan followed him.

"Maybe by the time Matt gets back, you'll have yourself a nice big garden to show him," Jon said brightly, climbing into the driver's seat of the wagon and taking the horse's reins.

She suddenly looked despondent. "I hope he comes back long before the crops are tall."

CHAPTER

13

"Your ticket, sir?" A uniformed porter held out his hand as he had to each preceding passenger on the train. Matt retrieved his ticket from his breast pocket and handed it to the gentleman who smiled politely.

"Pennsylvania. A beautiful state. Business or pleasure, sir?"

"Home," he said with a weary smile.

The porter touched the brim of his hat and bowed slightly. "We'll get you there as fast as we can."

The first Saturday of June dawned showery and warm. The woods surrounding the cabin were now lush with late-spring foliage and the increasing humidity of each day enriched the pleasantly mossy scent of the air.

As was her habit, Degan awakened early. When she heard the rain, she decided to lounge in bed a while longer instead of getting up to start her day's work. She felt decidedly lazy rising at mid-morning. The weather of late had been perfect for nurturing wild mushrooms on the forest floor, so in the afternoon, she set out, tucking into the waistband of her skirt a soft kitchen towel in which to carry any mushrooms she found. If the weather remained rainy all day, she thought, she would not be able to work in her garden at all. As early as tomorrow, she would see evidence of healthy weeds threatening to overtake her young crop of corn that had already grown several inches high. She remembered telling Jon many days ago that she hoped Matt would come home before the crops grew tall. Now that the corn was reaching higher for the sky each day, she longed for him to come home before the harvest.

She was grateful to Jon for all he had done, bringing supplies and visiting briefly every few days to ensure that she remained safe and didn't need anything. But she missed Matt more than she could have imagined. She missed his gentle smile, the sound of his voice, his strong, quiet presence.

She recalled her life with her husband years before he had been taken from her, when they were still so young. As all others in her people, their union had been arranged by the mothers, and she had barely spoken to her intended before going to live with him as his wife. But she had learned to care for him, and he had treated her well. Together they had come to share an intimacy and she had been content.

But now, her feelings for Matt were very different in their strength and depth. The idea of a woman sharing herself intimately with a man of her own choosing was unfamiliar to her. From somewhere in the back of her mind, she felt a nudging of self-reproach, as if she were doing something wrong. She wondered briefly what her mother and grandmother would have said if they were still alive and knew her feelings for this white man. But any sense of unease was far outweighed by her passionate longing for Matt. With apprehension, she wondered if he might have similar feelings for her.

When she saw Emma Miller some weeks ago, she suddenly knew an unpleasant sense of envy, and felt ashamed of herself. This woman of Matt's was very beautiful in her face and in her dress. Though such feelings of jealousy were frowned upon as unacceptable in her people, she could not silence her mind's comparison between herself and Emma, and it made her uncomfortable.

Since she was now recovered, she could go back to her people as soon as Matt returned. In fact, that had been their agreement. But with each passing day, her thoughts focused less on going home, and more on how much she missed the man who had saved her life, and made sure she was cared for, even while he was away.

So many times, she had recalled the night before he left, and how he had asked her to stay with him for the remainder of the night. When he held her in his arms, she had felt content and protected. And she remembered his tender kiss the next morning, the strong feelings he had stirred within her, how she would have given anything for him not to leave. The fierce physical yearning that he had awakened was undeniable and quite unexpected. She felt her cheeks grow warm as she imagined touching his bare chest again, stroking his strong arms and flat stomach. A mental picture of his muscular physique as he dressed the morning he left lingered in her mind's eye.

These thoughts of this white man surprised her, given that she had nearly died at the hands of the evil white captors just a few months before. She hated the white men, had even taken grim pleasure in killing one of them the night she escaped. Never would she have thought it possible to now yearn for the touch of another white man. But she knew Matt to be very different. When he looked at her with those kind eyes, and smiled his gentle smile, her heart seemed to tremble in her chest, and she longed to caress his handsome face.

"You will learn to care for the one you do not know," her grandmother had assured her before she became a wife. Her grandmother had been right—not once, but twice.

For two hours, Degan tramped through the underbrush, and along rough paths through a large area of the woods. Squirrels scampered, chasing one another from tree to tree. In the distance, she spotted a white-tail doe with a fawn. She sat for a while to watch the doe graze leisurely on the foliage, knowing the animal had surely picked up her scent, aware of her presence in the woods. Her search for wild mushrooms proved unsuccessful, and on such a cloudy day, darkness would come sooner than normal. So when a delicate rain began to tap gently on the canopy of leafy branches above her, she decided to make her way back to the cabin.

Some time later, her hair, blouse and skirt having taken on dampness from the weather, the misty light of the late afternoon grew brighter as the trees began to thin. The edge of the clearing came into view. When she lifted her eyes to the cabin, she stopped abruptly and gasped, her heart in her throat. There on the back porch stood Matt, leaning against the railing, watching her with a smile on his face.

She put a hand to her mouth as an unexpected wave of strong emotion washed over her, and her eyes welled with tears. When he descended the steps to approach her, her first thought was that she had forgotten how handsome he was. Joy mixed with relief shown in his eyes as he walked toward her, opening his arms in invitation.

Without thinking, she ran the rest of the way to leap into his embrace, and hung on as he lifted her off the ground. Pressing her face to the side of his neck, she breathed in the intoxicating scent that was distinctly his. His essence flooded her, quenching a desperate thirst that had taken root in her soul the day he left.

"Degan, Degan," she heard him say, "I missed you so." Setting her on her feet again, he took her face in his hands, smoldering anticipation in his eyes. He rubbed a thumb across her lower lip, opening her mouth slightly. She could hardly breathe as he leaned toward her. Closing her eyes, she felt his warm mouth on hers, softly at first, then more demanding. He kissed her leisurely, his tongue caressing hers, his hands pressing her body to his. She wrapped her arms around him, clinging to him.

After a long time that seemed far too short, he pulled back and looked down at her. Breathing heavily now, he smiled as he gazed into her eyes. She returned his smile, then reached to stroke her fingers gently across his bottom lip, and devoured his mouth again.

When he finally pulled back, she said, "I am so happy you are home. And I am sorry your father has left you."

"About Jon . . . I'm sorry but I needed to get word to you—"

She touched his mouth again. "It's all right. It is good you told him."

"It is?"

She nodded.

"Let's go inside." He put a hand on the small of her back as they made their way toward the porch steps.

In the cabin, Matt made himself comfortable by removing his tie, suit jacket, and boots, then set about unpacking his bags in the bedroom. As the rain and darkness fell outside, Degan sat on the bed watching him put away his things. She was full of questions about his visit, and he told her of his days spent with his family, the grand opening festivities for the hospital. He asked her how she had spent her days while he was gone, and she told him about the garden.

"A garden? I didn't notice it when I came home. You'll have to show it to me tomorrow."

She asked about Daisy, his mother, and his sister. He spoke briefly about his father's funeral, but then quickly changed the subject by removing a small, brightly colored box from one of his bags, and handing it to her.

"I think you'll like this," he said with a boyish grin, sitting down beside her on the bed. She stared at the box, then looked up at him.

"It's like the clothes. You have to take the paper off."

Her bewildered frown was quickly replaced by enthusiasm as she began tearing the wrapping paper to reveal a beautiful gold box with "Gold's Confectionery" scripted on the top. She looked up again.

"Open it."

When she lifted the lid, she saw several small dark cubes nestled in white tissue paper.

"Have you ever tasted chocolate before?"

"Chocolate?" she repeated, struggling with the unfamiliar word. "It is to eat?"

"Yes. Try one."

She carefully placed one square in her mouth, and as it began to soften on her tongue, she thought she had never tasted anything so delectable.

"You like it?"

She nodded eagerly. "I would eat the whole box."

Matt laughed. "You may want to save a few for later. There aren't any candy shops in Sylvan."

"Thank you," she said, watching him rise from the bed to reach again into his bag. This time he produced a beautiful shawl made of cream-colored lace, and a floor-length silk robe in lush shades of emerald green and royal blue.

"Oh, Matt," she said, as he unfolded them across her lap. She carefully touched the soft material of each, astonished by the beauty of the gifts. Once again, she was moved by his generosity.

"So lovely," she said, stroking the fine silk and elegant lace in her lap. "I want to thank you, but . . . it seems not enough to say. You are so kind to me."

There was a softness in his eyes as he moved toward her, his fingers smoothing the hair that framed her face. "I missed you, Degan."

"I missed you also. I am very happy you are home." He leaned closer and his mouth touched hers again, his hand cupping the back of her head before coming to rest at the base of her neck. When he pulled away, he touched his forehead to hers and closed his eyes.

"I don't want to frighten you," he said in a husky voice, "or suggest anything you don't want." He looked into her eyes. "I would never do anything to hurt you."

"I know."

"If the clan mothers were here, I would ask . . ."

She put a hand to the side of his face. "The mothers are not here. Only I am here."

"You know you can refuse me if you choose. I would never force myself on you. If you're afraid—"

"I will not refuse you," she whispered. "And I am not afraid."

With great care, she laid the shawl and the robe aside and, rising to stand in front of him, began to unbutton the front of her blouse that was still damp from the rain. His eyes never wavered as he watched her slowly progress to the last button. Freeing the material from the waistband of her skirt, she pushed the blouse off her shoulders, and it fell to the floor.

Matt took her hand and pressed her open palm to his lips. His mouth traveled to her wrist and back to her palm, and what felt like liquid fire coursed through her body from his touch. She would not have imagined this simple act could have such an effect on her, but she felt weak all over, and a moist heat was gathering between her legs.

She reached to remove the thin straps of her chemise from her shoulders. The bodice draped at her waist, exposing her delicately firm breasts for his gaze. The raw desire in his eyes was so strong she could feel its power envelop her. He stroked the side of her throat, then his fingertips leisurely traced a path across her collar bone and back, then down between her naked breasts.

"Do I please you?" she asked tentatively.

"Yes," he breathed, "very much so." Reverently, he reached to cup her breasts in his hands, feeling their firm weight, her soft skin. His thumbs stroked her dark nipples until they hardened. A throaty sigh escaped Degan's lips as she leaned her head back, closed her eyes, and prayed that he would never stop touching her. Then she felt his warm mouth gently sucking, his tongue caressing each nipple until she trembled, crying out in breathless pleasure.

To her surprise, he dropped to his knees on the soft rug in front of her, and reached behind her to unfasten the waistband of her skirt, which fell easily to the floor. He slipped the silky chemise over her hips before grasping the ribbons that held her pantalets in place. At this, he paused and looked up at her. Realizing he was seeking her permission and giving her the opportunity to stop him if she chose, she looked into his burning eyes and nodded once. He pulled the ribbons and the final garment settled at her feet.

His gaze upon her naked body was so intense, she thought his eyes would burn right through her.

"You have seen me before," she said, "that first night."

"Not like this," he said. He looked up at her. "I want to touch you . . . with my mouth."

"This is not . . . what I have done before."

"If I do anything you don't like, just tell me, and I'll stop," he murmured against her flat stomach below her navel, then kissed a trail to the tops of her thighs. His hands touched the crisp dark hair between her legs, and his thumbs spread the skin there to expose the most sensitive part of her body. Her breath caught in her throat when his tongue touched her there, and he began to lick softly. His tongue was cool at first against her hot skin, and she was sure she would collapse from the throbbing fullness he was bringing her to. She let go breathless moans of pleasure as her passion built until she feared her trembling legs would no longer support her.

His hands massaged her buttocks and the backs of her thighs, occasionally passing between her legs to feel her wetness, increasing his own urgency. He devoured her ravenously, a starving man enjoying his first nourishment in a very long time.

The force of her pleasure, an encompassing heat that was mounting uncontrollably, finally reached its peak, and she let out a loud scream as her legs gave out, and she collapsed into Matt's arms. He held her tightly as her whole body shook in climax. His fingers passed over the spot his tongue had brought to exquisite sensitivity, then he outlined her mouth with her own wetness, and kissed it away. Cradling her body against him, he continued to massage between her legs until the last of her passion had been drained from her. He brought his fingers to his mouth, murmuring "Sweet," as he tasted her again.

When the spasms began to subside, and some sense of reality had returned, she looked up at him, raising a hand to touch the wetness that glistened on his chin. He smiled at her with a soft look of satisfaction.

"You are so beautiful," he whispered with awe in his voice, "so beautiful. This was all I could think about while I was away."

After a time, she slowly sat up and moved behind him. Her warm breath, then her lips, were on his neck, just below his ear. She took his earlobe in her mouth and nibbled gently, pleased to hear him sigh with pleasure. Moving to his side, she pulled his shirt collar open, exposing more of his neck and chest, and felt him put a hand on the back of her head as she planted soft kisses on his skin. Then she straddled his lap and slowly began to unbutton his shirt.

Matt rested his hands on her hips, and drank in her nakedness. Her long hair fell about her shoulders as she worked at opening his shirt, and his pants were damp where she was sitting.

He reached to stroke her hair. "I want to taste you again."

"No," she refused gently, "now I taste you."

With a trace of apprehension in his eyes, he confessed, "It's been a long time for me."

"For me also," she murmured.

She pushed his shirt from his shoulders and, tossing it aside, laid both hands on his broad chest and caressed his bare skin. These were the strong arms that took care of her, and held her when she was injured and frightened. He had ministered to her so tenderly, and made her feel safe. Her desire now to pleasure him was overpowering. She wanted more than anything to see him naked and writhing in ecstasy beneath her.

Seeming to read her mind, he moved to lie down on the rug. She quickly unfastened his pants, and with one lift of his hips, she easily slid them down his legs and threw them aside. On her hands and knees, she moved slowly toward the pronounced fullness that was protruding from his undergarment. She reached to pull the material down, exposing him, completely and beautifully erect.

"Ooohhhh," she breathed hungrily. She pushed his last garment off and paused to take in the vision of his nude, muscular body in the soft glow of the lamplight.

Her hands, yearning to touch every inch of him, moved up and down his legs, stopping at the thick patch of hair between them. She heard her name escape him as her tongue caressed the entire length of his erection. Taking much of the shaft in her mouth, she leisurely sucked and licked until she knew he was at the brink of explosion.

"Please, Degan," he begged, "take me."

Then she was on top of him, guiding him inside her, raspy moans escaping his throat. With his hands on her hips, she moved up and down, slowly at first, then gradually faster. He watched her as she pleasured him, her body glistening with perspiration just as his was. He reached to pull her upper body close to his, and in one smooth motion, rolled both of them over so that she was now on her back and he was on top of her.

He paused for a moment, gentle concern in his eyes. "Are you all right?" He knew what she had endured in her captivity months ago. She nodded, touched by his thoughtfulness. Her trauma now seemed so far away, so distant from her, enveloped as she was in Matt's tender lovemaking that burned with such intensity that nothing of the past could intrude.

Still inside her, he stroked her breasts again, and she arched her back in ecstasy. He leaned to kiss her mouth, her neck, and she wrapped her arms around his back as his thrusting began again. Closing his eyes, he repeated her name against her ear until his breathing became rhythmic panting, and finally, his entire body stiffened as he cried out in shuddering climax.

At midnight, they lay quietly together, entwined under the damp sheet, exhausted. From the floor, their lovemaking had moved to the bed and now, hours later, tucked snugly under Matt's arm, Degan rested her head on his shoulder, her fingers caressing his chest. She listened to his steady breathing, felt the warmth of his bare skin along the length of her naked body, and felt contentment and bliss encompassing her.

Matt brought her hand to his lips for a kiss. "Degan, there's something I need to tell you," he began. She lifted her face to look up at him. "When I was away, I couldn't stop thinking about you. I couldn't wait to come home to you. I thought about . . . all the time you've been here, and . . . how much you've come to mean to me. I know you miss your home and your family, and if you want to go back to them, I'll take you, just as I promised. But . . . I want to ask you . . . to consider staying with me . . . a while longer." At this, she rose on one elbow. He took a deep breath. "I've fallen in love with you, Degan, and I don't want you to leave. I want you to stay with me."

She was very still, studying his face, which was filled with a mixture of anguish and hopefulness. Her own heart was full, overflowing, for the one who had shown her so much kindness. He was a strong man, yet at times revealed a sweet vulnerability that was so endearing, never more so than now. She had never intended to fall in love with the white shaman, never intended to stay with him beyond her recovery.

She put a hand to his cheek. "When you were away, each day was hard for me. I felt inside like . . . the garden with no rain, as if I would not live. But today when you are home, it rains again. Inside is alive again."

She watched his face fill with emotion as she spoke, as if he hung on every word. "You are very deep in my heart. I love you also."

He smiled at her and pulled her closer. She pressed her face to the base of his neck and felt him stroke her hair.

"Do you think you might . . . stay with me?" he asked.

She sighed gently against his skin, weighing this dilemma that had presented itself more forcefully each day. She was well aware that she could go back to her people at any time of her choosing. But when she tried to imagine herself leaving this man and this place, she felt such a compelling reluctance that even the strong pull of her own people and all that was familiar to her could not overshadow her desire to remain here with him.

"I miss my life from before, and my family."

"I understand," he said sadly.

She rose again on one elbow to look into his eyes. "But I do not want to leave you."

"Then stay," he replied, suddenly optimistic.

In the soft glow of the lamplight, his eyes were pools of tender anticipation. She felt at that moment she held in her hands the fragile possibility of happiness for both of them. She decided to give in to her heart. "I will stay longer."

Elation flooded his face and he gathered her again in his arms and held her tightly to him. Both were silent for a time, contemplating this new stage of their bond. Then Degan asked, "You were not happy with your family?"

"I've never felt as though I truly belong in that world. I don't . . . fit in."

She looked up at him. "What does this mean?"

He took a deep breath, considering how best to explain. "As I've gotten older, and especially since the war, I've come to value different things. I need a simple, quiet lifestyle, with simple, everyday people. When I'm in Washington, there are parties and social gatherings where the people are all well-to-do, and they're generally well-meaning, but . . . most of them would never understand why I would choose to live in a place like this, away from the finer things. I just don't belong there."

"But it is where you were a child with your mother."

"My mother didn't raise me, Daisy did. I guess I learned my values from her. And I'm very grateful for that, even though it's made it impossible for me now to truly belong in my family's world."

"But it is your home."

"No, this is my home," Matt said firmly. "I've made this home here for myself, and now with you, and . . . since you've come to live here with me, Degan, I've never been happier."

"I am happy here with you also," she said.

Sometime later, they both drifted into exhausted sleep.

The next morning, Degan awoke later than usual. Almost instantly, she remembered the night before, and when she looked to see that Matt was sound asleep next to her, she was delighted to realize it had not been a dream.

At some point in the night, his half of the sheet had been discarded to her side of the bed, and he now lay on his stomach, his pillow pushed out of the way against the massive headboard. Savoring the vision of his nakedness, her eyes followed a path across his broad shoulders, down his muscular back to his waist, his well-shaped buttocks, and strong legs. She longed to caress his body, but was afraid her touch would penetrate his deep slumber, and she did not want to waken him. So she lay beside him, happy simply to watch him sleep, and replayed in her mind their lovemaking from the night before. Never in her life had she experienced such ecstasy. When he had dropped to his knees before her, she had been uncertain of what to expect. But he had known exactly where and how to touch her body to bring her to heights of excruciating pleasure that she had not known before.

He had pushed her hand away from her mouth when she tried to quiet her own screams of release, telling her that he wanted to hear her scream. She had come to him hungry and burning, and under his skillful touch, he had rendered her helpless, then exquisitely fulfilled again and again.

His own arousal was evident from the time he stroked her breasts and unfastened her skirt and pantalets to drink in her nakedness. She had seen clearly the effect her body had on him, and when she had undressed him, his full passion had grown freely. He had let go a husky groan as he entered her, and she knew from his trembling climax later that his pleasure had been intensely satisfying.

And afterward, when they were lying together, he had shared his deepest feelings with her. She now realized she had loved him for a very long time.

She watched his back move up and down as he breathed. Without waking, he began to stir. In one motion, he reached to replace his pillow under his head and turned over on his back. His breathing remained deep and steady as he continued to sleep. In the morning light, Degan took in the vision of his full manhood. Now the temptation was too great. Unable to resist, she leaned forward to take him again into her mouth.

Moments later she heard his soft, waking moans, and felt his gentle hands on top of her head. "Oh my God," he whispered without opening his eyes. Continuing to pleasure him, she heard him say, "I don't think I have anything left in me, but what a way to wake up."

She smiled, depositing a trail of kisses across his flat stomach to his chest, then his neck and finally, his mouth. He reached to embrace her, then rolled her over on her back, and kissed her wantonly. She felt the sheet slipping down to her hips, then he took both her wrists in one hand and gently pinned her arms above her head. His mouth traveled to her bare breasts where he took one nipple, then the other into his mouth, leisurely stroking each with his tongue until they were hard and erect. She cried out in unbearable delight, arching her back involuntarily as the wonderful heat flooded her body once more.

The sheet flew off completely, and Matt was on top of her, his hardness prominently between them just before he entered her again. Her hips rose eagerly to meet every powerful thrust, and she wrapped her arms around his body, holding him close, feeling fresh perspiration surface on his skin. She felt her own passion building, and knew with every push that she was approaching her own sweet explosion. The two moved in concert, faster and stronger, until time itself seemed suspended. Matt opened his eyes and looked down at her, his face awash with tenderness and awe. She held his gaze as they moved together until finally, both let out cries of fierce, breathless release.

He collapsed on top of her just for an instant before quickly moving to her side. He draped an arm across her stomach, and she listened to his breathing slowly return to normal, along with her own.

After a while, he muttered into her pillow, "I'm completely worn out. I won't be able to walk for the rest of the day."

She laughed softly, stroking his disheveled hair. "I will bring you breakfast in bed."

"I won't put up a fight," he quipped. Before long, he was asleep.

It was mid-day when Matt awoke again, this time turning to see Degan sitting upright in the bed, chewing happily, the open box of chocolates in her hand, the sheet tucked under her arms.

He chuckled at the sight of her. "Enjoying your breakfast?"

"I try to eat slowly so the . . . chocolate . . . will last."

He sat up, rubbing sleep from his face. "I haven't slept that well in weeks."

"No bad dreams?"

"No, not last night," he said. "Do I smell coffee?"

"Yes. I will bring it." Setting the chocolates aside, she threw back the sheet and climbed out of bed. As she reached for her beautiful new robe, she felt his eyes on her body. When she turned to look at him, her suspicions were confirmed.

"Don't put that on," he requested softly, a playful smile on his face. "I want to watch you walk around naked."

The tone of his voice and the hungry look in his eyes sent shivers of renewed desire coursing through her. She felt her pulse quicken as she opened the bedroom door to go get the coffee.

CHAPTER

14

When Matt came out of the bedroom, he saw Degan standing at the stove, vigorously stirring liquid in a bowl. She had donned her new silk robe, and as she reached for thick slices of bread stacked in front of her, he approached her from behind. He playfully untied the sash of her robe and slipped his hand under the fabric to caress her breasts. When she turned to face him, his hands brushed her waist, and came to rest on her buttocks.

"Are you making French toast?" he asked, seeing beaten eggs in the bowl and the slices of bread.

"This is your favorite that you taught me." She returned his mischievous smile, but pushed his hands away and attempted to close her robe. "You are hungry for food or love?"

"Both." Kissing her lightly on the forehead, he moved to retrieve two plates from the cupboard. "I want you to show me your garden after we eat."

"With the rain yesterday, there will be many weeds today," she said, placing a cast-iron skillet on a hot burner. "The weeds always grow faster than the crops."

"When I was a boy, I used to help Daisy weed her garden. Maybe I can help you," he said, arranging two place settings on the table.

Degan frowned. "In my people, only the women work the crops. The man will never do the woman's work. The man hunts the animals for the people to eat."

When he did not respond, she turned from the heat of the stove to see him standing at his desk with Emma's book in his hands. He appeared to be studying the note she had written inside. Degan's heart sank.

He looked up at her. "Where did this come from?"

"Emma brought it when you were away."

"Emma was here? She saw you?"

"No. Jon was here. He went outside and took the book from her. She never saw me."

Nodding his understanding, he tossed the book on his desk.

"She still cares for you," Degan said quietly, turning back to the stove.

Matt returned to the cupboard, pulling out a drawer to retrieve two sets of silverware. "That doesn't matter to me anymore. The only person Emma really cares about is herself."

"Jon said this also."

"He's right."

"I believe Jon hates Emma."

"There's no love lost between them, that's for sure."

"He hates her because she hurt you?"

"He never trusted her, but when she betrayed me, that sealed her fate with Jon."

"What does this mean? Sealed her fate?"

"It means his dislike of her grew even stronger and now she can do nothing right in Jon's eyes."

Degan carefully turned the batter-soaked bread in the skillet. "Jon never took a wife?"

"No. The war ruined peoples' lives in so many ways. Some soldiers who made it back in one piece found the women they intended to marry got tired of waiting, and married somebody else. Some, like Jon, were betrothed before the war, but when he came back, she didn't want him anymore."

"Why?"

"He thinks because he lost his arm."

"He told me about that. It was terrible for him."

Matt closed his eyes and shuddered, the grisly ordeal of amputating Jon's arm still too fresh in his memory.

"I hope Jon will find someone to be his wife. A woman who is kind."

"Yes, he deserves that. He's a good man."

Degan smiled. "Yes, he is a good man. Now I know two good white men."

They had just settled at the table when a loud knock sounded at the door. Startled, Degan turned to Matt, who put a reassuring hand over hers before rising.

"Degan, it's me," came Jon's voice from the porch.

Relieved, Matt quickly reached to open the door. "Jon, it's good to see you!" He clasped Jon's extended hand, and wrapped an arm around his friend's shoulder.

"Welcome home," Jon said, stepping inside. Matt closed the door behind him. "When did you get back?"

"Yesterday afternoon."

"Sorry about your father."

"Thank you," Matt said stiffly, his eyes downcast. "Come in, sit down."

Jon and Degan exchanged warm greetings. When she rose to fetch a third place setting and to pour another cup of coffee, Jon saw that she was wearing a silk robe. Suddenly red-faced, he awkwardly averted his gaze until she sat down again.

"We were just starting to eat breakfast," Matt said, settling again at the table.

"You're just now eating breakfast? It's past noon!"

"We got a late start," he said with a look to dissuade further questioning.

Jon glanced at Degan, then back to Matt as a comprehending light came into his eyes. Saying nothing more, he gratefully accepted the platter of hot French toast, and helped himself to several pieces. While they ate, Jon inquired about Matt's family, and the new hospital. When he attempted to ask in more detail about Adam Tyler's death, Matt replied curtly and changed the subject.

"I understand you took good care of things around here while I was away," Matt said, leaning back from the table, coffee cup in hand. "I want to thank you for that."

Quickly becoming uncomfortable under the combined attention of his hosts, Jon studied the tabletop, embarrassment coloring his cheeks. "I was glad to do it." A moment of uneasy silence passed, then he looked up. "Have you seen the garden?"

"No," Matt said, pushing away from the table, "but I want to." He turned to Degan, who had begun to clear the dishes. "I'll help you with that later. Let's go look at your garden."

Smiling, she set the plates back down. "I will get dressed."

As she passed him to make her way to the bedroom, Matt gently caught her wrist. "Thank you for breakfast."

She looked down at him adoringly before passing into the bedroom, closing the door.

Alone now, the two men locked eyes, and Jon shook his head in disbelief.

"I can't believe she's been here for months and I didn't know about her," he said, careful to keep his voice low. "How the hell did you keep her a secret all this time?"

"She's afraid of anyone finding out about her," Matt said quietly. "So I just didn't tell anybody she was here."

"But I can't believe nobody's been out here from town. You know that's gonna happen sooner or later."

"We've been very lucky, I know. It's only a matter of time till she's found out. I haven't told anyone about her because she's terrified of white people. She was nearly killed by white men before she found her way here."

"She told me what happened," Jon said. "It's not my business, but . . . what the hell's goin' on between you two? I figure she's cookin' and cleanin' for you, like a servant . . . then that look you gave me before we ate, and the way she looked at you just now. I'm not blind—"

"She's not my servant," Matt said firmly. "Her injuries were substantial when she first came here. She nearly died. When she finally started feeling better, she wanted to do some work around here, just to keep busy, and I agreed. But she's never been my servant." He took another sip of coffee, searching for words to explain further. "Then yesterday, when I came home, we realized . . . our feelings have gone beyond . . . anything we expected."

"What do you mean?" He lowered his voice to a whisper, keeping a wary eye on the bedroom door. "You mean you're . . . courtin' her? An Indian squaw?"

Matt lowered his voice as well, and leaned forward. "Look, early on, we planned that she'd go back to the reservation once she was recovered.

But over the past few months, she's . . . become very important to me. I've asked her to stay here with me indefinitely and she's agreed."

"But you can't keep her a secret forever," Jon said, "and when people find out, they won't accept her, you know that. They'll think it's wrong that you're not with . . . your own kind."

Matt closed his eyes, frustrated with the same warning he'd heard before.

"And some you think are your friends will turn against you when they find out you're courtin' an Indian squaw. Hell, you're not courtin' her, you're livin' with her under the same roof. Like married folks!"

"I can't walk away from this," Matt shot back in a forceful whisper. "She's too important to me."

"Well, you're gonna have trouble when she's found out. People will say you oughta' be with a white woman."

Matt sighed heavily. "But what if that's not what I want? What if I want to be with a woman who doesn't happen to be white? What if I love a woman who doesn't happen to be white? Then what do I do?"

With a shrug, Jon fell silent.

"Where do you stand?" Matt asked him pointedly.

"What do you mean?"

"Where do you stand? Are you going to turn against me because of Degan?"

Jon frowned, and shook his head. "Who you court is your concern. The fact that she's Indian doesn't change anything between us. I just think you're askin' for big trouble is all."

"I know you're right. But I told you, I can't walk away from this."

"That day I got your letter and came out here, I didn't know what the hell to think when I saw her. And I thought she was gonna blow my head off. I come around the side of the cabin and walk right into a rifle stuck in my face—"

Matt laughed, relieved to break the thick tension between them. "Before I left, I made sure she could shoot. She's a damn good shot. She could defend herself if she had to."

"You don't have to tell me. I came close enough."

Matt was still chuckling when Degan emerged from the bedroom, dressed in a crisp, blue-and-white pinstriped blouse, and matching skirt of darker blue. She looked at the two suspiciously, knowing she had been the topic of their conversation.

"Jon was telling me how you almost shot him that first day he came out here," Matt said.

Degan looked tentatively at Jon, then at Matt. "I didn't know he is your friend." Seeing Matt's amused expression, she allowed a grin. "It's good I did not shoot him."

"See? You made a good impression," Matt told Jon, laughing again.

The afternoon sun was warm as they descended the front steps and rounded the corner of the porch. When Matt looked up, he saw the neat rows of small corn plants, soon to be stalks, emerging from the ground, which was dark with moisture from the previous day's rain.

"You did all this while I was away?" he asked in astonishment, strolling the perimeter of the garden, impressed by the plants that were now several inches high.

"Yes. Jon brought me supplies from the town. I found tools in your barn to work the ground." She bent to pull several small weeds that had poked from beneath the wet soil, and tossed them aside in the grass. "The women grow the crops that will feed the people."

"The women in your tribe grow all the crops?" Jon asked curiously. "What do the men do?"

"The men leave the village to hunt for many weeks. They bring back deer and bear and quail and other meat for the people to eat."

Jon looked askance at Matt before turning back to Degan. "Have you ever seen his shooting?" he asked with mischief in his eyes, and an irreverent grin. "I'm thinkin' you'll have to make do with your crops here."

Degan put a hand to her mouth to suppress her laughter.

"Yes, she's seen my shooting, you horse's ass," Matt replied with feigned offense.

"I make the garden not just for food," she continued. "It is good I do this for Matt because he healed me. I also do it because . . . this is what I know. The women work the earth and ask the Creator for the harvest in every season. When I plant this corn, I also burn tobacco so the Creator will hear my prayers and give a good harvest."

"So that's why my tobacco pouch is nearly empty," Matt muttered to himself.

"The people are thankful to the Creator for all the crops in the fields and the fruits from the trees." She looked out over her garden with longing in her eyes. "I miss my life before."

Standing at the garden's edge, Matt suddenly realized just how difficult an adjustment it must have been for Degan to have lived here during these past months. She had often talked of her life among her people, but today the contrast seemed more striking than ever. He recalled her description of communal living on the reservation. She had been surrounded not only by her immediate family, but by her extended family as well. All worked together to raise the children, grow and prepare food, and celebrate the harvest each year.

But for many months now, she had been virtually secluded in the cabin, with Matt her only connection to the outside world, a world with which she was largely unfamiliar. He was beginning to fathom how isolated she must feel at times, and why she often seemed so eager to hear about his days in the town, the people with whom he interacted, and the various activities related to his job. He felt remiss for not acknowledging this before.

Later, Matt and Degan sat in the two rocking chairs on the back porch. Twilight had begun to fall like a warm blanket over the woods, coaxing a whitetail doe and her fawn out of hiding to nibble on the tender grass that grew under the thick canopy of trees. A symphony of crickets chirped, and fireflies darted in criss-cross flight just above the grass. In the distance, a mourning dove cooed a melancholy cry.

The chairs creaked with a soft rhythm against the wooden planks of the porch floor, and the sweet, familiar smell of Matt's pipe smoke wafted in every direction as he puffed silently. Degan closed her eyes, and leaned her head back, taking in the elements of her present surroundings that had become so soothing.

"I missed your smoke," she said after a time.

Matt turned to see her tranquil smile. "Did the men in your tribe smoke often?"

"For many years, they smoke when they sit at council fires, to pray for wisdom," she said. "Now they also smoke for their pleasure, like the white man."

Matt removed the pipe from his mouth, gently tamped, then relit the tobacco in the bowl. "It relaxes me," he said, drawing on the stem. They sat quietly a while longer before Matt spoke again. "I was thinking about what you said earlier today, about missing your life from before. It must be hard for you to be alone here so much of the time."

Her eyes downcast, she suddenly looked sad. Her fingers absently rubbed an imaginary spot on the arm of the rocker as she searched for words. "I miss my life from before." She looked up at him. "But to leave you and go back to my people would be very hard. I am . . . not with my people or the whites. My only place is here with you."

Matt leaned forward to look into her eyes. "Degan, I love you, and I want you here with me. If you ever decide you want to be part of the white world, you can make that choice, and I would help you. You wouldn't be so alone if you decided to live among the whites."

She shook her head. "I am afraid of the whites."

"I know. Were you always afraid?"

"No. When the white holy men came to us many years ago, they were kind and I was not afraid. Some still come to the village. But when the evil white men came and took me . . ." Her voice broke, but she was determined to continue, her eyes wide, brimming with unshed tears. "What they did to me . . . I can never forget. They hurt me . . . in many ways. They killed so many in my family, even the children. I can never live among these people!"

Matt quickly reached to squeeze her hand. "Degan, honey, the men who did those terrible things to you are criminals and should be punished. The whites would call them criminals also."

She considered his words, but said nothing.

"I understand you're afraid," he told her gently. "But I promise you, no harm will come to you as long as you're with me. And maybe one day, you won't be so afraid. Look at Jon, you're not afraid of him."

"He is a good man. Like you."

"There are many good white people."

"Even if I wished to live among the whites, they would not accept me."

Matt remembered his conversation with Caroline, and with Jon earlier in the day. Both had expressed the same concern.

"It's true, some people would reject you because you're not like them," Matt admitted. "But they would be the lesser for it, not you."

Suddenly, she looked up with a brighter expression, her eyes filled with hope. "Maybe you will come to live with me among the Seneca?"

Taken aback at her suggestion, Matt sat in bewildered silence, not knowing how to respond.

"We have had whites live with the people. They learn our ways, and they are happy."

It was difficult for him to comprehend the implications of her suggestion. The thought of abandoning everything that was familiar to him to go live in a foreign society filled him with anxiety. Yet, it was not lost on him that this was exactly what he was asking Degan to do.

He chose his words carefully. "I don't know what I would do among your people. I wouldn't be accepted as a doctor."

"No, the people do not welcome the white ways to heal."

"Are there any whites living near your village?"

"No. On the reservation and in Salamanca, only the Seneca live there."

"Salamanca?"

"The town at the reservation."

"Then I would have to give up practicing medicine—"

Degan looked stricken. "No, you cannot! The Creator has chosen you to heal. If not for you, I would have died. You are the shaman for your people. You cannot choose a different path."

At an impasse, they fell silent.

"For now, I will stay here with you as I have been," she said with finality. "I am happy with you."

Her words warmed his heart, and with a smile, he brought her hand to his lips for a kiss. "I'm glad being here with me makes you happy."

Once darkness had fallen, they went inside and Degan set about cleaning the kitchen. Matt insisted on helping her.

"It is strange for me, when you help with the garden, and help with the food, and the cleaning," she said with a look of amusement. "You like the work of women?"

Matt chuckled. "It's how I was raised, I guess. I always helped Daisy in the kitchen when I was a little boy. She always said 'work is work.' But my mother never approved of me helping Daisy. She said I was 'much too familiar with the domestics.'"

"What is 'domestics'?"

"Servants."

"Like slaves?"

"No, domestics are paid for the work they do," he explained.

"When Jon was here the first day, he said I am your servant."

Matt came to stand next to her. "I set Jon straight on that account. I told him you're not my servant. He misunderstood."

She smiled at him, watching as he poured hot water from the stove into the large pan of dishes.

"Daisy is a servant?" she asked, washing the plates in the soapy water.

"Yes and no. In many ways, Daisy was more of a mother to Caroline and me than our real mother was," he said, retrieving a clean towel from the cupboard. "My mother was always busy with her social functions. It was Daisy who would teach us and discipline us."

"Discipline?"

"When we behaved badly, she would punish us," he explained, as a slow smile spread across Degan's face. "What are you smiling about?"

"I am thinking of you as a little boy," she told him, looking up from her work with a softness in her eyes that he had come to love. Handing him a plate to dry, she asked, "What did you do that Daisy would punish?"

He feigned a solemn expression. "Well, of course, I was a nearly perfect child," he teased, enjoying her laughter. "But there was one time—I was about seven or eight—I thought it would be funny to switch all the salt and sugar in the kitchen. So for a whole day, when Daisy thought she was adding sugar to a recipe, it was really salt, and salt when it was really sugar. We couldn't eat any of the food she prepared for the evening meal. She wasn't very happy with me when she discovered what I had done."

Laughing, Degan asked, "What did she do?"

"I was forbidden to go near the kitchen for a week, which was a fitting punishment since I loved being in the kitchen with Daisy."

When the dishes were washed and dried, Matt took Degan's hand and led her into the bedroom where he struck a match, holding the flame to the wick of the lamp that sat on the bedside table. As a soft glow warmed the room, he relaxed into the large armchair of buttery-soft black leather, and patted his legs in invitation for her to sit. She settled carefully onto his lap, tucking her bare feet between the cool leather of the arm and the thick cushion.

"Now, tell me something from your childhood," he challenged with a grin, draping his arm across her lower back. "I don't want to feel like the only misbehaving one here."

She considered her distant memories. "When we were very young, I lost my brother. We were playing far in the woods and we were lost. After a time, I found my way out, but my brother was not with me. When I am home, my grandmother asks where is my brother? I said he is lost. She became very angry, and very worried. My father took some men, and they searched. They found him before the night came."

"What did your father do to you?"

"He and my grandmother talked to me. The anger was fear. When they found my brother, the anger was gone. They said we should never go far alone because we are too young. We don't know how to come home. After that, my grandmother took us on long walks in the woods. She taught us how to look at the sun to find our way home."

Matt smiled. "Sounds like you had a good childhood."

"My grandmother and my father would have liked you."

Surprised by her comment, he said, "You think so?"

"Yes. My grandmother was wise. My father is a kind man, very strong. Always wants to do the right thing. I feel much love from him . . . like I feel from you."

He smiled, his head resting against the back of the chair, his eyes fixed on some distant point. "I would have liked to meet him. Do you think he survived the attack on your village?"

"I don't know. When the white men came, he left our lodge to get men to help us. I did not see him again before I was taken," she said. "Your father was a good man also?"

"Yes, he was. After the war, I said I'd never set foot inside a church again, but I did for his funeral. We couldn't have the funeral at the house because so many people came. We had to use the church, so I went. I felt I could do that much for him." Silence rested between them, Degan seeming to provide an open space for him to share more of his grief if he chose. "I wish I knew why God takes people when he does. You would think that in my work I'd be used to death. I saw enough of it during the war. Sometimes death is the best thing. But I don't understand what purpose it serves to . . . take people when they've got so much more to do in their lives. My father worked so hard, and was so proud of the new hospital. But he didn't get the chance to see it make a difference."

As Degan listened to his anguished questioning, Matt felt that she was lovingly cradling his soul, unguarded and vulnerable, in her hands. He sensed she understood the depth of loss he was feeling, understood him and accepted him. This was what he had longed for when he was in Washington, what he had longed for his entire life. This was what he had attempted to explain to Caroline, without much success. The freedom and luxury of letting his guard down and being his true self without judgment or penalty.

"And your father was proud of you?" she asked.

"The first night I was home, he told me he was proud of me."

Still unable to grasp the reality of his father's death, it seemed absurd to think of him in the past tense. Adam Tyler had always been a larger-than-life figure in his son's eyes, and the events of the last few weeks still seemed so unreal. He could not shake the certainty that he would return to his boyhood home, and once again see his father stroll from the library with a cigar between his fingers and a clever quip on his lips. He could still hear his father's laughter in his head, and would have given anything to have one more conversation with the man who had always been so loving and supportive of his children, even when he disagreed with their decisions.

Matt felt a tear trickle down the side of his face and onto his neck. Degan reached to touch its wetness with her fingers.

"I miss him," he whispered, his voice breaking. "I can't believe he's really gone."

Raw emotions lingered just beneath the surface. Trying to fight back the heavy sadness that threatened to smother him, he put a hand over his eyes, and took several deep breaths, which soon turned uncontrollably to sobs. He felt Degan cradle his head to her chest, and stroke his hair as he wept, her warmth helping to ease his misery. He listened to her voice echoing within her chest as she murmured words of solace to him, and thought he had never heard such a sweet, melodic sound, or felt so at peace in anyone's embrace.

Sitting up, he looked into her eyes, searching for any trace of disappointment or aversion to seeing a man weep openly, but she was looking at him adoringly, her dark eyes reflecting only empathy and concern. He could not remember the last time he had trusted someone enough to cry in front of them. His gratitude for her acceptance of him was deeper than words could reach.

"Your sorrow honors your father," she said simply.

"You lost so many of your family just a few months ago," he whispered. "How do you live with that?"

"I cried many times when you were away," she said. "Maybe I would be busy with work, but the memory would come very strong. I cried for a long time, until I was too tired to cry more."

A pained expression darkened his face, and he reached to touch her cheek with gentle fingers. The suffocating sadness of moments ago was now replaced by boundless affection for her. "I'm so sorry," was all he could think of to say.

"I am still very sad. I miss my family. But the Creator knows all things. The Creator brought me here to be with you. The Creator takes away, but also gives. Your father leaves, but I am here. My family leaves, but you are here."

Matt couldn't help smiling at her reasoning that was profound in its simplicity. He knew her faith in her Creator was unwavering, and whether or not he shared her beliefs, he could not deny she was a gift that had come into his life. A gift that he treasured more each day.

CHAPTER

15

For the farming families in the area, the months of summer and early fall were always demanding, full of activity and endless hard work. Children as young as six could often be seen working in the fields alongside their older siblings, tethered behind teams of horses. Applying all their weight to a plow that churned the earth, turning clumps of moist soil upside down in rows that stretched from one side of a field to the other, entire families worked from sunrise to sunset. Following the growing season, all family members were required to bring in the abundant harvest.

The long workdays began in the cool pre-dawn, and didn't end until the sun's magenta-gold glow slipped behind the foothills, taking with it the last of workable light. Only Sunday offered a few slower, lazier hours in which to attend church services and socialize with family and friends in respite from the previous week. There were few townspeople whose occupations did not in some way sustain the farmers. The blacksmiths and farriers, the millers who ground the harvested grain, and the wheelwrights who repaired wagon wheels and other equipment, all had a hand in keeping the local industry vital.

Matt and Dr. Bowman also kept busy treating routine injuries and illnesses of the entire population. Warm summer months often brought the scourge of cholera to some unfortunate families, and each year the doctors welcomed the cooler temperatures of fall, thankful to have passed another warm season without a widespread outbreak of the affliction that could take a life within hours of onset.

Degan's corn crop grew rapidly through the summer, reaching shoulder-height by August, with the beans and squash thriving alongside. The companion planting method of her people had worked well, with the beans dutifully climbing the corn stalks, and the broad squash leaves covering the ground to seal in moisture from which all three plants benefited.

Eventually becoming more accepting of Matt's assistance in her garden, Degan most enjoyed the days when his practice did not keep him away for long hours. He seemed to take pleasure in helping her work the ground, weed, and water the crops if rain had been scarce for a few days.

"You like working the crops with me," Degan said one afternoon in late August. She was crouched between two rows of tall corn, pulling weeds from between the stalks. Matt was doing the same a few feet away. "This is because you cannot shoot for meat?"

He smiled at her blunt assessment. "I guess so. But mostly I just enjoy being with you. Even though it's too damn hot to be working out in the sun like this."

"In my home, if it is hot like today, many times the women take off their clothes and work naked."

Matt stopped and looked up. "Well, don't feel obliged to keep your clothes on for my sake."

She met his playful stare. "You like working the crops more if I am naked?"

"I'd like just about anything more if you're naked."

Degan burst out laughing. His mischievous spontaneity often delighted her.

Their life together had fallen into a routine of comfortable intimacy that often eluded couples who had been together far longer. In the late evenings, they lay in bed, the open windows allowing the sweetly scented air from the woods to fill the room. Matt would read aloud to her as she rested her head on his shoulder. She loved to hear the sound of his voice as he brought to life the latest fiction of the day by authors such as Charles Dickens and George Eliot. Often asking questions about the descriptions in the stories, she listened to Matt's patient explanations of concepts and images, learning much about the white world. She was fascinated by page after page of printed words that comprised stories of people and events that were, in fact, not real.

"My people have stories also," she said, "but we speak the stories. And the stories are true. Why do the whites have paper stories that are not true?"

Matt held his place in the book with his finger, thinking of the best way to explain why fiction was so popular. "The whites have books that tell true stories also, and others that aren't true. The stories that aren't true are called 'fiction.'"

"I have not heard this word. Fiction?"

"Yes. Even though some stories aren't true, they're still interesting. I guess that's why people like to read them."

Degan frowned. "Many times I do not understand the whites."

He kissed the top of her head. "I know. But even though you know this story isn't true, do you find it interesting? Do you want to know what happens next?"

She shrugged. "Yes."

"Well, that's why we have these stories."

Listening to him read as he stroked gentle fingers across her bare back, she relaxed from her day's work. When she slept next to him, the night passed peacefully, neither of them terrorized by nightmares.

In the early morning hours, when sleep began to lift, he would reach to pull her close, and nestle his face in her hair. She would press her nakedness to his, feeling his warm skin against her body, so content that she wished they could stay in bed all day. He would deposit soft kisses on her neck, her shoulders, her breasts, and run his hand slowly down the length of her. He seemed fascinated by her naked body, gently exploring every inch of her, his touch almost always leading to fervent lovemaking long before the sun came up. Reluctant to leave her in the mornings, he would promise to return to the cabin to eat the mid-day meal with her if there were no emergencies to keep him.

At the end of the day, she relished hearing about his work, accounts that were often humorous and heartening. His demeanor was never more animated than when he was telling her of his work, and she knew he felt a genuine affection for the townspeople he served, especially the children. Though she had never met any of the families he spoke of, she felt she knew them quite well. His successes or failures in treating the injuries and illnesses of the people were often the determinants of his mood. She could tell immediately upon seeing his face if his day had gone well or not. But his low spirits never lingered. With a welcoming embrace from her, a quick recounting of the day, and a cigar before the evening meal, he was himself again.

One stormy afternoon, she had stayed inside, pleased that her garden was benefiting from much needed rainfall. The previous evening, Matt had brought home a dozen ripe peaches that had been given to him by a local farmer in exchange for helping his wife in childbirth. Degan had decided to make compote of peaches and maple syrup that her grandmother had taught her to make when she was a girl. She had just begun peeling the peaches when she looked out and saw Matt approaching the cabin on his horse. Grabbing a towel, she wiped her hands and went out on the porch to meet him.

He dismounted and tethered his horse to the post.

"Everything is all right?" she asked, watching him climb the steps toward her.

His face damp from the rain, he looked down at her, his eyes smoldering with hungry desire. "I needed to see you." He took her face in his hands and leaned to press his mouth hungrily to hers. Lightning flashed and thunder roared, startling her.

"Let's go inside," he said, taking her hand.

He led her through the great room and into the bedroom, cozy and dark from the storm. She reached to his collar and began unbuttoning his shirt as quickly as her fingers would move.

"How long can you stay?" she asked, her hands brushing his bare chest as she pushed his shirt from his shoulders.

"Until we're both satisfied." He watched as she sank gently to her knees to unfasten his pants. Pushing his undergarment down to mid-thigh, she took him into her mouth.

"Oh Degan," he groaned breathlessly, his firmness quickly becoming rigid within her warm, insistent mouth. He collapsed onto the bed, his hand slipping into her blouse, his fingers finding her taut nipples. She thought she would soon go mad with her own desire, a throbbing fullness between her legs growing stronger.

She quickly pulled up her skirt and straddled him. Amazement registered on his face when he saw that she wore no undergarments.

"The white woman's clothes are too hot," she replied to his surprised stare.

He smiled and reached to caress her wetness, then pushed into her with a throaty sigh of pleasure and closed his eyes as she began to move up and down. They moved in unison, faster and faster until both were panting with the effort. Watching his face, she knew a sense of fulfillment that she could barely contain. She felt complete, having Matt inside her and knowing that he was experiencing pleasure beyond description. She enjoyed nothing as much as seeing his upper body flush and stiffen and hearing him cry her name as he exploded into her.

His hands seized her hips, and she slowed her pace. His body very still, he finally whispered, "Stop," before opening his eyes and gazing up at her, a serene smile lifting the corners of his mouth. "You're an angel," he sighed. After a few moments, the intensity came back into his eyes. "Lie down on the bed."

She carefully climbed off of him and did as he said. He sat up, propping himself on one elbow, and leaned toward her.

"Put your hands above your head," he said. When she did so, he caressed gentle fingers from her neck to the top button of her blouse. As her breathing grew shallow and rapid, he took his time unfastening each button until she thought she could wait no longer for his satisfying touch.

"Please, hurry," she whispered, arching her back in anticipation.

"Am I going too slowly for you, my dear?" When her blouse was finally open to the waist, he pushed back the material to see her hard nipples straining against the delicate silk of her chemise. He carefully massaged each breast, paying special attention to each peak. Then he leaned to put his mouth against the silk and took her right nipple between his lips, gently pinching and sucking until she cried out.

"Put your feet on the bed," he said. When she complied, he pushed her skirt to her hips, exposing her nakedness. "Spread your legs for me." She obeyed, then watched as he sat up and bent to put his warm mouth between her legs, his tongue stroking her intimately. When Matt's expert touch brought her to this place of unbearable pleasure, she lost all ability to think. He was in command of her body, which responded to him with wild abandon that she could not control, even if she wanted to. She could hear herself crying out, soon reaching the pinnacle where she could take no more. But his skilled tongue kept the hot, tingling fire racing through her body until she lost awareness and exploded against him, suspended in time, convulsing in exquisite release.

After a while, she came back to herself, and sensed Matt's presence beside her on the bed. She felt drained, her arms and legs weak, and when she opened her eyes, he was propped on one elbow, watching her.

"I love you, Degan," he said with that little-boy expression that she adored.

She smiled. "I know. I love you."

He took her hand and reclined again beside her. "Don't let me fall asleep. I have to get back to town."

In late September, Matt returned to the office from a neighboring farm one evening to find the town sheriff waiting outside the front door. An imposing, burly man in his late-forties, Sheriff Daniel Wilkes had been providing law enforcement and security for the citizens of Sylvan and the surrounding area for nearly ten years. Usually an unexcitable, unassuming man, tonight he seemed agitated, pacing the length of the wooden sidewalk in front of the medical office.

"Hello, Daniel, what can I do for you?" Matt said as he rode up. Dismounting, he unfastened his medical bag from his saddle.

"Evening, Matt. I got a prisoner that needs your attention," Sheriff Wilkes said, following the doctor into the darkened office. As Matt struck a match to the wick of an oil lamp, the sheriff removed his hat, and ran a hand through his graying hair. "We finally caught up with the Collins boy. Him and his brother been robbing stages and causing all the trouble these last few months."

"I heard about them," Matt said, lighting a second lamp and turning the wick higher to brighten the room. "People say they're a couple of vicious criminals."

"Well, there's only the younger one now and we got him. Don't know what happened to the older one. We had lawmen from as far north as New York tracking them. They're damn slippery bastards."

"But you got them?"

"We got the youngest one, but he ain't sayin' what happened to his brother. And he took a bullet in the arm in the process of bringin' him in. He's over in the lock-up now. Can we bring him over?"

"You don't want me coming over there?"

Sheriff Wilkes shook his head. "No, Matt, we got a full house over there, too much commotion. It'd be better if we brought him over here.

Tom and I will bring him. With both of us, I don't think he'll get too far."

"All right. Once he's here, I'll chloroform him. He'll sleep like a baby for a while after that."

"Seems like a waste of good chloroform if you ask me," the sheriff grumbled as he opened the door to leave.

Matt chuckled. "Bring him over, I'll be here."

CHAPTER

16

Within half-an-hour, Deputy Tom Reilly knocked on the door of the medical office, accompanied by a wiry young man with downcast eyes and no expression.

"Evening, Matt," said the bearish deputy when the doctor opened the door. "This here's the prisoner Sheriff Wilkes was tellin' you about. The sheriff got called out on another matter."

"Bring him back to the treatment room," Matt said, leading the pair through the outer office.

His gait impeded by iron shackles around his ankles, the prisoner shuffled as best he could to keep pace. Handcuffs restrained his arms behind him, and his dirty clothes showed signs of the struggle of his capture. His left sleeve was torn and soaked with blood just below the shoulder.

A wooden examining table sat in the center of the treatment room. Against the far wall, an apothecary cabinet stood between a large desk strewn with papers and the back door to the alley. Several burning oil lamps sat around the room, collectively casting workable light.

Matt placed a tray of cutting and probing instruments on the examining table, then turned to Tom, who was eyeing the display with a noticeably ashen color.

"You'll need to remove the handcuffs so I can treat him," Matt said, ignoring the pall that had descended over the deputy's face.

Tom fumbled with a set of keys, addressing the prisoner sternly, "I'm takin' these cuffs off for the doctor, but don't you get any ideas about tryin' anything."

"What's your name?" Matt asked the prisoner as Tom slipped the metal restraints from his wrists.

"Stephen," the young man mumbled, gingerly massaging his left arm.

"How old are you?"

"Seventeen."

Frowning, Matt shook his head. "Just a boy," he said under his breath. "All right, Stephen, I need you to sit on this table and take your shirt off. I want to take a look at that arm before I remove the bullet."

With a long moment of hesitation, and exertion that seemed mostly exaggerated, Stephen mounted the table. He painstakingly began to unbutton his shirt, his eyes wandering aimlessly about the room. Matt could feel impatience and frustration swelling in the deputy standing next to him.

"Hurry up!" Tom finally shouted. "We don't have all night!"

"We wouldn't even be here if you hadn't-a shot me!" Stephen barked with hateful defiance.

The deputy drew back a fist, his face congested with anger.

"Tom!" Matt quickly put both hands on his arm. "Let's not give me more work to do beyond removing the bullet, all right?"

Scowling, Tom slowly lowered his fist. Matt noticed a hint of triumph in the boy's expression.

"Wipe that look off your face, you little piece'a shit," Tom snapped. "You got nothin' to be proud of. You bastards were on a killin' spree for months, but we finally caught up to you. Thought you could keep on runnin' from the law."

"Been runnin' from the law my whole life," the boy said proudly.

"Well, it's the end of the road for you," Tom growled. "Don't know what happened your brother, Joe, but—"

"A squaw bitch killed him. I tried to go after her, but she stole our horses. If I could'a caught up to her, I woulda flogged her good! But I shot her. I know I hit her too 'cause I heard her scream when she was hit."

Matt looked up. "You had an Indian woman with you?"

Tom spoke up. "We were trackin' these bastards with other lawmen around the state, even up into New York. They started out raiding the

Allegany Reservation. Killed some of the natives, took women captives, started makin' their way south."

A chill descended over Matt as he stared at the boy's dirty face. "Captives?"

Stephen raised defiant eyes, and Matt saw something in them that confirmed his suspicion.

"We don't know what ever happened to the women," Tom was saying. "There was nobody else with this kid when we caught him."

Stephen lifted his chin, an evil light glowing in his eyes. "That squaw bitch I shot prob'ly died. I hope she died. She killed my brother."

A murderous force was growing in Matt's chest. A bemused expression came over Stephen's face, as though he wondered how the doctor knew, and why it meant anything to him. With a good measure of pride in his tone, Stephan raised his chin and said, "We both had our turn on her. She fought us at first, then kinda seemed like she enjoyed it."

Matt steadied himself against the table, struggling with a bloodthirsty rage that was consuming him. He took a deep breath and closed his eyes, trying to control a strong impulse to seize his dullest scalpel and cut this boy's throat. His mind's eye tortured him with images of this filthy criminal molesting Degan, ignoring her injuries, ignoring her screams.

"Matt? You all right?" the deputy asked.

In a level tone, he said, "Tom, why don't you go out to the office and get yourself a cup of coffee? This won't take long."

"Are you sure?"

"He's in shackles, he's not going anywhere," Matt said, meeting the boy's cold stare.

The deputy shook a finger in the boy's face. "I'm right in the next room, so don't you try anything. I don't need much reason to shoot you dead."

Stephen silently watched the deputy leave the room before turning back to Matt, who suddenly clamped a hand over his wounded arm, and another tight around his neck. A strangled cry erupted from the boy, his face contorted in agony. Wild fury blazed in Matt's eyes as he pulled Stephen's face close to his.

"You son of a bitch!" he hissed. "I don't know whether to cut your goddamn dick off or slit your throat!"

"Let go'a my arm!" Stephen croaked.

Matt slammed the boy down onto the table. "You'll be begging for your life before I'm done with you!"

Stephen twisted in Matt's grip, his thrashing feet kicking the tray of instruments that crashed loudly to the floor. Suddenly from nowhere, his right hand flew up and the blade of a knife touched the side of Matt's face.

"Let go'a me!" Stephen grunted.

Stunned, Matt slowly released his grip on the boy's throat and arm. Raising his hands, he took a step back.

"Matt, you—what the hell—?" Tom bellowed from the doorway.

When Matt looked up, it happened swiftly. With no time to react, he saw the light glinting off the silver blade as it plunged forcefully into the left side of his chest. His knees buckled and with a strained "Ahhh goddammit!" through clenched teeth, he doubled over the examining table. In one quick motion, Stephen gave Matt a push, wrenching the bloodied knife from his chest. He jumped off the table and stumbled toward the back door.

Tom's pistol cracked loudly in the small treatment room, the bullet hitting the boy in the back and penetrating his heart. He fell against the door jamb and dropped to the floor.

The deputy ran to kneel beside Matt who had collapsed under the examining table, bright red blood soaking the front of his blue shirt.

Grasping Tom's collar, he said, "Dr. Bowman . . . upstairs."

Without a word, Tom raced to the second floor living quarters, and pounded wildly on the first closed door he came to.

"Dr. Bowman! Dr. Bowman!" He soon heard footsteps approaching from the other side.

The door was barely ajar before the deputy sputtered, "Come downstairs now! Matt's been stabbed!"

"What? What happened? I heard a shot—"

"The Collins boy we brought in stabbed him in the chest," Tom threw over his shoulder as he careened down the back stairs to the treatment room, Dr. Bowman following close behind. "The son of a bitch stabbed him!"

"Good Lord!" Dr. Bowman said when he saw Matt on the floor in a growing pool of blood. "Help me get him on the table."

The doctor ripped Matt's shirt from his chest while directing Tom to retrieve clean linen towels from the cupboard and apply the material to the wound.

"Hold that in place and put some pressure there," Dr. Bowman said. "Not too much! There, that's it."

"Jesus, what the hell was I thinking," Tom scolded himself miserably, "leaving Matt alone with this—"

"How the hell did he get his hands on a knife?" Dr. Bowman asked.

"I checked him myself, I must'a missed it. The son of a bitch had it in his pocket all along, just waitin' for a chance to use it."

"Look at me, Matthew," Dr. Bowman commanded, watching Matt's face closely for signs of shock. "Don't close your eyes, stay with us."

He nodded in response. "How bad?"

"Doesn't look good at the moment," Dr. Bowman replied, unwinding a length of bandage. He was reluctant to offer more of the bleak prognosis, but both doctors knew that if the blade punctured his lung or got too near his heart, Matt would not survive. "We're trying to get the bleeding stopped." Dr. Bowman addressed Tom. "Ease up some for a moment so I can see." Tom obeyed, tentatively lifting the linen towel from Matt's chest. Blood continued to seep from the wound.

"Damn it," Tom whispered, not waiting for direction from Dr. Bowman to replace the blood-soaked towel with a clean one. "If he dies it's my fault."

"Stay with us, Matthew," Dr. Bowman commanded in a firm voice, noticing Matt's face and lips growing more pale. "Fight the urge to close your eyes. You've got to stay with us."

Matt opened his eyes and murmured, "I . . . need to talk to Jon."

Dr. Bowman frowned and looked at him askance. "What?"

"I need to talk to Jon."

"Jon? Jon Monroe you mean?"

He nodded.

With no time to ask for explanation, Dr. Bowman looked at the deputy. "Once we get him upstairs, ride out to the Monroe farm and get Jon."

Within the hour, Jon burst through the front door of the small office and took the stairs two at a time before pounding on the door to Dr. Bowman's quarters. Once inside, the doctor led him down the hallway to the sparsely furnished bedroom that served as an infirmary.

"Tom told me what happened," Jon said as the two approached the open bedroom door. "How bad is it?"

"If he makes it to morning, I think he'll be all right," Dr. Bowman said with a heavy sigh. Jon could not remember ever seeing him look so distressed. "I'm hoping he lives through the night."

"My God," Jon breathed wretchedly, his mind fighting against the frightening implications of the doctor's words.

"He said he needed to talk with you," the doctor said, looking as though he expected an explanation from Jon, who offered none.

Jon approached the bed where Matt lay with eyes closed, his hands folded across his waist. Several yards of white linen bandage wrapped his left shoulder and bare chest, a sliver of red soaking through where the blade had punctured his body. A faded quilt covered him to the waist. He appeared to be sleeping, but when Jon came closer to sit carefully on the bed, Matt opened his eyes. He struggled to speak through a heavy dose of laudanum. Jon waited without saying a word, knowing what his request would be.

Finally, he breathed, "Degan."

"You want me to bring her here? Into town?"

Matt nodded.

"All right," he whispered to his friend, and rose from the bed. Turning to the doctor, he said simply, "I'll be back shortly," and was gone.

A dim shaft of lamp light shone through the front windows of the cabin as Jon rode up. Barely waiting for his horse to come to a halt at the porch, he dismounted and leapt across the steps to pound on the door.

"Degan, it's Jon!" his voice was louder and more panicked than he intended. When the door opened, he wasted no time. "Matt's been hurt. It's bad. He's askin' for you. I have to get you into town."

Taking a step back as though she had been shoved, Degan stared wide-eyed at Jon as shock washed over her.

Jon brushed past her into the cabin. Without thinking, he crossed the room to the stove and extinguished the low flame that was keeping supper warm.

"What . . . what happened?" she finally managed, turning toward him as if in a trance.

"I have to get you into town!" he said forcefully.

She appeared paralyzed.

Jon approached her and grasped her shoulder firmly. "Degan, Matt's been hurt bad and he's askin' for you. He needs you."

"I will go," she heard herself say, the words coming from nowhere, and yet from everywhere inside her.

He grabbed her shawl hanging on a hook beside the door, handed it to her, then took her arm and led her out the door.

The brief ride to town was a numbing blur for Degan, scarcely allowing her time to realize what was happening. Until now, she could never have imagined traveling to Sylvan, much less sitting behind Jon atop his horse and on her way at a full gallop. She only knew that Matt had been hurt, apparently badly enough to render him unable to come home. The look on Jon's pallid face and the urgency in his tone added to her growing sense of dread.

As they reached the edge of town, Jon slowed his horse to a trot, and made his way through the back alleys toward the medical office. He turned to offer Degan his hand as she dismounted, then he followed, quickly tethering his horse to the railing at the rear of the building.

When Jon opened the back door to the treatment room, Degan gasped at the body of Stephen Collins still lying just inside. Terrified, she stood frozen in place, unable to look away.

"This . . . is one of the men who . . . hurt me," she said, pointing to the body.

"Well, he's dead now. He can't hurt anybody ever again." Jon said, taking her hand and pulling her inside past the body. "They brought him in tonight for treatment, and the son of a bitch stabbed Matt in the chest. Dr. Bowman was here and took care of him right away, but it's a bad wound."

Degan said nothing as she followed Jon up the stairs to the second floor, but she thought she would collapse from the weight of what she had just heard. Matt had been stabbed in the chest. Her heart was pounding, and the blood drained from her face as an odd, cold tingling slithered down her arms. Trying to remember to breathe as she followed Jon, she watched him open the bedroom door, then saw an older man bent over Matt who lay bandaged and pale in the bed.

She rushed to Matt's side, nearly oblivious to Dr. Bowman, who stepped back and abruptly turned to Jon.

"Who is this?" he demanded.

Jon put a hand on Dr. Bowman's arm and pulled him to the side. "Matt asked me to bring her here. It's a long story."

Degan sat on the edge of the bed and took Matt's hand, pressing it to her cheek. Fearful eyes swept his upper body, taking in the bandage wrapped across his bare chest. Swipes of blood had dried on the side of his neck. His eyes opened slightly, and upon seeing her, he tried to smile.

"Jon told me what happened," she said. "Do you feel pain?"

He shook his head slowly. "Laudanum."

She gently kissed the back of his hand. "I will not leave you."

In a raspy voice, and with difficulty forming words, Matt began to speak. "Dr. Bowman says . . . I might not live through the night."

She closed her eyes tightly, his words bringing unbearable agony. "No. Please, please!" she whispered, tears spilling down her cheeks.

"Listen to me," he pleaded, "I want you to know . . . if I do live through this? I'm going to marry you."

Now the sobs that had been building in her chest broke free and she began to cry, rocking back and forth, pressing his hand to her wet face.

With his other hand, he reached for her, touching her hair momentarily before his arm dropped back to the bed. "Not the way I . . . wanted to ask you," he murmured, "but if I don't wake up . . . I want you to know . . . what my intentions were. Understand?"

She nodded, opening her eyes. She put a hand to his face, and stroked his cheek, feeling the whiskers at his jaw line and the warmth of his neck. "I am already your wife," she said softly, then watched him close his eyes peacefully.

"Matt?" she called in a panicked cry.

"He's just asleep. It's the laudanum," came an unfamiliar voice from the other side of the bed. Startled, she turned to see Dr. Bowman hovering over them, with Jon at his side.

"Degan, this is Dr. Bowman. He and Matt work together here in Sylvan," Jon told her.

"The old shaman," she whispered.

Not hearing her comment, Dr. Bowman said, "Jon explained your situation to me. If you're a friend of Matt's, you're welcome here."

"Will he live?" she asked bluntly, wiping her wet face with her sleeve.

"I certainly hope so," he said. When he realized she was waiting for more information, he bent to indicate the small bloodstain on the bandage at the left side of Matt's chest. "This is where the knife went in. I'm hoping that the blade missed his lung, and didn't do any major damage to the arteries near his heart. I don't know how deeply into his chest the blade went. But he hasn't been coughing, and his breathing hasn't been labored, which are good signs that his lung is intact. There's been no bleeding from his mouth, or elsewhere other than the wound site. He's a strong man, and in good health. The longer he goes without coughing or showing any other signs of distress, the better his chances."

Degan hung on each word as Dr. Bowman described his patient's prognosis. Though she did not understand some of what he said, she found this older shaman's knowledgeable demeanor comforting, and was grateful that Matt was in experienced hands.

"I've done everything I can. We'll just have to wait it out now," Dr. Bowman told her earnestly, offering his handkerchief. "Do you understand?"

She bobbed her head once in response, then turned back to watch Matt as he slept, drying her tears with the doctor's handkerchief. She dabbed a corner of the material against her tongue, and tenderly wiped the smudges of dried blood from Matt's neck.

Dr. Bowman turned to Jon. "We have a long night ahead of us."

CHAPTER

17

As if Matt's very survival depended solely upon her unwavering vigil, Degan spent the night at his side, never closing her eyes. He barely moved throughout the endless hours, his drug-induced sleep heavy and quiet. For long periods, she sat watching him breathe, and finally lost count of how many times she put her ear to his chest to hear his heart still beating.

In a chair on the other side of the bed, Jon's watchful concern, along with his occasional soft snoring when he dozed, kept her company. Dr. Bowman had stayed with them until after three o'clock before retreating to his own bedroom just across the hall, insisting that if Matt stirred, he should be notified immediately.

Wanting nothing more than to climb into bed with Matt and stroke his hair and his handsome face, she longed to take away his pain. She longed to take his hand and lead him gently back from the threshold of the spirit world. She would have much preferred to take the knife in her own chest rather than sit here helplessly while Matt hovered between life and death. Daring not even to consider the possibility of his death, she quickly pushed that thought aside each time it surfaced to threaten her sanity. As she had done so many times over the last several hours, she begged the Creator to spare him, not to take him from her, then buried her face in her hands and cried as silently as possible so as not to awaken either Matt or Jon.

At five-thirty, the first pale light of morning began to seep through the curtains at the windows. Gradually, the sounds of the town awakening in the street below, foreign to Degan's ears, wafted upward to the second-story bedroom. After a very dark eternity, morning had finally come, and Matt was still breathing, his heart still beating. Degan remained at his side in the chair she had occupied all night, and waited for Dr. Bowman.

Presently, Jon shifted in his seat across from her and sat up, seeming a little disoriented. Then he looked across the bed and their eyes met.

"I fell asleep," he murmured apologetically, looking apprehensively at Matt. "How is he?"

"He is alive," she said simply.

"I'll get Dr. Bowman," he said, and left the room.

In a few moments, the doctor came in wearing the same clothes as the night before. Degan sensed that he had not slept much. He gave her a cursory nod. "Let's see how our patient is doing."

As he approached, Degan stood up and stepped back from the bed. Dr. Bowman leaned down to press his stethoscope carefully against Matt's chest in numerous places. As he listened, a tense silence descended over them as Degan and Jon waited for his report.

"We've got a good strong heartbeat," he finally announced, looking hopeful for the first time.

Jon let out a loud sigh of relief, and glanced at a distraught Degan who stood with her hands clamped over her mouth. He went to her, putting his arm around her shoulders.

"Matthew," Dr. Bowman said in a firm voice, placing the stethoscope back on the table. "Matthew, can you hear me? Open your eyes, son, if you can hear me."

His head moved almost imperceptibly, then a little more. He took an audible breath and sighed, "Degan?"

Dr. Bowman stepped back as Degan rushed to the bedside. "I am here," she said. Taking his hand, she reached to stroke his cheek.

Slowly, his eyes opened and he looked up at her. He smiled more like himself this time, and squeezed her hand. Relief and gratitude flooded her, and she bent to briefly touch her lips to his face.

"How do you feel?" Dr. Bowman asked. "Any difficulty breathing?"

"Don't think so," Matt murmured. "Wound site burns some."

"Any notable weakness in your arms or legs?"

"Just . . . coming out of the laudanum," he said, his voice still thick from sleep.

"Do you feel feverish at all?" the doctor asked, touching a hand to Matt's forehead, and to the side of his face.

"No," Matt answered. The doctor bent to listen again to his heart, pressing the stethoscope to his chest and abdomen.

"Your color looks better," Dr. Bowman observed, looking relieved. "Your heart and lungs sound good, but I don't want you moving around for a while."

Suddenly, a pounding on the front door of the office downstairs caught their attention.

"I'll see who that is," Jon offered, and quickly left the room.

Dr. Bowman turned back to Matt. "You lie still. I'll go fetch some coffee. It's been a hellish-long night for all of us." He then looked pointedly at Degan and gave her firm instructions. "You keep an eye on him, and make sure he stays put. No moving around. I'll be back shortly."

She nodded solemnly, then turned back to Matt who had a look of concern on his face. "You look tired," he said slowly. "Did you sleep at all?"

"No. All night I watched you breathe and listened to your heart . . ." her voice broke and she put a hand to her mouth.

He reached to caress her cheek. "I think I'll be all right now." Then astonished realization dawned. "You came into town for me."

She nodded.

"You must have been so afraid."

"You needed me."

He smiled. "I remember what I said last night, and I meant it. It's my intention to marry you."

She returned his smile with misty eyes. "In my people, I am already your wife."

He brought her hand to his mouth, and breathed against her skin. The sounds of Jon's footsteps up the stairs grew louder as he returned to the bedroom.

"That was Sheriff Wilkes. He was asking about you."

"The Collins boy . . . what happened?" Matt asked.

"After he stabbed you, he tried to run out the back door, and Tom shot him. The undertaker picked up the body early this morning," Jon said.

Matt turned to Degan. "The boy who stabbed me was one of the men who captured you."

"I saw him last night," she said. "They are both dead now."

"Yes, they're both dead. They can't hurt you or anyone else ever again."

"This is good," she said, visibly relieved. "When will you be better to come home?"

"As soon as I'm able to get on my feet," Matt told her, placing a hand under his back, trying to sit up.

"No!" Degan quickly put a hand against his shoulder. "The old shaman says not to move."

"My back is aching from lying in one position all night," Matt complained, grimacing with the effort of raising himself. "I want to sit up."

"No, be still," she said. "The old shaman says not to move. You must be careful."

"I don't think just sitting up will hurt me."

"No, be still! Maybe your heart is not strong enough."

"There's nothing wrong with my heart. The knife . . . missed my heart or I'd be dead by now," he insisted, struggling to sit up before collapsing back on the bed.

"No, Matt, do as the old shaman says."

Jon's soft chuckling drew Matt's attention. "What are you laughing at?"

"The two of you, bickerin' like old married folks."

Matt looked up at Degan whose expression had softened.

Dr. Bowman returned carrying a tray laden with a coffee pot and four cups, which he placed on a small table at the side of the room.

"You should know, Miss, that doctors make the worst patients," he told Degan, a trace of teasing in his voice. He had obviously heard their exchange coming down the hallway. "I just want you to know what you're getting into. During his recovery, Matt will be stubborn as a mule, and he won't want to listen to anybody."

Matt pleaded his case. "I want to sit up, my back is killing me."

"We'll fluff up the pillows a little," Dr. Bowman conceded, "but I want you to be still and lie flat for at least forty-eight hours. You're very lucky to be alive, but you have a serious wound and you need to rest."

Matt sighed heavily in defeat, while Degan repositioned the pillows behind him.

Throughout the morning, the news of the attack on the doctor spread quickly from house to house, business to business. By lunchtime, nearly every citizen in Sylvan had heard the details of Matt's close brush with death the night before. Jon took a permanent position in the downstairs medical office, delivering frequent updates on the popular patient's condition to those who stopped by inquiring of his welfare. Some asked to see him personally, but their requests were gently denied, his need for rest offered as the reason.

By mid-afternoon, when Dr. Bowman was satisfied that Matt's condition had stabilized, he set out to make brief house calls to other patients. Before leaving, he waved a finger sternly in Matt's direction.

"No getting out of that bed." Then, turning to Degan, he said, "I'm putting you in charge of him until I return. You take a firm hand if you need to." With a pat on her shoulder, he was gone.

Degan turned to Matt and smiled. "He cares for you."

"He saved my life," Matt said.

"I saw blood on the floor when I came last night."

"It's a good thing he was here. I might have bled to death."

Degan closed her eyes tightly, for a moment reliving the long hours of suffocating dread that had encased her as she waited for morning.

"They hurt and killed so many," she said.

Matt took her hand again. "Why don't you lie down beside me and get some rest?"

She considered his suggestion, then carefully climbed atop the quilt, and rested her head on the pillow beside him. Turning toward him, she took his warm hand in hers, and for the first time in many agonizing hours, felt secure and relaxed. Before drifting into sleep, she silently thanked the Creator for hearing her cries the night before, and for not taking him from her.

When the town had fallen quiet again that evening, Jon returned Degan to the cabin after she had received Dr. Bowman's assurance that Matt would continue to improve, and would likely be well enough to come home the following day. Noting her expression of concern, Matt added his own assertion that he was feeling stronger, and would surely be back at the cabin by suppertime the next evening. Besides, he said, he was worried about her, and wanted her to get a good night's rest. With that, as well as Dr. Bowman's promise to check on Matt within the next few days, Degan reluctantly agreed to go home.

Shortly after sunset, with his patient resting quietly in the second-floor infirmary, Dr. Bowman set about tidying the downstairs treatment room from the activity of the night before. The tattered remnant of Matt's bloodied shirt still lay where he had tossed it. The linen towels the deputy had used to stop the blood flow were still on the examining table and the floor.

The events of the past twenty-four hours seemed unreal, and Dr. Bowman was just now beginning to realize how close he had come to losing Matt. But as shocking as the attack had been, the revelation that his apprentice had, for months, been harboring an Indian woman in his home was even more astonishing, and still difficult to believe. Jon had briefly explained their history and their arrangement, and there was certainly no mistaking the depth of feeling and connection they shared. Their bond was obvious from the moment Degan entered the infirmary. Dr. Bowman understood from experience that her presence could well have contributed to Matt's very survival.

Still, overhearing Matt's proposal of marriage to this squaw was very troubling, and Dr. Bowman felt a compelling responsibility to counsel Matt against any permanent attachment to such a mismatched companion.

Matt is too skilled a physician to compromise his career by taking as his wife someone so far removed from his station. His next thought, and of greater concern, was Matt's mother, Kathleen. He hoped fervently that no one in Matt's family, particularly Kathleen, was aware of this ill-advised liaison. Dr. Bowman had developed a strong feeling of protectiveness toward Adam Tyler's widow. The thought of Kathleen's reaction to the news that she would be expected to embrace an Indian squaw as her daughter-in-law made him cringe. The further thought that she might even hold him responsible if he failed to intervene was unbearable. He resolved to speak to Matt at his earliest opportunity.

A knock at the office door interrupted his thoughts. He answered to find Emma standing on the stoop. On her arm was a sizeable basket laden with dishes of home-cooked food.

"Come in, Emma," Dr. Bowman said, taking the basket from her, and marveling that a small woman could carry such weight for any distance. "Whatever you've got in here smells mighty good!"

Emma pushed the hood of her dark woolen cloak from her head, nudging light wisps of blond hair out of place. "I was here earlier today, but Jon refused to let me see Matt. So I thought I'd make supper for you gentlemen," she announced proudly. "Roast chicken with all the fixins' and a blueberry cobbler for dessert."

"That's very kind of you," Dr. Bowman said enthusiastically.

"I've been just sick with worry all day," she said. "If I promise not to stay long, do you think it might be all right if I visited with him?"

"Well, I don't see the harm," Dr. Bowman amiably. "He's feeling better this evening. Perhaps a brief visit would be all right."

Emma stepped closer to the doctor and favored him with her sweetest smile. "Thank you, Dr. Bowman."

Without waiting for a proper escort from her agreeable host, and without delay lest he change his mind, Emma swept past him and up the back stairs. On the second floor, she noticed that the door to the infirmary was ajar. Giving it a push, she saw Matt lying in the bed with eyes closed and one arm propped behind his head.

She quickly took in the sight of her former suitor, weakened and vulnerable, and decided that this was indeed a providential turn of events. As she approached the bed, it occurred to her that the present circumstances afforded her the opportunity to assert her rare upper hand, and she was not about to squander her good fortune.

CHAPTER

18

"Oh, Matt!" Emma cried, rushing to the bed.

Startled, Matt instinctively pulled the quilt higher over his chest.

"Emma," he said uneasily, "I didn't hear you come up the steps."

"I brought you some supper," she said, removing her gloves and unfastening the clasp of her cloak. "I heard what happened. How are you feeling?"

"Better, thank you," he replied stiffly.

Leaning over him, she reached to touch the bloodstained bandage. "Poor thing," she murmured, then stroked the side of his face. He shrank back involuntarily. She positioned herself on the edge of the bed. "I've been just sick with worry. As soon as I heard what happened, I ran over here, but Jon turned me away and wouldn't allow me to see you. He can be so rude at times!"

Her solicitous manner felt artificial and Matt's guard went up. He knew her too well to believe her primary concern was for his well-being.

"Now I insist that when Dr. Bowman releases you, you must come over to the hotel and let me take care of you," Emma demanded, running her hands up and down his arms. "No sense you going back to that cabin all by yourself with no one to look after you."

Matt shook his head. Even if he still lived alone, the thought of confinement at the Miller Hotel under Emma's care filled him with dread. "That won't be necessary, Emma—"

"Now, Matt, after all you've done for Mama and me, please let us help you. You know I'll take good care of you," she purred, gazing at him seductively.

"I think by tomorrow morning, Matt will be feeling like himself again," Dr. Bowman said from the doorway.

Emma turned abruptly, visibly irritated at the interruption. Flustered, she turned back to Matt as Dr. Bowman approached the bed.

"I'll be checking on Matt every day until he returns to work. You don't need to worry yourself."

Grateful for his colleague's well-timed rescue, Matt reinforced the point before Emma could argue. "He's right. I'm feeling better this evening, and—"

"And after he enjoys that delicious supper you brought, he'll be good as new, I'm sure," Dr. Bowman put a hand under Emma's elbow and eased her to standing. "Now why don't you come downstairs and help me prepare Matt's supper tray. We don't want everything to get cold after you worked so hard fixing it."

Matt breathed a sigh of relief as Dr. Bowman led a sputtering and outnumbered Emma from the room.

Two hours later, Dr. Bowman pressed his stethoscope against Matt's upper body. Emma had reluctantly left earlier, taking with her the basket of empty dishes and a petulant attitude, as her plan to take in the injured Matt had failed.

Nodding his satisfaction, Dr. Bowman straightened. "Well, Matthew, if you promise me you'll stay in bed and rest the next few days, I think you can return home tomorrow."

"Good. I'll be glad to get home."

Dr. Bowman frowned thoughtfully, easing into the chair beside the bed. He looked as if he had something to say but was unsure how to say it. Leaning forward to rest an elbow on each knee, he pressed his fingertips together before his gray whiskers. Matt had seen this gesture enough times to know that he was pondering a distressing subject.

"You're troubled about Degan, aren't you?"

Dr. Bowman took a deep breath and exhaled heavily. "You know I've always had your best interests at heart—"

"I think I know what you're going to say. That I'm going to have a difficult time bringing her into white society, and that I should be courting a white woman."

"Who you court is your concern, of course. But I must tell you that a permanent liaison with this Indian woman will effectively ruin your career."

His mentor's blunt assessment took Matt by surprise. Until now, he had not allowed himself to consider how his union with Degan might affect his future as a physician. Now that the risk had been voiced, he wondered if Dr. Bowman's prediction might be true.

"Have you thought about this?"

Matt studied his hands folded at his waist. "I always thought when people learned of her, they might be disapproving at first, but they'd eventually come to accept her. Just as everyone here accepted me when I arrived."

"I think you're being naïve, Matthew," Dr. Bowman said. "This is a very different situation. Degan is . . . from another world entirely. And with the Indian wars and all the killings going on out West, people are bound to look at her as the enemy."

"But she has nothing to do with that!"

"It doesn't matter. She's one of them . . . a hostile. People won't see any further than that. She'll never be accepted, and you'll be ostracized as well. Think of your poor mother, Matthew."

"What's my mother got to do with this?"

"She's all alone in the world now that your father is gone. She'll be looking to you for support, more than anyone else. Think of how she'd feel about you marrying an Indian squaw. For God's sake, Matthew, I'd hate to think of what that would do to her, especially now in her fragile state."

Matt almost laughed. His mother was many things, but she was not fragile.

"You're turning your back on everything you once held dear," Dr. Bowman continued. "Your vocation, your family—"

"I won't walk away from Degan. I can't."

"Matthew—"

"I can't! I love her too much. In my mind, she's already my wife. All that's missing is the ceremony and the piece of paper. Once I'm back on my feet, we'll have that as well. I'm tired of living with this secret. I want to live with her openly, as my legitimate wife."

"It's good that you finally want to do the honorable thing and make her your wife after living in sin for so many months, but—"

"I came very close to dying last night. It's made me realize what's important to me. It's Degan I want."

"More than being a physician? More than healing people?"

Matt hesitated. "I believe I can have both."

The doctor recognized Matt's determined tone as a harbinger of an arduous battle ahead, and he decided not to press the point for now.

"All right, let's put this aside for tonight. It's late. You need to get some sleep."

"How can I sleep now?"

"I'll give you something." At the apothecary cabinet, the doctor uncapped a dark brown bottle and poured a small amount of laudanum into a glass. "What's your pleasure? Brandy? Whiskey?" His attempt to lighten the mood fell on disgruntled ears.

"Brandy," Matt growled.

Dr. Bowman returned to the bedside and handed him the glass. Matt hastily threw back the shot. Slamming the empty glass on the nightstand, he closed his eyes and waited for the medicine to take effect. Settling more comfortably between the sheets, he began to feel the soothing warmth of the liquor flow down his arms and legs. Already feeling closer to sleep, he sighed. "She's everything I could ask for in a wife. I've loved her for a long time. I can't imagine my life without her."

"I understand how you feel, Matthew," Dr. Bowman said. "It's just too bad she isn't white."

"I don't care about that," he whispered, drifting further from his surroundings. He wanted to assert that none of the conventional standards of white society really mattered to him, had never mattered to him. He knew that now. At his core, he had always rejected the strict elitism and intolerance he had seen so often in his parents' world. His father had been able to bridge the two worlds quite well—serving the underprivileged and less fortunate, while navigating the exclusive circles of Washington society. But regardless of his parents' station, Matt had never felt at home in the upper classes.

The brandy and the sedative had taken hold, and his mind was shutting down. Without opening his eyes, Matt took another deep, cleansing breath and smiled to himself. "She is beautiful, don't you think?"

The doctor did not respond as Matt floated into slumber.

The following evening Matt returned to the cabin. Knowing he would be unable to care for his horse for a few days, he had asked the proprietor of the livery stable in Sylvan to keep his mount a while longer.

"We'll take good care of him, Dr. Tyler, don't you worry about a thing," Benjamin Nichols promised his loyal customer. "After what happened, you shouldn't be lifting that saddle or tending to the stable. We'll be glad to look after him for a few days, till you're back to your old self. I'll have one of my boys give you a ride home."

He was barely in the front door before a jubilant and thankful Degan urged him into bed to rest while she prepared a light supper, which she served him at the bedside.

"You are feeling good tonight?" she asked apprehensively.

"Yes, I'm going to be fine." He took her hand as she sat down on the edge of the bed.

"You are troubled about something," she ventured with a frown of concern.

Matt smiled. "What could possibly be troubling me, now that I'm back home with you?"

She looked at him askance, as if she sensed he was keeping something from her, but she said nothing more.

Early the next morning, a knock sounded at the cabin door. Matt had alerted Degan that Dr. Bowman would likely be visiting early, as was his habit when checking on patients following initial treatment. When she opened the door, the doctor bowed politely.

"Good morning," he said, touching the brim of his hat.

"Good morning," she replied softly, stepping back to allow him entry.

"How is our patient this morning? Did he have a restful night?"

"Yes. He is still sleeping."

"Ah, well, I don't want to waken him just yet. He needs his rest. If I may, Degan, I'd like to have a talk with you."

Removing his coat and hat, the doctor settled on the sofa. The fire felt good after the chilly ride from town. Degan sat at the opposite end, watching his face expectantly as he cleared his throat and gathered his thoughts.

"Degan, I've known Matthew's family for many years, even before he was born. In fact," a bit of pride squared his shoulders, "you might be interested to know that Matthew's father and I served together in the

Mexican War at Buena Vista. We served under the command of General Zachary Taylor. Have you heard of him?" Degan shook her head, and the doctor deflated a little. "No, of course you haven't. Well, as I was saying, I've known Matthew since he was a boy. He's been like a son to me. I've always wanted what's best for him."

He paused to stroke his gray whiskers, searching Degan's face. She waited silently for him to continue.

"Matthew is a very gifted physician, as was his father. And like his father, Matthew has always derived great satisfaction from helping people, from healing people."

"He has told me many stories about his work. He has great love for his people. This I understand."

"And they love him. That's why when I overheard Matthew proposing marriage to you the other night, I was very troubled indeed. Degan, the whites will never accept you as Matthew's wife."

She frowned. "What does this mean?"

The doctor took a deep breath. "It means that the whites will not approve of the marriage, and will reject Matthew . . . push him away . . . because of you."

"Because I am not white."

"Yes. You see, people feel strongly that whites should marry whites, and Indians should marry Indians, and so on. Each with his own kind. Why, even the Bible warns against marrying outside your own kind. Are you familiar with the Bible?"

"This is the book the whites say the Creator gave to them. My people have no book. The Creator gives this book only to his white children."

"Yes, well, white people live their lives by what the Bible says, and it warns against such intermarrying. If you and Matthew were to marry, the white people would be so angry that they would no longer allow Matthew to heal them. And that would be a great loss because Matthew was born to heal. Do you see why this can never happen?"

Degan's expression changed and she sat back, the import of his meaning taking hold. He waited silently, allowing his words to penetrate, as they seemed to be having the intended effect.

When she looked up again, her eyes were full of sadness. "The Creator has chosen Matt to heal. I believe this is true. But if the whites learn that I am his wife, he will no longer be allowed to heal them. They will push him away. This is what you believe?"

"Yes, I do," the doctor said.

"His people want him to marry a white woman. Maybe Emma?"

"You know about Emma?"

"Yes, Matt told me about her."

"They were together for a while last year. I know she still cares for him. In fact, she came to see him in the infirmary last night." *Matt taking Emma as his wife would be little improvement over an Indian squaw, but at least she's white, and Kathleen need never know of her family's unsavory background.* The doctor briefly wondered why Matt always seemed drawn to inappropriate women so far beneath his station. "Emma would be a much better wife for Matthew, you must understand that."

Degan bowed her head and soon Dr. Bowman saw a tear splash onto her hands in her lap. His voice was softer now, as a father's telling a child she can no longer play with a beloved toy. "We must think of what's best for Matthew. It would be better for him if this union between you came to an end and you return to your people—"

"What the hell are you doing?" Matt's voice startled both Degan and Dr. Bowman, and they looked up to see him standing in the bedroom doorway.

"I—"

"What the hell are you doing?" he repeated, coming to sit across from them. Yards of linen bandage still bound his bare chest. His face was pale, but anger and the sting of betrayal burned brightly in his eyes as he waited for an answer.

"I came out to check on you this morning. When I arrived, you were still sleeping. I was just having a talk with Degan—"

"I heard your talk," Matt said. "I heard you telling her that I should marry Emma because she's white. I wouldn't marry Emma no matter what color she was!"

Degan rose quickly from the sofa and went to sit on the arm of Matt's chair. Her worried expression and gentle hand on his arm seemed to defuse his rage.

"Forgive me, Matthew, I know I'm overstepping my bounds here, but I had to say something. A decision of this magnitude affects so many other people. I've seen the satisfaction your practice brings you, the rapport you have with your patients. People trust you, and think highly of you. Think about your family, especially your dear mother, and the effect this union would have on her. You're choosing to throw away everything that's important to you for this . . . woman!"

"That's the way you see it," Matt said, taking Degan's hand and pressing it to his chest. "But you're wrong. For God's sake, I'm not the first white man to take an Indian wife! People might be disapproving at first, but they'll get used to the idea."

"Gentlemen from fine families such as yours do not take Indian savages as their wives. That happens out West on the prairie where there are no decent white women. Men from your lineage served in Congress, and signed the Declaration of Independence. I dare say, some of your ancestors were likely murdered by this woman's people!"

"I love Degan too much to allow your prejudices to influence me. Perhaps you lack the courage to pursue what would make you happy and fulfilled, but I don't. And I won't allow the narrow-minded bigotry of other people to stand in the way of what I want."

The doctor sighed. Matt's jaw was set as he waited for a reply, and Degan's face was unreadable. The room shouldered a heavy silence and Dr. Bowman could think of nothing more to say to support his case. His attempts to protect Kathleen from unendurable shame had failed. His only hope now was that his conversation with Degan might influence her against this unthinkable plan of Matt's. If she really cared for Matt, she would remove herself from his life and return to her own people where she belonged.

Finally, the doctor spoke quietly. "I did come to examine you this morning."

"That won't be necessary," Matt replied flatly. The request to leave was unspoken, but nonetheless clear.

"Well, it looks as though I've said enough for one day." The doctor stood, retrieving his coat, hat, and medical bag, "I'm sorry to have caused distress by expressing my opinions, but I wouldn't have been able to live with myself otherwise. Matt, you've been like a son to me. I want nothing more than your happiness. Degan, you seem civilized enough. I hope you'll think about what I've said."

With that, he walked unaccompanied to the door and left.

Her eyes filled with profound sadness, Degan turned to Matt, who still had her hand pressed tightly against his chest.

"Don't listen to him. He's getting senile in his old age."

"He is right," she whispered.

"Degan, I know what I want. Do you love me?"

"Yes, I do love you," she said without hesitation. "But the old shaman is wise—"

"Why would you so readily take to heart what he says?"

"He is old and wise. Like the elders who sit at the council fires, his eyes have seen his people for many years. He knows the people. He knows what is the right thing to do."

"But you said that when the elders make a wrong decision, the women oppose it. You're not opposing him?"

"Only the clan mothers, who are also old and wise, can say no to the laws of the council fires."

Matt put a hand to his eyes in frustration. Of course, he realized, Dr. Bowman's words would carry significant weight with Degan. As was the custom of her people, an elder's view of a situation and how it should be resolved would not be questioned by a younger person.

"In my people I am already your wife," she said. "But I can never be your wife in the white world. I can be your wife only here in this place, where we are apart from the people."

"That's not what I want. I want you to be my wife in every aspect of my life. I don't want to hide you anymore. I don't want to live in secret anymore."

"I can never be your wife in the white world."

She spoke softly and he could hear the resignation in her voice. Her words fell hard on his heart. It became clear to him that he, too, was caught between two worlds, just as she was. While he was willing to take the risk of accompanying her into white society, he couldn't force that transition on her. He struggled with the fear that Degan might never be willing to step beyond the safe border of their current arrangement.

"Your people want you to take a white woman as your wife. Like Emma."

"But that's not what I want," he said quietly. "I want to marry you. And I want you to be my wife everywhere, not just in this cabin."

"I cannot be the cause of your people turning against you. The old shaman is right. The Creator has chosen you to heal. If you can no longer heal because I am your wife, then I cannot be your wife."

Matt sighed heavily, and leaned his head against the back of the chair.

"You are pale," Degan said, standing. "You must rest."

Despite a determined effort to resume their normal life together, the dark cloud of Dr. Bowman's words hung over Matt and Degan like a sinister apparition that had moved into the cabin with them. Their unspoken agreement not to talk further about the issue held for a few days.

October brought the first snap of cold on the evening air. Hours spent on the back porch after supper had gradually shortened as the weather cooled.

"I heard some interesting news today," Matt began with a smile one evening. As Degan sat beside him on the top step of the porch, she realized it had been a long time since she'd last seen him smile. The sun was drifting lower through the trees, and she pulled a blanket more snuggly around her shoulders. "I told you about the new church that was built a few weeks ago? A new minister, Reverend Baines, just moved here with his family. I heard today that the Reverend's daughter is sweet on Jon."

Pleased by this news, she was eager to hear more. "What does Jon think of this?"

"Well, you know Jon. He's embarrassed by the attention, but I think he's pretty happy about it."

"You know this woman?"

"Not very well. I met her and her family briefly the other day. Her name is Anne. She's got red hair and blue eyes—"

"Her hair is red?" she asked, wide-eyed.

"Yes. Have you ever seen someone with red hair?"

She shook her head, unable to picture in her mind's eye a woman with red hair. "She is beautiful?"

Matt shrugged. "She's pretty. I wouldn't call her beautiful. But what matters is what Jon thinks, and I think he's smitten."

"Smitten . . . ?" she repeated the unfamiliar word.

"He wants to court her," Matt translated.

As comprehension sparked, Degan looked relieved. "This is good. I hope she is kind to him."

They sat in silence for a few minutes before Degan spoke again. "How does the white man court his woman?"

Matt pondered her question. He had never before tried to explain the delicate process of courtship between a man and a woman.

"In my people, when we are still very young, the mothers say who will marry," Degan said. "Then when the time is right, the man brings fresh game he has killed to the woman's family, and the woman brings cornbread or cakes that she made to his mother. This is to show that each can provide for the other, and they will not know hunger in the marriage."

Matt waited for her to continue before realizing she was finished. "That's it?" he asked, astounded by the simplicity of the process.

She nodded. "Then they are together, husband and wife."

Matt chuckled. "It's not that easy with the whites. We've made it pretty complicated. Jon will have to let Anne know that he's interested in courting her. He'll do that by going to her father and asking permission to court her. If Reverend Baines thinks Jon is a good prospect for his daughter, he'll agree. Then Jon will probably approach Anne in church, and maybe ask to sit next to her during a service. If that goes well, then he might ask to call on the Baines family in the evening and visit with everyone in the parlor. This goes on for a few months. Jon and Anne won't be spending any time alone together until much later."

Degan listened with fascination. "It is a long time!"

"In white society, courting moves very slowly. But some couples don't wait until they're married to . . . know each other . . . physically, as we do. They only go through the courting ritual out of respect for their families."

"And to marry is a joyful thing for the whites?"

"Yes, the two families are usually happy that their children are getting married, and will be starting a family of their own."

"You did not . . . court me like this. This is because I am not white?"

"Our situation was different from the start," he said, reaching to take her hand. "When you first came to live with me, I . . . fell in love with you early on."

"When?"

"The day I bought the clothes for you. We were sitting by the fire that night, and you were telling me that the white man treats his woman like a dog. I wanted so much to convince you . . . to show you that not all white men are like that. You looked so beautiful sitting there in the firelight. I knew then that I never wanted you to leave."

She smiled. "In my people, we are already married. You take care of me, and I take care of you."

"In the eyes of the whites, we're living in sin because we haven't been married by a minister of a church."

"This troubles you? That you have not courted me and married me according to your people?"

"I do want to marry you, but not because of what my people think. I don't want to live in secret anymore." He chose his next words carefully. "It's only a matter of time before someone rides out here from town and discovers you. If you were my lawful wife, I think people would eventually accept us."

She looked uneasy and her eyes drifted downward. "The old shaman says no."

"I know he does, and you believe him. But he's wrong."

"He cares for you. He protects you."

"He does care for me. But it's my mother he's trying to protect. He knows she wouldn't approve of me marrying you."

"I cannot be the cause of your people turning against you." The familiar sadness washed over her and her eyes welled with tears. "But I would be a good wife to you."

"I know you would," he whispered. "You already have been."

She quickly wiped her eyes with her sleeve and attempted a smile. "I hope Jon is happy with Anne. He will start courting her soon because it takes a long time. Maybe they will marry some day."

"Maybe we will marry some day," Matt said quietly.

"We can live here as we have been. Only Jon and the old shaman know about me, no one else."

"This secrecy can't last much longer. And I don't want to live like that anymore. I want to take you into town. I want to take you to Washington to meet my family."

"No! I cannot be your wife in the white world. I can only be your wife here, where it is just us."

"That's not enough anymore," he said firmly.

"The old shaman is wise. He knows the ways of the whites, and he knows the gift of healing the Creator has given you. When you were near death, the Creator saved you because you are special. In my people, when one is called to walk a path, they must walk that path. They never choose a different path. The Creator has shown you the path of shaman. I cannot be the cause of your people pushing you from this path."

He shook his head. "Degan, the night I was stabbed, I heard Dr. Bowman telling Jon that he wasn't sure I'd live till morning. When I heard him say those words—that I might die—something happened inside me.

I saw your face in my mind. How I felt and what I wanted became so clear to me. I knew that if I lived, I wanted to live openly with you as my wife."

"We cannot—"

"I know. That's not what you want." They sat in silence for a long moment before Matt spoke again. "So what do we do?"

Without looking up, she replied, "Maybe now I will go back to my people."

Hearing this monstrous suggestion given voice, he was too stunned to respond. Of all possible resolutions to their dilemma, the thought of losing her brought a sickening dread to his stomach. Finally, he managed, "Is that what you want?"

"Maybe it is the right thing."

He put two fingers under her chin, and lifted her face to look at him. "There's nothing right about it and you know it." He dropped his hand and turned away from her. "If you go back to your people, you'll remarry?" A cold chill pierced him and he did not want to know the answer.

"Yes," she said miserably.

He shook his head in disbelief. "How can you?" He turned to her, desperation and hurt in his eyes. "Degan, regardless of where you are, or who you're with, I will always consider you my wife. I could never be with someone else now, because it would feel as though I'm being unfaithful to you. Wouldn't you feel the same?"

"It is the way of the Seneca—"

"That's not what I asked!"

She answered in a barely audible whisper. "Yes, but . . . it is the way of the Seneca."

"Well, damn the Seneca!" he shouted, and did not apologize for startling her. "Damn the Seneca! And damn you!" In a burst of anger fueled by pain, he turned to grip her shoulders, and shook her. "How can you leave me? After all we've been to each other? Goddammit, how can you—?"

"I cannot stay here! The whites will hurt both of us if I stay with you!"

The space between them was tense, then just as quickly, Matt seemed to come to his senses. He relaxed his grip, a strange exhaustion descending over him. He realized there was no way to bridge their opposing views of the situation. Ever since Dr. Bowman's visit, she had been telling him she would not enter white society as his wife. He now realized her mind was made up, and there was nothing he could do about it.

He looked into her wide eyes that were filled with anguish, then turned away. "I told you from the beginning that when you were ready to go home, I would take you. I'll make the travel arrangements immediately."

"Maybe wait a few days?"

His gaze was fixed on the trees behind the cabin. The leaves, though more sparse each day, still boasted vibrant shades of red and yellow, with some of the burnt orange and brown leaves floating to join others on the ground when the breeze picked up strength.

His voice was flat and unemotional. "At the moment the Collins boy stabbed me, I didn't really feel anything. You would think that if the blade of a knife pierces your body, it would hurt. But that's the funny thing about the body. It has a protective feature to it . . . causes you to go numb when you need it most. Prevents you from feeling the intense pain until later." He turned to face her again, but his eyes were different now, looking through her, and far away. "That's where I am now. And I need to take you back immediately, while I'm still feeling numb. Before the pain sets in. Otherwise, I won't be able to let you go."

She wanted to reach out to him, touch his arms folded across his knees, touch his expressionless face. But something in his demeanor prevented her from doing so. She sensed an impenetrable wall had risen between them, a wall that was more formidable even than her fear of him in the beginning. She watched as he rose from the porch, and without looking at her, went inside.

Then she was alone with the weight of her decision that felt so heavy and black that she longed to cry, but could find no tears at this depth. She felt as though some mysterious, thieving force had descended over her, and stolen the air from her lungs, the very blood from her veins. She felt empty and cold, envious of the numbness he spoke of that allowed him to walk and speak and breathe.

CHAPTER

19

"Here, take these with you," he remembered Caroline saying months ago as he was preparing to return to Sylvan from Washington. She had handed him a pair of her own black traveling gloves. "When you take Degan back to her home, she can wear these on the train. They'll hide the fact that she's not married."

His sister's generous forethought had surprised him. An unmarried woman traveling with a man would draw unwanted attention, especially when it was clear she was not a blood relative. The hood of Degan's cloak would help obscure her face, but she had nothing to cover her hands. It was a small but important detail, and he was grateful Caroline had thought of it.

Now, Degan was back with the Seneca, and he sat alone on the train as it clacked and rumbled through the countryside. Acres of dormant farmland, abandoned until spring, passed his unseeing eyes. Bound for the town of Landers, he would take the stagecoach back to Sylvan, back to his cabin, back to his life without Degan. He pressed the small black gloves to his lips, closed his eyes, and felt a deep emptiness in his soul that he feared he would not survive.

During her last days with him, Matt had remained respectful to Degan, but distant, able to communicate only on the most superficial level. The easy, nurturing intimacy they had shared for so many months seemed to evaporate as soon as she made her decision to return to the reservation. Surprisingly, he found himself grateful that his heart and mind felt encased in ice.

He knew she keenly felt the chasm between them, and that she, too, was in pain. She had been withdrawn and seemed physically ill much of the time. Her emotions fluctuated from teary and raw one minute to stoic and reticent the next. A few times, he had discovered her crying in private, but made no effort to comfort her. As unfathomable as it seemed, she remained convinced that leaving him was the right thing to do.

Her decision to return to her people had produced a deep pain that was now seething under many layers of anger. He had remained too vulnerable for too long and in the end, it had brought him only emptiness and sorrow. Now a survival instinct had risen to defend him, and he could not reach beyond its formidable walls. Swirling about in his mind remained the unending, unanswered plea, how can you leave me? How can you leave me?

Two days ago, when the train had finally chugged to a halt at the Salamanca station, the white-gray sky was spitting a cold drizzle, and the morning fog had not yet lifted. As Matt offered his hand to assist Degan from the passenger car, he noticed they were two of only a handful of travelers who were disembarking hastily from the train to seek the warmth of the station. The world around them seemed oblivious to the fact that his life was ending at this moment, here on this platform. He felt like a sleepwalker, mechanically going through the proper motions, fearing at any moment his sanity would collapse, and he would tumble into a dark unknown from which he would never recover.

A smiling porter set Degan's bag at their feet, waiting unobtrusively as Matt extracted several coins from his pocket for the tip. Degan leaned to grasp the handles of the bag, tightening her grip against Matt's attempt to take it.

"Let me help you," he offered plaintively.

"No."

"I'll order a carriage."

"No, I will walk from here."

"Degan, it's cold and miserable, I don't want you walking. I'll order a carriage—"

"No, please," she said, her eyes filling with tears as she held up a hand, and began backing away from him toward the edge of the platform. She stopped, set the bag down, and removed the gloves. She stepped toward him, holding out the gloves, which he numbly took. "Thank you," she whispered.

Barely able to breathe for the weight of sadness in his chest, Matt could only manage, "Are you sure this is what you want?" When she did not answer, he said simply, "Take care of yourself." The words sounded trivial and ridiculously inadequate.

She turned and quickened her steps to the stairs that led to the street-level walkway. Matt stood motionless, watching as she made her way past the station and into the street. The cold air picked up the hem of her cloak, and she reached to grasp the sides of the hood to hold it in place around her head.

When Matt returned home the next evening, he saw Jon pacing across the front porch. He did not direct his mount to the cabin to greet his friend, but instead rode to the barn. A few moments later, the barn door creaked open. Matt looked up.

"How long have you been here?" he asked, unfastening the leather billets of the saddle.

"Not long," Jon answered. "I figured you'd be back by day's end."

Matt hoisted the heavy saddle from his horse's back, and swung it to the top railing of the stall. An awkward silence drifted between them before Matt spoke again.

"I appreciate you being here, Jon, but there's nothing you can do. She's gone back to her people, and that's the end of it."

Looking at the floor, Jon bobbed his head. "It's just a damn shame, that's all. I wish things coulda turned out different."

Matt made no reply, but continued the mindless routine of caring for his gelding by replenishing his water supply, and scooping fresh grain into his feed bin. As the horse munched contentedly, he removed the saddle blanket from the animal's back and began to stroke his coat with a brush.

"She wanted to remain hidden from white society," Matt said. "She was afraid people wouldn't accept her as my wife, and that I'd be rejected because of her. I don't want a wife I've got to keep secret. It was only one obstacle, but it was a big one. We couldn't resolve it."

Jon was nodding. "What will you do now?"

Matt shrugged. "Go back to the way things were before she came, I suppose. I don't know what else to do." He looked up from his task to meet Jon's stare. Neither said a word, but they both knew that nothing would ever be the same.

At well past midnight, Matt sat alone in the great room, warming himself in front of the hearth. Physically and emotionally, he was exhausted, but his mind would not quiet. His thoughts moved slowly backward, musing over the past year. Thankfully, a blessed numbness had descended over his soul, and he contemplated his life with the dispassionate view of a bystander. Degan's voice and laughter seemed to resonate all around him. He thought of her warm smile, her warm body, her dark, playful eyes. Those eyes in which he could see a reflection of himself and their life together, in which he found not just happiness, but contentment and peace.

By now, she had reunited with family members who had lived through the attack on her household. Undoubtedly, her sudden reappearance after so many months would stun the survivors, and he imagined a joyous reunion. He resolved to cling to the image of her gratefully rejoining her people and her familiar way of life after being away for so long. But loneliness quickly overpowered him like a deep, rushing tide that he was too tired to fight. Jon's question, "What will you do now?" echoed in his brain. Reluctantly, he dragged his thoughts from the past and attempted to formulate a future.

But that felt too dangerous. Any thinking or planning would compete with the numbness that was shielding him like a suit of armor, and he could not risk dispelling that protection.

From old habit, he rose to retrieve a cigar from the humidor on his desk, but decided he was not in the mood for a smoke. Smoking was a relaxing pastime he had enjoyed in the evenings when he and Degan sat before the fire talking of his day, her life before, the people and events that had shaped each of them. Tonight, a cigar would do little to soothe him.

He dropped the lid of the humidor and reached instead for the brandy snifter.

Her light tapping on the cabin's front door went unanswered, so Emma opened the door cautiously.

"Matt?" she called as she removed her riding gloves. The fire in the hearth had gone out, and the cabin had taken on a fierce chill, so she kept her heavy wrap draped around her shoulders.

When there was no answer, she crossed the room to tap on the bedroom door that was slightly ajar. Still no answer. She peeked around the door's edge to see that the empty bed was an unmade mess.

"He must be on the back porch," she murmured to herself, passing through the bedroom, and reaching for the latch to open the back door. A frosty gust swept across the porch to greet her before she stopped abruptly. She saw Matt slouched in one of the rockers, his eyes closed, a nearly empty bottle of brandy in his lap.

"Matt?" When he did not answer, she called his name again.

He stirred, straining to open blood-shot eyes, squinting against the gray afternoon light. He slowly put a hand to his brow and looked up with no expression. "What are you doing here Emma?" he croaked.

"I came to see if you're all right. I spoke with Jon and Dr. Bowman this morning. No one has seen you. I told them I'd ride out here to check on you. I thought something happened to you."

He closed his eyes again, his arm dropping back to his side. With a scowl, he turned his head away and slurred, "Nothing happened. Go back to town."

As she took in his condition, she became more alarmed. He looked as though he hadn't shaved in days, and his hair was in tangled disarray. He wore no coat or protection whatsoever against the late fall chill. His white shirt was deeply creased, as though he had slept in it for several nights. It draped loosely, unbuttoned and untucked from his pants.

She approached the rocker and knelt at his side, putting a hand on his arm. The smell of brandy and stale cigar smoke hung on him. "Matt, what happened? I've never seen you like this."

Keeping his head turned away, he muttered again, "Nothing happened. Get out. Go back to town."

Her mind racing to find a reason for such an uncharacteristic descent to this condition, she recalled his father's death a few months back. She had recently heard a rumor that Matt had been seen with a mysterious woman boarding the stage, but she swiftly pushed that unpleasant thought aside. She had been unable to ferret out any further information, as the two people who knew him best, Dr. Bowman and Jon, had remained tight-lipped at her questioning.

She reached to lift the brandy bottle from his hand, and suddenly his grip tightened. He turned his head abruptly to glare at her.

"You'd better be replacing that with a full one!" he growled.

Saying nothing, she held his stare, wrenched the bottle from his hand, and set it down with a thump on the porch.

"Are you trying to drink yourself to death?"

"That would be fine," he said miserably, putting his head down with a hand over his eyes. "Just leave me alone."

"Why don't you let me help you to bed so you can sleep it off?"

When he did not respond, she rose to stand in front of him with arms crossed, trying to determine how best to get him up. Taking a deep breath, she leaned forward and grasped Matt under each arm with the intention of hoisting him to standing.

He roused to put firm hands on her shoulders and glowered at her with stormy eyes full of pain.

"Emma, leave me the hell alone!" he roared, wincing at the sound of his own voice.

"I'm trying to help you!" she shrieked.

He grimaced again. "Please," he pleaded, "just go away and leave me alone."

"All right, I'll make a bargain with you," she began in a softer tone. "I'll leave you alone if you let me help you to bed so you can sleep this off."

He frowned as he weighed her proposition. "If I let you put me to bed, you'll leave?"

"Yes."

He considered her a moment longer before nodding his consent.

"Put your arms around me, and I'll help you up."

He brushed her hands away. "I don't need your help," he said, bracing himself on the arms of the rocker. He rose unsteadily to his feet, only to topple forward into Emma's arms, nearly knocking her over.

She struggled to remain upright, backing into the porch post to steady herself. "No, you don't need my help at all, I can see that," she spat.

With an arm around his waist, she led him back into the bedroom where he collapsed onto the bed, and promptly fell sound asleep. She stood over him for a moment, shaking her head in disgust before retreating to the great room.

She restarted the fire in the hearth, all the while silently berating Matt for allowing the original blaze to die. When the renewed flames caught fresh wood, she stood up, brushed her hands clean, and smoothed her skirt. She had a fleeting thought that the bedroom was undoubtedly as chilled, but she quickly decided not to bother with restarting that fire. *It's not my fault he let all the fires die out. Besides, if I restart the bedroom fire, I'll probably wake him.*

The matter dismissed, she removed her wrap and riding bonnet and went to the icebox to find something to eat.

The sun had set when Matt opened his eyes. He raised his head, immediately struck by the frostiness of the room. The throbbing pain that had cinched itself mercilessly from the base of his skull around to his eyes was nearly gone, but his body still ached. He rose from the tangled sheets to make his way unsteadily to the hearth, and bent to reignite the fire.

He allowed the warmth of the blaze to fill the room before removing his shirt and shuffling to the washstand. When he caught his image in the mirror, his reflection startled him. Red-rimmed eyes looked back vacantly. His haggard face was pale under several days' growth of beard, his hair disheveled from sleep. When he leaned forward to stroke his whiskers, his hand shook. Obviously, his days spent drinking were taking their toll, but at the moment, he could not think of a good reason to stop.

Lifting the porcelain pitcher, he poured water into the basin, trembling with the exertion. He reached for his shaving mug, soap, and brush.

"Matt?" Emma's voice called from the doorway before her footsteps rounded the partition. "What are you doing?"

He stood bracing himself against the washstand, trying to summon the motivation to continue. "I'm going to shave and get cleaned up," he said. "I thought you left."

"I decided to stay until you woke up. How do you feel?"

"I've had better days," he answered hoarsely.

She stepped closer. "Let me do that," she said, pulling the mug from his tenuous grip. Taking the shaving brush, she mixed the soap with water to create a foamy lather, then reached for a towel, and draped it over her shoulder. Matt stood silently, unresisting, as she smothered his whiskers with the foam, dabbing in soft, circular motions. When she picked up the blade and brought it to his face, he recoiled involuntarily.

"Try not to cut my throat."

The blade poised at his cheek, her voice dripped with feigned innocence. "Now why would I do a thing like that?"

He did not answer, thinking it best to remain as motionless as possible while she wielded the sharp razor at his face and neck. With no words exchanged between them, a skilled Emma methodically scraped away his beard with precise strokes. Matt considered that she had certainly done this before, and he vaguely wondered for whom.

She used the towel to clean the last swipes of lather from the edges of his smooth face and neck, then picked up his comb. Standing on tiptoe, she brought his hair back to a semblance of order. Suddenly, his tolerance for her nurturing gestures reached its limit. He took a step back, relieved her of the comb, and tossed it on the washstand.

"I'm afraid I'm not very good company, Emma," he said curtly, reaching for his dressing gown. "Thank you for your help."

Choosing to ignore his sour mood and icy dismissal, Emma summoned her sweetest smile. "You don't have to worry about that, Matt. I'm here to help you. Can I fix you something to eat?"

He shook his head. "I'm not hungry."

She stepped forward and put a hand on his arm, looking up at him with eyes that were seductive and alluring. Moving closer, she nuzzled against the base of his neck.

"Emma, what are you doing?" he whispered.

"I know how to make you feel better, honey, don't you remember?" she purred, bringing her hand up to lightly stroke his bare chest. He felt her lips gently touch his neck, her breath warm on his skin.

"I . . . I can't be with you, Emma, I'm sorry," he said, closing his eyes. Somewhere in his head, an alarm was going off, but he made no move to disengage himself from her embrace. In his mind, he could see only Degan's face, could hear only her voice, could yearn only for her hands and her mouth on his body. But the painful reality that she was gone pierced him deeply, and he had been left to navigate his anguish as best he could.

"Why not?" she murmured, her hand slipping down to the bare skin of his waist. "I know what you need. Where's the harm?"

He kept his eyes closed. Against his better judgment, he allowed himself to savor her touch, though it was distinctly different from what he had come to prefer. Every cell of his body cried out for Degan. Yet Emma was here and willing. Through the murky turmoil of his thoughts of Degan and her leaving, he chose not to stop Emma from her course. Her question, "where's the harm?" echoed blasphemously in his head, and he found himself clinging to the hope that perhaps she could somehow repair the gaping hole in his heart.

"I know how to make you feel good," she was saying, unfastening his pants as deftly as she had shaved him moments before. She looked up at him with a grim hunger in her eyes, her jaw set. "Whatever is troubling you, take it out on me."

He felt his pants loosening around his hips, then felt Emma's warm hand inside, touching him, arousing him easily. His own body betraying him, he moaned aloud, clutching her tighter to him. With little success, he tried to push aside the fact that while her touch felt good, it was depressingly empty of any real affection.

Instinctively, his hands reached to remove several hairpins that held her chignon in place, then coaxed her long blond hair to its full length down her back. His fingers found the buttons at her collar, and he opened them quickly without meeting her eyes. More brusquely than he intended, he pulled her blouse open, stripped it from her shoulders, and threw it on the floor. Not bothering to unfasten the corset at her waist, he pushed the straps of her chemise down her arms, baring her breasts, which he groped roughly with both hands, then his mouth.

"Yes, yes! Take it out on me!" she commanded breathlessly, pressing her hand against the back of his neck.

A glimmer of reason surfaced through his foggy mind. He stood upright to search her face for any signs of uncertainty or unwillingness. But her expression suddenly clouded with anger, her brow furrowed, her teeth clenched.

"Don't stop!" she hissed, reaching to unfasten the waistband of her skirt.

He made quick work of the hooks under her breasts that held her corset in place, then tossed the stiff instrument to the floor. Without looking up, he grasped the delicate lace at the top of her chemise and ripped it from her body in one loud tear. He slipped his hands beneath the ribboned waist of her pantalets and yanked powerfully, the shredded garment dropping to her feet.

Throughout the process of callously stripping her naked, he could barely recognize himself, and somewhere in the back of his mind, a revulsion against his actions was festering. But a distant memory surfaced to remind him that rough treatment had always aroused her, and she was not protesting.

Her damaged clothes in a heap, he looked up at her with fiery eyes. He took her face in his hands and kissed her mouth ferociously, then pressed her against him, his hand across her bare buttocks. With his other hand, he grabbed a breast, and pushed its peak upward to meet his mouth.

He took one erect nipple between his teeth, sucking hard until she cried out in pain.

Catching her breath, she ordered, "Take me, now!"

In one motion, he picked her up bodily, her legs straddling his hips, and shoved her against the wall. With a violent thrust, he was inside her, pushing into her again and again with a power so reckless and fierce they both soon were grunting in unison from the exertion. Then unexpectedly, he slowed his pace and looked down at her. When their feverish eyes locked, he pulled out of her, then watched her face as he thrust back into her with such savage force that she flinched, but held his gaze. She raised her chin slightly, her eyes defiant, as if challenging him to overpower her, to break her if he thought he could. He slammed into her again with all his strength, again and again, watching her wince and gasp with each crushing jolt, sensing she was nearing her climax.

"Is this what you wanted?" he demanded through clenched teeth.

Struggling to take a breath before the next thrust knocked the air from her lungs, she could not find her voice.

"Is this what you wanted?" She could only hold his stare, her jaw tight, her fingers digging into his shoulders. "Answer me or I'll stop!" he roared hoarsely.

"Don't stop!" she managed feebly. "Let me finish, please!"

"Say it again!"

"Please!"

Then she cried out in shuddering release, her body stiffening in the culmination of her passion. She did not breathe for what seemed an eternity, then gasping and clinging to him like a helpless rag doll, her face slowly began to relax. Her eyes closed and her head dropped against his chest. He gripped her chin and tilted her head up.

"Is that what you wanted?" he whispered.

She nodded weakly, looking exhausted, as he gently wiped the sheen of perspiration from her forehead. He eased her back to standing, supporting her for a moment until she was steady on her feet. He reached to lift and refasten his pants. Without looking back, he made his way to the bed and flopped onto the sheets, worn out and miserable.

In the dim light of pre-dawn, Matt turned on his side to see a slumbering Emma lying on her stomach, her face partially obscured by the wrinkled sheets. His eyes were immediately drawn to several tender-looking abrasions across her upper back, which he realized she must have sustained when he was thrusting into her against the wall. He reached to brush aside a tendril of blond hair to look more closely at the marks. Taking care to ease quietly out of bed, he went to the apothecary cabinet in the great room for a pot of salve.

She was still sleeping soundly when he returned. He dipped his fingertips into the salve and touched it gently to the red scrapes on her back, feeling very guilty for being responsible for the wounds. It was not his habit to forcefully strip a woman naked, then cruelly shove himself into her like a rutting animal. The more details he recalled from the night before, the more embarrassed he became. The memory of her demanding this behavior of him did little to assuage his discomfort. He remembered stopping at one point, looking into her eyes to search for apprehension or distress. Instead of anxiety or even the soft burning of desire, he had seen fury and frustration that her passion had been interrupted. So he had abandoned himself to the primal urges of the moment.

The salve applied, he replaced the lid on the metal pot and set it on the nightstand. He lay back to stare at the ceiling. Now more awake, he was beginning to realize that the implications of what he had done were reaching like tentacles to defile the sanctity of his union with Degan. Whether or not Degan was still part of his life, she would always own his heart, and he had allowed his desperate suffering to drive him to compromise his commitment to her. Considering that by now she had surely married a Seneca man and resumed her life did not diminish his mounting guilt and disgust at his own behavior.

He turned to watch Emma as she slept peacefully on Degan's side of the bed, feeling as though he had willingly thrown himself into a bottomless pit. It seemed a lifetime ago that Emma's pretty face had been the object of his fantasies, and her affections eagerly anticipated. Though she lay next to him now, warm and naked, he never felt so alone in his life. Instead of filling a deep and hungry void in his soul, their encounter left him feeling more hollow than before. There had been no emotional connection between them whatsoever, only her violent, physical release.

He closed his eyes, and as always, saw Degan's face clearly, as if she were standing next to their bed. His only hope, he thought miserably, was that with time, her face would fade from his mind's eye, and he might eventually be able to find some measure of comfort in another's embrace. But this prospect was neither consoling, nor even believable.

When he awoke again some two hours later, Emma was gone.

At mid-afternoon, Matt secured his mount in front of the Miller Hotel. Near the edge of town, the two-story clapboard building always looked forlorn and in disrepair. No one in town could fathom how the enterprise stayed in business.

A stunned Charlotte looked up from her ledger at the front desk to see the doctor approaching, removing his hat.

"Matt!"

"Good afternoon, Charlotte."

"I haven't seen you in a while," she said, unable to hide a look of concern at his haggard appearance. "Are you feeling all right?"

"Yes, I'm fine," he lied. "I've come to see Emma, is she here?"

Charlotte's eyes brightened. "I'll fetch her for you."

"Thank you," he said, as she scurried through the dining room, into the kitchen.

Emma appeared quickly, an odd expression, almost anticipation, on her face. Without saying a word, she motioned for him to follow her to a private seating area in the nearly vacant dining room. A handful of stragglers from the lunch crowd sat finishing their coffee on the opposite side. Matt pulled out a chair for her to sit, then settled across from her at the small table. He cleared his throat, finding it difficult to meet her eyes.

"I . . . I don't know how to say what I've come to say," he began awkwardly.

Emma smiled sweetly and reached across the table to take his hand. "It's all right, Matt, take your time. I know what you're going to ask me, and we're both going to be very happy when I answer."

Confused as to her meaning, he continued. "I . . . I owe you an apology. For my behavior at the cabin yesterday evening."

Emma's smile faded.

"I'm afraid I haven't been myself lately, but that's no excuse for my actions. I certainly never meant to hurt you." He looked up. "How is your back?"

"My back?" she asked tersely. "You came to ask me about my back?"

"I came to apologize." His words seemed to be irritating her, and he did not know why. "I don't blame you for being angry with me, and I don't expect you to forgive me anytime soon. But I want you to know how very sorry I am for what happened."

Her face quickly hardened. "Matt, you can save your apology," she said, sitting up straight and squaring her shoulders. "And I don't need your pity. I thought you were going to ask me to . . ."

Suddenly, comprehension took hold. "You thought . . . ? I . . . I wasn't—"

"Well, it doesn't matter," she said with a lift of her chin. "Seems you haven't heard that Zebulon Baines has asked me to marry him."

"The minister's son?" His wide eyes gave away his astonishment before he could manage a more courteous reaction.

Indignant, Emma snapped, "Yes, the minister's son! He's been courting me for a while. He asked for my hand in marriage last week. If you hadn't been hiding out at your cabin getting drunk, you'd have known. The news is all over town."

"I'm sure it is," he muttered sardonically.

With a tense smile and patronizing tone, Emma said, "You waited too long, Matt."

"I beg your pardon?"

"How long did you think I'd wait for you to ask for my hand? I can't wait forever. You could have had a good wife in me, but you didn't treasure me the way Zebulon does. You were fool enough to throw everything away. Zebulon has promised to take care of me, and Mama as well. We'll have a good life together."

Unable to believe what he was hearing, Matt leaned forward to stare at her. "Does Zebulon know that you seek out intimate relations with other men behind the back of your betrothed?"

Emma's face flushed to her hairline. Matt couldn't tell if the cause was rage or shame. "I came to your cabin yesterday because I was worried. When I saw you, I felt sorry for you. I tried to comfort you, but obviously, you didn't appreciate me. You never did. But I've put all of that behind me, and I'm marrying someone who does appreciate me."

Matt gripped the edges of the table in frustration. Emma would never change. He closed his eyes and decided he did not have the stamina to continue this discussion.

"I'm sorry if you're upset," Emma said in a quiet voice, "but my mind is made up."

She had misinterpreted his reaction, innocently or deliberately, Matt could not tell. When he opened his eyes, the inscrutable expression had returned to her face. He rose from the table, put his hat back on, and politely touched the brim.

"I wish you all the happiness you deserve," he said, and turned to leave.

Dr. Duncan, please accept my humble gratitude, sir, for your kind letter of three weeks ago, Matt wrote in his response. A letter to his mother would follow his return correspondence to the hospital administrator, informing her and the family of his plans. *You and Dr. Williams have bestowed a great compliment upon me with your request that I reconsider my decision regarding employment on the medical staff of Hamilton General.*

Though I could never hope to fill the void left by my father's untimely passing, I would be most honored, sir, to gratefully accept your generous offer of employment at Hamilton General . . .

CHAPTER

20

The morning sun, unusually warm for late autumn, seemed to scorch Degan's body as she crumpled weakly into the grass. The mounds of earth in the garden, faded now from summer heat and lack of moisture, rose up in waves that echoed her churning stomach. She put her head in her hands. Recent experience had taught her that fighting the sickness was useless. When the next strong wave of nausea washed over her, she leaned over and vomited into the dry grass. Reaching quickly to the pocket of her skirt, she snatched a handkerchief and brought it to her mouth. Another wave of sickness flooded her and she vomited again.

When the queasiness passed, she sat up. She moved slowly to the shade of a nearby oak tree, and leaned back against the rough bark. Wrestling with the unrelenting fatigue that had plagued her for weeks, she closed her eyes. As always, the image of Matt's handsome face surfaced in her mind. Those gentle eyes that she loved, so filled with pain and misery because of her. She knew his face would remain with her until the day she died. Sadness rose from deep within her, its weight crushing her.

"Degan?" The sound of her sister's voice startled her. "Something is wrong?" Gowesan asked, concern on her face as she approached and knelt close. "You are so sad. You think again of the white shaman."

Degan could only nod, sadness and longing drowning words. "My husband," she finally said.

"You are not happy here with us."

"For a while, I wanted to come home," she said in a small voice. "But it is a mistake. He comes to me in my dreams. My home is with him. He is my husband and I have hurt him deeply. My heart is sick. My body is sick."

An understanding light shone suddenly in Gowesan's eyes and she reached to press her hands firmly against Degan's lower stomach. When their eyes locked, awareness rushed over her and she now understood the signs. "I must return to my husband."

When the thick stand of trees began to thin, Degan's expression changed.

"We are near the cabin," she said, turning excitedly to her father beside her on the small wagon seat. "It will be soon now."

He slowed the horse's pace. "You are sure?" For nearly a week, they had been traveling through the cold wilderness of northwestern Pennsylvania toward Matt's cabin.

"I am sure," she said.

Her father looked at her doubtfully, still concerned that their long journey had been for nothing. He hoped his daughter would not be disappointed. Her mood had improved considerably ever since she had made the decision, against his better judgment, to return to the white shaman's lodge. Fur traders passing through Salamanca on their way to nearby Buffalo had provided him instructions on how to get to Sylvan.

"You are sure this white man will want you still?" he had asked repeatedly.

She had been insistent. She knew now that leaving Matt had not been the right thing to do. Nearly every night, the Creator sent him to her in her dreams, and had given her his child. These were unmistakable signs. The Creator was showing her that Matt was her husband and she his wife, despite what the old shaman had said. She must now return to him and make amends.

"He will still want you to live with him among the whites," her father had told her.

"This I will do," she had replied, mustering every shred of courage she had.

Now, Degan moved to the edge of the seat as the wagon approached the cabin. The day was fading. If Matt was not here, she would start a fire in the great room hearth, as she had done so many times before, and wait for him to return from the town.

But as her father reined the horse to a stop at the porch post, something about the cabin looked different. Wrong. Cold tentacles of heartbreak began to grow and clutch at her heart. She dismounted from the wagon carefully, a protective hand over her rounding belly. The cabin looked dark, and when she climbed the steps and peered in the windows, she saw that it was completely empty.

She opened the door and went inside. The cabin was unoccupied. She gazed at the corner beside the cold hearth, imagining the small bed on which she had recovered, Matt tending to her injuries, saving her life. But there was nothing there. A heavy sadness descended on her with a weight that made her knees buckle. She collapsed slowly to the hard floorboards in front of the hearth.

Her father came to kneel beside her. "No one is here?"

"No," she said miserably.

"Where is he?"

"I don't know," she whispered. "He is gone from this place." She covered her face with her hands and cried.

PART II

December 1867, Washington

CHAPTER

21

Sophia Thornton's sparkling earrings caught the light from a hundred tiny candles illuminating the Christmas tree. The resplendent decorations, along with fresh pine boughs draping the mantel, gave the parlor of Tyler Mansion a warm, holiday glow.

"So you grew tired of seclusion in the country, Dr. Tyler?" she said, lifting a cup of eggnog to her lips. Her dark eyes looked up at him over the crystal rim. "What better time to return to family than at Christmas?"

Matt smiled politely. "When my apprenticeship ended, I needed a change. I'm looking forward to the challenges at the new hospital," he said, the well-rehearsed line sounding trite.

"I'm sure the citizens of little Sylvan will miss you," Ian Thornton said, smoothing his thick, gray mustache. "But their loss is our gain."

"You're very kind."

Though he had not been in the mood to entertain guests, Matt had to admit that Mr. and Mrs. Thornton were proving to be engaging conversationalists, just as his mother had predicted. Kathleen had planned a small dinner party two days before Christmas as a way to "bring some joy back into this house." Her own gloomy demeanor, combined with that of her son, had produced a dark cloud over the entire household which was still heavy with sorrow. Just days before the holiday, she decided that entertaining might be the remedy for her sadness and whatever was ailing her son. So she sent invitations to several hospital board members and their families. An "intimate holiday soiree," she had called it. Ian

Thornton, a recent addition to the hospital board, had also been invited, along with his wife, Sophia.

"I'm delighted that you've expressed an interest in our property in Georgetown," Mr. Thornton was saying. "Sophia has been impatient to relocate further from the city."

"I'm very grateful to you for agreeing to show me the property. If it meets my needs, I'd like to move in as soon after the holidays as possible. I hope that won't be an inconvenience."

"If you find the house to your liking, I'm sure we can arrange immediate possession." Mr. Thornton addressed his wife. "Perhaps we can include Dr. Tyler in our dinner party on Friday." He turned back to Matt. "That will give you an opportunity to view the property and meet your new neighbors at the same time."

"Darling, don't rush Dr. Tyler in his decision," Sophia Thornton gently admonished her husband.

"Friday would be fine," Matt said.

"Excellent," Ian replied.

When Matt arrived at the Thornton residence Friday evening, he could hear an array of laughter as he alighted from his carriage. Though he had known others would be there, he cringed and his heart sank. Even small crowds always made him uneasy. He dreaded the suffocating tedium of such social engagements, at which he was expected to make pointless small talk with strangers.

"Dr. Tyler, do come in," Ian Thornton said cordially when he answered the door. "We're so pleased you could join us this evening."

Matt swept off his hat and stepped into the foyer. "I appreciate your kind invitation."

As a matronly servant helped him off with his coat, the host waved a hand toward the parlor. "Come say hello to our other guests. This distinguished gentleman and his lovely wife are Mr. and Mrs. Hughes, our neighbors," Ian said as the pair nodded toward Matt.

"Good to meet you, Dr. Tyler," Mr. Hughes said, extending his hand. "And welcome back to Washington. I hear you've joined the staff at Hamilton General. Your father's presence is sorely missed, I dare say."

Any mention of his father's passing still brought a sense of the unreal, even now. But Matt smiled politely and took Mr. Hughes' hand.

"Thank you, sir."

Mrs. Hughes took a step forward. "Your mother and I are very good friends. We serve together on the Sanctuary Beautification Committee at the church. Perhaps she's mentioned me?"

Matt's thoughts raced to find any reference to this woman that may have stuck in his mind, but none surfaced. "Yes, I believe she has mentioned you," he lied. "It's very nice to finally meet you. Mother enjoys her church committee work immensely." *Two lies in a row, how I hate these tiresome engagements.*

An odd expression came over Mrs. Hughes' face. Her eyes suddenly took on a glint of purpose and something close to condescension. "I hope we will soon see *you* at church, Dr. Tyler. I'm sure you'd find many rewarding opportunities to serve. We do find it so fulfilling, doing the Lord's work."

Matt resisted the urge to tell her just what he thought of the frozen hypocrites who sat detached and critical in those hard wooden pews. And even worse, what he thought of the God they worshipped who allowed the insanity of war to rage out of control, destroying wholesale the lives of those he supposedly loved.

"I'll see if I can fit it into my schedule," he replied casually.

Just as Mrs. Hughes opened her mouth to respond, Ian hastily took Matt's arm and stepped toward another couple.

"This is Mr. Prindle and his wife. They are also neighbors of ours."

With his graying hair and thick mid-section, Mr. Prindle looked at least fifteen years older than his wife.

"Ian tells us you may be moving into the neighborhood, Dr. Tyler," Mr. Prindle said, extending his large hand.

"I'm considering it, yes," Matt said.

Sophia entered the parlor to announce that dinner was ready. As the guests slowly filtered into the adjoining dining room, she moved toward Matt and her husband. Auburn highlights in her dark hair caught the candlelight, a relaxed smile softened her face.

"Good evening, Dr. Tyler, I'm so glad you could join us this evening."

"It's my pleasure, thank you for having me."

"Darling, please show Dr. Tyler where he'll be sitting," Sophia told her husband, then turned back to Matt. "After dinner, Ian will take you on a tour of the house."

Once the dessert dishes had been cleared, the ladies settled in the parlor for coffee, while Ian offered Mr. Hughes and Mr. Prindle his best brandy and cigars in his study before excusing himself to join Matt in the foyer.

"Let's start on the second floor, shall we?" Ian said, approaching the stairs.

The house was not large, but the four bedrooms upstairs were spacious. The floorboards in the hallway creaked pleasantly under the carpets as they passed from room to room.

"I always envisioned this room as a small library," Ian said when they entered the fourth bedroom, "though I never found the time to make it so. The windows along that wall look out onto Sophia's flower gardens in back. Exquisite view, especially in the spring."

Matt took a few steps around the room and nodded his approval.

"I'll show you the kitchen," Ian said, leading the way downstairs.

The kitchen was much smaller than Daisy's workspace at Tyler Mansion, but Matt could picture a cook and a maid functioning comfortably in the area. He looked toward an open door at the rear of the kitchen.

"I see there's a sunroom?"

"Yes," Ian said. "It's really regrettable that you aren't seeing the house in daylight. That's one of the features of this house that Sophia will miss the most. She spends hours sitting in the sunroom reading and doing her needlepoint."

Matt imagined the room awash with light and warmth. He tried to shake off the pang of loneliness that had once again twisted its familiar ache around his soul.

"What do you think of the house?" Ian asked. "Is it to your liking?"

"Yes, very much so. It's not overly large, so I won't need to employ more than two or three servants. I like the fact that the house sits near the end of the street. It must be very quiet."

"Yes, it's a peaceful neighborhood. Your neighbors next door would be, of course, Mr. and Mrs. Hughes. And the neighbors across the street are Mr. and Mrs. Prindle. Good people. I'm pleased that you like the house."

"I'll be making an offer for the property," Matt said.

"Excellent! I think you'll be very happy with your decision."

"If I may ask, where will you and your wife be moving to?"

"I have my eye on a larger property just outside the city."

"But you will be living close by."

"Yes," he said, "we'll still be within a carriage ride of the city."

Early the next morning at Tyler Mansion, Kathleen was happier than anyone in the household had seen her in months. She was inspecting the breakfast items displayed atop the sideboard when Daisy entered the dining room carrying a platter of hot, crisp bacon.

"Daisy, your pancakes look light as air and delicious," she chirped.

"Thank you, Miss Kathleen," Daisy replied, pleased but puzzled. "It's nice to see you're in such a good mood this morning."

"Well, our dear Matthew spent last evening at the Thornton residence. I am hopeful that the Thorntons provided a suitable dinner companion for him. Someone whom he found interesting and engaging."

"Ah," Daisy said, smiling. "yes, that would be nice."

"It's time Matthew took a wife," Kathleen said firmly. "I knew he'd never find anyone suitable in that backward little hamlet in which he was living. He wasted too much time there. But now he's finally come home where he belongs, and I know it's only a matter of time before he—"

"Good morning, Mother. Daisy," Matt said as he entered the dining room. Both women stared at him in hushed anticipation. Mystified by their gaping, he slowed his pace as he made his way to the end of the table and eased slowly into his seat. Looking at each of them, he finally said, "I feel as though I'm about to give birth."

Kathleen tried to sound nonchalant. "Well, Darling, I was just telling Daisy that you spent last evening at the Thornton residence."

"I did," he said, casually draping his napkin across his lap. "Daisy, that bacon you're holding looks delicious. Is it your intention to serve it?"

Daisy snapped to attention and set the warm platter beside his plate, then went to the sideboard. She lifted the small chafing dish of pancakes from its flame, and placed it next to the mistress of the house.

"Is there anything you'd like to tell us about your evening?" Kathleen asked. "Please, don't keep us in suspense."

"We enjoyed a wonderful supper, then Ian Thornton showed me their house," he began, pausing to take a sip of hot coffee. "I intend to make him an offer for the property, and I hope to take possession in early January."

Ignoring this news, Kathleen pressed, "Was there anyone interesting among the dinner guests?"

"I met two couples who will be my neighbors," Matt replied. "By the way, I met a friend of yours from church. A Mrs. Hughes?"

"Oh, yes. Mrs. Hughes and I serve on the Sanctuary Beautification Committee at church," Kathleen said. "Did the Thorntons provide a dinner companion for you?"

"No, they did not," he replied, noticing that familiar spark of purpose in his mother's eyes. "Is that what you're so curious about?"

Kathleen was stunned and clearly disappointed. She shook her head. "Allowing a gentleman to sit by himself, unaccompanied, at a dinner party? The idea! I do not know what's happening to people's manners these days."

"Well, they did," Matt said, hoping the subject would be dropped. He longed for his father's presence at the table, realizing for the first time how often he had intervened to stem the onslaught of disapproval from Kathleen. In an attempt to redirect the discussion, he asked, "Where is Cara this morning? She won't be joining us for breakfast?"

Kathleen waved a hand dismissively. "Oh, she's gone down to that dreadful dispensary again. She goes there nearly every day now."

"Good for her. I'm glad to hear that," Matt said.

Kathleen huffed in disgust. "How can you say that? You don't know what that place is like. It's embarrassing."

"No, I don't know what the place is like, but I intend to find out today. Cara's been wanting me to come down ever since I moved back to the city."

"I don't understand her devotion to that place. It's bad enough that she feels she must work like a common servant, but then why in the world would she not pursue employment at the hospital your father worked so tirelessly to establish?"

"Mother," Matt said firmly and as respectfully as he could muster, "I would think you'd be supportive of the dispensary. It is, after all, affiliated with the church and Hamilton General as well. Father's hospital provides manpower and supplies—"

"I am well aware of how the dispensary is supported, Matthew," Kathleen snapped, "and I am in favor of the church running a dispensary for the underprivileged. I am not completely heartless. After all, those people are constantly ill with afflictions that you and I can only imagine."

"But you just don't want your daughter working with those people, is that it?"

Kathleen pursed her lips and squared her shoulders. "That filthy dispensary is certainly no place for a refined young lady such as Caroline. I can barely hold my head up in this community, knowing that everyone is aware of how Caroline has chosen to spend her days. And nights, for that matter."

"I believe she's following in Father's footsteps. I remember Father always having time for the underprivileged and those who could not afford to pay for private medical care. Cara feels a sense of purpose in doing the same."

A hard glint came into Kathleen's eyes that Matt had never seen before. All color drained from her face and she glared at her son. "Your father spent far too much time caring for the common masses of this city. Far too much time! And his attention was too often misinterpreted."

"What are you talking about?"

"That's all I intend to say on the matter."

Matt shook his head. His mother would never change. Apparently, it was acceptable for the poor and indigent to require medical care, as long as no one associated with Kathleen provided that care. She had always expressed similar outrage and embarrassment when the elder Dr. Tyler donated his time and expertise to the poor. During his childhood, Matt had overheard many arguments between his parents over his father's untiring dedication to the poor. He had grown up witnessing his father never turning anyone away, even if they were unable to pay for his services. Now, Caroline was following their father's model and Matt admired his sister for doing so.

He decided to change the subject. "What I really want to discuss is my employment of servants in my new home. How would you feel, Daisy, about me taking Sara with me when I move?"

Kathleen's back stiffened. "Sara is my employee, Matthew."

"Very well. I'd like to take Sara with me when I move. Have you any objections?"

His mother was silent for a moment, as though searching for her answer. Everyone in the household knew that she rarely troubled herself about who worked under Daisy. She simply wanted to be asked first.

"Well, I suppose it matters little to me one way or the other," she finally said. "I'll let Daisy make that decision, as she will be the one most affected by your choice."

"Fine! Daisy? How would you feel about me taking Sara? And please don't defer to Mother."

"You'd have a hard worker in Sara," Daisy said. "She learns quick and she's made good progress in the time she's been here. You'll have to hire a cook, though. Sara makes a good downstairs maid, but she's no cook."

"Is there anyone you could recommend?"

"I'll put the word out that you're looking. There are a couple of young ladies in other households that might be interested."

"I'll be generous with pay and time off. And I'm easy to please," he added with a grin.

"You won't have trouble finding someone," Daisy said. "The Tyler family is known for treating servants well. When will you be taking possession of the Thornton house?"

"As soon as they can vacate. They'll be moving to a larger property just outside the city. If all goes well, it shouldn't be more than a few weeks."

"Sara will be very happy that you asked for her, Matthew," Daisy said. "I'll let her know today to prepare to move."

"Thank you. And if there are any final instructions that she'll need before leaving your supervision, I trust you'll take care of that as well."

"Yes, of course."

CHAPTER

22

A forty-minute carriage ride from Tyler Mansion, the dispensary near the end of Alexander Street was smaller than Matt had imagined. The modest, red brick building sat back from the street, its entrance along an alleyway adjacent to an abandoned warehouse, several blocks from the busy merchant district. The location of the dispensary had a deserted feel to it, spawning in Matt renewed concern for Caroline's safety.

A middle-aged woman looked up from her work of alphabetizing patient files to greet Matt with a smile.

"Good morning, sir, may I assist you?"

Matt removed his hat. "Good morning. I'm here to see Caroline Tyler. I'm Matthew Tyler, her brother."

The woman's face brightened. "Oh, hello, Dr. Tyler. Caroline has told us about you. She said you might be visiting." Extending her hand into Matt's, the woman said, "I'm Mrs. Howell. I'll fetch her for you."

He watched the clerk disappear into the room beyond the reception area and quickly scanned his surroundings. A large wooden filing cabinet sat behind the small desk, and a dozen wooden chairs lined the walls. He noticed a young woman sitting along the back wall with a squirming little boy in her lap. The child was wrapped in a blanket, protectively holding his misshapen left arm. The woman met Matt's stare and something in her eyes told him to approach.

"If I may," he said, indicating the chair next to her with his hat. She nodded once and he sat down, pointing to the boy's obviously broken arm. "How long have you been waiting here?"

"'Bout an hour," she said. "Guess the doctor got called out on another emergency. I don't mind the wait but my boy here's in pain."

Matt leaned forward to address the child directly. "What's your name, son?"

The boy quickly buried his face in his mother's coat collar.

"It's all right. Tell the gentleman your name," his mother coaxed in a soft voice. Without looking up, the boy made a muffled sound into the thick fabric. The mother looked at Matt, her expression part amusement and part embarrassment. "He can't hear you if you're talking into my coat. Look at the gentleman and tell him your name."

The boy lifted his face and made tentative eye contact with Matt. "Caleb," he said barely above a whisper.

"Well Caleb, I'm going to see what I can do about getting you some help, all right?"

The boy nodded.

"Matty, I'm so glad you're here," Caroline's voice rang out. Matt turned to see her standing in the doorway behind him. He rose and motioned for her to join him in the next room.

"I was just speaking to this woman," he began in a low tone. "Her little boy has a broken arm and she tells me your doctor has been delayed."

"Yes, poor thing has been waiting for more than an hour," Caroline replied, her face full of compassion. "Dr. Wallace had another emergency and had to leave. I don't know when he'll get here."

"I don't mean to intrude into the operation of the dispensary, but . . ." He glanced toward the reception area, then back at Caroline. "I'd like to take a look at the boy myself. I can set the bone in a matter of minutes."

"Matty, that would be very kind of you."

"Show me your treatment room and supplies," he said.

Caroline quickly escorted him through the dispensary, settling in a large treatment room at the rear of the building. "All the supplies we have are here," she said, pulling out the drawers of a cabinet along one wall.

"I'll need chloroform and towels," Matt said, raising the blinds at each of three large windows. He removed his coat and tossed it over a chair, then began rolling up his sleeves. "I'll also need a small splint and a roll of bandages."

Caroline hurried to place all the supplies at one end of the examining table in the center of the room. She turned to Matt and suddenly noticed the long scar on his right forearm. "Oh! What happened to your arm? I haven't seen this scar before."

Matt looked down and attempted to brush off her concern. "Just an accident I had at the cabin a while back."

"It looks as though it was a very serious wound."

"I'm ready for Caleb," he said shortly.

"Of course, I'll bring them in."

Moments later, Caroline escorted the mother into the treatment room, the boy being pulled by his good arm behind her. His attempt at bravery on the edge of failure, his face was flushed and he looked ready to burst into tears.

"Mrs. Morris, please meet Dr. Tyler," Caroline said cordially. "Dr. Tyler, this is Mrs. Morris and her son Caleb."

"Mrs. Morris," Matt said with a slight bow. He then extended his hand to the boy, whose wide eyes came to rest on the scar on his arm. "Hello again, Caleb. I'm Dr. Matthew Tyler. I'm going to take care of that arm for you today."

The boy hesitated, then reached and allowed Matt to shake his hand.

"If you need anything, I'll be in the next room," Caroline said before turning to leave.

"Thank you," he said, then addressed Caleb. "I'm going to lift you onto this table. I promise I will be very careful not to touch your injured arm, all right? I know it hurts and I don't want to make it worse."

He grasped the boy under his arms and easily lifted him to sit on the examining table. The mother stood close by, a protective hand on her son's back.

"You know, Caleb, when I served as a doctor in the war, I helped many brave young men just like you," Matt told him as he reached for the towel and the chloroform, "soldiers who were hurt or had broken bones. Now I'm going to do for you what I did for them. I'm going to pour a little of this liquid into this towel and I'm going to ask you to breathe into the towel. You'll fall asleep, just like you do every night in your bed. And when you wake up, your arm will be fixed and you can go home."

"You mean my arm won't be broke no more?"

"It will still be broken, but the bone will be back in place and ready to start healing," Matt explained. "Your arm will be wrapped with a splint and bandaged in a sling for a few weeks, so the bone can heal. And you can show all your friends your injury and tell them how brave you were when the doctor treated you. How does that sound?"

"All right," he said tentatively.

"Are you ready to be a brave soldier for me?"

The boy looked to see his mother's reassuring smile, then back at Matt. "Yes, sir."

"Good man," Matt said, soaking a section of towel with chloroform. Supporting Caleb's head with one hand, he held the towel over his nose and mouth. "Just breathe deeply for me and relax, there's nothing to be afraid of, I've got you." Caleb complied and with minimal struggle, his eyes soon drifted shut as Matt slowly eased him down onto the table. He grasped the boy's wrist and elbow, then looked up at Mrs. Morris. "You may not want to watch this."

She turned toward the windows and closed her eyes while Matt made quick work of setting the bone. He grasped the wrist and forearm just below the elbow, then gently pulled with a slight twist, moving the broken ends back into place.

"Finished," he said. "You can look now." When she turned, he showed her Caleb's straightened arm.

"Thank you kindly, Dr. Tyler," she said. "I don't know how much longer we would have been waiting if you hadn't come by."

"I'm glad I could help," Matt said, wrapping the splint tightly to the boy's arm with a length of clean linen. He then wrapped the end of a bandage around Caleb's wrist and secured it within a sling knotted around his neck.

"How long will he sleep?"

"Not long. He'll have to rest for at least a few days so as not to risk further injury."

"Oh, asking a seven-year-old boy to rest?" Mrs. Morris said with a tease in her voice.

Matt smiled. "Not an easy task, I know."

By late afternoon, Matt had scarcely had a respite from a steady procession of patients in and out of the treatment room. No sooner would he clear the supplies and wipe down the instruments and the examining table from the previous patient, when Caroline would peek around the corner to announce that someone else had come in needing to be seen by a doctor. Most of the patients were children, but many were women, obviously poor and malnourished, who had come from miles away to be seen for free.

Dr. Wallace finally slipped in the back door just after six o'clock, offering his apologies for being gone so long, and gratefully acknowledged Matt's day of hard work. Matt had already met and worked with Dr. Wallace on several occasions at Hamilton General, but had not seen him around the hospital much of late.

"I don't know how you keep up with the work here," Matt told the doctor as he was placing unused bandages back in the cabinet. "Now I know why I rarely see you at the hospital. Is every day this busy?"

Dr. Wallace chuckled. "Most days are quite hectic. I've been the only doctor working here for a while. We could certainly use your help, Dr. Tyler, if you'd be willing to commit to a few hours a week. I know your administrative duties at the hospital keep you busy."

Matt contemplated his suggestion for a moment. "I did enjoy helping out today. The need is so great. I didn't realize until today how much I miss working directly with patients. I fear I'm not much of an administrator. I don't have that gift that my father had."

CHAPTER

23

When Matt heard the faint tapping of the brass knocker at his front door, he rose quickly from the table in the parlor.

"I'll get the door, Sara!" he called upon entering the foyer, and reached to open the door. "Good morning, Daisy, come in," he said warmly.

"Good morning, Matthew," Daisy said, stepping inside and carefully wiping her feet on the carpeted mat at the door.

"May I take your shawl?"

"Thank you. As warm as it is this morning, I could have left my shawl at home. It seems we've gone from winter straight to summer, with no spring. Where is Sara?" she asked, looking puzzled that the master of the house would be taking a guest's wrap at his own front door.

Matt looked around behind him. "I think she's in the kitchen with Chloe. I told them you were coming over this morning. They're probably making fresh coffee."

"Matthew, I shouldn't be using your front door," Daisy said, lowering her voice. "I know you told me to, but . . . it just isn't proper. What if someone sees me? It's better if I use the servants' entrance at the back of the house—"

"Daisy," he said firmly, "in my house, you will use the front door, just like any guest or family member. Let's have no more discussion on the matter." Ignoring her scowl of disapproval, he put a hand on her elbow and guided her toward the parlor.

"How is Miss Chloe working out for you?" Daisy asked. "The Jemisons said her cooking was excellent, except that she needed to work on her timing."

"She's fine. As you know, I don't do much entertaining, so there's really no need for her to have such an impeccable sense of timing. I just eat when it's ready," he said with a grin, knowing what her reaction would be.

"No wonder these girls like working for you," she said with exasperation. "You don't enforce any rules or exercise any discipline, then you pay them handsomely and give them an extra day off!"

Matt laughed. "I'm not quite that lenient. The other day, Chloe made a béarnaise sauce that I simply could not eat. I think she burned it or something."

"See? Timing!" Daisy sat down in the chair he had pulled out for her across from his place at the table.

"Anyway, I told her I was going to send her over to spend the afternoon with you to learn the finer points of making sauces."

"Of course, Matthew, I'll be happy to help you get your household running smoothly. I can see why you don't entertain. You don't have reliable help in the kitchen! And why on earth are you taking your breakfast here in the parlor instead of the dining room?"

"That was my idea," he said, settling across from her. "I like having breakfast here because this room faces the street and there's a view. There's no view in the dining room."

Sara scurried into the parlor with a basket of warm muffins and a pot of fresh coffee.

"Good morning, Miss Daisy," she said when she reached the table.

"Good morning, Sara. How are you?"

"Fine, thank you, ma'am," Sara said, arranging the items on the table, then turned to Matt. "Miss Chloe just took these muffins out of the oven, sir. She said to let them cool a bit before you eat them."

"Thank you, Sara."

The maid bobbed an awkward curtsy and hurried from the room.

Matt looked at a grinning Daisy, shook his head, and sighed with resignation. "Please, no more curtsies," he muttered. "Did you teach her that?" He reached for a muffin and grimaced when it burned his fingers.

"No, I did not. That is her own idea," she said, stifling a chuckle at his mild annoyance. She reached for the coffee pot and poured each of them a cup. "So who is the lucky servant who'll be in charge of this garden you want to plant?"

"I've asked Sara if she would want to take charge of it," he said. "But she knows nothing about what to plant or when to plant. That's why I asked for your help. Once we get things going, I can help with the upkeep."

"Taking care of a garden is hard work, Matthew. With your duties at the hospital, I'm surprised you want to take on a garden as well."

"I need a diversion. I enjoy my work with patients at the hospital, but the politics of running the place . . ." he said, frustration seeping into his tone. "I don't know how Father did it. Too often I'm pulled from the patients and brought in to settle disputes among the staff and the administration. I suppose they think that because Father was a skilled and diplomatic administrator, I will be also. But I have very little patience for the squabbling. Lately, Dr. Duncan has been taking over more of the administrative duties, as I've been spending more and more time at the dispensary. Gives me more opportunity to work directly with patients."

"I'm sure Miss Caroline and the others are glad to have your help."

"I enjoy the work, and I feel as though I'm making a difference. The patients are so appreciative. And knowing they have no other alternative for medical care when they're in need . . . it's very fulfilling. The days are long, but I don't want to be anywhere else."

"So you haven't found a young lady to—?" Daisy caught herself and quickly added, "I'm sorry, Matthew, that was a very prying question. Forgive me. I forget my place with you sometimes."

"Daisy, please don't apologize," he said. "Your place with me is very special, you know that. You've been like a mother to me my whole life."

She smiled warmly at him and felt again the ease of their relationship.

Matt looked up at her and grinned. "And I see what you're doing. You're trying to get me married off, aren't you?"

"Some would say it's time."

"They would, would they? And my guess is that Mother is at the head of the pack."

"We just want you to be happy, Matthew, that's all."

"I know," he said, his smile fading.

Daisy longed to know if he had met a woman or had his eye on someone to court, but she would not allow herself to ask. She couldn't imagine any suitable woman turning Matthew down if he asked to court her. And if he had not yet chosen a woman to court, she couldn't imagine why. It was a quandary that she and Kathleen had tried to solve on more than one occasion.

"If I may say, Matthew, you look tired."

"I haven't slept well in a very long time," he said, reflecting on the terrifying dream he'd had just the night before. The nightmares had returned ever since he first moved into the house and he could not remember the last time he had slept the whole night through. From Sara's alarmed expression at breakfast some mornings, he knew she must hear him yelling in his sleep during the night, just before jumping awake, drenched in sweat and breathing hard.

He suddenly rose from the table. "Come, I'll show you where I want the garden to be."

Morning sun bathed the back of the house and the lush grass still held its dewy moisture. Putting a hand up to shade her eyes, Daisy paced around the backyard for a few moments before coming to stand next to Matt.

"There's a bit of slope to the ground, which means you'll have more moisture at the far end of your plot," she explained. "That's good. You won't need to water as much down there, and your plants will grow better."

"Wait, let me get Sara," Matt said, striding toward the back door. "She needs to hear what you're explaining." Moments later, Sara emerged, wiping her hands on her long cobbler's apron.

"Sara, we'll plant sweet corn across the bottom of the plot where there'll be more moisture in the soil. Corn needs a lot of moisture. We'll plant potatoes in the middle, and the other vegetables along the far side. We can line the bean poles along that far edge—"

"If you plant beans next to the corn, the vines will climb the corn stalks," Matt interjected. "Then there's no need to put poles in the ground."

Daisy looked up, amazed. "Matthew, I thought you said you didn't know much about planting. That's an excellent idea." She turned to Sara. "We'll plant the beans and the corn together."

Cold dread wrapped itself around him like a heavy blanket as he approached the cabin, and he could hear her screams growing louder. He burst through the door to see three men surrounding the table, cheering on a fourth who was bent over Degan, her knees at his sides, her arms pinned by his filthy hands. In a blind fury, he tackled the man, but the other three quickly overpowered him, dragging him off to the side to watch in horror as her attacker continued his assault, thrusting hard into her as she screamed and struggled against him. She looked to the side and their eyes locked, her expression one of wild desperation, begging him to help her . . .

"Dr. Tyler! Wake up!"

Whose voice was that?

"Degan?" he called frantically, then abruptly sat up in bed. Breathing hard, he looked around, disoriented and panicked.

"Sir? It's me, Sara. You were having another nightmare." A dim circle of light glowed around the flame of a small lamp, illuminating Sara's face that showed concern mixed with confusion and fear.

His breathing fast and labored, Matt dragged a hand across his face and realized where he was. "I . . . I'm sorry I disturbed you. I'm all right. Please, go back to bed."

"Yes sir," she said. Lifting the lamp from the nightstand, she tiptoed out of the room and softly closed the door.

Matt reclined again, but was wide awake, reliving the sickening terror of the dream repeatedly in his mind, wondering if he would have to endure the torment of nightmares about Degan for the rest of his life.

CHAPTER

24

"Cara, you know how I feel about such matters—"

"No, Matty, I don't," Caroline said, filling the top drawer of the wooden cabinet in the treatment room with rolls of bandages. It was the late end of a long, tiring day and both had stayed to organize new supplies and clean the treatment room in preparation for the following day. Matt was sitting next to the cabinet handing his sister the bandages in order of size. "I must say, I'm surprised by your reaction to Rev. Peterson's offer. I thought you'd be as pleased as I am that the church is donating more money to the dispensary."

"I am glad they're giving us more money, I just don't want to have to attend a church service to get it. Can't you go alone?"

"Matty, as representatives of the dispensary, it would be unseemly for the two of us not to attend the service at which the church is presenting us with a generous monetary gift. Surely you can agree."

He fell silent. He knew his sister was right and he was being petulant and unreasonable. But the thought of attending any church service filled him with dread and he would be very glad when it was over.

"You've been working long days here for months," Caroline was saying. "A little recognition is overdue."

"You're right, I know," he finally said. "Of course we should both be there."

"Think of all the patients we'll be able to help with that money," she said in a softer tone. "I never realized how you felt about church. Have you always felt this way?"

Matt's eyes drifted downward without really seeing. In a small voice, he said, "Just since the war."

"Oh," she said quietly. "You never speak of the war, and I'm never sure if I should ask you about it."

"I still have nightmares about it. Almost every night, I can hear the men screaming for help." He decided not to mention that more frequent were his nightmares about Degan and the gnawing emptiness of being separated from her. He knew his sister would not truly understand the damage done by war or the relentless ache of having lost Degan.

"I'm sorry," Caroline said, turning from her work. "Wouldn't church be comforting for you? I often feel better in church because I feel closer to God."

Matt shook his head and let go a humorless laugh. "I don't know that there is a God."

"Matty!"

"Honestly, Cara, how can there be? How can there be so much pain and suffering of innocent people if there's a loving God? The war took such a toll, you could never understand unless you had been there. So many . . . I couldn't help them. Hundreds, thousands of young men, just boys really, riddled with disease and infection, wounded beyond anything human, enduring hideous deaths. I couldn't save them, Cara. I couldn't even ease their suffering while they died. I couldn't—"

"Matty, look at me." She quickly knelt in front of him to pull his attention from the grasp of horrific memories. "Don't think about it. Don't talk about it anymore, it's over and done with. It's in the past. Think about the future."

"The future?" His stare broke from the unseen recollection and he looked down at her with a depth of sadness on his face that she had not expected. She had never seen her brother so close to tears and it made her uneasy.

"The future of the dispensary, and how many people we will help," she said, trying to sound optimistic. "Those in the city who would have to go without medical care if we weren't here. These are the people you can help now. Think of the children."

Matt was silent, but she thought his expression had brightened just a little.

"The money we'll receive on Sunday will help us in our mission. And it may even prove to be an interesting service," she said, standing to resume her task. "Rev. Peterson told me that in addition to presenting the dispensary with a donation on Sunday, the church is also hosting two missionaries who are passing through the area. They will be speaking about their work during the service, and afterward, there will be a reception in their honor."

Matt said nothing, but glanced up at his sister and tried to look less miserable.

The church was packed the next Sunday. Elegantly dressed couples, along with their equally stylish and starched children, paraded into the pews until the sanctuary was filled to capacity.

Mrs. Hughes had taken her usual post at the entrance of the church, greeting parishioners with a chilly upturn of her mouth and a limp handshake. When she spotted Matt and Caroline, her face beamed with triumph.

"Good morning, Miss Tyler, Dr. Tyler. Isn't it a beautiful day the Lord has blessed us with? I'm so pleased you could join us this morning."

Caroline extended her gloved hand. "Good morning, Mrs. Hughes. We've been looking forward to the service all week."

Matt cringed inwardly at Caroline's polite response and wordlessly returned Mrs. Hughes' icy smile with one of his own.

"I am so sorry your dear mother cannot join us today," Mrs. Hughes said.

"Yes, we are as well," Caroline said. "She awoke with a headache this morning and decided it best to rest. Nothing serious, I'm sure."

"But how awful for her," Mrs. Hughes offered with feigned compassion. "Well, I do hope she soon feels much better."

"Thank you, we will tell her you asked about her," Caroline said, turning to Matt, "won't we Matty?"

"Yes, of course," he answered absently.

When the usher escorted them to a pew near the front of the church, he motioned for its occupants to make room for two more. Matt ignored the dour looks hurled in their direction by the ladies as they were forced to stand, move two steps to the right, and reseat themselves. Caroline smiled sweetly and thanked them kindly for their trouble.

As the service got under way, Matt recalled the services he had attended in childhood. Nothing much had changed. The lethargic singing of melancholy hymns, the vague promises of rewards awaiting the godly, and the harsh punishments in store for the wicked. When he glanced over, Caroline's eyes were fixed obediently on the Reverend Peterson who was droning on about how the church needed more money from the parishioners. For a moment, he was tempted to lean over and whisper in her ear that the minister sounded drunk, but he decided to behave himself and hoped the missionaries would prove more interesting.

Between the third hymn and the sermon, Rev. Peterson's face brightened as he approached the pulpit to announce the church's monetary gift to the dispensary. He mentioned briefly the "tireless work with the poor" performed by Caroline, Matt, and others at the dispensary, and thanked them all for their time and dedication. He said it was "regrettable that Dr. Adam Tyler's widow could not be in attendance at the service this morning," but that he knew she was extremely proud of her children and the work they were doing, following in their father's footsteps. Matt wondered silently what the church members would say if they knew how Kathleen really felt about her children providing medical care to the city's poor.

Near the end of the service, Isaiah Webster and Jonah Butler were introduced with all the fanfare the staid Reverend Peterson could muster.

"These two servants of our Lord have sacrificed their own comforts—their very safety and welfare—to venture into the wilderness," Reverend Peterson told his congregation, "seeking to share the Lord's message with godless heathens."

Bored and unimpressed, Matt struggled to pay attention as the first young missionary, Mr. Butler, spoke of their work for the Lord. But his mind wandered.

" . . . traveled through northwestern Pennsylvania, to the town of Sylvan, on our way to western New York," Mr. Butler was saying from the pulpit. Matt snapped to attention and looked up. "We stopped at Fort Gibson and were picking up supplies and medicine to take to the native reservation on the Allegany River." Matt's pulse quickened. He sat very still, listening intently. "But when we arrived in the town of Salamanca in western New York, we learned of an epidemic on the reservation, an illness spreading among the natives, so we left the supplies at the fort and turned back."

An illness spreading on the reservation. Matt was suddenly desperate to know what kind of illness, and how widespread. Typhoid fever or diphtheria could sicken hundreds in a matter of days.

" . . . disappointed that we couldn't share the gospel on the reservation," Mr. Butler was saying. "Some of the natives have been converted to Christianity, thanks be to God. But some still cling to the godless religion of their ancestors. They need to hear the word more than anyone . . ."

Fidgeting in the pew, Matt felt trapped under a strong urge to dash out the door and jump on the next train to Salamanca. After so much time had passed, why was this news causing such an intense reaction? It had been more than a year ago that Degan had returned home to Salamanca and resumed her life among her people. *She's probably never given me another thought since that day at the train station. But what if she's ill? What if the illness on the reservation has already taken her?* The thought made him sick to his stomach.

Over the din of his own thoughts, Matt heard very little of the remainder of the service. Afterward, the parishioners filed out of the sanctuary and into the adjacent church hall for the reception. As the crowd meandered toward the exit, Caroline busily greeted friends and neighbors, shaking hands and chatting, telling all how grateful they were for the church's generous gift to the dispensary. Matt was too preoccupied, his mind set on speaking privately with the missionaries to learn further details of the sickness on the reservation.

When they finally made their way to the church hall, Matt's heart sank when he saw the missionaries had been corralled into a corner by throngs of parishioners.

"Dr. Tyler! Over here!" a voice called out. He saw Mr. and Mrs. Hughes standing among the inner circle beside the missionaries. Mr. Hughes was reaching above everyone's head, motioning for him to join them.

"Mr. Webster, Mr. Butler, may I present Miss Caroline Tyler and Dr. Matthew Tyler," Mr. Hughes said, as a flurry of handshakes were exchanged.

"Miss Tyler, Dr. Tyler, I'd like to offer my congratulations and admiration for your work at the dispensary," Mr. Butler said with a slight bow toward Caroline, seeming to address only her. Young and lanky, with gray eyes and a full mustache that was slightly darker than his hair, Mr. Butler exuded a fresh enthusiasm and social ease beyond his years. "Rev. Peterson has told us of your steadfast dedication to the poor."

"Thank you, Mr. Butler. I believe very strongly in the work we do," Caroline replied with a smile. Their eyes locked for a long moment.

"Gentlemen, you may be interested in talking with Dr. Tyler," Mr. Hughes said, breaking the spell between Caroline and the young missionary. "Dr. Tyler spent two years living in northwestern Pennsylvania."

"Where were you living in Pennsylvania, Dr. Tyler?" Mr. Webster asked.

"Sylvan," Matt replied. "I was an apprentice with the physician there, Dr. Henry Bowman."

"Ah yes, when we passed through Sylvan some weeks ago, the Methodist church invited us to speak. I do remember Dr. Bowman," Mr. Webster said. "A bustling little town, what with the railroads coming closer."

"If I may, gentlemen, I'd like to ask you more about the sickness you mentioned on the Allegany Reservation," Matt said, his tone sounding more urgent than he intended. "Have you any idea of the affliction? Typhus? Cholera?"

"I'm afraid we don't know for sure, Dr. Tyler," Mr. Butler replied, "but some said it was diphtheria."

"Is there a doctor in Salamanca?" Matt asked.

"No," Mr. Butler said. "Very few whites living up there at all. With the railroads coming in, more whites will likely migrate, but up to now, it's been only the natives."

With a contemptuous chuckle, Mr. Hughes said, "I doubt the hostiles would allow a white doctor anywhere near them. The savages have their own ways of healing, so-called. It's said their medicine men burn tobacco and shake rattles over the sick."

"Which is why we're spreading God's good word to the natives," Mr. Butler interjected.

Matt wondered how God's good word would improve the lot of the sick any more than burning tobacco and shaking rattles, but he kept quiet.

"The reservations are not hospitable places to live," Mr. Butler continued. "Despite the government's promises of providing for the natives, conditions are harsh, and the people are very poor. The Office of Indian Affairs is a corrupt bunch. The very agency assigned to care for the natives has made their plight far worse through neglect and unscrupulous dealings. Disease is a constant plague on the reservations."

"But they are savages," Mr. Hughes said hotly. "They want no part of civilized society. Why must our government be responsible for their welfare? I say let's put our government's resources to good use instead."

As the conversation shifted to the U.S. government's policies toward natives and the Office of Indian Affairs, Matt could not keep his thoughts focused. With great effort, he forced himself to remain where he stood, determined to be the first customer at the train station in the morning to purchase a ticket to Salamanca. It was now clear to him that his bond with Degan ran deep and strong and would never fade. He had been deluding himself to think otherwise.

"Matt?" a voice echoed from somewhere, pulling his attention back to the present.

He quickly reoriented to the room and realized Caroline had been speaking to him. "Forgive me," he offered awkwardly.

"Mr. Butler and Mr. Webster have requested a visit to the dispensary," she said.

"Yes, we'd enjoy a tour of your facility while we're in town," Mr. Butler said, smiling softly at Caroline, "if it wouldn't be an inconvenience. We certainly would not want to interfere with your work, Miss Tyler."

"Not at all," Caroline said. "I'd be happy to show you the dispensary."

Early the next morning, Matt arrived at the dispensary to find Jonah Butler hovering over the cabinet in the reception area listening attentively to Caroline's explanation of the facility's patient records system. When Matt caught her eye, she looked up and smiled.

"Good morning, Matty," she said, noticing his tense expression and purposeful stride.

"Good morning. Mr. Butler, good to see you again," he said stiffly, extending his hand. "Mr. Webster decided not to join you?"

"Oh, well, as I explained to Miss Tyler, he wasn't feeling well this morning, so, regretfully decided to excuse himself from our visit," Mr. Butler explained, though Matt noted he did not look overly disappointed to have Caroline all to himself.

"That is regrettable," Matt said.

"Matty, Mr. Butler has invited us to lunch today. Can you join us?"

"I'm afraid I can't," Matt replied. "Cara, if I may have a word with you?"

"Of course," she said, glancing at Mr. Butler, who nodded his consent.

"I can't stay long," he said, leading her back to the empty treatment room. "I've got a train to catch."

"Where are you going?"

"To Salamanca," he said. "To the Allegany Reservation. I'll be out of town for a time."

Caroline frowned. "But why on earth . . . ?" Then comprehension dawned. "Matty, you aren't going after that Seneca woman!"

"Yesterday, the missionaries spoke of an illness on the reservation. I have to go and see if there's anything I can do. I have to see that she's all right."

"Oh, for heaven's sake," she groaned with disappointment. "What about the dispensary? We need you here. Our patients need you. Don't do this."

"I'm sorry but I have to go. Dr. Wallace can cover for me while I'm away. I won't have any peace until I know Degan is all right."

"But I thought . . . you had forgotten about her by now."

The idea that he could ever forget about Degan brought a fresh wave of pain that he could not put into words.

"And anyway, don't the hostiles have their own medicine?"

"They have herbs and prayers. That won't help if it's serious."

"You may not be able to help either. And what if you get sick?"

Matt was silent, but Caroline knew he was determined. A look of resignation settled on her face. She threw up her hands in frustration. "The idea! Leaving our patients here and chasing after a—" His eyes darted to her face in warning. "You're going into a pack of savages all by yourself. At least take someone with you."

He shook his head, undeterred. "There's no time. I'm sorry you have to be the one to tell Mother of this, but I cannot wait."

"When will you be back?"

"I don't know."

Caroline sighed, "I'll convey your message," cringing at the thought of explaining to Kathleen that Matt was on his way to an Indian reservation to see to the welfare of the woman he loved.

The afternoon was wintry and bleak. Heavy, iron-gray clouds spat icy needles as Matt stepped from the train onto the wooden platform of the depot, carrying his medical bag, surgical kit, and small valise. He pulled the collar of his coat higher against the raw chill and walked a few paces to the end of the platform, reorienting himself to the area.

Remembering Degan's path from months ago, he walked from the train depot further into the town. A dozen men had gathered on the front porch of a small general store. Intent on their conversation, they did not notice him until he stepped up to the wooden-plank sidewalk just a few yards away. He moved toward the group, and they silently turned from one another to face him.

At that moment, he more fully understood Degan's unwillingness to immerse herself in white society. These men looked decidedly different from him in every way, and for the first time in his life, Matt felt outnumbered and vulnerable. Though made of the familiar fabrics of cotton, flannel, and wool, their clothing presented unmistakably native design, with intricate patterns of beading and colorful embellishments. All had long, black hair worn either loose about their shoulders, or bound from their faces with strips of leather and cloth. As they stared at him, a daunting mix of pride and suspicion formed an invisible wall between them.

"I've come to see Degan," Matt announced simply.

At those words, the group stepped aside to reveal an elderly man sitting in a rocking chair behind them. The man's long hair, completely gray, hung freely to his waist. The dark skin of his face was leathery and deeply creased. He rose slowly to his feet and walked confidently to stand face-to-face with Matt. His eyes, though sunken with age, held an expression that was curiously familiar.

"You are the white shaman," he said, with no trace of questioning in his voice.

Surprise registered on Matt's face. "Yes."

"I am Degan's father."

Matt opened his mouth to speak, but could muster no words. He could only extend his hand to the older man, who looked down before taking it firmly in his.

"Please come," he said. "There is a sick child."

CHAPTER

25

The father did not speak as they walked briskly along the frozen dirt street.

"Is Degan all right?" Matt asked fearfully.

"Degan is well. The sickness did not take her."

Matt let out a heavy sigh of relief, only then realizing he'd been holding his breath. "What is your name?"

"Nagonda," the man answered, not changing his pace.

Finally they stopped at a modest, wood-frame house on the edge of town. A thin ribbon of smoke drifted horizontally from the chimney. Two women and two teen-aged boys lingered outside. Like the men at the general store, all wore clothes of native design, and all turned to stare when they saw the white man approaching. Each woman held a colorfully patterned blanket around her shoulders against the chill. When the women offered shy smiles, Matt instinctively touched the rim of his hat to return their wordless greeting. Nagonda spoke to them in what he surmised was the Seneca language. The only word he could distinguish was Degan's name.

Inside, the small house was meagerly furnished, clean and tidy. One oil lamp burned, the wintry day granting the interior almost no light through two small windows. A dying fire did little to warm the room beyond the bricks of the hearth.

Matt followed Nagonda into an adjoining bedroom where several women in native dress encircled a young child lying on a faded bare mattress. When he entered, the women looked up to stare in hushed fascination. His heart leapt to his throat as his eyes fastened on Degan.

Jolted by disbelief when she saw him, she took a step back, her eyes wide, her hands over her open mouth. With a cry, she separated from the group and rushed forward into his arms. He clutched her tightly, fighting to keep his head above a flood of emotions, and feeling as though his very soul had finally returned to its proper place. Her embrace was equally fervent, but she quickly stepped back, her face awash in torment.

"Please, can you help?" She took his hand to lead him to the bed. The child was obviously feverish and having difficulty breathing.

He placed his medical bag and surgical kit on the mattress before taking off his hat and coat and rolling up his sleeves. He was only marginally aware of the other women who kept their eyes on him as they reluctantly drifted from the room at the urging of Degan's father. He wanted to say so many things, to ask where her husband was, but he forced himself to focus on the emergency at hand.

"Tell me how long he's been sick," he said, pulling a wooden chair closer to sit by the bed. He reached to turn the lamp flame higher.

"Four days," she said. "He has a fever now. His breathing is very hard."

"How long has his breathing been labored like this?"

"Since this morning, he is worse."

Matt leaned to press his fingers gently to either side of the child's warm neck, which seemed to cause discomfort. He turned the child's head toward the light and, murmuring sweetly, "What's the matter, little man?" he carefully opened the tiny mouth to view the back of his throat. When he looked up at Degan, Matt knew his expression had given away the seriousness of the child's condition.

"It's diphtheria," he said, watching speechless horror descend over her. She wavered on her feet, and he quickly stood, grasping her shoulders to steady her. "There's a way I can help him breathe easier. It'll give him a chance for survival. I need to make a cut in his throat—"

She drew back in shock. "No!"

"Degan, listen to me, it's the only way. Diphtheria causes a membrane to cover the windpipe. It's preventing him from breathing. If I don't cut through it, before long, it'll suffocate him."

She buried her face in her hands.

"I've done this before," he continued with intensity in his tone. "It's the only way, and we don't have much time. You have to trust me."

She raised her head, her dark eyes swimming in anguish. He felt the familiar swell of love for her that he had hoped would eventually wane, but now was stronger than ever.

"He's your little boy, isn't he?" When she nodded, his heart stopped. "I'll do everything in my power to save him, you know that."

She looked across the room to her father, then down at the feverish child fighting to breathe. "All right."

Having gained her consent, Matt quickly got to work. From his medical bag, he retrieved chloroform, bandages, and several linen towels, then opened his surgical case to select his smallest scalpel. He had performed this procedure on two children before, neither as young as this little boy.

"I'll need some kind of small, hollow tube," Matt told her, illustrating the necessary size with his fingers. "I'll insert it into his throat and he'll breathe through it."

She looked again to her father, who quickly left the room.

"He will find something," she said.

Matt poured chloroform into a cloth in his palm and gently placed it over the boy's nose and mouth. Within seconds, the child slipped into deep sleep.

"Would you remove his shirt?" he asked, and Degan complied. He then rolled a linen towel into a tight cylindrical shape and tucked it securely under the child's neck and shoulders, lifting and extending the front of his throat. When Nagonda returned with a small piece of hollow tubing made of smooth, sturdy wood, he presented it to Matt for inspection.

"That will work," he told him, amazed that he had located a suitable instrument so quickly. "It needs to be very clean. Wash it thoroughly with hot water. Hurry."

When Nagonda left the room again, Matt turned to Degan, who seemed to anticipate his question.

"We have snow snake we play in winter. He cut the wood from a small snow snake he makes for a child."

Matt recalled that long ago, she had explained snow snake, a favorite winter amusement among her people. The precision with which the hickory rod had been carved and finished was impressive, and the tiny version of the toy was perfect for its current purpose.

With all instruments assembled, Matt grasped his smallest scalpel by its ivory handle. He took a deep breath and briefly met Degan's wide eyes.

"I need you to hold his head steady," he said. "Are you all right?"

"Yes," she said unconvincingly. She placed one hand firmly across her little boy's brow, pressing his head to the mattress.

"There may be some blood when I make the cut. I'll need you to clean the wound site as I work so I can see what I'm doing. We have to work fast. Can you do that?"

She nodded, taking the linen towel he handed her. With great care, Matt touched the sharp blade to the base of the child's throat. When he pushed in to make a vertical incision, Degan cried out and turned her head.

"Don't look away, Degan! Stay with me. Take the towel and clean the blood."

She followed his instructions, dabbing at the blood on her baby's neck at the edges of the incision. The child continued to sleep. Matt quickly pressed to cut again, enlarging the opening, spreading the sides of the incision with his fingers.

"Degan, clean the blood," he said. She complied, her hands shaking. Glancing up at her, he realized she wasn't breathing. "Take a breath, it'll be over soon. Stay with me."

He pushed the blade deeper to make a small cut in the trachea, then rotated it in a circular motion to create a round hole.

"Clean the blood," he said calmly. Still holding the incision open, he tossed the scalpel aside and reached for the small tube.

Degan touched the towel to her baby's neck, looking as though she would faint. "How can he survive this?"

"Trust me," he murmured without looking up.

Holding the little tube up to the light, he inspected it quickly, then carefully inserted one end through the incision into the trachea. Within seconds, the child's breathing quieted as air now passed unobstructed through the tube.

Seeing Degan's tormented expression change to astonished disbelief, he took the towel from her and carefully touched it to either side of the incision.

"This . . . this will stay in his throat?" she asked incredulously.

"Just until the fever passes and the membrane falls away." He looked up to meet her questioning face. "There's no cure for diphtheria. He's still a very sick little boy, but at least now he can breathe. If we're very lucky, he'll be able to recover."

"We have to wait?"

"I'm afraid so. I'm sorry I can't do more for him right now."

"You . . . you saved his life."

Matt took her shoulders and fixed his eyes to hers. "I may only have bought him some time. There's nothing else to do with diphtheria. He may still . . . not recover."

The possibility of her child's death did not seem to penetrate. "You will stay with us?"

"If you want me to stay, of course I will." He reached for the linen bandages, tearing them into thin strips that he wrapped carefully around the small tube, and around the child's neck to secure the breathing device.

Degan watched as he worked. "When he wakes, he will be hungry. How will I feed him?"

"He should be able to nurse normally, but you'll have to be very careful of the tube. Keep it clean and dry. We'll have to watch to make sure no fluids enter the tube and go into his lungs."

"Thank you," she whispered. Their eyes locked, the torrent of emotions between them nearly palpable. "How did . . . how did you know to come here?"

"From missionaries traveling in this area. I met them in Washington," he said, cleaning the scalpel and wrapping the unused bandages in clean towels. He looked around and saw that her father was no longer in the room. "They said there was an illness here. They weren't sure what it was."

"We have lost many," she said, gazing at her slumbering child whose breathing was now quiet and steady. She passed a hand over the delicate tuft of wavy black hair atop his head, then pulled the threadbare blanket higher to his shoulders and tucked it around his body.

"I know how much you wanted to be a mother," Matt said softly. "I'm happy for you. He's a beautiful boy. He looks like you."

"Matt—"

"Where's your husband?" he asked with guarded caution, bracing himself for a fresh wave of pain.

"I have no Seneca husband," she replied.

He stared at her blankly. "I don't understand. Didn't you remarry?" To his surprise, she shook her head. "But . . . you said you'd remarry. That's your custom. I thought—"

"I will not remarry." Her voice was firm and full of unshed tears. "I am your wife. I cannot be with another because my place is with you."

Matt sat motionless, taking in the magnitude of what she was saying. "Well then, who is this boy's . . . ?"

She held his questioning stare, and in her eyes, he saw an intense, unbreakable bond that struck him like a physical blow. Comprehension took hold and he found himself quickly tallying the months in his head. Realizing she must have been pregnant when she left him, his brain was slow to connect with his voice. He swallowed hard and stumbled over the question to which he already knew the answer.

"I . . . I'm . . . the father?"

She confirmed this revelation with a nod. "I have not been with another."

He struggled with disbelief. "I . . . I just operated on my own child?" As this realization swept over him, he leaned to put his head in his hands. "When were you going to tell me?" He looked up at her. "Did you know you were expecting when you left me?"

"No, I did not know. We came back to you in the beginning, before he was born," she said, her words tumbling out urgently. "My father and I went back to the cabin, but you were not there. No one was there. Where were you?"

Matt rose from the bed on shaking legs. He stepped to the window to look out at the dreary winter twilight, placing both hands on either side of the window to steady himself. "I moved back to Washington after you left. I took a position at my father's hospital."

"Why did you come here?"

"I was worried about you. When I heard about the illness here, I wanted to see that you were all right." He turned to see abject sadness on her face. "I wish I had been with you when you gave birth."

"I wished for you also. I was afraid I would die."

"Most women think that with their first child," he said dismissively.

"No. I was afraid I would die and you would never know about your son. And we would not be able to come back to you." She rushed to pour out her heart before he could stop her. "When I came back here, I tried to be happy with my people . . . but . . . without you, I did not want to live. And I was very sick. Then I knew I will have a baby. I knew my place is not here. My place is with you. So my father and I traveled many days to the cabin to find you. To tell you. But you were not there. I wanted to die, but they said I must live for the baby. And today, I see you here. I think you have come back for me. But you did not come to take us back. You came only because of the sickness."

"Degan, I need time," he said, broken beneath the crushing pain and anger that had twisted around his heart. "Do you have any idea what I went through after you left? I couldn't face the day. I couldn't . . . I only wanted to sit alone in the cabin and drink brandy until I passed out . . . to make the pain stop *for just five minutes!* I tried to go back to practicing medicine, but I couldn't. I was good for nothing."

"Your people would push you away because of me. I did not want this to happen. This is why I left you."

"Since you left, I've been no use to anybody."

"You saved our son's life," she whispered. "You are my husband. My place is with you."

Though her words would have been a rescuing lifeline months ago, Matt now turned back to face the window, peering into the darkness. He suddenly felt so weary of cold, dark emptiness, he thought he would go mad. He longed for warmth and light, and the committed affections of someone with whom he could relax and share his life.

"How can I trust you," he murmured.

He felt her hand on his shoulder, urging him to face her. When he looked down into her dark eyes, he knew that her suffering had been as piercing and unrelenting as his.

"Even before he is born, I want my son to know his father. He would know his father," she said firmly. "He will always be Seneca, but he is also white."

Matt raised his eyes to look at the little boy breathing steadily, sleeping peacefully on the bed. Trying to make sense of a multitude of conflicting emotions, he took a deep breath and exhaled slowly.

"What did you name him?" he finally asked.

"Adam."

Tears stung his eyes and his throat tightened with emotion. "After my father."

For the first time since he arrived, Degan smiled. "He will know he is half Seneca and half white. He will know about you. I hope you will teach him."

Matt suddenly felt like a child himself in need of solace. Degan took a step forward and tentatively placed her arms around his waist, pressing her body to his, resting her head against his chest. Her embrace was sweetly familiar, her essence flooding him with a powerful wave of completion and yearning that he could barely defend against. He made no move to return her embrace, but closed his eyes, hopelessly fighting the longing that rose from his soul.

"No," he whispered through clenched teeth. "No! You left me. How can I trust you?"

"I left you. It was a mistake. I ask you to forgive me."

"Degan," Nagonda's voice came from the doorway. When they looked up, her father summoned her. With a frown of confusion, she slowly pulled away and left the room.

Alone now, Matt leaned against the window frame and felt a cold draft seeping in from the wintry night outside. Feeling the chill keenly, he looked to the shrinking fire in the grate at the opposite side of the room, and went to feed fresh logs onto the embers. The new wood caught, and he stood to enjoy the warmth.

It occurred to him that perhaps the baby had taken a chill, and he turned from the fire. Seeing no extra blankets or bedding of any kind, he reached for his coat and layered it atop the thin blanket. He sat down gingerly on the side of the bed and studied the sleeping boy. He put two fingers against the little face and felt the heat of fever, then stroked the black hair that draped fine curls around tiny ears.

"Black hair . . . like your mother's," he whispered, "but wavy like mine."

The knowledge that he was caressing his own child struck him like a locomotive. He recalled the dozens of babies he had delivered, always seeing expressions of astonishment on the faces of new parents when they reached to touch the miniature fingers and toes of their newborns, hardly able to fathom that this tiny person could be real. Now, for the first time, he knew at a very deep level exactly what they had been feeling.

He reached to stroke the boy's small hands that curled in loose fists at his sides. To his surprise, the child stirred and, without waking, opened a fist to encircle and grip tightly his father's finger. Matt pulled gently to free himself, but the little hand held, unyielding.

At that moment, Matt knew that nothing of this world could ever separate him from his son. No sacrifice would be too great, no obstacle would prevent him from giving his son everything he could possibly need for the rest of his life. The power of this new reality had begun to settle into his core, and he knew he was now a different man from the one who had arrived at this place just a few hours ago.

He gazed down at his son, a spontaneous smile spreading across his face. "That's quite a grip you've got there, boy," he said softly. "Long fingers. A surgeon's fingers."

The boy squirmed under the warmth of his covers and began to whimper in his sleep. Matt knew the chances for survival of diphtheria were not good. He closed his eyes tightly and, for the first time in years, pleaded with God.

"Please don't let him die," he whispered, fighting back a desperation that was deeper than tears, much deeper than words. "You took my father from me, don't take my son, too. Please, don't take him."

A presence beside him startled Matt. He turned to see Nagonda standing by the bed.

"He will live?" he asked simply.

Matt turned back to his son. "I don't know. All we can do now is wait."

"Others are sick and need this," Nagonda said, touching the base of his wrinkled throat.

Suddenly, Matt knew a paralyzing reluctance to move from the bed. As if reading his mind, Nagonda said, "You do not want to leave the boy. This is good."

Matt looked up to see pleased satisfaction on Nagonda's face. "I wish I had known about him from the beginning."

"We came for you."

"Degan told me. I wish I had been there."

"You are here now." Nagonda sank wearily onto the bed. He drew a long breath, looking into the fire that cast a golden flush on his leathery skin. "My daughter was happy before the white men took her. But I see she is different now. I see she is very unhappy, even when the baby comes. Her love for you is very strong."

"It wasn't strong enough to keep her from leaving me," Matt said. "I wanted her to stay with me. I wanted to marry her. But she's too afraid of the whites."

"Maybe her love for you is stronger than she knew. Stronger now than her fear."

"Only she can answer that."

"You love my daughter?"

Matt closed his eyes and allowed the profound simplicity of that question to penetrate to his heart. "I would die for Degan," he said softly. "I love her more now than I did when she left me. The only person in the world I could possibly love more than Degan is this little boy." He reached to lay a gentle hand across his son's chest that was floating up and down with each breath.

Still gazing at the flames, Nagonda's face crinkled into a smile. He turned, his eyes revealing the insight of age and experience, and Matt found himself wishing he could talk with the old man all night. His mind was flooded with questions about his early life, his family, his thoughts of white men, his hopes for his grandson.

"I don't know what you think of me," Matt said, "but I'll be a good father to this boy. I'll give him whatever he wants."

"That could be trouble," Nagonda replied, a teasing playfulness in his eyes that was familiar to Matt, as he had seen it so many times in Degan's eyes.

He smiled. "What I mean is, I'll provide whatever he needs. I'll take good care of him."

Nagonda nodded, then slowly creaked to standing. "Please come with me," he said. "There are others who cannot breathe." When Matt looked down in hesitation, Nagonda said, "Degan will sit with the son."

CHAPTER

26

Matt poured a small amount of laudanum into a cup and handed it to Degan. "When he wakes up, he'll feel the pain of the incision. Give him a teaspoon of laudanum, slowly. Put some sugar in it, it's very bitter."

"I remember," she said.

"He'll soon quiet. Don't give him too much."

She nodded her understanding.

"Every few minutes, I want you to check the tube to make sure it's clear. As soon as you see any liquid in the tube, put your mouth on the end of the tube and suck out whatever is in there. Nothing can enter his lungs except air. Do you understand?"

"I want you to stay here with us," she said, her expression grave.

"No, daughter," Nagonda interjected before Matt could respond. "There are others who cannot breathe."

"When will you return?"

"As soon as I can," Matt said.

"Do as he says, daughter. He cuts quickly. We will return by sun-up."

With no regard to the late hour, Nagonda led Matt from house to house, knocking on doors and explaining their mission to weary occupants. Standing over feverish loved ones, Matt gave concise direction to the caregivers. Those who understood English acted quickly, while others looked to Nagonda for interpretation. Meeting with less skepticism than he would have imagined, Matt was astounded at the willingness of strangers to allow a white surgeon to walk in and perform a tracheotomy on their child in the middle of the night. It was obvious that Degan's father carried some influence and authority among his people.

Just before daybreak, the two made their way back to the house, Matt desperate to check on his son. Nagonda had assured him through the night that if Degan needed them, she would send word to find them. Nevertheless, Matt was tremendously relieved when he learned that all in the area who could be saved had been visited.

As they approached the house, Nagonda could barely keep pace with Matt, who bounded up the porch steps in one leap.

"Degan?" he called on his way to the bedroom. She was sitting in the chair by the bed. Her blouse open to the waist, she was holding her nursing child against her breast. When she looked up and smiled, Matt thought he would collapse with relief at the sight.

"How is he?" he asked anxiously, removing his coat and kneeling in front of her.

"He no longer feels too warm with fever," she said.

"That's good." He reached to inspect the bandage that held the small breathing tube in place. In doing so, he inadvertently brushed against the warm skin of her breast and she gave a little yelp.

"Your hands are cold!"

"I'm sorry," he said, grinning at her reaction. She smiled at him and, warming his hands with his breath, he could feel his soul healing under her adoring gaze. "If you can pull him away for a moment, I want to look at the bandage."

Putting a gentle hand to the side of the baby's face, she pulled his demanding mouth from her nipple. Matt examined the bandage and nodded his satisfaction.

"You've been watching for fluid in the tube and keeping it clear?"

"Yes. I gave him the medicine. It makes him sleep, and keeps the pain away. I remember this."

"Good," Matt said. The baby stared at him for a moment, then returned to his mother's breast.

Degan grasped his cool hand. "You are tired."

"I was out performing tracheotomies all night. Your father took me from house to house."

"I know. The people are talking about my white husband." She suddenly looked apprehensive. "How long will you stay with us?"

"Diphtheria is very contagious. Since I've been exposed to the virus, I'll have to be quarantined here for a few weeks."

"What is . . . quar . . . ?"

"Quarantined. It means I can't leave here until I'm sure I won't come down with diphtheria myself."

"What will we do if you are sick?"

"I'm not worried about that," he said, stroking the baby's head. "I just want to make sure he's all right."

"I am glad you will be with us. It's good you are with the baby. Please, can we be as we were before, at the cabin?"

Feeling his defenses rise, he shook his head. "No, Degan. Part of me would give anything to go back to those days when we lived together at the cabin as husband and wife. I was so happy then. But I'm not ready for that. I don't know if I ever will be. The pain . . . I wouldn't survive it a second time."

Tears welled in her eyes. "I will not leave you again," she said firmly.

Matt put a gentle hand on the baby's head. "For as long as I'm here, I just want to make sure he's safe and well. That's all."

She nodded, unable to speak past her need to cry.

"I want to hold my son," he said.

Degan pulled the baby from her breast and carefully handed him over. Matt supported Adam's head and back as he cradled the drowsy child against his chest.

"You know how to hold the baby," she said, surprised at his skill.

"Of course I know how to hold a baby," he said, never taking his eyes from his son, who was quickly falling asleep in his arms. He leaned to place a soft kiss on the tiny forehead.

"Degan?" A woman's voice came from the doorway. Matt looked up to see an older woman who resembled Degan, standing with her hands on her hips, staring at him suspiciously.

"Gowesan, this is my husband," Degan said, buttoning her blouse, then addressed Matt. "This is my sister."

Under different circumstances, Matt would have approached her to offer his hand in greeting, but something in her demeanor made him freeze where he stood. Gowesan was obviously older than Degan, a few inches shorter, with lighter hair and small eyes in a plump face.

Without a word, Gowesan marched toward him with outstretched arms and open animosity. "The man does not hold the baby!"

"Gowesan!" There was a sharpness in Degan's tone that Matt had never heard before. "The father will hold the son."

Gowesan glared at Matt, who made no move to turn over the child. She then turned to Degan and said something vehemently in their native tongue.

"This white man will love the son and teach him many things, as our father taught us," Degan retorted. When her sister made a heated reply, Degan said, "I will talk the English words so my husband will understand!"

Gowesan looked exasperated, but said nothing more as she turned and stomped out of the room. The baby began to squirm in his father's arms, a frown creasing his brow.

"Shhhhh," Matt whispered, leaning to touch his lips to Adam's forehead. "It's all right, don't cry. Your Aunt Gowesan means well, but she doesn't understand how much I love you."

Degan rose from the bedside chair. "Maybe you want to sit with him."

Matt kept his eyes on Adam as he took her place in the chair, never noticing the tears she wiped from her face.

The pale January sun cast little warmth as Matt sat on the narrow wooden steps at the back of the house. Recent days had been a curious mix of awkward introductions and explanations. He learned that in addition to Degan's mother, two brothers had also perished in the attack on her household the day she was captured. Aside from her father, two sisters had survived, one married and living with her husband and children a few houses away; the other, Gowesan, living in the house with Nagonda, Degan, and the baby. Though Degan's father had greeted him with respectful tolerance, Gowesan remained cool. Wary of whites in general, she was especially suspicious of the white shaman who had cut her nephew's throat within minutes of his arrival. The fact that this action had saved the boy's life did little to assuage her hostility. For Nagonda, it was enough that Degan trusted him, but the sister would prove more difficult to soften.

Just as the missionaries had described, the Allegany Reservation was largely rural and poor. Degan had explained that the Seneca people had once numbered in the hundreds of thousands with vast acreage of orchards and productive farm land. Now, because of disease and forced relocation to reservations in the west, the population had dwindled to just under a thousand on the Allegany. Degan and her family lived on the outskirts of Salamanca, the only town on the reservation, which totaled a few thousand acres, significantly smaller than the lands of her ancestors. The old way of life had been preserved as much as possible, with small gardens nurtured and cultivated, and seasonal celebrations observed throughout the year. But the Seneca had lost much of their former wealth and holdings through the fraudulent dealings of greedy white men who felt entitled to native lands.

Though it was difficult, Matt had successfully held his emotions in check since his arrival. Living once again in the same house with Degan, he was careful never to step beyond the bounds of polite deference. Even so, the fierce aching for her at his core remained constant. When she looked at him with those soft, dark eyes filled with love, he thought he would go mad with the longing to reach out and clutch her as a drowning man clutches a life preserver. But he remained resolute that while he was trapped in this house under threat of illness, he would not allow himself to yield to his desires against his better judgment.

On this cold afternoon, Matt had slipped quietly outside, glad to be away from what seemed a daily argument between Degan and Gowesan. Though they argued mostly in their native language, which he did not understand, the heated exchange was still uncomfortable to witness.

The back door creaked open and Matt turned to see Nagonda peering out. Without a word, the old man came to sit next to him, though there was barely enough space on the narrow step for more than one person. Matt noticed Nagonda reaching into his coat pocket to withdraw two thin cigars. In his rush to leave Washington, he had neglected to bring cigars or tobacco of any kind, and he had felt keenly the absence of smoking since his arrival in Salamanca.

When Nagonda wordlessly handed him one of the cigars, Matt asked, "What are they fighting about in there?"

Without turning his head, Nagonda replied, "You," and struck a match to light first his cigar, then Matt's.

Taking a long, satisfying draw, Matt sighed, "Thank you," already feeling more relaxed.

"It's good when the men leave the women to smoke for a time," Nagonda said, shifting uncomfortably on the step. "The white man's lodge is too small. In the old days, all the family lives together in one big lodge. Today, in the white man's lodge, only a few people can fit."

"How long have you lived here?"

"Many years. Degan does not know the long houses of the old days. She only knows the white man's house." His voice sounded tired and resigned. "Many years ago, they thought to separate our families would be good, make us live in many small lodges like this one. This makes us more like the whites."

Matt shook his head in exasperation, feeling ashamed of his government and the narrow thinking of his own people.

"You did not know of this," Nagonda continued. "Your people do not know about this place—the reservation—and how we live."

"No," Matt whispered, now ashamed of himself for somehow missing the fact that an entire civilization had declined considerably, their centuries-old way of life altered forever on the whims of a powerful and oblivious foreign government.

Nagonda fell silent, puffing on his cigar.

"I thought you would smoke only during religious ceremonies," Matt said.

"This is the old way. Now we also smoke the white man's way."

The women's voices from inside the house rose against each other, and the two men could hear the baby fussing as well.

"If I've been the cause of conflict in your house, I apologize," Matt said sheepishly.

Nagonda shrugged. "Gowesan does not trust the white man."

"I don't blame her. Many white men should not be trusted."

"Gowesan is not happy that Degan loves a white man. Now you are here, and you will take Degan from us again."

"That is not my intention. I didn't come here to—"

"I know why you came here," Nagonda said quietly, gazing at the small plot of dirt that was the backyard.

"I just want to make sure the baby is all right."

"The son is getting better. Maybe better than the father."

Matt tapped the gray ashes from his cigar before bringing it to his mouth for another draw. "It's been good to see Degan again," he admitted, exhaling. "But . . . I can't allow myself to . . ."

"Your love for her is great, but there is no trust."

"She destroyed that when she left me," he murmured.

"But you still came for her."

"I'm only here for the baby—"

"You did not know about the baby when you came. You came for Degan."

Faced with the truth of his purpose, Matt fell silent. By coming here, he had given in to his impulse to see that Degan was well. His plan had been to see to her safety, then leave. But now that he was here, he struggled daily with the prospect of leaving her and Adam.

Nagonda stared straight ahead for a time, puffing contentedly on his cigar. "My wife was killed by the white men who took Degan. We were together many, many years. But on the night the white men came from nowhere, my wife was outside. They shot her." He held up a weathered finger. "One shot in her heart."

Matt was watching his face, wishing he could ease some of the pain. "I'm so sorry," he whispered.

Nagonda turned with a look of resolve in his moist eyes. "I see what is in my daughter's heart. I see what is in your heart. You must make the trust again. Do not waste what the Creator has given you."

Matt sighed heavily and looked away with a humorless chuckle. *You people and your Creator.*

"The Creator led Degan to you," Nagonda said. "And now he has led you here."

"Your Creator has taken more than he's given," Matt said. "What makes you think I was led here? I came of my own choice."

"You said you heard about the sickness in a church. This is how the Creator brought you here."

Matt pondered his statement, but dismissed the notion that he had been led to the church service weeks ago by anything other than Caroline's sensitivity to social decorum. No matter how he got here, his aim now was to somehow survive this agonizing proximity to Degan. Once it was safe to do so, he would leave, he told himself, with the intention of returning regularly, but only to be part of his son's life.

"I don't care much about your Creator," Matt said bluntly, "but I do care about my son, and I'll never abandon him. I'll be leaving this place in a couple of weeks, but I'll return as often as I can. I want to see my son grow up."

Nagonda frowned disapprovingly.

"Matt!" Degan's voice suddenly screamed from inside the house.

Matt jumped to his feet and bolted through the back door. "What's wrong?" he called, making his way to the bedroom.

"The baby!" she replied frantically. "The wood is out of his throat!"

Matt raced to the bedside and bent to inspect the bandage, which had loosened, causing the breathing tube to dislodge.

"He will not breathe now!" she shrieked.

"Shhhhh," he said, holding up a hand. He held the tube to the side of the incision. "He may be able to breathe without it."

They waited a few tense seconds, Degan's own breathing stopped as she watched her child squirm on the bed. Suddenly, the baby took a tentative breath and began to whimper, obviously taking in air through his nose and mouth.

Matt looked up to meet Degan's distraught stare. "He can breathe on his own now. He'll be all right."

She let go a cry and reached to pick up her child, cradling him against her. With tears flowing freely, she pressed her face to his, then turned to Matt and leaned against him, crying into the front of his shirt.

At that moment, Matt's self-imposed restraint gave way, and he reached to embrace her and their child. He closed his eyes and rested his face against her hair, drinking in the essence of her that had once nourished him. He allowed himself to savor her and this familiar wholeness for a few moments, then forced himself to pull away.

She looked up at him, her face wet. "Please stay with us."

Had she reached through his skin and pulled his beating heart from his chest, she could not have stirred him more. Unable to muster any words, he turned from her and left the room, passing Nagonda in the doorway.

Degan was still crying when her father approached.

"The baby?" he asked, his face awash with concern.

"The baby will live," Degan replied. "He can breathe now, without the wood."

"This is good!" Nagonda said, confused. "Why do you cry?"

Degan laid the child back down on the bed and covered him with the thin blanket before sitting on the edge of the mattress. She put her hand on Adam's stomach and stared straight ahead, fixing her eyes on some distant point that her father could not see.

"I have lost my husband," she finally murmured.

"Why do you say this?" Nagonda asked, sitting down beside her.

"He no longer feels for me as he once did."

"I believe you are wrong, daughter."

Degan frowned and turned toward her father. "Why do you say I am wrong?"

"Because he is here. He will not leave this place without you."

"No," she said miserably. "I have hurt him too much. I tell him many times that I will not leave him again, but he cannot believe me. He cannot forgive me."

Nagonda sighed. "You told me when you were with the white shaman in the beginning, he said he will not hurt you. But you did not believe him. You were sure he would hurt you. All the time, you waited for him to hurt you. But he never did."

Degan nodded. "This is true."

"You did not believe his words."

"No."

"You had to see that he will not hurt you. Only then did you believe him. It is the same now. The white shaman must see that you will not leave him. You must show him."

She sat in silence, allowing his words to sink in. "How can I show him?" she asked.

Nagonda patted her knee, then rose and left the room.

Over the next few days, Matt and Nagonda returned to the homes they had visited the first night to check on the children. Nearly all had begun to recover, and the families expressed gratitude to the white shaman and to Nagonda for bringing him.

"I'm running out of supplies," Matt said as they bounced along the rutted road on the way to the last house. He had dispensed enough laudanum to each family to help ease the pain of surgery, but his supply was nearly gone. "Is there another white doctor anywhere near here?"

Nagonda shook his head. "Maybe the white army."

Matt remembered the missionaries mentioning Fort Gibson in the area. "Where is the Army outpost? Is it nearby?"

"Outside the town. On the north side. Maybe they have the medicine you need."

Still under self-imposed quarantine, Matt knew he could not leave the reservation for at least another week. He hoped that by continuing to ration his supplies, they would hold out.

"Sometimes, men from the white army ride through," Nagonda continued. "If they come to us, you can ask them for supplies. Since you are white, maybe they will give them."

Matt looked at him curiously. "I would hope they'd give needed supplies no matter who asked."

Nagonda smiled, and Matt sensed the old man was amused at his suggestion. "This is not the way of the white army. They live in this place for themselves, not for us."

"Then why do they ride through?"

"To watch us. To keep us quiet. Not to help us."

Matt fell silent. He remembered what the missionaries had said about the government's Office of Indian Affairs. They were fundamentally corrupt and could not be trusted to provide for the natives, according to their purpose. The personnel at Fort Gibson would have been a suitable point of outreach toward the natives in this area, but apparently they, too, had neglected that portion of their mission.

The old man frowned. "You do not know your people."

"I guess I don't," Matt replied. "But if I have to go to Fort Gibson myself to get more medicine and supplies, I will."

When they returned to the house at mid-day, a meager assortment of food had been placed on the table for them. A small pot of soup sat warming on the stove, and a plate of bread had been placed on the table, along with two small apples and two boiled potatoes. Matt took Degan's arm and pulled her aside.

"Have you eaten at all today?" he asked her in a low tone.

An odd expression crossed her face. "I am not hungry."

"Degan, you're nursing the baby, you have to eat."

She looked uneasily at the table, then back to him. His hand on her elbow, he led her to the table and said, "Sit," then took a bowl and ladled it full of watery soup from the pot on the stove, and set it before her. Selecting a piece of bread from a plate on the table, he placed it at the edge of the bowl.

"Eat," he told her sternly. Only then did he look up to see Nagonda and Gowesan standing motionless, watching him. Degan looked at her father and sister hesitantly, then took a spoon and sampled the soup. Matt sat down beside her and said to them defensively, "What are you staring at? A nursing mother has to eat."

Breaking from their trance, Nagonda and Gowesan exchanged glances, then Nagonda helped himself to a bowlful of the soup. Gowesan went to the cupboard to retrieve a small knife, and sat down across from Degan. Carefully slicing one of the apples into wedges, she placed the pieces beside her sister's bowl. Matt watched her, and when she looked up, he smiled his gratitude.

After the mid-day meal, Matt walked out onto the small front porch to smoke. He caught sight of two riders in the distance, and wondered if these were two of the men that Nagonda had said sometimes rode through. He scrutinized the men as they approached in the dirt street. One wore civilian clothes, the other the dark blue uniform of the U.S. Army. He descended the steps and walked out into the street to meet them. They reined their horses to a stop in front of the house and dismounted.

"Good afternoon," Matt said, approaching them with an outstretched hand. "Matt Tyler."

The men shook hands. "James Grey, with the Office of Indian Affairs. This is Lieutenant Stockton. We don't usually see white folks out here among the natives when we make our rounds, Mr. Tyler. What are you doing all the way out here?"

"It's a long story. I'm a doctor. I was in Washington and heard there was a sickness here on the reservation. I came to see if I could help. You gentlemen are taking chances riding through. There's been a diphtheria outbreak here."

"There's always some outbreak of illness," Mr. Grey said with a dismissive wave of his hand. Then a perplexed look came over his face. "Why does your name sound familiar? You say you were in Washington?"

"Yes. Perhaps you knew my father, Dr. Adam Tyler? My family has lived in Washington for many years."

"No, sir, I don't believe that's how I know you. Did you serve in the war?"

"I did. I was on the medical staff. Assistant surgeon with the 177th Pennsylvania Regiment."

Mr. Grey shrugged. "Well, I expect it'll come to me eventually."

"How far is Fort Gibson from here?" Matt asked.

"Just a mile or so north," Lieutenant Stockton replied, pointing behind him.

"I've been treating some of the natives," Matt said, turning to Lieutenant Stockton, "but I'm running out of supplies. Any chance you could spare some laudanum and chloroform?"

"For the natives?" The lieutenant looked pessimistic. "I can put in a request with my superiors, but the supply chain moves pretty slow, Dr. Tyler."

"If you would please put in the request as soon as possible. Unfortunately, I'm not able to leave here because I've been exposed to the virus."

"We'll see what we can do."

The provost marshal, Captain Jeremiah Ross, crossed his arms obstinately and leaned back in his desk chair. Lieutenant Stockton had seen this stance enough times to know that the doctor's supplies would be a long time coming, if the request was ever officially put in at all.

"What was the doctor's name who made this request?" Captain Ross asked.

"Dr. Matthew Tyler," the lieutenant replied. "Says he was with the 177th Pennsylvania Regiment. The name sounds familiar, but I can't place him."

A flicker of recognition shone on Ross's face. "I'll tell you who he is, Lieutenant. Remember hearing about Colonel Garrison? The colonel who died in the field hospital at Fredericksburg?"

"The Garrison family from Buffalo?"

"Yes. This Dr. Tyler was the surgeon in charge of his care the day Col. Garrison died. Captain Matthew Tyler, I'm positive that was his name."

"How do you know, sir?"

"Colonel Garrison was good friends with my superior officer, Colonel Timmons. The Garrison family tried to press charges of neglect against Dr. Tyler, but the case was never pursued. Colonel Timmons once told me he felt it was his personal responsibility to follow through on the charges on behalf of the Garrison heirs, but the Army Medical Corps lost track of this Matthew Tyler shortly after the war. No one knew where he was."

"Well, he's right under our noses now, sir," Lieutenant Stockton said, "living among the damn hostiles, God only knows why. I'm sure Colonel Timmons would consider it a personal favor, and be indebted to you, if you brought him in for questioning."

"Degan, come here!" Matt called from the bedroom.

When she rushed to the doorway, wiping her hands on a kitchen towel, she saw Matt sitting on the floor, his arms outstretched, with Adam between his legs.

"Watch this," he said, as Adam gripped his father's thumbs and pulled himself to standing. Since the baby had begun to recover, he had quickly learned to crawl, to sit up on his own, and now to stand with assistance. "He'll soon be walking by himself!"

Degan smiled, her heart bursting with love for her husband and pride in her son. "And when he walks, you will watch him always to keep him safe?" she asked teasingly.

"Ah, he's too smart to get into any trouble!" Matt said, helping the baby sit, then stand again. "Look, the more he practices, the better he gets."

She laughed at the two of them, the baby grinning at his father as he pulled himself to standing again and again. Over the past two weeks, Matt had been inseparable from his son, and absolutely amazed at every move he made, as if no other child in the world had ever accomplished the same developmental tasks. He had all but completely taken over the baby's care—bathing him, comforting him when he cried, and changing diapers. Even Gowesan could not help but comment on the white man's unusual attentiveness toward his son.

"You're going to grow up to be a strong, wise man of good character, just like your grandfather," Matt said, picking Adam up to nuzzle his neck, which brought soft giggling from the baby.

Nagonda's voice came from behind Degan. "There are men here. From the white army."

Matt looked up. "They brought the supplies already?" But when he saw Nagonda's grave expression, an inexplicable pang of dread shot through him. Two uniformed Army officers were standing on the porch.

"Dr. Matthew Tyler?"

"Yes."

"I'm Lieutenant Stockton, we met the other day. This is Lieutenant Wright. I'm sorry, sir, but you'll have to come with us. The provost marshal at Fort Gibson, Captain Ross, has some questions he wants to ask you about the Garrison case. I suspect you know what that's about?"

Matt took a deep breath and looked briefly at Degan, who had come to stand beside him. "I do know what it's about," he said. "But as I told you, I've been exposed to diphtheria here. It would be risking the health of every man in your detail if I were to come near them."

"I don't expect that would matter much to Captain Ross, Dr. Tyler," Lieutenant Stockton said.

"Lieutenant, diphtheria is highly contagious and I've been living with the virus for days. As a doctor, I can't risk—"

"Sir, we will take you by force if necessary. But one way or the other, you're coming with us."

Matt saw in the young man's eyes the blind determination to follow orders.

"Allow me to get my coat," he said, and pushed the door shut. He took Degan's shoulders and looked into her questioning eyes. "I have to go with these men."

"Why?"

"During the war, a colonel died under my care, and the family is pressing charges."

"What does this mean?" she asked, panic rising in her voice when she saw apprehension in his eyes.

"The colonel's family wants to punish me for allowing him to die while he was in my care. I have to answer for the actions I took back then."

"What will happen to you? Where will they take you?"

"They're taking me to the provost marshal's office at Fort Gibson for questioning. Beyond that, I don't know what will happen. I don't know how long I'll be gone."

He quickly donned his coat and hat, and put a hand to her cheek as he reached the door. "I'm sorry. I'll be back as soon as I can." Confused and forlorn, Degan watched him descend the porch steps with the two men.

Fort Gibson, located on the northern edge of town near the railroad depot, was no more than a small collection of buildings. The provost marshal's office was located on the first floor of a two-story stone house. Matt was escorted into a small outer office crowded with military personnel in the dark blue uniforms of the U.S. Army. The outer office gave way to a larger gathering room with a long wooden table in the center, at which sat a woman and a man in civilian clothing. A captain stood with his back to the door as Matt entered.

"Please sit down, Dr. Tyler," Lieutenant Wright said, closing the door behind him.

The officer turned. "Good afternoon, Dr. Tyler, I'm Captain Ross, the provost marshal. These folks are the Garrison children. They've come down from Buffalo to be present at your questioning."

Matt nodded a silent greeting to each of them, the woman glaring at him with cold, loathing eyes. He turned back to Captain Ross. "The Lieutenant did tell you I've been exposed to diphtheria? It's a risk to all of you for me to be in this room."

"We finally found you after all this time, Dr. Tyler," the woman said, her voice shaking with emotion. "We're not about to let you get away so easily again. Did you think you could hide forever?"

"Miss Garrison, I've asked that we try to keep these proceedings civil," Captain Ross said. "Please sit down, Dr. Tyler."

Matt took his place at the opposite end of the table from the Garrisons. Captain Ross settled at the table and spread a file of papers before him.

"I suppose formal introductions should be made," Captain Ross began, plainly uncomfortable with social etiquette, especially given that Col. Garrison's daughter was so blatantly on the verge of angry hysteria. "This is George Garrison and Virginia Garrison."

Mr. Garrison acknowledged Matt with a bob of his head, while his sister looked away.

"I'll get right to the point," Captain Ross continued. "The purpose of these proceedings today is to try to find out what happened on the day of Colonel Garrison's death. This is not a court-martial, obviously. It's a court of inquiry. A chance for everyone to hear what happened on the day in question. I'll be asking you, Dr. Tyler, to recount to the best of your ability what happened that day, and what actions you took. We'll then determine if there's cause for charges to be filed, or if we need to call in witnesses in your behalf, or on behalf of the Garrisons. At that point, we will—"

A quiet knock sounded at the door behind Lieutenant Wright who was standing guard. He looked to the marshal with raised eyebrows. Captain Ross nodded his permission and the lieutenant reached to open the door. Low whispers were exchanged, then Lieutenant Wright came to lean over the marshal's shoulder.

"Sir, a member of Dr. Tyler's family is here to witness the proceedings," he said.

Hearing this, Matt frowned in confusion and his mind raced. Who from his family could be here, unless they had been given advance notice of the questioning, and that seemed unlikely.

The marshal looked to Matt, then cleared his throat. "By all means, bring them in."

Lieutenant Wright motioned to the sentry waiting at the door. He pushed the door open and stunned silence fell over the room as Degan walked in. She stood perfectly still, slowly meeting all eyes as they brazenly took in her appearance. Her gaze settled on Matt, who looked as astonished as everyone else.

Finally, the marshal found his voice. "Miss, do you speak English?"

"Yes," she replied.

"Just how is it you're a family member of Dr. Tyler's?"

She raised her chin and spoke clearly. "I am his wife."

An audible gasp escaped Virginia Garrison, and an incredulous Captain Ross turned to Matt. "This is your wife?"

Keeping his eyes on Degan, he nodded. "Yes, sir, she is."

With a heavy sigh, Captain Ross waved a hand at the young officer. As Lieutenant Wright approached Degan, she suddenly looked fearful and took a step back. He stopped a distance from her and said, "With your permission, ma'am, I'll escort you to a seat near Dr. Tyler."

Visibly relieved, she nodded and followed the officer to the table. Matt kept his eyes on her, slowly absorbing the significance of her presence. He knew quite well the courage it had taken for her to come here, among all these white people, mostly U.S. Army officers at that. The powerful message she was sending hit its mark.

Lieutenant Wright pulled out the chair next to Matt and motioned for Degan to sit. When she was seated, the marshal continued. "As I was saying, this is not a court-martial, but a court of inquiry—"

"Yes, we understand, Captain Ross," Miss Garrison said, throwing a caustic sneer at Degan. "Now that this little sideshow is over, can we please get to the questioning? I am eager to hear how Dr. Tyler is going to explain why he killed my father."

Captain Ross gave Miss Garrison a stern look before turning to Matt. "Dr. Tyler, can you tell us what happened the day Colonel Garrison died?"

Matt took a deep breath and leaned forward to fold his hands on the table. "My memory of that day is very spotty. I remember they brought

Colonel Garrison in sometime in the afternoon. The fighting had been intense that morning. There were hundreds of casualties. We were dangerously low on supplies, and somebody said the colonel was suffering from typhus."

"My father never had typhus," Miss Garrison said dismissively.

"Miss Garrison, please," Captain Ross said.

"I'm sorry, but he did have typhus," Matt said, meeting the woman's angry stare. "The high fever, the cough, the rash, all the symptoms were there. But it was the bullet wound to his chest that finally took him."

George Garrison leaned forward. "Dr. Tyler, can you tell us how quickly you were able to tend to my father once he was brought in?"

Matt shook his head. "I don't remember. I have no idea how long he was there before I got to him."

"Was it still light when you got to him?" Captain Ross asked.

Matt lowered his eyes. "No, sir."

Miss Garrison cried out and buried her face in her handkerchief.

"You let my father suffer for hours before you even looked at him?" George Garrison asked. "Why didn't one of the other surgeons tend to him?"

"Mr. Garrison, there were hundreds of wounded and dying soldiers waiting to be treated. There were only three surgeons, counting myself. We had been working sixteen hours straight with no rest, not even a chance to sit down."

"But my father was an officer!" Miss Garrison shrieked. "You should have tended to him as soon as he was brought in. Just what were you doing that kept you from helping my father immediately?"

Matt's polite restraint snapped, and something sprang to life in his eyes. "I was trying my damnedest to save as many soldiers as I could! I was pushing a boy's intestines back into his abdominal cavity because a cannon ball had blown him apart. I was up to my elbows in blood and shit, but I thought if I could somehow get this boy's guts back into his body, I could sew him up, and he might live to see his mother again!"

A cold silence gripped the room, and even Degan sat stunned by his intensity. The only sound was Matt's rapid breathing as he slowly recovered from his outburst. Everyone else sat perfectly frozen until finally, George Garrison said in a measured tone, "Dr. Tyler, we would be grateful if you would mind your language." He waved a hand in the direction of his sister. "There is a lady present."

"She asked," Matt growled.

After a long moment, Captain Ross spoke quietly, "Dr. Tyler, your rank was Captain, is that correct?"

"Yes sir," he murmured.

The marshal rifled through his papers before focusing on one. "It says here that the chief surgeon in charge of the field hospital that day was a Major William Fenton?"

"Yes sir."

"As an assistant surgeon, you were under Major Fenton's command and direction, is that correct?"

"That's correct."

"Well, then, I believe we need to summon Major Fenton to these proceedings to question him on the events of that day."

Miss Garrison's small fist hit the table. "He's already admitted that he allowed my father to die! You're going to delay justice when you have my father's murderer sitting right here?"

Captain Ross stared at her pointedly. "Miss Garrison, please. We must get all sides of the story before we pass judgment, if any judgment is to be passed. Major Fenton may have a clearer memory of the events of that day. I, for one, would like to hear Major Fenton's accounting of that day. Then we can determine—"

"At the very least, then, hold him in custody until Major Fenton arrives," she said. "Otherwise, he's likely to escape into the wilderness with the savages and never be seen again. Your army lost track of him once, now you're going to let him get away again?"

"At this time, no charges have been justified in my mind. I cannot hold a man in custody if he has not been formally charged!"

"It's taken us over two years to find him," she said. "Now you're willing to let him walk out of here, even after he's admitted that he willfully neglected my father's need for medical care that day!"

George Garrison grasped his sister's white hand and said in a quiet, but determined tone, "Perhaps a conversation with your superior officer, Colonel Timmons, would change your mind. Need I remind you that Colonel Timmons and my father were close friends? If this man slips through your fingers again, Captain Ross, the colonel will not be pleased."

Matt watched as the provost marshal's resolve collapsed. When the marshal took a deep breath and turned, Matt reached under the table to squeeze Degan's hand.

"Dr. Tyler, we will need to take you into our custody until Major Fenton can join us. Once he arrives, we will reconvene."

"For how long?" Matt asked in an anguished voice.

"That depends," Captain Ross said. "We'll send a telegram to the War Department in Washington this afternoon. We'll start there."

"Sir," Matt said, "my wife is here. We have a son, who is also here. I've been exposed to diphtheria. You have my word, sir, I am not going anywhere. When Major Fenton arrives, I will be at the home of my wife's family, where your officers found me this morning—"

"No!" Miss Garrison cried. "You let my father die without doing anything to help him. Now you're finally going to have to answer for that."

"I'm sorry, Dr. Tyler, but I have no choice," Captain Ross said miserably. "You'll be in our custody here in town. Your family will be close enough."

Miss Garrison leaned back in her chair, a tight smile on her face. She glared triumphantly at Degan, then at Matt.

"Until Major Fenton arrives, these proceedings are adjourned. Lieutenant Stockton, please escort Dr. Tyler to a cell."

His hand resting on his sidearm, Lieutenant Stockton approached Matt. "Come with me, sir."

A panicked cry broke from Degan's throat. Lieutenant Wright anxiously looked to his superior, who caught his silent request and waved a hand toward Degan.

"Ma'am," Lieutenant Wright said, quickly approaching Degan to touch her arm. "He'll be all right." He helped her to stand, pulling her away from the table. Matt stood, keeping his eyes on her as the lieutenant pulled her to the side of the room.

"Don't worry," Matt said, his face pale and too tense to give her a reassuring smile. "Go home. Take care of Adam. I'll be all right."

She watched in horror as they led him from the room.

CHAPTER

27

Lieutenant Wright led Degan to a wooden bench that sat along the wall behind them and urged her to sit.

"Where are they taking him?" she asked, on the verge of tears.

"To the jail here in town."

"But why? My husband has done nothing wrong."

"Captain Ross doesn't want to take his word for that. He wants Dr. Tyler's superior officer to corroborate his accounting of events on the day Colonel Garrison died." Degan frowned as he spoke. "Do you understand?"

"I only know my husband has done nothing wrong. I want him to come back to us."

"That might take a while. But you can go visit him at the jail if you want."

"Please, tell me how to go there."

"With your permission, I'll be happy to take you there myself."

She nodded. "Yes, please."

Lieutenant Wright stood and offered Degan his hand, but she stood unassisted. She looked at him fretfully, wrapping the colorful blanket tighter about her shoulders. The young lieutenant stopped at the quartermaster's desk on the way out and requested permission to borrow a wagon.

"What for?" the quartermaster barked, irritated at the interruption.

"I'll be escorting Mrs. Tyler to the jail to visit Dr. Tyler," the lieutenant replied.

The quartermaster leaned to peer around the lieutenant and glare at Degan. He shamelessly looked her up and down, taking in her native clothing and unwavering stare. He then looked back to the lieutenant with a sneer.

"Takin' good care of the doctor's little squaw, are ya?" he spat sarcastically.

Lieutenant Wright squared his shoulders and his face hardened. "I'll bring the wagon back before sun-down." With that, he turned toward Degan, positioned his hat firmly on his head, and motioned for her to precede him out the door.

"I apologize for the quartermaster's conduct just now," he said sheepishly, offering Degan his hand into the wagon. She settled onto one end of the seat and watched the lieutenant climb up beside her and take the reins. She studied his profile as he steered the horse into the muddy street.

"Why are you kind to me?" she asked him.

He glanced at her uneasily, then focused intently on the street before them. "I figure it's the Christian way. I got nothin' against the Iroquois. My great-grandma was an Iroquois." He turned to her. "She was Oneida."

Degan smiled at him and said nothing more.

When Lieutenant Wright reined the horse in front of the jailhouse, Degan did not wait to be assisted from the wagon. By the time he jumped down and fastened the reins to the hitching post, she was already standing at the door.

"Afternoon, Lieutenant," the guard said when they entered. "Who's that you got there?"

"This is Mrs. Tyler. She'd like to see Dr. Tyler."

The guard gave Degan a hard look. "Well, I'll be damned! He does have a squaw wife. I figured that was just an ugly rumor." He paused as if trying to decide whether to balk at the request, then saw something in the lieutenant's eyes that brought his more obedient nature to the surface. "All right, go on in."

Wright led Degan through the outer office and back a dark, chilly hallway with individual cells along one side. Each cell held a flat, bare mattress on a low cot, and a small window that allowed pale light in from the gray day outside. As they progressed to the last cell, Matt stood up and walked to the bars.

Degan cried out and rushed to take his hands. Without a word, he reached through the bars to caress her cheek, then looked to the lieutenant.

"Thank you for bringing her," he said quietly.

Degan turned to the lieutenant. "Please, may I go in with him?"

He shook his head. "I'm sorry, ma'am. That's not allowed."

She looked crest-fallen. "Why?"

"It's for your own safety, ma'am."

Incredulous, Matt said, "Lieutenant, she's my wife. Surely you don't think I'd do anything to harm her."

"I'm sorry, Dr. Tyler. It's regulations."

"Lieutenant, you out-rank the guard with the key," Matt said. "You could make an exception."

When Wright looked down at Degan's imploring eyes, she reached to put a gentle hand on his arm. "Please? He is my husband."

He seemed to melt under her touch and turned to leave. Moments later, he returned and when Degan saw him reach to unlock the door of Matt's cell, she breathed a sigh of relief and thanked him.

"Yes, ma'am," he said, pulling the heavy iron door open for her.

She flew into Matt's open arms and he lifted her off the floor in a fervent embrace. Neither noticed that Wright had stepped quietly away to the opposite end of the hallway to allow them privacy.

He set her on her feet again and took her face in his hands. He leaned to kiss her mouth, and she wrapped her arms around his neck, pulling him closer. Despite their present circumstances, when he pulled back to gaze down at her face, he felt giddy and more joyous than he could remember feeling in a very long time.

"Now you know I will not leave you," she said firmly, delighted to finally see a glimmer of trust in his eyes. "Now you know I love you."

He smiled softly. "I love you . . . Mrs. Tyler."

The sound of this new name she had heard for the first time today brought a smile to her face. "This is the name of your wife? Mrs. Tyler?"

He nodded. Then, his expression turned serious and he looked around the cell. "I'm sorry about all of this, Degan. I don't know how this will turn out."

"What will they do to you?"

"I don't know. Once Major Fenton gets here, hopefully, he'll be able to clear my name."

"I know nothing of this," she said, frustration building. "I only want you to come home to me and our son."

Matt took her face again and met her eyes. "Listen to me," he said firmly, "when I get out of this, I want to return to Washington with you and Adam. I want nothing less than that. We can come back to Salamanca to visit from time to time, but I want our son to have the opportunities I can provide him in the white world. Can you live with that?"

"Yes," she said without hesitation. "I will teach him the Seneca ways, and you will teach him the white ways. We will not leave you."

Relief flooded him. He closed his eyes and touched his forehead to hers. Before he could say any more, Lieutenant Wright stepped to the door of the cell.

"I'm sorry, ma'am, I'm afraid it's time to go."

Degan looked quickly around the cell, and removed the blanket from her shoulders. "Take this. You have no fire and no blanket here."

Matt refused. "No, you keep it. I'll be fine. You'll need it to keep warm on the ride back to the house."

"No! You will be cold here—"

"I'll see he gets a blanket, ma'am, don't you worry about that," Wright said.

Matt replaced the blanket around her shoulders. "I'll be much better here if I know you're taking care of yourself and Adam."

He kissed her forehead, and she promised to return the next day.

The gray day had turned sharply colder when Lieutenant Wright and Degan stepped outside the jailhouse. Several soldiers in uniform had gathered on the sidewalk, talking and laughing quietly among themselves. They fell silent when they caught sight of Dr. Tyler's Indian wife with the lieutenant. Feeling their bold stares, Degan instinctively stepped closer to the lieutenant.

"Don't you gentlemen have someplace to be?" Wright asked the group in a stern tone. Watching as the soldiers slowly dispersed, the lieutenant turned to Degan. "Ma'am, perhaps you'd allow me to escort you back to your home. It'll be dark soon. You shouldn't be riding by yourself . . . in the cold."

Degan smiled gratefully and nodded her acceptance of his offer.

"How long will my husband be in the jail?" she asked as their horses ambled through the rutted street.

Wright shrugged. "That's hard to say. The marshal will try to contact Major Fenton, Dr. Tyler's superior officer at the time of Colonel Garrison's death, to get his recollection of what happened that day."

"When this man tells that my husband did nothing wrong, you will free him?"

"Well, it's not up to me. If it were up to me, I'd let him out right now." The lieutenant thought it best not to reveal the real reason the doctor had been locked up. It was a most unusual circumstance, putting a man behind bars without formal charges. But everyone knew the influence of the Garrison family, and their close ties with Captain Ross's superior, Colonel Timmons. If the Garrison family wanted to punish Dr. Tyler by holding him in a cell for a few weeks, Captain Ross would comply. Wright knew the provost marshal to be generally well-intentioned, but not particularly principled under pressure. Besides, the doctor had made it harder on himself by openly acknowledging a native wife, a move that would garner him little sympathy in most quarters.

The next morning, as Degan was preparing to leave for the jailhouse, Nagonda insisted on accompanying her.

"No," she said with finality. "I must go alone."

"Why do you go alone?" Nagonda asked. "This is foolish."

"My husband must see that I am not afraid to go among the white soldiers. He must see that I will not leave him. This is what you said, and you are right."

Her father looked bewildered. "You are not afraid?"

"I am afraid," she replied. "But I must go alone. I must . . . carry my fear with me." She wrapped the blanket around her shoulders and turned toward the door. "There is a young officer who is kind to me. Maybe he will be there when I reach the town."

"You know where to find him? This kind officer?"

"No. But if he is not there, I will still go to the jail."

"Why do you do this alone?"

Degan raised her voice. "If I am to live in the white world with my husband, I must do many things alone. You will not be there to help me. The kind officer will not be there. Only I am there, alone!"

Nagonda's expression softened and he came to take hold of his daughter's shoulders. "Go to your husband."

A gust of cold wind swirled around them as she opened the door to leave.

"Wait," Nagonda said, rushing to open a small cabinet that sat to one side of the hearth. He retrieved two cigars and a small box of matches, and wrapped them in a length of cloth from the kitchen. When he handed the bundle to Degan, he said, "Give these to your husband, from me."

When Degan reined her horse in front of the jailhouse, it had just begun to snow lightly. Scanning the nearly deserted streets for Lieutenant Wright, she dismounted and tethered the horse to the post. She hoped that the kind lieutenant might be waiting inside.

"I'll be damned, look who's back for a visit!" the guard said with a sneer as he looked up from his desk.

Degan quickly looked around the small office, and her heart sank when she saw that she was alone with the guard who was rising to approach her.

"I have come to see my husband," she said, knowing he must have heard the quiver in her voice.

"Is that so? Well, you'll have to get past me first," he said with an arrogant smirk.

He began to step toward her, and she backed away. Feeling her courage evaporate as he continued to approach, she suddenly felt the wall at her back. His arm above her head, he leaned against the wall behind her, his face just inches from hers.

"There's no nice young lieutenant to protect you today, is there?" he asked, clearly enjoying his intimidation of her. "I'm just tryin' to decide what I'm gonna make you do before I let you see your husband." Then he noticed the small package in her hand. "What's that you got there?" he asked, snatching it from her. She reached for it, but he held it from her, grinning maliciously. Unwrapping the cloth, he said, "Well, look here, cigars for me!" He tucked both cigars and the matches into his coat pocket and leaned forward. "Do you know what the punishment is for bringin' contraband to a prisoner?"

Before she knew what was happening, he brought his hand firmly under her jaw and slammed her head against the wall, pinning her tight. "I heard you squaws have nice soft tits. I'm gonna see for myself." A choked cry broke from her throat as he fumbled at the front of her blouse. Barely able to breathe, she felt his sweaty hand grab at her left breast. She forced herself to meet his bold stare, and suddenly her fear turned to fury, her backbone straightened, determination taking hold. Quickly, she brought both arms up and knocked his hands away, then forcefully shoved him back a few steps.

"Whatever you do to me, I have survived far worse from the whites!" she hissed, the intense rage in her chest spilling into her voice. "I have no time for your foolishness! My husband waits for me."

He instinctively raised his hand to strike her but she did not flinch. Holding his stare, she watched his sneer dissolve into confusion, almost disappointment. "Well you take all the fun out of it, don't ya?" With defeat in his eyes, he grabbed her arm and gave her a hard shove that nearly knocked her down. "Go to your husband, then, you squaw bitch."

"Degan?" she heard Matt call out from his cell.

"I am here," she called back, giving the guard a final glare. Just inside the hallway, she paused a moment to collect herself and straighten her clothing. She could not allow Matt to sense distress in her that would cause him concern. As if time were moving in slow motion, she wondered briefly if this was the treatment awaiting her in the white world. Then she realized that for the first time, she had stood up to the white man's cruelty and it made her feel strong.

"I'm so glad to see you," Matt said as she approached, his eyes soft and full of love. He reached through the bars to take her hands. "I don't suppose the guard will let you come in with me since the lieutenant isn't here to order it."

Degan looked askance toward the outer office, her reluctance to ask the guard for a favor written plainly on her face.

"It's all right, I'm just so glad you came. Here," he pulled a thin blanket from the cot and passed it through the bars to spread it on the floor just outside the cell. "Sit down."

They both settled on the cold stone floor, holding hands through the bars.

"Tell me about Adam," he said eagerly, watching her face as though deriving sustenance from her.

"Our son is well, but he misses his father," she said with a sad smile. "He is almost walking. It will be very soon."

"I hope he doesn't forget me while I'm in here."

"He will not forget you. You will see your son grow and do many things. You saved his life . . . just as you saved mine."

Matt leaned to kiss the back of her hands. "I'm curious about something. When you left, you were so convinced that leaving me was the right thing to do. What changed your mind?"

"Every night, the Creator sent you to me when I am sleeping. In my people, what we see in our dreams is from the Creator . . . telling us what we will do. You came to me in my dreams, and then the Creator gave me your child. This is when I know I am your wife. The old shaman says I cannot be your wife, but the Creator has made it so." Matt smiled at her, marveling again at her simple faith that she always embraced without question. "Did the Creator also send me to you?"

"Did I dream of you? Yes, many times. Every day I thought of you. I tried to . . . move on with my life . . . to get over you, but I couldn't. I couldn't stop thinking of you. I hoped that my love for you would fade over time, but . . . it only grew stronger."

"You were with another?"

Matt's eyes drifted downward and he paused. "There were beautiful women in Washington," he said, looking up. "But when I was in their company, I longed for you even more. I couldn't . . . give myself to anyone. I belong to you."

She reached to stroke his face, her eyes growing moist.

"Dr. Tyler?" a voice startled them and both looked up to see Lieutenant Wright approaching from the outer office. Nodding toward Degan, he swept off his hat. "I have good news, sir. Major Fenton has been contacted. He'll be here in a few days."

"Thank you, Lieutenant," Matt said gratefully. "That is good news."

"Ma'am, would you allow me to get you a chair to sit on? That floor doesn't look very comfortable."

"Please, may I go in with my husband?" she asked.

Meeting with less resistance than the day before, they watched as the lieutenant turned and went to fetch the key. When he returned, he said, "I'll leave instructions with the guard to allow you to enter the cell if I'm not here," as he unlocked the door. "If he gives you any trouble, you let me know. I'll wait for you in the office. When you're ready to leave, just call for me."

Degan smiled at him. "Thank you," she said, pausing to touch his arm before she entered the cell.

Matt waited until the lieutenant was gone, then whispered, "I'm grateful for his help, but I'm not sure I like his attentive manner toward you."

"He is very kind to me," she said as they settled on the small cot.

Matt frowned. "He's a little too kind. I think he's sweet on you, and I don't like it."

A flicker of amusement shone in Degan's eyes. "My husband is angry when another man is kind to his wife?"

Raising an eyebrow, Matt looked disapprovingly toward the outer office. "As long as it doesn't go beyond what's proper. I saw the way he looked at you when you touched his arm just now."

"His kindness allows us to be together here, instead of the bars between us. This is good."

Matt relaxed a little. "Yes, I much prefer having you in here with me, although I feel terrible, subjecting you to these conditions. A jail cell is the last place I want to be with you."

She reached to take his hands. "I want to be at the cabin with you. Where we were so happy."

"At the cabin," Matt agreed with a grin, "in bed."

She laughed and kissed his mouth, slowly at first, then more urgently as she felt his hands on her back, holding her tightly against him. Then she felt one hand slip from her back around her side to stroke her breast through the fabric of her blouse. Both breathing harder now, they pulled back.

"We need to stop, or I'll go mad," Matt whispered. "I can't . . . take you here."

She turned to steal a quick glance at the doorway to the office. Turning back, she placed her hand firmly on the prominent bulge between his legs and moaned hungrily.

"I want you to take me," she murmured.

He gently pushed her hand away. "Not here. I don't want to give them a reason to punish me further. We'll have our time together . . . when I get out of here."

Degan rode to the jailhouse each morning. The guard who had taken great pleasure in bullying her at first, grudgingly unlocked Matt's cell door for her every day upon her arrival, she assumed on Lieutenant Wright's orders. As each day passed, Matt became more despondent with his situation, and she more worried about his condition. Despite his assurances to the contrary, she was certain he was not getting enough to eat, and was not being allowed to care for himself properly. Upon learning that the guard had confiscated the cigars and matches he had sent with her the first day, Nagonda sent replacements.

"Your father is a saint," Matt sighed, exhaling smoke from his first satisfying draw. "Tell him I said thank you."

Nine days later, they heard loud voices outside the jailhouse, as though men were arguing in the street. Then, a deep-voiced man came bellowing into the outer office, and immediately down the hallway. Degan stared at him as he walked purposefully toward them. He was an imposing figure, taller and much heavier than Matt. Streaks of tobacco juice glistened in his full whiskers, his dark eyes piercing and lively. Wearing a U.S. Army uniform, he looked fully in command and comfortable with his authority.

"Well I'll be goddamned!" the man roared as he stopped in front of Matt's cell. "Tyler, what the hell are you doing in a goddamned jail cell?"

"Waiting for you to arrive and clear my name, sir," Matt replied. Degan knew this must be Major Fenton and she breathed more easily than she had in many days.

Fenton spat tobacco juice on the floor, and pointed to Degan. "Who's this?"

"This is my wife," Matt said.

"What's she in for?"

Matt stifled a smile. "Keeping me company, sir."

Fenton's eyebrows shot up. "That's one dedicated little squaw you got there, Tyler." His eyes met Degan's. "You Seneca?"

"Yes," she said in a clear voice.

Fenton nodded agreeably and looked back to Matt. "You'll never find a more loyal companion than a Seneca, Tyler."

"Yes, sir, I know."

Fenton turned and took a few steps toward the outer office. "Corporal!"

"Yes, sir?" the guard answered, rushing toward them.

"Get in here and open this cell. You've mistakenly locked up an accomplished surgeon and a fine man."

The guard hesitated. "Sir, my superior officer, Captain Ross—"

"I'm your superior officer at the moment, son. Now do as I say and unlock this goddamn cell!"

"Yes, sir!" Clearly intimidated by this bear of a man, the guard fumbled awkwardly with the keys. Degan felt a rush of satisfaction when she saw that his hands were shaking. "I'll have to shackle him for transport to the provost marshal's office."

"You'll do nothing of the sort, Corporal," Fenton barked. "I'll be escorting Dr. Tyler to the marshal's office. Consider him released into my custody. Now let's get on with it, I'm a busy man."

The guard said nothing more as he unlocked the cell and pulled the heavy iron door open.

In the provost marshal's office, Captain Ross said, "We certainly appreciate you attending these proceedings, Major Fenton," as everyone took their seats at the large table. Matt and Degan sat at one end of the table, while the Garrisons took their places at the opposite end. In the center, Captain Ross and Major Fenton sat facing each other. "These are Colonel Garrison's children, Mr. George Garrison and Miss Virginia Garrison."

Fenton nodded in their direction. "You have my sympathies. Your father served his country well."

"Thank you," George Garrison said quietly.

"Major Fenton, were you in a position to witness the events in the field hospital the day Colonel Garrison died?" the provost marshal began.

"I was," Fenton began. "It was a hellish couple of days, Captain. I don't have to tell you about the horrors of battle. And I can assure you that Dr. Tyler acted properly that day—as did all my surgeons—with proper care to all the soldiers it was humanly possible to save."

"But what about our father?" Miss Garrison asked impatiently.

"If you could elaborate, sir," Ross said, "and tell us about the care that Colonel Garrison, in particular, received."

Fenton took a deep breath. "I was in charge of the field hospital at Fredericksburg. As such, the three surgeons working that day, including Dr. Tyler, were under my direct supervision. The U.S. Army suffered enormous casualties in Fredericksburg. The damn Rebels beat us soundly. Hundreds of men were brought in the day Colonel Garrison died. Hundreds more lay on the battlefield, dying of wounds that would have been survivable had they been brought in, but we just didn't have the man power to treat everybody. We never did. I ordered my surgeons to work on the soldiers who could be saved, before infection and gangrene set in. We needed every man at the front. We needed infantrymen, not commanders. The foot soldiers with rifles in hand-to-hand combat saved this union, not the generals and colonels on horseback, beggin' your pardon," he said to the Garrisons. "I ordered my surgeons to tend to the foot soldier first. That's the way I ran my field hospitals."

"Did our father have typhus, sir?" George Garrison asked.

"Yes, Mr. Garrison, he did," Fenton replied. "Typhus, as you know, is very contagious. I didn't want a contagious man brought in among the other injured soldiers who were already fighting for their lives. So we kept Colonel Garrison quarantined at the edge of the hospital grounds. I told Dr. Tyler to leave Colonel Garrison alone, but he thought he could save him, and he worked damn hard to do so, despite my orders. He worked on him, tried to revive him for more than an hour. I was the one who finally pulled him off, told him to give up, the colonel was already dead at that point."

Matt had been staring at his hands folded on the table in front of him as Major Fenton spoke. He had no recollection of his treatment that day of Colonel Garrison, no memory of trying to save him, no memory of any specific actions taken. That day, along with so many others, had melted together into a blur of agony, filth, and exhaustion that continued to haunt him. Barely able to recall his superior's clear instructions not to tend to Colonel Garrison, he sensed no rancor now in Fenton's demeanor for his orders having been defied. When Matt looked up, all eyes were on him. He looked at the Garrison children at the opposite end of the table and, for the first time, saw no bitterness in their eyes.

"If your father hadn't already had typhus," Fenton said, addressing the Garrisons, "he might have survived his wound, especially in the skilled hands of Dr. Tyler. But in his already weakened condition, an otherwise survivable gunshot wound . . . finally took him."

"Is it your opinion, then, Major Fenton, that Dr. Tyler should not be charged with any crime related to the death of Colonel Garrison?" Ross asked, glancing toward the Garrisons.

"That is my opinion," Fenton replied.

"Well then, if there are no further questions for the major," Ross said, "these proceedings are adjourned. Dr. Tyler, you're free to go."

Relieved beyond words, Matt turned to embrace Degan, then stood to shake hands with Major Fenton. "Thank you for coming, sir."

"I'll have one of my men provide you transportation to the train station, Major, when you're ready," Ross said. "There's a boarding house in town that can accommodate you until your train leaves."

Fenton picked up his hat and bowed politely toward Degan, then the Garrison family before leaving. George Garrison stood up and assisted his sister to standing. Miss Garrison stared blankly toward Matt and Degan, then turned and swept from the room. George Garrison approached Matt with an outstretched hand.

"Thank you, Dr. Tyler, for trying to save our father."

All the strain and fear of the past two weeks suddenly rose to settle in Matt's throat. He took Mr. Garrison's hand firmly and nodded, unable to speak.

Matt waited a few more days before purchasing two tickets on the passenger train to Washington—giving the weather time to clear, and Degan time to say a proper good-bye to her family. When they had returned from the jail the day Matt's name was cleared by Major Fenton, Nagonda had met them with elation that was bittersweet. He had been happy for his daughter, whose husband was once again a free man. But he was also heartbroken, having known all along that the white shaman would eventually take his daughter and his grandson away, to the white world and a future that he could not begin to imagine.

The night before their departure, Matt and Nagonda sat in their usual spot, on the back steps of the small house, smoking. It had become a routine that Matt had grown to look forward to, and that he now realized he would miss. Tonight, Nagonda was more quiet than usual, and Matt knew why.

"I'll take very good care of Degan and the baby," Matt said softly. "I love both of them more than I could ever express in words." Nagonda stared straight ahead for a long moment, so Matt continued. "I know you must be worried about them entering white society, but . . . they will know boundless love from me. And they'll never want for anything."

"I see how you love Degan and the son," Nagonda finally said, his voice barely above a whisper. "My grandson will have a good life in the white world. He will know the ways of the Seneca. His mother will teach him. And he will also know the thoughts of white men. This is good. When our two people live apart, this is not the way for the white man and the Seneca to learn about one another, and live in peace. My grandson will grow to know both people, and he will tell our stories to the whites . . . so they will know us also."

"He'll grow to be an honorable man," Matt said, feeling pride swell in his chest as he imagined his son's future. "I want to thank you for your kindness and generosity toward me since I arrived here back in January. You've been very gracious in accepting me."

Nagonda turned to Matt. "This I do at first for my daughter. But now, I see for myself that you are a good man. Even Gowesan sees, but she will not say. Maybe when you return to the white world with Degan, your family will be kind to her also."

Matt nodded, but fell silent. Over the last few days, he had successfully avoided thinking about the reception that awaited them in Washington. He did not want to imagine his mother's reaction to the news that not only did he bring his Seneca wife back with him, but their child as well.

PART III

March 1869, Washington

CHAPTER

28

"Would you be in need of a carriage, sir?" A young man dressed in full livery stood outside the train station and addressed Matt with a polite tip of his hat.

"Yes, my wife and I need transportation to Georgetown," Matt replied, placing a hand on Degan's back.

The driver looked at her curiously. The style of her pale blue frock and matching wrap was the same as every other woman traveling through the station. But the driver's smile faded as he looked at her face, then at the child in her arms. Silently, he reached to take the bags from Matt's grip and quickly secured them to the luggage rack at the back of the carriage. He opened the carriage door and bowed slightly as Degan climbed in.

"How far is your home?" she asked, trying to find a comfortable position for Adam on her lap as the carriage jolted into the street.

"It's a few miles. Here, let me hold him," Matt said, reaching for the baby, who immediately grinned and stretched his little arms toward his father. Degan watched as Matt held Adam close to the small window of the carriage so he could look out at the passing street.

"See all those people out there?" he murmured to his son. "Look at all the new buildings and all the workers, see that? What do you think of all that?" Then he turned to Degan with a broad grin full of pride. "He's watching everything so intently."

She smiled as he turned back to the baby and continued to comment on the passing activity as they made their way through the city, and finally into Georgetown. Matt's house sat on a quiet street lined with mature trees that were still bare from the winter. The houses stood close to one another, just like in Salamanca. But these houses were much larger, built solidly of red brick, many with green ivy wrapped like a blanket around the sides. When the carriage pulled to a halt at the front stoop, Matt didn't wait for the driver to open the door. The baby still in his arms, he alighted and offered Degan his hand as she stepped out.

"May I take your bags inside for you, sir?" the driver asked courteously.

"Yes, please," Matt replied, then turned to Degan and motioned for her to follow the driver into the house. Once inside, she stood transfixed, bright afternoon sun bathing the open foyer and the wide staircase leading to the second floor.

"Sara? Chloe?" Matt called out, closing the heavy front door behind the departing driver. Degan turned to him with a questioning look. "My maid and my cook," he explained.

Within a few moments, Sara appeared on the second-floor landing, smoothing the front of her cobbler's apron as she hurried toward the stairs. She stopped abruptly on the top step when she saw Degan.

"Yes sir?" she said tentatively.

"Hello Sara. Please come down and meet my wife," Matt said casually.

Sara's eyes grew large and her mouth dropped open as she slowly began her descent, unabashedly gaping at Degan the whole way to the downstairs landing. Her wide eyes darting from Matt to Degan and back, she slowly made her way across the foyer to stand in front of them.

"You're looking well, Sara," Matt said cordially. "I'd like you to meet Mrs. Tyler."

"Afternoon, ma'am," the young maid murmured, keeping her head down and bobbing an awkward curtsy.

Degan smiled at the girl, who seemed reluctant to meet her eyes.

"I know this must seem like a rather sudden turn of events, Sara," Matt said, "but it's actually quite a long story. I've known Mrs. Tyler since I lived in Sylvan. She'll be the mistress of the house now. I think you'll find her to be very kind and generous."

"Yes, sir," Sara said, raising her chin slightly to offer Degan a timid smile.

"And this is our little boy," Matt said proudly. "His name is Adam."

Sara's eyes softened as she looked at the baby in Matt's arms. "Aw, would you look at that?"

"Would you please fetch Chloe?" he said. "I'd like her to meet Mrs. Tyler as well."

"Miss Chloe went to the market to shop for dinner, sir," Sara said.

"When do you expect her back?"

"Later this afternoon. We didn't know you were comin' home today."

"I understand. Mrs. Tyler and I will get settled in, then."

"Which bedroom did you want for the nursery, sir?" Sara asked. "We don't have no crib for a baby."

"For now, prepare the smaller bedroom next to mine as the nursery. We'll make do with what we've got."

"Yes, sir. Oh, the postman brought your letters by. I put them on the sideboard in the dining room," she said, picking up their bags and making her way back upstairs.

With eyes as wide as Sara's, Degan turned to Matt.

"What?" he asked with a grin.

She looked uneasy. "This is strange for me."

"I know it is," he said, putting his arm around her shoulders and pulling her close. He kissed the side of her head. "I hope you'll soon become accustomed to living in this house and having servants around. I think you'll like Sara. She's always been eager to please."

"What will she do?"

"She's the maid. She keeps the house clean, serves the meals, and she'll help you take care of Adam. In fact," he said thoughtfully, "I should probably look into hiring another servant now that you and Adam will be living here."

Degan wandered the perimeter of the foyer, looking tentatively into the parlor, then into the formal dining room. His home was much larger than she had imagined, the beautifully furnished rooms filled with light from the early spring day. She would live here in this house with him, and they would raise their son here, in these plush surroundings, and with the assistance of young women she did not know. Unable to grasp all the implications of her role as Matt's wife, she closed her eyes, took a deep breath, and reminded herself how deeply she loved him.

"Let's go see who wrote Father a letter while he was away," Matt said to Adam as he carried him toward the dining room. The child squirmed in his arms and turned to reach for Degan. "I think he wants his mother."

Degan unfastened her heavy cloak and draped it over a chair in the foyer, smiling as she reached for her son.

"If you'd like to take him upstairs for a nap, Sara should soon have the room prepared."

She nodded and made her way to the stairs. On the second floor, she paused to gaze out the window at the end of the hallway. Looking down at the backyard, she saw a rectangular plot of ground a few paces from the back of the house and surmised this must have been Matt's garden last season. For a moment, her thoughts wandered back to that day at the cabin so long ago, when she had discovered a similar plot on Matt's property and decided to make a garden for him. How her life had changed since those days. She nuzzled her son, who was watching a robin flutter on a tree branch just outside the window. Sensing that someone was watching her, she turned to see Sara standing in the doorway of one of the bedrooms with a bemused expression on her face.

"The nursery is ready, ma'am," she said softly, waving her hand toward the room behind her.

Degan nodded, carrying Adam past a large, masculine-looking room which she knew instinctively was Matt's. The smaller, adjacent bedroom was more sparsely furnished, but still lavish, with thick carpets on the floor and heavy draperies at the windows.

"I made a space for him in the middle of all these pillows so he won't roll off the bed when he sleeps," Sara said, a bit of pride in her voice for having thought of such an ingenious solution to their lack of a crib.

"Thank you," Degan said as she placed her son on the bed and began to remove his traveling clothes. "The small bag we brought is for Adam. Where is it?"

Sara hurried next door to Matt's room and soon returned with the bag. She set it on the bed and opened it. Degan watched as she began removing Adam's clothing, diapers, and the corn-husk doll her father had made for his grandson. She stared at the doll curiously, then put it aside.

Degan sat with the baby in one of two armchairs by the window, and proceeded to unbutton the front of her blouse to the waist, then slipped the lacey strap of her chemise down her arm, exposing her left breast. As the baby hungrily devoured her nipple, she smiled down at him, then felt Sara's eyes on her. The girl stood by the bed, mesmerized by every move she made.

"Are you an Indian, ma'am?" she finally asked, wide-eyed.

"I am Seneca," Degan replied, rubbing a finger lightly across her son's cheek. "My people live on a reservation many miles north from here."

"Do you scalp people?"

Degan frowned. "This word I don't know . . . scalp?"

Sara illustrated with her hands. "You know, do you cut off people's scalps? I hear that's what Indians do."

"No," she cringed. "Why would I do this?"

"I don't know," Sara said, looking relieved. "Maybe you're not that kind of Indian. You look like an Indian, but in white woman's clothes. Do you wish you was white?"

Degan smiled and shook her head. "No."

"I don't think the white people are gonna like you much, ma'am, especially Dr. Tyler's family," Sara said earnestly. Degan detected no malice in the girl's tone.

"Why do you say this?"

"Because you're not white."

"Sara!" Matt's voice boomed from the doorway, causing both women to jump. Clearly angry, he had a stern look on his face and his arms were crossed in front of him. "I expect you to make Mrs. Tyler feel welcome in this house. Have you forgotten your manners?"

Suddenly looking as though she might faint, Sara's cheeks flushed and her eyes fastened to the floor.

"It's all right," Degan said gently. "We are getting to know each other."

Matt's outrage somewhat diffused, he addressed the young servant in a quieter tone, "I believe Chloe has returned from the market. Please go down to the kitchen and see if she needs assistance."

"Yes sir," Sara whispered through trembling lips, and without looking up, forced herself past Matt and escaped downstairs.

"I'm sorry about that," he said, coming to sit in the other armchair beside Degan.

"She has not seen a Seneca before. I was teaching her."

"I don't want her making you feel more uncomfortable than you already do. Especially in this house."

"Many of your people will have these questions. Sara will learn about me only if she asks. Maybe you are . . . uncomfortable," she said, struggling with the word.

He had to chuckle at himself in the face of her insight. "Maybe you're right," he admitted, feeling a little embarrassed by his outburst. All along, he had been concerned about Degan's adjustment to the white world. He now realized that perhaps the adjustment would be significant for him as well.

Having nearly forgotten why he'd come upstairs, he pulled two sheets of folded paper from his breast pocket. "I received a letter from Jon, with good news. Do you remember me telling you about the minister's daughter in Sylvan who was sweet on Jon? Her name was Anne and I told you she had red hair?"

"Ah yes," Degan said as the memory surfaced.

"Well, Jon and Anne have gotten married."

Degan gasped with joy and took hold of Matt's arm. "This is very good!"

"It gets better. He says they're taking their honeymoon trip to visit some of her relatives in northern Virginia, which is not far from here. They also want to visit Washington."

"They will come here? When?"

"According to his letter, they'll be arriving sometime next week."

"It will be good to see Jon. I am glad we will meet his wife also."

"Jon will be surprised to see you, and especially Adam," Matt said with a grin, folding the letter and placing it back in his breast pocket. "He doesn't know that I went to Salamanca."

"He will be pleased?"

"Yes. He knows how I feel about you," Matt replied, "and what I went through when you left."

Degan reached to take his hand. "I am glad you came for us. Our son will grow to be a good man in the white world. I am glad you are his father."

Matt brought her hand to his lips for a kiss, his throat tight with emotion.

"Your family is here also?" Degan asked.

"My mother and sister live a few miles from here."

"You will go to them?"

"I want to settle in for a few days before I visit them," he said, fighting a vague sense of obligation he felt to call on his mother after being gone so long. He was not looking forward to that day and had decided to put it off as long as possible.

"I would like to meet your mother," Degan said. "But maybe she will not be happy that I am your wife."

Matt reached to lovingly caress the top of Adam's head. "When he's asleep, I'll show you our room."

She glanced down. "He will be asleep soon," she said, and rose to carry him to the bed. She nestled him between the rows of pillows that Sara had fashioned, covered him with the soft blanket from the foot of the bed, then closed her blouse.

Matt's adjoining bedroom reminded Degan of his room at the cabin—distinctly masculine, with furnishings dark and rich. As soon as she entered, she felt a sense of familiarity that was comforting. She recognized the four-poster bed, the focal point of the room. Across from the foot of the bed was a massive fireplace in which robust flames were chasing the chill from the room. A tall wood-framed mirror stood in one corner, and Degan went to peer into it, always fascinated by the whites' desire to see their reflection. Matt removed his coat and settled comfortably into an oversized leather armchair at the side of the fireplace. He retrieved a cigar from his coat pocket and snipped one end.

"You must be tired from traveling," he said, striking a match. "Maybe you'd like to sleep before dinner. The bed is very comfortable."

In the mirror, she watched him slowly rotate the cigar between his fingers as it lit. She had always loved his hands. Warm and strong, they had saved her life so many months ago, and more recently, their son's life as well. They had comforted her, provided for her needs, and brought her indescribable pleasure. As he puffed on the cigar, she studied his handsome features, dark wavy hair that now had just a few strands of gray at the temples, his green eyes that so often revealed his vulnerability, eliciting gentle protectiveness in her.

A playful mood came over her and she turned from the mirror. She went to lean against the foot of the bed across from him, and bent to unbutton and remove her ankle boots. Slowly lifting her skirt and petticoats to just above her knees, she pushed one garter, then the other, toward her ankles, loosening each stocking and pushing it over each foot. Looking up, she was pleased to see that he was watching her closely. Holding his stare, she stood and unbuttoned her blouse, slipping it from her shoulders and tossing it to the floor. Her voluminous skirt and petticoats unfastened and dropped to her ankles, she stepped out of them and threw them to land near her blouse. Slowly, she pushed the straps of her chemise from her shoulders and eased it over her hips, loosening the waist of her pantalets and sliding both to the floor.

Forgotten gray ashes were accumulating at the glowing tip of Matt's cigar while his eyes remained fixed on his disrobing wife. Just before the ashes dropped into his lap, he placed the cigar in the ashtray on the table beside him, barely aware of what he was doing.

She stood facing him, naked, feeling the fire of his gaze burning into her skin. Sinking to the floor in front of him, she settled between his legs and reached to cup her hand around his fullness, massaging until he closed his eyes and moaned aloud. Her fingers worked urgently to unbutton his trousers and soon, with a lift of his hips, she managed to pull his garments down to his thighs, exposing his firmness already glistening moisture at the tip. Without a word, she devoured him with her warm mouth, knowing once more the fulfillment of hearing his breathing become heavier as he grew rigid at her touch.

"Oh Degan," he sighed. She savored his taste, his scent, his passion that she knew was building beyond control. His hands touched her hair, and when she looked up, he was watching her with a smoldering hunger in his eyes that she yearned to satisfy. He grasped her shoulders and pulled her up to sit astride his lap, entering her easily.

He touched her breasts reverently, as if seeing them for the first time. Her dark nipples taut, he brushed them lightly with his thumbs before encircling them in his mouth and gently sucking one, then the other. She cried out with pleasure and laid her head back, hearing him murmur her name against her warm skin.

She took his face in her hands and gently touched his lips with hers. Opening her mouth, she felt him caress her with his tongue, his passion unyielding inside her. She began to move up and down, slowly at first until their rhythmic breathing grew stronger and faster. His warm breath on her, she felt him grasp her buttocks in a massaging grip. She moved faster, watching his face flush and his eyes close as he surrendered to intense passion. Finally, he cried out in powerful release. He clutched her to him, panting against her. The fabric of his vest and cotton shirt felt cool against her body.

When he pulled back and reached down to touch her, they both heard Adam start to cry in the next room. Degan's eyes darted to his face and she sat paralyzed for a moment. Then just as quickly, they heard Sara's voice cooing to the baby in a soothing tone.

"Sara will take care of him," Matt whispered to her.

She turned toward the adjoining room, sat very still and listened, but all they could hear now was Sara's voice singing a sweet lullaby. She turned back to Matt to see a gentle smile on his face, which she returned. He pulled her naked body tightly against him and stroked her hair.

"I'm glad you're the mother of my son," he murmured into her ear. When she sat up, he took her face in his hands and said, "I think you'll be more comfortable if we finish this in bed."

Four days later at Tyler Mansion, Kathleen sat as though paralyzed, a fixed stare boring into her son. She had been sitting in the parlor with her needlepoint, which she hastily put aside when her son entered.

Having finally decided he could no longer avoid calling on his mother, the look on William's face when he answered the door told Matt everything he needed to know about the reception he would face. He knew Caroline would have told her the reason he left town so abruptly weeks ago. Now, after a brief, tense greeting, Matt got right to the point.

He recounted how Degan had come into his life, and how their relationship had evolved throughout the previous year. He chose his words carefully, watching his mother's face grow pale. Her eyes had a vacuous quality that he had seen often in his life, always when she was receiving news that she would subsequently refuse to accept.

"I love her," he concluded simply. "We have a son together."

After what seemed an eternity, Kathleen finally exhaled, and to Matt's great surprise, smiled tenuously at him. She actually seemed more relaxed than he had expected, and he found himself clinging to the hope that he might be spared the histrionics he had known her to display when she was upset.

"Matthew, darling, I know exactly what this is," she began, her voice even and controlled.

He frowned. "You know exactly what *what* is?" he asked, cautiously intrigued.

"Your attachment to this . . . woman. This is nothing more than what many physicians have experienced when they've rescued a female patient from a life-threatening situation. The woman always takes on . . . an irresistibly helpless quality that few men can resist." Matt was speechless, so Kathleen continued. "This woman that you found on your property was badly injured and in need of medical attention, which, being a decent man and compassionate physician, you provided. You probably saved her life, and she might even be capable of gratitude. Now you're feeling that because you rescued her in her time of need, there's some sort of emotional bond between you. And you're calling it love. But it isn't love, my darling. It's simply that she was in need of your services and your talents to treat her, and now she's recovered and should go back to her own kind. And take the child with her."

Matt sat motionless, trying to decide if he had the fortitude to counter his mother's conviction that his feelings for Degan were nothing more than fantasy born of his successful treatment of her wounds. He leaned forward in the chair and met her confident stare.

"Mother, if it makes you more comfortable to be dismissive of my feelings for Degan, there's nothing I can do about it. But I can assure you that what I feel for her is not the result of having saved her life. I love her. She is my wife now."

"How can she be your wife? Surely you weren't married by a Christian minister!"

"We're as committed to each other as any other husband and wife," Matt said evenly.

Kathleen exhaled slowly, trying to keep her emotions in check. "Matthew, I know whereof I speak. I have seen this before."

"I don't know what you mean."

"I've never mentioned this," she began, keeping her voice low, "but years ago, your father fell into this same trap with a woman who was from a disadvantaged background and suffered violence in her home. She had been injured by her husband and she came to Adam for treatment. Of course, your father treated her and was kind to her, but this woman misinterpreted his generosity for affection, and . . . well, let us just say it was an absurd misunderstanding that took some time to clarify."

"What woman? Why haven't I heard about this before now?"

"Because it was nothing!" Kathleen asserted with a forced laugh. "Whatever affection this woman thought was between her and your father was based upon nothing more than a compassionate physician doing his job, treating a patient as he would any other patient. It was simply a misunderstanding on her part, that's all. You've never heard anything about it because it was nothing. Just as your feelings for . . . this woman . . . are nothing."

"Stop—!" Matt caught himself and took a deep, calming breath. "You must stop saying that if there is to be peace between us."

"Matthew, think about this for a moment. Perhaps you don't mind harboring a godless savage under your roof, but in this house, we feel quite differently. God in heaven, how can you be so naïve? Have you not read the newspaper accounts of the savages in the western wilderness who take great delight in torturing and scalping the poor, defenseless settlers? I've heard that some of the savages even feast on the bodies afterwards in wild celebrations. How do you know this creature you've innocently brought into your home won't one day turn on you in such a way?"

Having nearly reached his breaking point, Matt immediately caught a mental picture of Degan, knife in hand, scalping him in his sleep, then gleefully devouring his dead body. Suddenly, uncontrollable laughter burst from him and, covering his face with his hands, he guffawed loudly.

"I do not appreciate being laughed at," his mother said indignantly.

Finally catching his breath, he replied, "Then don't say funny things."

"I don't know why I should be surprised by what you're telling me," Kathleen sniffed, her controlled demeanor crumbling. "You always did have more of an affinity with the domestics than you did with refined individuals of your own station. And to think that the heir to the Tyler name is half ignorant heathen. Your father must be turning over in his grave!"

With that, Matt stood, his jaw clenched in anger. "Mother, you must accept the fact that Degan and I are husband and wife. We have a child—"

"I do not have to accept anything of the kind!" Kathleen shrieked. "And don't even think about bringing that savage into this house! I will not allow it!"

He felt her words penetrate, their implication slowly stabbing to his core, just as the Collins boy's knife had done so many months ago.

His voice quiet, he asked, "Have you no interest in seeing your grandson?"

Kathleen sat up straighter and lifted her chin. In her eyes, he saw something close to satisfaction as she spat, "No!"

The word stung, just as she had intended. "As you wish," he replied, feeling a stone wall rise between him and his mother. Finally, he turned and left the house, slamming the door behind him.

A while later, Caroline cautiously peeked around the corner of the parlor door to see her mother sitting on the settee, staring into space.

"Mother?" she said tentatively before entering the room.

Kathleen looked up at her daughter with a blank expression.

"Mother, what's wrong? I thought I heard Matty's voice," Caroline said gently, sitting down next to her mother.

Kathleen began to shake her head in disbelief. "I can barely take in what just transpired in this room," she said. "In thirty-three years of marriage, your father never walked out on me in the middle of a disagreement. Now, my Matthew has abandoned me—in my own home, mind you—just as we were discussing his tragic situation."

"What tragic situation?"

"He's taken in this . . . savage woman and, God have mercy, they've had a child together!" Kathleen closed her eyes and put a hand to her chest.

"What? He's . . . a father?"

Kathleen nodded, reaching for her handkerchief and dabbing her eyes. "I simply cannot accept that he's chosen to turn his back on everything your father and I taught him . . . everything our family has held precious." She held her handkerchief over her mouth and seemed to be crying into it, though Caroline saw no tears. "What has happened to this family since your father passed?" she asked, her words muffled into the cloth. "My children have strayed so far from a suitable path, and I am left all alone to endure it."

Caroline moved forward to take her mother's cold hand in her warm one. "Mother, Matty is a good man, very sensible and compassionate. You and Father did a wonderful job of raising both of us," she paused, hoping her mollifying words would penetrate her mother's outer coating of stubborn fear. "Now, I think we must trust Matty's judgment on this."

"Caroline, I will not allow that feral heathen into this house! I cannot change the fact that Matthew has chosen to throw his life away, but I do not have to be a participant in this tragic situation."

Kathleen suddenly looked tired and worn out from the fight. She squeezed her daughter's hand and closed her eyes. Caroline had a fleeting thought that her mother looked like a little girl who was afraid to jump a short distance into the waiting arms of a loved one.

"Mother, if Matty has chosen this woman as his wife, we must accept it," Caroline said, watching a tear trickle down her mother's cheek. She quickly moved to sit closer and put an arm around her mother's shoulders. "Let's be brave and enlightened about this. If those in our circle choose to attach a dishonorable label to us because of Matty's choice, perhaps we can rise above it."

Kathleen sat up straight, lifted her chin slightly and gave her daughter a cool glare. "Both of you have been a disappointment to me." Stung anew by her mother's latest barb, Caroline sat back and was silent. She knew what was coming. "I told you that dispensary would be your ruin and I was right. You should have taken heed of my warnings."

"Mother, my meeting Mr. Butler had nothing to do with the dispensary directly—"

"Perhaps not directly, Caroline, but when you associate with those types of people day in and day out, your standards naturally become much lower. You begin to accept for yourself that lifestyle, and you're willing to associate with those who are far beneath your station."

"Mr. Butler is a fine man," Caroline said in a small voice, frustrated that her throat was growing tighter and tears were rising to the surface, as they always did when she argued with her mother.

"Regardless of what kind of man he is, he certainly is not a proper suitor for you. Oh, if only your father were here," Kathleen said, exasperated to be shouldering the burden of parenting alone. "Why on earth would you not accept Mr. David Lawson's offer of courtship? He is a much more worthy prospect. His family is well-to-do and quite prominent in Annapolis."

Caroline realized her mother would never approve of Jonah Butler as a suitor, simply because he did not come from a financially comfortable background. But she herself cared very little about such things. And she knew exactly what her father's reaction would have been to the news that she and Mr. Butler were courting. He would have approved as long as he knew that Mr. Butler was a man of integrity with honorable intentions. She realized that when Kathleen bemoaned her fate as a now-single parent, it was not because Adam Tyler would have supported her elitist stance, but because he always provided her insulation from the unpleasant task of discussing with her offspring their poor choices.

Kathleen sighed loudly, smoothing her skirt and straightening the lacey collar of her dress. "I simply don't know how I'll face my friends, or anyone in the church. What will they think of me? I thought I could endure the worst of it when you and Mr. Butler began courting, but I can never forgive Matthew for shaming me like this!" After a moment,

Kathleen waved her hand dismissively. "But, at least I made it clear to Matthew that his . . . wife . . . is not welcome in this house. I'll never see her, which is a great blessing."

Caroline decided that for the time being, a little progress had been made. Her mother had begun the process of resigning herself to the notion that Matt's decisions were his own affair, and that she was left with no alternative but to somehow live with them. Martyrdom would sit well on her mother's shoulders. She wondered if Kathleen's banishment of Matt's wife from the house would hold, especially given that the Seneca woman was now the mother of her only grandchild. But she had known her mother to deny herself joy in the name of stubborn principle many times before. She decided to leave that battle for another day. For now, she would go to Matt and try to soothe his wounded spirit.

Caroline lifted the brass knocker to tap on the front door of her brother's house. When Matt himself opened the door a few moments later, a dejected expression on his face and a smoldering cigar between his fingers, he wordlessly stepped aside and waved a hand toward the foyer.

"Have you come to plead Mother's case, or try to make peace?" he asked, closing the door behind her.

"I've come to tell you how happy I am that you're home," she said, watching him take a deep draw on his cigar and slowly exhale gray smoke into the air. His smoking always reminded her of their father, and so she found it comforting. "And to congratulate you on . . . taking a wife."

"Thank you," he replied flatly, accompanying her across the foyer.

When Caroline entered the parlor, she saw a petite woman sitting on the divan. The woman looked up and smiled, her face serene and strikingly beautiful. Her deep brown eyes were soft and bright, long dark hair flowed freely down her back. On her lap, she held an adorable little boy who so closely resembled Matt, Caroline's breath caught in her throat.

"Oh!" she said with delight, clasping her hands in front of her. She looked to Matt, whose face had finally broken into a smile. "Is this my nephew?"

"Yes, this is Adam," Matt replied as they approached the divan.

"Adam! After Father," Caroline said, sinking into a chair next to the divan. "And you must be Degan?"

"Yes," Degan said, noticing Caroline's blond hair beneath her bonnet, and how elegantly she was dressed. "I am glad you are here."

Adam stood on his mother's lap and reached toward Caroline's dangling earrings that sparkled above her collar. He giggled excitedly as Caroline reached for him, taking him into her arms and situating him on her lap.

"What a beautiful little boy you are," she cooed as he reached again toward her ears.

"If you don't want to lose those earrings, I'd suggest either taking them off or distracting him with something else," Matt admonished with a grin.

"That's all right, I don't mind if he wants to play with my jewelry," Caroline said, then touched the little scar at the base of Adam's neck. "What happened here?"

"When I arrived in Salamanca the first day, I learned that Adam was suffering from diphtheria. I had to perform a tracheotomy on him immediately so he could breathe."

"That was the illness on the reservation you spoke of when you left?" Caroline asked.

"Yes. Once I had been exposed to the virus, I had to remain quarantined there for a few weeks. But that first day, I learned that Adam is my son."

"Matt saved our son's life," Degan said softly.

"How fortunate that you left for Salamanca when you did. Otherwise, the diphtheria might have . . . oh, I hate to think of what might have happened!" Caroline said, giving Adam a quick hug.

"Thank you for coming," Matt said quietly, and when his sister looked up, she saw the hurt still fresh in his eyes.

"Matty, I'm so sorry about what happened between you and Mother. I hate to see you so troubled."

"She said some very hurtful things. I expected she would have difficulty with the news, but I didn't expect her to stoop to mean-spirited name-calling and insults to my character."

"I'm sorry it's come to this. But I do think Mother may eventually come around . . . as best she can, and in her own way. She reads stories in the newspapers about—" Caroline's eyes darted to Degan, then back to Matt "—well, about the killings and such in the West. That's the only impression she has of . . . Indians."

"It's an inaccurate impression," Matt said firmly, settling beside Degan on the divan.

Caroline decided it best to change the subject. "We've missed you at the dispensary while you've been away. Dr. Wallace was able to recruit two additional physicians to help, and our new-patient visits have increased."

"I'm glad to hear that more doctors are volunteering their time." Matt said, noticing Degan's confused expression. "The dispensary is a place where the poor can receive medical care that they don't have to pay for. Before coming to Salamanca, I was working there nearly every day."

"You healed many at this place?"

"Yes, he did," Caroline chimed in. "Many poor people, mostly women and children, who would otherwise go without medical care, came to the dispensary to receive free care from Matty and the other doctors who were generous enough to volunteer their time."

Degan turned to Matt and smiled softly, her eyes filled with pride.

"I do have more good news to share," Caroline said. "I'm quite sure Mother didn't mention it."

"Frankly, she said nothing worth hearing while I was there."

"You remember Mr. Jonah Butler? The missionary who came to tour the dispensary the day you left?"

"Yes, I remember," Matt said with a grin. "He was quite smitten with you. He was able to convince his companion to claim illness and miss the tour so he could have you all to himself."

Caroline's cheeks flushed a rosy pink. "Matty!"

He chuckled at her embarrassment. "That's what happened, is it not?"

She glanced up sheepishly. "Yes, he confessed much later that Mr. Webster was not truly ill that day. Anyway, Mr. Butler and I have been courting."

"That is good news. I'm very happy for you, Cara," Matt said, noticing a blissful glow about his sister that he had not seen in a very long time.

"Of course, Mother doesn't approve," Caroline said, her smile fading, "but Mr. Butler is a fine man."

"I'm sure he is," Matt said. "But what about his work as a missionary? Won't he be traveling?"

"He's awaiting his next assignment. He's expecting that the Board will be sending him to the continent of Africa. He's been assisting at the dispensary these last few weeks."

"The Board?"

"The American Board of Commissioners for Foreign Missions. They sponsor many missionaries when they go overseas."

"And what will you do when he leaves for his next assignment?"

"I'll continue with my work at the dispensary," she said quietly, her happy expression of a moment ago dissolving from her face. "I'll be sad to see him go, of course. He's a wonderful man. But I'll have my work at the dispensary, which I find so satisfying." She looked up with a brave smile that was clearly forced. "Your sister will likely be a spinster, Matty."

"You haven't discussed marriage?"

"No," she replied. "We haven't been courting very long. And anyway, if I am here in Washington and he remains a traveling missionary, I don't see how marriage would work."

"Perhaps when he's faced with leaving you, he'll decide to give up the missionary field and stay."

"Oh, I would never want him to give up the missionary field for me," Caroline said quickly. "That has been his calling. I couldn't ask him to abandon his calling."

Matt glanced at Degan, then back to his sister. "Sometimes things work out without anyone having to abandon their calling."

"I'm very happy for you, Matty. Months ago, when we talked that night after the party, I was discouraging of you. Perhaps at the time, I was echoing Mother's sentiments more than my own. I've come to realize that in order to be fulfilled, one must often defy societal tenets and follow the heart."

"You were right about the path being more difficult. But the rewards are greater."

"Still, I know it's hurtful that Mother reacted to you the way she did," Caroline said. "You must be very disappointed that she showed no interest in meeting her grandson."

"It's not just that. My conversation with her made me realize that we may encounter that same sentiment elsewhere. My greatest fear is that Adam will be subjected to that kind of unfounded hatred throughout his life. I couldn't bear that."

Caroline looked down at her nephew, who had fallen asleep in her lap, and put a gentle hand to his cheek. "Yes, it's too bad we're not as enlightened as most Europeans I've met. When I was living in Europe, I found them to be much more accepting of . . . mixed marriages and the offspring of those unions." Caroline looked up. "You remember, when

Father took us to London years ago? There was a couple living across the street, and the wife was from Africa. In fact, I remember other couples of mixed origins living in the city. I can't imagine people in this country ever being so accepting of mixed couples."

"Yes, I remember," he replied. "But we were children at the time. Perhaps those couples faced difficulties that we couldn't fathom."

"They spoke openly of their lives together. They were happy, and said they were treated well. I found the same to be true when I was living in Paris."

Matt was silent for a moment, then turned to Degan. "I wish that were the case here, but I fear we will never know acceptance and neither will Adam."

The clock on the bedroom mantle chimed eleven-fifteen as Matt removed his smoking jacket and draped it over the arm of the chair before the fireplace. Degan had retired earlier, and he looked down at her now, nestled in bed beneath a thick comforter, dozing contentedly. Her dark hair contrasted sharply with the snow-white pillowcase. She breathed softly, her lovely face relaxed in sleep. At times, it was still hard to believe that she had come into his life, that she was now his wife, and they had a son together. Despite his mother's scathing reaction earlier in the day, tonight as he gazed at his sleeping wife, his heart was so full of love he thought it might burst from his chest.

He undressed and climbed into bed carefully so as not to awaken Degan, but she stirred. Silently, she reached for him and pressed her body to his, resting her face against his neck. He took her hand and held it against his chest.

"My husband is troubled," she murmured.

Matt sighed heavily. "I'm afraid for Adam. I don't ever want him to experience the kind of reaction I endured from my mother today. I would do anything to protect him from that. I fear we have a difficult road ahead of us."

She sat up to lean on one elbow, studying his face. "I hear the fear in your voice. You were never afraid before. I was afraid, but you were not. Now you are afraid?"

"It's different now, with Adam. You and I have chosen each other, but Adam never chose to have parents who . . . All I'm saying is, there are some who would punish the child for what they see as the sins of the parents.

We have a difficult road ahead of us, but for Adam, it may be even more so."

Degan contemplated his meaning, her eyes now reflecting his fear. "I have known hatred from the whites. I do not want our son to know this hatred also."

Matt reached to pull her to his side, looking into the future a few years and seeing Adam going off to school among other children whose parents would both be white. He imagined the teachers reacting to his son in the same manner his mother had, and his son's classmates being even more malicious or ostracizing him altogether. A heavy dread filled his core. "My God, Degan, what have we done?" he muttered.

She stroked light fingers across his chest. "Adam may know hatred, but we will love him enough so he will forget. And we will have more children."

He looked down at her. "You want more children?"

"Yes."

He gazed thoughtfully at the ceiling, a soft smile coming to his lips. "I'd love to have a little girl. A tiny version of you running around the house."

"I wish for our children never to know hatred."

"They will at times, there's nothing we can do about that. But you're right, all we can do is love them enough to make up for it. If we raise them right, they'll be strong enough to withstand whatever they may face out in the world."

"I am glad you are the father of my children," she whispered.

Matt pulled her closer. As he felt her relax against him and drift into sleep, he was filled with great love for her and intense apprehension for Adam and their future children.

CHAPTER

29

"I'll be fine, Mrs. Howell," Caroline called out from the back of the dispensary. "I'm just going to tidy the treatment room, then I'll be leaving myself."

"It's so late, Miss Caroline, why don't you come in early tomorrow morning and put things away?" Mrs. Howell suggested.

Caroline let go a self-conscious laugh. "It would be difficult for me to leave the dispensary in a mess. I'm a bit of a stickler in that way."

"Well, all right. I have the reception room straightened, all the filing is done, and the clocks are wound," Mrs. Howell said, coming to stand in the doorway of the treatment room. Caroline was recapping and alphabetizing medicine bottles, arranging them neatly on a shelf. "I'm sorry I can't stay to help you, but Mr. Howell expected me home two hours ago."

"No, please, do go ahead and leave, I'll be fine," Caroline said. "Mr. Butler said he might be stopping by after the church service this evening."

"Very well," Mrs. Howell said tentatively, turning to leave. "I'll see you in the morning."

"Good night, Mrs. Howell, and please apologize to Mr. Howell on my behalf, for keeping you so late. I hope tomorrow is not as busy as today."

"I hope so too. Good night, Miss Caroline."

Moments later, Caroline heard the familiar slam of the front door and the click of the lock as Mrs. Howell left. She had been alone in the dispensary on several previous occasions, but never this late in the evening.

She had hoped that Jonah would meet her here and escort her home, but he had evidently been delayed from some reason.

The last of the medicine bottles organized, she looked around the dispensary to assess her remaining work. Bloody towels lay on the floor from an earlier patient whose cough from consumption had led to admission to Hamilton General. Instruments needed to be cleaned and examining tables wiped down in preparation for the next day's work. At that moment, she wished her father could be here to see the dispensary, particularly the treatment room, where patients came every day to receive care. She knew he would approve and might even respectfully offer suggestions as to how things might be run more efficiently. Suggestions she would greatly appreciate. Dr. Wallace and Matt had both demonstrated their dedication to the dispensary by working long hours there. Caroline knew that Matt had recently begun to recruit other doctors at the hospital, hoping they would donate some of their time to helping the poor. Each month, the dispensary treated more and more patients and she felt good about the work, especially helping the children.

Just then, she heard footsteps on the wooden sidewalk at the back door. Startled at first, she then realized that Jonah had likely gone to the front door, found it locked, and decided to come around back. Having lost herself in her thoughts, she was glad he had come around to the back door, as she wouldn't have heard his knock at the front. Excited to see him, she rushed to the back door and opened it.

She gasped when she saw a strange man, disheveled and dirty, leaning against the door jamb. His clothing was torn and soiled and his unkempt beard was streaked with tobacco juice and filth. His eyes were glassy and red-rimmed, and Caroline caught the strong smell of whiskey as he opened his mouth to speak.

"Beggin' your pardon, ma'am," he mumbled in a low, raspy voice. "I 'pologize for . . . disturbin' you . . . at this late hour. I need . . ." The man fell forward against her and she staggered back under his weight. Frantically, she reached behind her toward the examining table for support, but her hand found nothing and she cried out as they both crashed to the floor. Her left leg and much of her skirt were trapped under him as he struggled to roll away from her. Pushing against him, she was able to free herself just before he collapsed again to the floor.

"Sir?" She scrambled to her knees and bent over him. His eyes looked sunken, his breathing was shallow and rapid, his face was an ashen-gray color. "Sir?" She reached to take his hand, startled at how cold it was, and knew instinctively that it would never be warm again.

With great effort, the man opened his eyes. "I can't . . . feel my legs."

Caroline swallowed hard, a helpless panic overtaking her. She wished fervently that either Matt or Dr. Wallace were still here, but they had left hours ago. Her mind raced to think of which doctor would be closer, or should she just run out to the street and beg any passerby to transport this man to Hamilton General?

"You need a doctor, sir, and there's no doctor here."

"Nothin' a doctor can do for me now, ma'am," the man whispered, closing his eyes.

Caroline knew he was right. She looked around the treatment room for something to make him more comfortable, knowing he would not have the strength to move from the floor. *I can at least fetch a pillow for his head and a blanket,* but when she tried to get up, he gripped her hand tightly.

"Please don't leave, ma'am—"

"I'm only getting you a pillow so you'll be more comfortable. I'll be right back."

Moments later, she knelt again on the floor beside him and without hesitation, removed his hat and lifted his head to place the pillow underneath. She unfolded the blanket and draped it over his lower body.

"In my coat pocket," he managed, his breath coming from his chest in raspy gulps.

She searched the man's pockets and found a small, crumpled photograph showing the likeness of a woman and a young girl of about twelve.

"Is this your family?" she asked.

"My daughter, Amanda. And my wife."

"Do they live here in Washington? Do you want to see them?"

He shook his head. "Both dead. House fire, three years ago."

"Oh, I'm so sorry," Caroline said, feeling a lump of tears building in her throat. "You've been alone since then?"

"Yes ma'am. But . . . today is . . . happiest I've been . . . in a long time."

She frowned in confusion. His body obviously ravaged by drink and disease, and on the edge of death, he lay here on the hard wooden floor of the dispensary, with only a stranger for company as he died.

As if reading her mind, he answered her. "In a little while, I'll be . . . with my family again." A weak smile lifted the corners of his mouth and his eyes drifted shut.

"Caroline?"

She looked up to see Jonah Butler standing in the open doorway. "Jonah!"

"Are you all right? What happened?" he asked, closing the door behind him and coming to kneel at her side.

"This man came for help. He says he can't feel his legs. I think he's . . . dying."

Jonah quickly took in the man's appearance. He had seen imminent death many times. The man's labored breathing, his color, the pinched look of his face, all the signs were there.

"Shall I fetch one of the doctors?" he whispered, knowing that would be futile.

Caroline shook her head, sadness filling her eyes. "I'll just hold his hand until he passes," she whispered. "No one should die alone."

Jonah nodded, then moved to the man's other side and took his other hand. They sat quietly for a few minutes before Jonah addressed the man in a raised voice. "What is your name, sir?"

The man did not respond for a long moment. Finally he managed, "Nelson. Edwin Nelson."

"Would you like a word of prayer, Mr. Nelson?"

"You a man of the cloth, son?"

"Yes sir, I am," Jonah replied.

"All right then."

Jonah glanced at Caroline, then bowed his head. "Father in Heaven, please look kindly upon your servant here, Edwin, and welcome him into your kingdom tonight. We ask that you forgive whatever sins he's committed in his life, and allow him to receive your grace and redemption, according to your promise. In the name of your son, Jesus Christ, amen." Jonah raised his head and said, "It's all right now. You can go if you want to. A place has been prepared for you."

With that, the man's chest rose and fell with a final hoarse groan. A trickle of dark liquid seeped from the corners of his mouth into his beard, and he drifted into perfect silence.

Caroline let out a little cry, and sat staring as though paralyzed, taking in what had just happened. She gently placed the man's hand at his side and looked at his now-peaceful face. She returned the photograph to his coat pocket, knowing it would be buried with him. Jonah reached to pull the blanket up to cover the man's head.

She looked up at Jonah who had been watching her. "He's with his family now," she said quietly. "Thank you."

A look of bewilderment crossed his face. "For the prayer, you mean?"

"For coming when you did, and for helping this man pass peacefully."

Jonah smiled at her. "Will you be all right if I leave to go fetch the undertaker?"

She nodded.

Two hours later, Caroline was sitting at the desk in the front office, staring at her partially written account of what had transpired in the treatment room earlier. She knew she must complete the note before going home, as tomorrow would be another busy day, and she would need to work at her typical pace, as if nothing had happened tonight. Jonah had gone to alert the undertaker that his services were needed at the dispensary, and the body had been retrieved forty-five minutes ago. Jonah had offered to finish cleaning the treatment room while Caroline wrote her note, and she could hear his movements in the back as he worked.

After a time, he came out to join her. "Are you making any progress?" he asked, unrolling his shirt sleeves and buttoning the cuffs.

Pulled from her thoughts, Caroline looked up at him, then glanced at the clock. "It's after eleven. I didn't realize it was so late."

Jonah smiled. "You must be bone-tired," he said, pulling a chair up to the desk and settling next to her.

"I'm so glad you were here tonight," she said softly.

"Me too," he said. Then he took a deep breath and said, "I have news, Caroline."

Noting that his expression had turned serious, she braced herself.

"I received my next assignment today. As I expected, it's in Africa, the western coast of the continent."

She nodded, unprepared for how quickly overwhelming sadness was flooding her heart. Swallowing hard, she finally said, "Oh. I see."

"I don't have to leave for a couple of weeks. They're expecting me to make travel arrangements and report in three months. That gives us plenty of time."

"Plenty of time?" she echoed, not knowing exactly what he meant. A couple of weeks and then she would likely never see him again? She turned away from him, tears suddenly filling her eyes and spilling down her cheeks.

"Yes, plenty of time," he said, "for us to get married."

She whirled back around with wide eyes. "What?"

"I want to marry you, Caroline Tyler. If you'll have me. I know I should be asking your brother for permission, but—"

"But . . . you . . . You want to marry me?"

"Caroline, I've wanted to marry you since that day I first saw you in church." He suddenly looked uneasy and a little frightened. "Oh, I'm so sorry, how stupid of me. Tonight of all nights . . . I should have waited for a more proper time to ask you, not tonight after we've witnessed—"

"No, Jonah," she said, wiping tears from her face with her sleeve. He quickly fumbled in his pockets and produced a white handkerchief and handed it to her. "It's just that I . . . I mean, how can I leave the dispensary? You know that I believe this is my calling. I can't leave our patients—"

"There are others who can take care of the patients here." He leaned forward and took her hands, enthusiasm fueling his words. "I was hoping you would agree not just to marry me, but . . . to help me start a dispensary like this one in Africa. The Board is interested in providing medical treatment for the natives there, as well as for other missionaries in the area. They've had success supporting what they call . . . medical missionaries in these regions. They've taken notice of the work we've been doing here and they feel we could make an enormous difference with a similar dispensary in Africa."

She stared at him, wide-eyed and unable to speak, her mind racing to absorb both of his life-changing proposals.

"Dr. Tyler and Dr. Wallace have been working toward securing other doctors to volunteer here, and while the need is great here at home, it's even greater overseas in places like Africa. We can work to provide medical care and spread God's word at the same time. It's the highest calling."

Still speechless, she finally exhaled and dropped her gaze, but Jonah could see that she was already processing the information.

Finally, he said, "I know this is a lot to take in at once. Take some time to think about it. I can wait. I will wait for you."

CHAPTER

30

Unusually warm for early April, the weather had cleared after several days of rain. Many of the unpaved streets of Georgetown remained muddy and deeply rutted from passing carriages, and the street in front of Matt's house, though less traveled, was no exception.

When the rains began, Sara had placed extra mats on the porch and just inside the front door to protect the tiled floors she had worked so hard to wax and buff. Her new mistress had, so far, proven to be kind and appreciative of her efforts, and she was eager to remain in her good graces. The master of the house had relaxed a bit since those first days of his return with his new family, and for this, Sara was grateful. He no longer watched her so intently, as if waiting for her to say something wrong to his Indian wife. She surmised this protectiveness was normal, given his obvious affection for her, and Sara had to admit, Mrs. Tyler returned his affections equally. On many occasions, Sara had entered the parlor or the dining room and found the couple holding hands, laughing softly at a private joke, or murmuring sweetly to each other.

On her days off, when she visited with her young friends who worked in other households, all were curious and full of questions about working for such a mixed family. What was the mistress really like? Did she run through the house naked and shrieking? Did she eat with her hands and babble in her native tongue? Sara now found these questions amusing, though she remembered having the same questions herself when she had seen Mrs. Tyler standing in the foyer that first day. Her friends were pleasantly surprised to learn that the mistress of the house was actually very easy to work for, amiable in disposition and liberal with praise. They were also decidedly envious when she told them that Dr. Tyler had substantially increased her salary now that there were two more people living in the house, one a young child. Though the youngster definitely made more work for her, Sara had grown to care for the little boy whose soft eyes and sweet personality mirrored his mother's. Despite her extra duties, she took great satisfaction in her job. And unlike some of her friends who were employed in other households, Sara witnessed open affection and respect in the Tyler home. Any conflict came from outside the home, she quickly learned.

Within a few days of the Tylers' arrival in Washington, Mrs. Tyler and Adam had been playing together in the backyard when Mrs. Hughes' grandson wandered over. The little boy was close in age to Adam, and he seemed delighted to discover a playmate in the yard next door.

But the two toddlers' play time was abruptly cut short when Mrs. Hughes came storming out her back door and across the lawn, shrieking at her grandson to get away from Adam and Mrs. Tyler. Sara had witnessed the entire exchange from the kitchen window.

"Robert!" Mrs. Hughes had barked, grabbing the little boy and pulling him away. "You mustn't go near these people! They're dirty!"

Without another word, Mrs. Hughes marched back into her house with her squirming grandson in her arms, leaving Mrs. Tyler and Adam sitting in the grass looking stunned and dejected. Sara had never liked Mrs. Hughes, and now she detested her even more. That same evening, she had overheard Mrs. Tyler recounting the incident to Dr. Tyler, and had been disappointed that her mistress had dissuaded Dr. Tyler from going next door and "breaking that bitch's neck" as he had threatened.

"We will have visitors in a few days, Sara," Mrs. Tyler had said last week. "Please make the guest room ready."

"Yes ma'am," Sara had replied, thinking that Mrs. Tyler had taken to her role as mistress of the house quickly and with relative ease. It had taken only a few days for her to learn that it was Sara's job, not hers, to perform basic household tasks.

Now, as Sara busily polished the dining room table to a high sheen, she heard a tapping at the front door.

"Good afternoon!" came the greeting from a man with only one arm, accompanied by a woman with bright red hair beneath her sage-green bonnet.

"Afternoon, sir," she replied.

"Is Dr. Tyler at home?"

"Yes, sir, please come in," Sara said, taking a step back.

"Jon!" Matt shouted from the second-floor landing, making his way quickly down the stairs.

"There's the master of the house!" Jon said, removing his hat and crossing the foyer. They met at the last step for a raucous embrace.

"My God, it's good to see you!" Matt said, standing back to look at his friend, who hadn't changed much except for a few strands of gray hair at his temples.

"You remember Anne, from Sylvan, now my wife," Jon said proudly.

"Of course," Matt said, approaching her with an outstretched hand. "Welcome, Anne, and congratulations! You'll have your hands full with this one."

Anne took Matt's proffered hand and giggled, her cheeks flushing. "Thank you for having us. It's very kind of you to accommodate us for a few days."

"We've been looking forward to your visit."

"We?" Jon asked with a frown.

Grinning, Matt looked up to the second-floor, and Jon followed his eyes. When he saw Degan standing at the railing with a young child in her arms, his mouth dropped open and he stood motionless for a long moment.

"What the—" Jon finally managed, turning to Matt, then looking up again. "Well, I'll be damned!"

"Jon!" Anne gasped.

"Beggin' your pardon, honey . . . I'll be damned! How did—?"

"It's a long story," Matt said, watching as Degan began her descent. "Anne, I'd like you to meet my wife, Degan. And this is our son, Adam."

Matt could not have said whose eyes were wider, Jon's or Anne's, as Degan swept across the foyer toward the couple. When she put out her hand, Anne hesitated noticeably and took a step back, looking to Jon with a mix of disbelief and anxiety on her face.

"I am happy you are here," Degan said warmly. Anne looked down before cautiously touching her hostess's hand in a fleeting grasp.

When Degan turned to Jon and smiled up at him, he wordlessly embraced her and the baby in a warm hug.

"This is your son?" he whispered, stepping back.

"Yes," she said.

"I'll explain how everything happened," Matt said, putting an arm around Jon's shoulders.

"Well, you don't have to explain how you got your son," Jon said with a teasing wink at Degan.

"Jon!" Anne chided with a flush of embarrassment.

After dinner, with their guests settled in the parlor, Sara served coffee and freshly baked sugar cookies, one of Chloe's specialties.

"Miss Chloe has another special dessert planned for later," Sara said, enjoying the mysterious promise of better things to come. Degan had asked for Sara's assistance in putting Adam to bed shortly after dessert was served.

"You feelin' all right, ma'am?" Sara asked as she began removing Adam's day clothes in the makeshift nursery. "I don't mean to offend, but your color's not quite right. And your appetite hasn't been any too hearty of late."

While Sara retrieved a clean night shirt for Adam from the dresser drawer, Degan collapsed into one of the armchairs at the window. "I am grateful to Chloe for her work, but . . ." her voice trailed off and she leaned to put her head in her hands.

"Pardon me asking, ma'am, but . . . are you with child?"

Degan looked up at the young maid, astonished at herself for having missed the signs a second time.

In the balmy twilight of early spring, Matt and Jon decided to take a walk through the neighborhood after dessert. Smoldering cigars in hand, the two strolled leisurely through the red-brick streets that lined the Georgetown quarter.

"You seem happy with Anne," Matt said.

"I'm a lucky man," Jon replied. "I still can't believe she agreed to marry me."

Matt chuckled. "I know what you mean. I feel the same about Degan."

"You know, I used to think I'd never be able to take a wife because . . . I'm not a whole man. But now I see that doesn't matter. Anne doesn't care that I'm missing an arm. She accepts me the way I am." Matt searched his friend's face and saw forgiveness in his eyes. "It's all right now," Jon said, and Matt briefly put an arm around his shoulders. They walked in silence for a time before Jon spoke again. "After all you been through, you must feel like you're dreamin', especially with that little boy you got."

"It's so much responsibility though. I was never afraid of being with Degan and what we might face as a couple. But now, with Adam, it's different. I'm . . . terrified."

"Of what?"

"Of what he'll face with parents who . . . aren't both white. You know, before, I was so defiant, ready to reject the conventions of white society with no regrets. But now, it's not just myself I'm making those decisions for. All my choices are . . . choices that Adam will have to live with as well."

"Damn, I see what you mean," Jon murmured. "I always thought folks would give you a hard time because your . . . wife is an Indian, but I never thought about a child."

"If you could've heard my mother the other day . . . my God, Jon, she was brutal. And I'm afraid she's typical. I can't bear the thought of Adam facing even a small measure of that kind of bigotry. He's just an innocent baby."

"You can't protect him from everything."

Matt felt again the agony of knowing that eventually, his son would experience prejudice from whites. "I wish we lived in a society that didn't care so much about a child's lineage. I know he'll have great opportunities, but I fear he'll also have to fight more than his share of battles."

Jon sighed. "Maybe a hundred years from now, things'll be different."

"We'll all be long gone before that day comes."

Jon looked up just as they rounded the corner of the block. "Looks like a carriage has pulled up in front of your house."

The carriage door opened and Matt watched as Jonah Butler stepped out, then turned to offer his hand to Caroline. He remained with his hand out to assist another person. Daisy slowly emerged from the interior. Without a word, he picked up his pace.

"Daisy!" he said, embracing her warmly. "I'm so glad to see you."

"Welcome home, Matthew," she said as he released her and stepped back. The look in her eyes told him that she had already accepted the man he had become, whatever that might mean. His throat tightened with emotion and he felt at once boundless gratitude and boyish excitement.

"Thank you," he finally managed, and turned to exchange warm greetings with Caroline and Jonah. After Jon's introduction, Matt turned back to Daisy. "Come see the baby and meet Degan."

As Daisy climbed the three steps into the house, Matt noticed she was slightly stooped, moved more carefully now, and at times, twisted her face in discomfort. Her hair was completely white under her evening bonnet, and her fingers looked a little more crooked and gnarled than he remembered.

"Degan?" he called from the foyer. When she emerged from the parlor, he presented her first to Daisy, then to Jonah. He savored the sight of Caroline greeting Degan with a cordial embrace and telling her it was good to see her again.

"Matt has told me many things about you," Degan said to Daisy, extending her hand, which Daisy took.

"It's very nice to meet you," Daisy replied.

"You are a mother to him, and taught him to be a good man," Degan said softly. "Thank you."

Stunned by her forthright statement, Daisy's eyes grew moist and she turned to Matt, then back to Degan. Hearing herself described openly as Matt's mother sounded absurd, given their obvious differences in race and station. But in many ways, she knew in her heart that Degan's assessment could not have been more precise.

"I can see that our Matthew is very happy," Daisy said. "That makes me happy. I'm glad he found you. Now, where is this little boy that Miss Caroline has told me so much about?"

"He's sleeping upstairs. Come, I'll show you," Matt said, putting a gentle hand on her arm to guide her toward the stairs, while Degan escorted their guests into the parlor. Once upstairs, they tip-toed down the hallway and into the nursery. Leaning over the slumbering child on the bed, Daisy said, "Oh, Matthew, he's beautiful!" with as much enthusiasm as she could express in a whisper.

"I think he looks like Degan, but everyone else says he looks like me."

"He does look like you!" she said. They watched as Adam stretched in his sleep, spread his little toes on both feet, then relaxed again. Daisy chuckled softly and pointed. "You used to do that same thing in your sleep when you were a baby."

Matt laughed quietly. "Did I?"

She reached to put her hand gently on Adam's head, stroking his dark, wavy hair. "Caroline says you're traveling to London soon?"

"Yes, I've been invited by a former colleague of Father's."

"Your father would be so proud of you, Matthew. And he would dearly love this little boy of yours," she said, and was surprised to see a look of consternation come over Matt's face.

"Oh Daisy," he began, "I don't know what to do. I fear for Adam, and how he'll be received. Mother's reaction the other day—"

"I overheard your discussion with Miss Kathleen," she said quickly. "May I offer you my thoughts on this matter?"

"Of course," he said, leading her to the armchairs at the window.

"This country is still so divided," she said, easing slowly into a chair. "The way I see it, the war did nothing to bring the North and the South together. We may have preserved the Union for the politicians, but if anything, there's more division now in folks' hearts and minds than ever before. I've seen a few mixed couples in my time. It can be mighty hard on the little ones when the mother and father are not . . . both white."

Matt studied his folded hands, nodding his understanding with a dejected look on his face. "I love Degan more than I could ever express, and I love my son even more, but . . . I wonder what we've done in bringing Adam into the world."

"Matthew," she said, reaching to put a warm hand over his, "you must take heart. Don't let your misgivings get the better of you. You have the woman you love at your side, and a beautiful little boy to raise. Teach him to rise above whatever he may face."

He looked up and she could not remember ever seeing so much fear in his eyes. "But how? I don't know that I can," he whispered.

"You can and you will. You must."

"I can't express how much it means to me that you came here this evening. And that you said those kind things to Degan downstairs."

Daisy squeezed his hand. "Don't forget, you and Degan are not alone here. Your mother may choose to reject you and your family—for now—but Caroline and I are here. And you will find others who are accepting of your family."

Matt took a deep breath, seeming to hang on her every word.

"You waited a long time for this happiness," she said. "Try to enjoy it."

Putting an arm around her shoulders, he held her close for a long moment. "Thank you, Daisy."

"Matty?" He and Daisy looked up to see Caroline and Jonah standing in the doorway of the nursery. "May we come in?"

"Of course," Matt said quietly, watching as his sister took Jonah's hand and led him closer to the bed to look adoringly down at a sleeping Adam. He watched Jonah's expression as he looked first at the baby, then at Caroline, and was gratified to see his face glowing with affection.

Caroline turned toward them. "We have news."

Matt motioned for everyone to step out to the hallway, pulling the bedroom door shut behind them.

Looking as though she might burst with excitement, Caroline said, "Jonah has asked me to marry him and I've accepted."

"Cara, that's wonderful!" Matt said, embracing his sister, then shaking Jonah's hand and congratulating him.

"Thank you, Dr. Tyler," Jonah said.

"Jonah, if you're going to be my brother-in-law, I think you should start calling me Matt."

Daisy embraced the couple, and Matt was pleased to see Jonah accept her caring gesture without hesitation.

"There's more," Caroline said, bracing herself. "The Board is sending Jonah to Africa for his next assignment. And . . . I've decided to go with him."

This news was received with more surprise than joy, and left Matt and Daisy momentarily too stunned to speak.

"Matt?"

All turned to see Degan reach the top step, a tentative smile on her face as she immediately felt the tension of the group. As she approached, Matt instinctively put his arm around her shoulders and pulled her to stand beside him, explaining his sister's news to her.

"We're very happy for you both, but of course, we will miss you," Matt said. "How long will you stay in Africa?"

"Our plan is to start a dispensary there, much like the one here," Jonah said. "The Board has been impressed with how hard Caroline and the rest of the staff have worked, and they've agreed to support a similar facility there. There's a great need for medical missionaries and good medical care to be made available to the people there."

"I'm very proud of you, Cara," Matt said softly, then turned back to Jonah. "Who will provide the direct care to the patients? Have you any doctors prepared to staff the facility?"

"No, not yet," Jonah said, his smile fading. "That's a major deficiency in our plan. We don't expect to find well-trained physicians among the population there. But perhaps we—"

"Matty?" Caroline broke in, anticipation mixed with hopefulness on her face. "Would you consider . . ." Then she looked at Degan and remembered her young nephew sleeping in the next room and her face fell.

Jonah had picked up her thought. "I don't suppose you would consider joining us in Africa? Even temporarily, just to get the dispensary started, until we can recruit a permanent staff of physicians?"

Matt stared at them, speechless, then looked down at Degan who was awaiting his response.

"We would have to discuss it," he finally said. "I'll admit, it's an intriguing proposition."

Caroline gave a little squeal of delight and clasped her hands to her chest before spontaneously hugging Matt, then Degan, and even Daisy.

"Evidently, she thinks you've already agreed," Jonah said jovially. "What do you think, Miss Degan?"

"I will go where my husband goes," she answered quietly. "My home is with him."

Still chuckling at his sister's exuberant reaction, Matt looked down at Degan. "We have a lot to talk about."

"Yes, we do," she replied, a soft smile on her face. Something in her eyes made him look at her curiously before turning back to Jonah.

"I do like the idea. Of course, we have the London trip coming up—"

"That would give us time to get the facility built and equipped," Jonah said. "Then by the time you arrive, we'd be up and running."

"Excuse me, sir?" Sara interrupted from the top of the stairs, catching everyone's attention. "Miss Chloe says her special dessert is ready."

Degan turned to Matt. "She says it is called 'ice cream.' She says this is very good."

With a mischievous grin, Daisy looked at Caroline, then at Matt. She moved to Degan's side, put an arm around her waist and pulled her toward the stairs. "Let me tell you about a time when Matthew was a little boy and ate too much ice cream."